BENEATH THE BROKEN OAK

LORI ALTEBAUMER

For Tucker, Travis, and Tanner

Mighty oaks from little acorns grow.

I will not leave you orphans; I will come to you.

John 14:18

PROLOGUE

Long before the soul of man touched the soil of El Hueso

A biting wind growled up the rugged slope to gnaw its way through the tenacious scrub brush clinging to the West Texas plateau. Year after year it returned, punishing the cursed ground until nothing remained but a hardscrabble land. The scarred hill upon which the town of El Hueso would one day exist seemed to hunch its rocky spine against the blast.

Only the surliest of plants chose to grow in the harsh landscape, and only the hardiest of them survived. Tasajillo, catclaw, juniper, yucca, prickly pear, shin oak, skunkbush, and eventually the invasive thorn-covered mesquite tree.

Until one day the acorn of a live oak found itself abandoned atop the inhospitable plateau.

With determination, it wedged itself into a narrow pocket of deep soil surrounded by rocky ground and braced itself against the angry wind. With tenacity, it sent its roots deep beneath the surface until it found a hidden spring. There it quenched its thirst in the cool, life-giving water.

With unshakable hope, it flourished in a hopeless place.

Year after year the winds came, bending and whipping the oak until a fork formed in its trunk. Two branches now spread from one. A day would come when the tree would break. Weakened by the split, one branch would succumb to the storms that raged over the plateau.

But that day had not yet come when the Charidy family settled beneath the mighty oak on the wild Texas frontier in the fall of 1858.

CHAPTER 1

A tree must grow toward the light, or it will succumb to the darkness.
~Anonymous

*D*awn was coming. The darkness couldn't last.

Sweat beaded on Harrison's forehead and trailed along his hairline until it ran beneath his collar. He didn't stop to wipe it. The steady scrape of his shovel jabbing into the hard ground shredded the night air like a wild beast ripping the flesh from its prey. Every so often, he surveyed the distant edges of the night.

The house made his mission risky. The woman who lived there worked nights at the hospital, but she could be home soon.

He ran a hand over his right hip, reassured by the presence of the firearm hidden beneath his shirt. He didn't want to kill her. But if he had to, he would. A hundred years hadn't lessened the truth's power to change everything. To ruin everything. The sins of the fathers—or something like that.

Darkness throbbed with the screak and click of frogs and crickets. Honeysuckle sweetened the air. *Like the scent of rotting death.*

His insides prickled as the memory edged its way up from where it lay buried in his soul. He cut it off with another thrust of his shovel, burying one thing while he worked to uncover another.

"Aidan!" a woman called, her voice tight with panic. "Aidan Truett, where are you?"

The boy's mother. He froze, shovel suspended above the hole. A few more inches and he'd find it. He was certain.

A ray of light bounced along the ground near the voice coming from the direction opposite the house. The bobbing beam grew larger, as though she headed straight toward him. But why? The oak tree's deep shadows hid him well. She couldn't see him.

A scuffing against the rough bark rasped above him. In the fork of the tree, a glint of light winked at him.

That would change everything.

The woman's voice cried out again, braided with equal measures of urgency, anger, and fear. The reflection in the tree shifted.

His fingers curled around the smooth wooden handle, grip tightening as though to strangle the unfairness of his life. If the truth wouldn't stay buried, he'd find another way to destroy it.

He'd been so close tonight. He could feel it.

The idea to kick off his campaign for a seat in the state legislature by making an appearance at the nursing home had been a mistake. The old man was crazy. Everyone knew it.

Maybe *he* was crazy for letting the man's rantings drive him to this desperate mission. But he wouldn't risk it.

He'd silenced the rantings of the old man, but that didn't mean the doddering fool hadn't already told others.

Forced to abandon his quest, he slipped into the night as a small form dropped from the tree's branches to the ground.

Another problem to eliminate.

CHAPTER 2

A lone tree is a vulnerable tree. Without a forest to protect and sustain it,
the tree must face the perilous forces of nature alone. ~Anonymous

ain zinged up Jodee Trevaine's leg as her foot touched
the ground. One of the many occupational hazards of a
forest service employee—stepping in holes. Of the long list of other
sources of pain, she'd take a hidden hole over rattlesnake bites,
poison ivy, killer bees, and her least favorite—the business end of a
double-barrel shotgun.

The latter only happened once, but she'd since carried a taser.
She'd have preferred her SIG, but while Texas was an open carry
state, her job was not an open carry job.

Still in uniform, though off-duty, the impossible-to-conceal-
under-the-required-forestry-service-uniform firearm remained
locked in its box inside the console.

She rolled her ankle to stretch the tight muscle. The walk across
the parking lot would help loosen it. With her keys clutched in her
right hand, she scanned the lot of Tooley's Truck Stop. It was the in-
between time when sensible people had gone home, and the night
ghouls hadn't yet slunk from their hiding places. A survey of the

area didn't trigger any alarms. No suspicious characters loitering about, and still . . .

Tooley's Truck Stop was not a place she would stop if she'd had another option. The building's long neglected appearance evoked more watchfulness than welcome. If there were security cameras, they probably didn't work. But the nausea churning inside gave her no choice.

She lifted her hair from the back of her neck, hoping the brush of air against her damp skin would bring comfort. The air was still —too still.

The forecast predicted a wave of volatile spring storms to kick up before long. Already flashes of lightning cut jagged lines along an evening horizon darkening like a fresh bruise.

Between the rapid thumping of her heart and the persistent churning nausea, she needed to find a source of relief.

What she needed most was time to think—to stop the world for long enough to make sense of what she'd done and what she planned to do next. The great monster of guilt trekked up her body, stomping on nerves and trampling her confidence.

She'd made a mistake. A careless, life-changing mistake. And now she couldn't care more.

Her stomach pitched. Truck stops had their own peculiar fragrance—diesel fumes, truck exhaust, and a cement surface marinated in decades' worth of discarded gum and spilled sodas. Depending on the time of day and season, trash cans covered in baked on ketchup and filled with scraps of fermented food—a fly's delight.

She swallowed the last of the protein shake attempting to climb its way up her throat and headed toward glass doors covered in fingerprint smudges and paper flyers that curled around the edges in the damp air. Just a quick dash in for saltine crackers, Sprite, and a tub of hopefully unexpired peanut butter.

Halfway across the lot, she froze. Speaking of things that had expired.

Blue Sunday.

The lanky cowboy stood beside a mud-crusted truck, his back to her as he faced the pumps.

An unexpected sense of longing and relief loosened the tightness inside her, as though the sight of him took her to a forgotten place, a shelter she could run to. The emotion surprised her. She scowled. Indigestion. Never eat at the Yellow Dog Burrito or Bust food truck again.

Inside she knew her troubled emotions weren't the result of bad tacos. She placed her palm against her stomach. *Not now.* She'd think about this later.

Her heart shuddered into the maddening tempo she'd fought against all afternoon. She adjusted her trajectory and sped her steps. Retreat had never been her way. Avoidance. Well, that was a different story.

Blue had been a sweet-talking cowboy who'd given more than one girl a toothache.

Though she'd escaped his charm with no cavities, that didn't mean he wasn't still a pain in certain other areas. Like her foolish heart.

She hurried on, her steps as unsteady as her frantic thoughts. *Why now and why here?*

She deserved to carry her load by herself. Her current condition might have been an accident, but the solitary life she'd built wasn't. Jodee Trevaine would take care of herself.

The queasiness that had her stopped at this shady truck stop contradicted her declaration. If she'd done a better job caring for herself, she wouldn't be in this situation. The sight of him caused an unwelcome desire for a friend to grab at her heart. But not Blue.

Never Blue.

Lightning flashed in the distance. Moist, breezeless air hovered over the heated asphalt. That would change when the storm broke.

"Well, well, well. Are my eyes playing tricks on me or is that the backside of the notoriously aloof Jodee Trevaine I see trying like the dickens to pretend she didn't see me?" His drawl poured out like warm honey. His words parted the thick air and two-stepped across the asphalt between them.

"Not interested, Blue." She continued on. A conversation with him would make her remember things. It would make her feel things. She was doing more than enough of that already.

"So, you did see me and chose to ignore me. I stand corrected. Not aloof, just plain rude."

She stopped, inhaled, then attempted to purge the emotions she didn't want to deal with in a heavy exhale. She'd become good at hiding her feelings, burying them deep enough others couldn't find them. The fact she sometimes buried them so far down she couldn't find them either was a problem. They just kept accumulating somewhere far beneath the surface, dulling her to the next emotional upheaval.

She turned to face him because he was right. Her problem was hers. She didn't have to blame him because her life was on the brink of falling apart.

Mischievousness sparked in the blue eyes that met hers. Never a care in the world touched Blue Sunday. Of course, an alcohol induced indifference usually compensated for a great many of those cares.

A few years older and the son of a hired hand on her grandfather's ranch, they'd grown up living completely different lives on the exact same piece of land. But they were forever connected by a night she'd rather not remember.

And a future she couldn't have. Not now.

Facing him, the hardness inside her started to crumble. "What do you want?"

"All I said was hey."

"You didn't say hey." She put her hands on her hips and cocked her head to the side. "And even if you had, with you *hey* is never all that's being said."

He shook his head as his gaze ran over her frame with an appreciative glance. "You think you know me."

"You're a pretty open book." She grinned. "And not a terribly complicated read."

"Hurtful." He placed a hand over his heart. "Especially since you haven't seen me in . . .how long has it been?"

Eight years, seven months, and fourteen days. Her indifferent façade caved. Jodee folded her arms over her middle and looked away.

When you were responsible for the death of your best friend, guilt ticked like an eternal clock that never ceased.

His expression sobered, and she knew he remembered that night as well. "Yeah, I still miss him too."

She wasn't the only one who had lost a best friend. Chris had been more than a rock in their lives. He'd been the thread that stitched them to the hope of a better future than the one promised by the chaos of their dysfunctional home lives.

"It is what it is." Another time, maybe even another world. One she couldn't go back to. She offered him an indifferent shrug that caused his brow to furrow. What did he see? Whatever it was, it wasn't real.

"What brings you around these parts?" he asked. Though he tried to imitate her indifference, she read the question in his eyes. *When will you stop running and come home?*

"A Ford F-150 with a Texas A&M Forest Service decal on the door."

"Same ol' Jodee." Blue widened his stance and crossed his arms, the curves of his shoulders pressing against the faded gray t-shirt he wore.

Her eyelids fluttered in contradiction. She shifted her gaze to something farther away, guarding the secret behind the tattered curtain of her soul. She wasn't the same old Jodee, but it was easier if he kept believing she was. What he didn't know couldn't hurt her.

He moved closer. "It's good to see you again, girl."

The familiar scent of horseflesh, saddle leather, and spearmint gum danced over her senses. Blue. The warmth in his voice washed over her like sweet cream. Up close he didn't look so lanky. A broader chest and shoulders rounded out with new muscles gave his t-shirt a pleasant fit. She hugged herself tight as though chilled in the sultry air and aimed her gaze at his truck instead. It was good to see him again but in all the wrong ways.

She couldn't do this. She couldn't go down the "for old time's sake" path. The moment had to end, and she had to be the one to end it. "Well, enjoy the view while it lasts which won't be much longer."

"Dang it, Jodee. When did talking to you become like trying to roll up old, barbed wire? A man practically needs a new shirt, and a tetanus shot just for being civil."

His words cut deep. He wasn't wrong.

"So that's it? After all this time, I tell you it's good to see you, and you can't find anything nice to say?"

She had plenty to say but little of it nice, and none that she'd share with Blue. She'd done this to herself. Her secret metastasized inside her, attacking her from every side. She blinked, her hand covering her mouth then dropping to rest against her stomach. Was that how she felt—as though she were being consumed from within by a deadly disease? The wrongness of her thought numbed her.

"You know Jodee, you really need to work on your social skills. Someday you'll wish you had a friend. A more reliable friend than me."

If only she could accept being friends as if that were all she and Blue were meant to be. But after what she'd done, she didn't deserve even friendship from Blue.

They'd both lost too much the night Chris died. In a strange way, they'd lost something they never had. Maybe that made the sorrow all the more painful.

"See ya later, Blue." She forced a smile she hoped hid the loneliness strangling her. She turned and walked away, certain he watched her go.

"What's a guy gotta do to get a chance with you, anyway?"

The same thing he'd always said when she refused to fall prey to his charms. She followed it with the same thing she always said. "If you have to ask, you don't have one."

The truth was, Blue was the only one who had ever come close to having a chance, and that chance had expired long before either of them saw it coming. A raw, burning agony stung her nose and blurred her vision.

"Atta girl, Jodee." His unexpected reply carried on a soft, rain-scented breeze, a butterfly kiss to her soul. Murmured words as she wasn't meant otherwise hear them.

Her steps faltered. She bit her lip to silence the sob that threatened to escape.

The heart-sick ache tore at her resolve, tempting her to turn around and run to him. But it was too late. There was no undoing the mess she'd made.

The refrain from an old George Strait song played in her head. Right or wrong, she was still in love with Blue Sunday.

Yeah . . . the past was dead and buried. It needed to stay that way. She didn't need Blue and the demons he battled to be part of her uncertain future.

CHAPTER 3

A stricken tree, a living thing, so beautiful, so dignified, so admirable in its potential longevity, is, next to man, perhaps the most touching of wounded objects. ~Edna Ferbe

Blue watched Jodee walk away as though his soul were made of yarn snagged on the jagged edges of the broken woman trailing his unraveling heart behind her.

He was over her. Had been for years, right? His adolescent infatuation had met up with the adult reality that he'd never understand Jodee Trevaine. And after what he'd taken from her, he'd never deserve her.

But it didn't erase the truth. A part of his heart had always been hers and always would be. Maybe one day he'd be strong enough to cut that cord and stop letting her tie him in knots.

His palms pressed against the warm hood of his truck, the heat of the engine radiating through the metal as he closed his eyes and prayed for guidance and strength.

The pump clicked off. He finished his transaction by ripping the paper receipt before the printer finished spitting it out.

Seated in his truck, he flipped the visor down, forgetting the stack of receipts he'd already stashed there. The slips of paper rained down on him and scattered across the floorboard. He punched the steering wheel, growling out a string of half-syllabled nonsense. Expressing his anger remained a challenge ever since cleaning up his vocabulary.

He hardly recognized the man he used to be, but that didn't undo the damage that man had done. Actions had consequences. And he'd been a very active boy.

He exhaled a breath laden with regret.

Why now? Jodee's presence might not be the last thing he needed, but it came close. He'd been given a chance to prove he'd changed, that he was more than a good-for-nothing chip off the ol' block. He didn't intend to let down the man who'd saved his life.

A reflexive shiver scuttled down his back as he recalled the long night he'd spent locked in that tiny brick building while Oliver Matthews doused him in ice water every thirty minutes like clockwork. By the time the sun dawned, he'd been sober, starved, half-frozen, and humbled enough to listen to the lecture he received from both Matthews and Blue's Memaw, Dovey Sunday. But it worked. The lesson stuck.

He rested his head against the seat and stared at the glass doors Jodee had walked through.

It didn't matter how much he wanted to go after Jodee, he had to let her go. He owed it to Matthews. Even if it meant leaving a part of his heart on the grimy concrete surface of a truck stop parking lot.

He put the truck in gear and headed to the exit. If he didn't go now, he might do the thing he shouldn't. Sometimes it was best to leave a tangle of barbed wire be.

His phone rang and he pulled it from his pocket to check the caller ID. Oliver Matthews. Had the man sensed Blue's doubts and called to make sure he stayed committed to the plan?

With one hand on the wheel, he answered. "This is Blue."

"Any news?"

"Nothing. You're right. Can't find anyone who'll talk. At the first mention of his name, they start looking over their shoulders and clam up like someone replaced their Chapstick with Gorilla Glue."

"What about his son?"

"Nolan is interesting." Blue switched to speaker mode and placed his phone on the console.

"Explain."

He smiled. Sheriff Oliver Matthews was a man who liked to get to the point.

"Sometimes he's friendly and almost talkative."

"And the other times?"

"He goes silent like he's scared of his shadow."

"If that man was your father, you'd be leery of your shadow too." Matthews coughed. "I'm tellin' you, that man's as crooked as a barrel of fishhooks. He has to be stopped before he gets his hands into the state government."

He bypassed the on-ramp to stay on the access road.

"He's got women who work for him. You tried sweet-talking one of 'em?" Matthews asked.

A flash of lightning blazed across the sky as Jodee's face blazed through his mind. "In case you've forgotten, you and what must've been a tanker truck load of ice water are the reason I stopped *sweet-talking* women." As much as he wanted to help, he'd changed the night he sobered up.

He glanced in his rearview mirror, his recent encounter with Jodee still clinging to his thoughts.

"What about Syrah? She says she's his daughter even though he don't acknowledge it."

"I've talked to her a few times, but . . ." He left off without saying something about the woman unsettled him in a way he couldn't put to words.

"Don't think for a moment she wouldn't play Judas with you if it served her purpose," Matthews said.

Blue wouldn't argue. Syrah moved and talked and breathed with a restless hunger, as though she could never be satisfied.

Matthews continued, "I just can't believe one family could run roughshod over an entire county for over a hundred and fifty years and not leave a clue. Not one piece of evidence against them."

"I've been to the ranch. Checked out the barns, but I haven't been invited into the big house yet. And I've spent more time at Roots than I want to." Only took setting one foot in the door of the disreputable bar to hit the *more than he wanted to* mark, but he didn't say it. "Nothing."

"He ain't gonna make it easy."

"I'm pretty sure the bartender knows things, but he doesn't talk much. And I've never seen our guy in there. You sure he still keeps an office there?"

"He owns it. The place has been in his family since before *El Hueso* was founded. And he ain't ever been of a mind to sell it. Had an offer from some development company to buy it at a premium several years ago, but he wouldn't part with it. In fact, the deed says that as long as there's a descendent living, it stays in the family."

"Sounds odd."

"It is. I did a little research and there isn't a similar clause on any of his other properties. Wouldn't let them put a historical marker on the place either."

"Well, if the people won't talk, maybe the building will." Blue coaxed the last piece of gum from the package. He needed something to chew on besides his problems. He wadded the wrapper and flicked it into the empty cupholder.

"How's that?" Matthews asked.

"No idea, but I'm tired of hitting dead ends and closed mouths. Don't forget, my grandparents were a part of this community. My grandmother still is. I spent a decent amount of time hanging around. I didn't think much of it back then," Okay, maybe he'd been too busy being a part of the problem to see anything but the good time in front of him. "But looking back, yeah, there's something not right about this place."

"Look, I ain't feeling a hundred percent here." The weariness in Matthew's voice confirmed his words. "I darn sure won't have your back if anything goes down. I'm going to text you two phone numbers. One's a Texas Ranger you only call *if and when* you have something solid, something he can corroborate. The other number, you get into any kind of bind, you text that number. When he sees it's you, he'll come running.

"And Blue, just remember, you ain't law enforcement. You look and listen, but you keep it on the right side of the rule book. It'd grieve me greatly to have to lock you up." Matthews cleared his throat. "Or bury you."

CHAPTER 4

A wounded tree carries hidden weaknesses. A severe windstorm can wreak havoc on such a tree. ~Unknown

The signature aroma of a derelict convenience store—greasy and stale beneath a layer of cheap sanitation—assaulted Jodee as she shoved through the glass door. The only difference between here and outside was the cooler air. A sign for the restrooms hung askew on the back wall. She hurried in their direction, driven by the desire to escape Blue's presence as much as her desire to splash cold water against her clammy skin.

As if that would make it all go away.

A brown-headed, freckle-faced boy, maybe five or six years old, played with toy cars in the empty hallway. She cringed at the sight of him on the filthy floor as she bolted into the restroom.

With cupped hands, she sloshed her face with tepid water. An empty paper towel dispenser forced her to dry her face with the hem of her uniform shirt. She allowed Blue enough time to have moved on before exiting.

She opened the door, hopping to the side to avoid stepping on a tiny red corvette speeding over the scuffed, grime-covered tile. The boy looked up at her. Her heart stopped for a lifetime of a second with a future she wasn't ready for staring at her.

How had this happened? Okay, she knew *how*. A better question was *why* had she let this happen?

But the most important question was what she planned to do about it. Did she really have a choice? She'd closed the door on her desire for a family years ago. Did her current circumstances change what she believed?

She inhaled, then released her breath in a slow stream, letting it carry the stabbing ache with it. She wanted to move, but something about the boy held her captive as he continued to roll his cars across the dirty floor.

"The red one's my favorite," she said, nodding toward the car as it whizzed past her foot again.

"Mine too." His inquisitive eyes studied her for a moment. "Are you a police lady?"

The innocence of his question made her smile. It wasn't uncommon to be mistaken for a Game Warden when she was in uniform, and to a boy his age, uniforms probably looked the same.

It also wasn't uncommon for people to run for cover when she showed up. "Nope. Just a tree lady."

"Oh." His brow furrowed, as though her answer needed a thorough examination. Then he turned his attention back to his cars.

Another wave of dizziness unbalanced her.

Lord, help me. An ironic request since she wouldn't have accepted help from anyone, even if it had been offered. Not even the Lord she told herself.

Only one other customer stirred inside the store. A burly man examined the rack of locally processed beef jerky. He side-eyed her, then turned his back as though he were sensitive about his dehydrated meat selections.

She found the peanut butter and saltine crackers, swung by the cooler for a cold Sprite, and deposited them on the counter.

"You coming to the Old Settler's Reunion this weekend? You can buy your pass here." The cashier recited the pitch by rote as she swept a curtain of limp brown hair aside to reveal a pale face. The young woman wore the frazzled and exhausted look of someone trying to make life work but failing. She bore the same thin nose and wide eyes as the boy she'd seen in the back.

A single mom? In her early twenties, Jodee guessed. Too young to have a child as old as the boy she saw in the back, though not impossible. The notion knotted in her chest as though the arrhythmia that pestered her had finally contorted her heart. Her spoken *no* answered the cashier's question. But inside it responded to the anxious question only she asked.

One only she could answer.

The girl coughed, the kind of wheezing sound that drew the concern of others. She coughed again and fanned the air in front of her, becoming aware of Jodee's scrutiny. "Cigarette smoke. It doesn't take much to trigger my asthma." She dug beneath the counter and produced an inhaler.

The swoosh of the door when another person entered the store drew her attention as she pulled a handful of crumpled dollar bills from her pocket.

Few things pricked her suspicions more than a face hidden in the dark recesses of a hoodie. These days one never knew if the person chose the mode of dress as a fashion statement or if they were headed to a drug deal.

The cashier, whose shirt said her name was Kimberly, glanced toward the hallway where the boy played, but the man stopped at the cooler where the energy drinks were kept.

She handed Jodee her change.

"Keep it," Jodee said. Considering the small amount, she dug a hundred-dollar bill from the emergency stash in her front pocket and placed it on the counter.

A flicker of a smile, gone before it had time to exist, flashed over the woman's face. Her eyes cut to Jodee, a mixture of gratitude and fear softening her features before the guarded expression returned.

"Are you sure you're okay?" Jodee asked.

"Happens all the time. I'm used to it." This time she offered her a more convincing smile.

Jodee scooped up her purchases to leave. A niggle of unease made her pause, but it disappeared as quickly as it came.

A weathered cowboy opened the door and held it for her. He dipped his head, the brim of his worn gray felt hat hiding his face in the shadow. Constructed of sinews and joints made knobby by years of hard labor, the browned hand that held the door told her more about the man than anything else could have. "You be careful out tonight. Foul weather's coming. Feelin' it in my bones."

"Thank you." She slipped through the door with a quick nod. Always trust the weather report from the bones of an old cowboy.

"Remember, though," he said. "No matter how bad the weather gets, the sun's still shinin' on the other side."

The angst she'd tamped down all day broke free to stampede over her, bringing a herd of other emotions with it. Moisture pooled in her eyes, blurring her vision.

In contrast to the wild emotions, her heart settled into a calm, steady rhythm.

There are times when words are more than just words. The impression this was one of those times pierced her. Her grandmother—a woman with far more faith than Jodee—used to say *God often sends unknown messengers to people in times of need.*

The illogical urge to turn back to the man seized her, but he was gone, disappearing between the aisles inside the store.

Foul weather's coming, the old man had said, his words conjuring Blue's face in her head.

She rested her hand against her stomach. More like a perfect storm.

A fresh wave of nausea crested over her. Her heart resumed its erratic flutter kicks. She stumbled, the back of her hand pressed to her mouth.

In a place where no one would see, she lowered herself to the ground next to a parked box truck and leaned against a tire. Drawing her knees up, head lowered, she held the cool soda bottle against her forehead. The symptoms had first started this morning. Much too soon to know anything for certain. But she'd become so consumed by the possibility, it now felt like fact.

A gust of air swept over her, chasing away the smell of rubber and diesel exhaust that filled the air. In its place, the comforting aroma of baking bread drifted over her. The unexpected scent soothed her.

She sipped her soda, then closed her eyes, letting the carbonation burn her throat. She had to get it together. This wasn't like her.

"I'm not supposed to be out here." A boy's voice captured her attention.

Apprehension skittered over her in cold prickles.

"It's okay. I asked your mom. She feels bad you've been stuck here tonight while she works. You're going to love my red car. Looks just like yours, only bigger." The pleasant, friendly quality of the man's speech may have enticed the boy, but they didn't reassure Jodee. Her intuition screamed danger.

"And yours is real." The boy stated it with childlike certainty.

"Sure is."

"As long as Kimber—I mean my mom—said it was okay. She said if I wander off again, they'll take me away from her."

"You wander off a lot, do you?"

"I like to explore. I'm going to find a treasure so she won't have to work so much and maybe we can live in a nice house with a swimming pool and maybe an indoor treehouse. I maybe already did."

"That right? Did you hide it someplace safe?"

"I can't tell. It has to be a secret."

"Well, we're friends now, right? And friends keep each other's secrets."

Alert, Jodee eased to her feet, adrenaline-filled concern snuffing out the last of the queasiness. A vehicle approached from her right, the tires grinding to a slow stop. Not good.

"Hey mister, I don't see any red cars."

"I'm really sorry about this little guy."

"Hurry up! Stop conversatin' with him and get in." A woman's voice shot from the vehicle to stab through the air.

"You be a good boy, and everything will be fine." The man's words twisted up as though from a guilty conscience.

A muffled cry propelled her forward.

She hit the end of the row of tractor trailers at a full run. No plan, just a primal response activated by fear.

"Sheesh, Syrah. We aren't trying to scare the crap out of him. He needs his seatbelt," he said.

"Shut up and get in before someone sees us."

"I ain't sure that wouldn't be for the best."

Jodee lunged forward as the man hoisted the boy into the back seat.

Unable to close the distance between them, she threw the open soda. The bottle struck him in the back, showering him in soda.

"Get in!" The man lunged into the truck as the driver gunned the engine. The tires screamed against the asphalt, drowning out Jodee's shout as the door slammed shut, sealing off the boy's cries.

As she scrambled for her cell phone, fingers tangled in her hair, jerking her backward. Fire-like pain raced over her scalp as someone dragged her into the shadows of the massive trailers. Her heals scraped across the ground as she struggled to keep her footing. Panic and pain twisted together, silencing her scream. Even if she had, they were at the rear of the lot now. Party row—where no one ever sees anything.

Rough hands shoved her, slamming her against a trailer. Her head bounced off the metal. An explosion of light blinded her as her phone slipped from her hand. *Fight. You have to fight. But how?*

Her brain stalled.

A thick arm snaked around her waist, pulling her against a wall of flesh. The stench of cigarette smoke and beef jerky burned her nostrils as he stomped her cell phone into the pavement.

Fight. Protect. Protect. Fight. Protect. The words pounded through her.

She brought her foot down hard along the inside of his shin, snagging it on the boot he wore, throwing her off balance. She fell. Instinct curled her into a ball. She pulled her knees to her chest, covering her midsection a second before he landed his first kick. A second and third followed, each one striking pain along her shins.

He drew back for another kick and she rolled, struggling to escape beneath the trailer. Not fast enough. The rough asphalt scraped away the flesh of her palms as he dragged her backwards.

Releasing his hold, he dropped to straddle her. Thick fingers clamped around her neck, squeezing.

The world grew dim as she clawed at the hands.

"Lady, around here folks know they got to mind their own business and keep their noses out of everybody else's."

Pain seared her lungs as a black haze crept up around the corners of her consciousness. She dug her nails into the hands crushing her throat. Like a fire with no oxygen, her strength drained away.

Then the pressure around her neck ceased. She gulped air into burning lungs.

"You go on and get out of here," the man said, his voice low and deep like the growl of a hungry dog. "This ain't none of your business."

She blinked hard, confused. Was he talking her?

From the corner of her eye, the silhouette of a man in a cowboy hat an a duster took shape. He didn't move, yet an aura of fierceness radiated from his presence.

An unexplainable peace wrapped around her. Somewhere, someone was baking bread. The warm aroma wafted over her.

Her attacker grabbed a handful of her hair again, lifting her head so his hot, jerky scented breath steamed against her ear. "We're not finished yet."

He let go with a shove, and her head struck the asphalt.

A groan slipped from her lips as darkness rolled over her.

CHAPTER 5

*Character is like a tree and reputation like a shadow. The shadow is what
we think of it; the tree is the real thing. ~Abraham Lincoln*

*A*cting Sheriff, Logan Adams, tore his gaze from the weather
app covering his computer screen in green, yellow, and
way too much red. He checked the caller ID. "I'm watching it."

"Didn't doubt you were. If the waters rise, you'll need to get
someone out to Blood Cut Creek to put up the barricades on both
sides. Never fails, some yahoo will try to drive off in it." Sheriff
Oliver Matthews barked out orders as though he were speaking to a
rookie.

"I got it, Sheriff. It's not my first rodeo. Remember, I grew up
here."

"Yeah, yeah, I remember. Just habit. Truth be told, I rest a whole
lot easier knowing you're in charge than I would if it was anyone
else."

"I learned from the best."

"Hopin' those years in Dallas didn't ruin your good instincts."

"Just grew my desire to be off the concrete and back on real solid
ground." Logan pushed the painful memories away. His desires

weren't that simple. "How's it going down there? They're not pumping you full of an improved personality, are they?"

MD Anderson Cancer Center was the best place Matthews could be considering his diagnosis.

"You ever heard of stuff called Cisco wine? Pretty sure that's what they're shooting through my veins, and they're backing it with turpentine. If the cancer doesn't get me, this blasted treatment will."

"So that'll be a no on the improved personality." Sorrow stitched through him at the implications of Matthews' diagnosis. He flicked at the tattered edges of the desk calendar in front of him, his thumb rubbing absentmindedly at the paper as though it might free a different reality from the one his friend was forced to endure. When that didn't happen, he changed the subject. "How's Rachel?"

"She missed her calling. Should've been a drill sergeant the way she keeps everyone hopping around here. They kicked her out of the room the other day for giving orders better than she takes 'em."

"You got a good woman." Matthews' wife Rachel descended from some of the first families to settle in West Texas. Folks like her had been seeded with a tenacious determination. Logan wouldn't be surprised if Matthews recovered just because she willed it so.

"Which reminds me, you need to find you one before too much longer. You ain't getting any younger or prettier," Matthews said.

"I don't think they make 'em like Rachel anymore."

"How would you know? All you ever do is work. The ones you'll meet while on duty aren't marriage material, if ya know what I mean."

"Guess you'll need to get well and come on back so I can step down from the job of Acting Sheriff. Give me some time to get out there and scout out the fillies." He twanged his statement with a note of humor, but a face blossomed in his imagination. *Marriage material?* Not by some expectations, but still she hovered in his thoughts. "Or maybe I'll just stick with having Sunday dinner with you and Rachel for the long term."

"Don't threaten me or I'll find one for you myself." Matthews released a half chuckle, half cough. "Back to the weather, be sure you have everything you need in your unit when you head out. You never know what might come up. Get ready for a long night, especially if the power lines go down."

"Yes sir, I'm on it."

"No, you're not. You're sitting in a comfy, dry office yacking on the phone with a dead man."

Logan flinched at Matthews' assessment of his condition, but arguing with his stubborn superior wouldn't change anything. "Point made. I'm about to head out."

"Be sure you drive Blood Cut Road and keep an eye on Jacob's Ladder. The wind always does strange things there. If there's going to be a wreck, that's where it'll be."

"Yeah, don't I know it." Logan's words were quiet as another memory sprang to life.

"There's something else I need to talk to you about." Another round of hacking cough rattled in Logan's ear. "But it'll keep 'til tomorrow. Now get back to work," Matthews said, before ending the call.

Logan's phone rang again the moment he disconnected. "Hey Aunt Grace, what's up?"

"Just letting you know I've been called in to work tonight. They were short staffed, and you never know what might happen with these spring storms."

Grace lived in the decaying community of El Hueso but worked as a nurse at the New Plenty Regional Hospital fifteen-minutes away. With no one else left to care for her, Logan made it his job to see to his widowed aunt's safety, though she was more than capable of caring for herself. "Take the long way and stay off Jacob's Ladder." He didn't need to say it. She'd remember another rainy night on that windy stretch of road, too.

"It never gets any easier, does it?"

"Not on nights like this."

"Swing by the hospital if you need anything . . . like maybe a hug."

A smile twitched on Logan's mouth. He knew how that would

look—the acting sheriff needing a hug from his aunt because old memories still upset him. "I should be good. Looks like the storms will pass through pretty fast. If they don't leave too much damage, it'll be just another night like the rest."

A long silence filled the space.

"Everything okay?" he asked.

"Everything's fine. Just take care tonight, and I'll see you in the morning." She hung up, the tone of her parting words stirring his unease. Grace's intuition was a fact he'd learned not to ignore.

He stood to retrieve the Stetson hat he'd already covered with a rain protector, then picked up the waterproof jacket it was still too hot to wear. There had been a time when he loved rainy days and nights. Becoming a law enforcement officer had cured him of that misguided romanticism.

His phone chirped again. He frowned, "Miss me already?"

"Logan, something's happened."

He waited, once again perplexed by her ability to sense when trouble was coming.

"It's Aidan. Kimberly just called from Tooley's and asked if I'd seen him. She took him to work with her tonight, but she can't find him now. She's looked everywhere."

He straightened as though called to attention, his fingers tapping the side of his holster. Emotions he refused to acknowledge churned inside him. The boy was well-known for his wandering escapades, but most of the time he only wandered off from his house or the school. Finding him never proved difficult since the boy wasn't trying to hide. But disappearing from a truck stop on I-20 was a different matter, especially with storms headed their way. "I'll check it out. Is she still at work?"

"Yes. But Logan," Grace hesitated. "She's afraid to call it in. You know how Aidan tends to wander. Someone put it in her head that they'd report her to CPS if she didn't do a better job watching him."

Maybe someone needed to talk to her. A truck stop in the middle of the night was no place for a kid to be running around.

His radio squawked. "I'll head over."

Grace's *thank you* still sounded in his ear when the dispatcher's voice stated his call sign.

"630. Go ahead."

"Start to a man down at the Blood Cut Road intersection of I-20. Going to be Tooley's Truck Stop for a female lying on the ground in the parking lot. RP states she may be unconscious but is unsure."

"Ten-four." Logan's attention shot up as he listened to the information. Instinct rattled along his nerves. A possible missing boy and an unconscious woman at the same truck stop at the same time. Assuming a connection was premature. Assuming it wasn't was a long shot.

The chance it might be Kimberly knotted in his stomach.

As scenarios played out in his head, the situation with Aidan took on an even greater urgency.

This had the makings of a long, cold, wet night.

He prayed that was the worst of it.

CHAPTER 6

The apple cannot be stuck back on the Tree of Knowledge; once we begin to see, we are doomed and challenged to seek the strength to see more, not less.
~Arthur Miller

Blue pulled into the parking lot at Roots and killed the engine. Drumming his thumbs on top of the steering wheel, he stared at the building. There was a time when a bar—even a dive bar like this one—would have promised him a night of blissful forgetfulness. But tonight, it dredged up memories he didn't want or need.

He exhaled. It seemed like a lifetime ago when he believed a drink offered the only way out. The only way to forget he was the son of Doug and Jolie Sunday—a couple with more baggage than an overbooked commercial airlines flight.

He wasn't that man anymore, yet that didn't make him any less antsy about his presence in Roots or his reason for being here.

The two-story building constructed of locally quarried stone should have served as something more worthy than a run-down bar. Though somewhat distinguished, the rusted pipe rails once painted white, wisps of seedy, overgrown weeds crowding against the rocks, and the peeling sign hanging at the edge of the lot by an act of will more than structural integrity gave the structure a ramshackle appearance, though not enough to keep folks from coming here on a regular basis. It was the unofficial hub of local activity.

Tension braided his shoulders. He rolled his head to loosen it. He continued to study the limestone structure. Treasure hunts were easier when you knew what you were hunting.

And if what you were looking for couldn't either save a community or destroy it.

He might not have any friends left when it was over if this went south. And thanks to his past and the family tree he branched out of, real friends were already in a short supply.

Seeing Jodee tonight upped the stakes.

More vehicles had parked in the gravel lot since he'd arrived. The Old Settler's Reunion and Rodeo had drawn in a larger-than-usual crowd. Most of them would either be staying with locals who were family or friends, or in a hotel in New Plenty. But with nothing else to do before the festivities started, sooner or later they'd wind up at Roots.

Inside, he found a barstool and inventoried the occupants. Country music, accompanied by the crack of pool balls colliding on green felt, offered a familiar greeting. The bartender—a short, middle-aged man with thinning hair and a thickening middle—eyed him as he popped the top off a longneck and slid it to Blue. They'd done this dance a few times already.

Blue lifted the bottle, tipping it toward the bartender in an unspoken thanks before feigning a drink.

This wasn't where he wanted to be, not by a long shot.

The fresh notion that by helping Matthews he might gain a bit of respect from Jodee troubled him. He shook his head. Still the eighteen-year-old kid trying to impress a girl. But not just any girl.

A young woman walked by. She smiled as she ran her eyes over Blue in a way he didn't relish.

Blue ducked his head before she could take it any further.

Tonight, it was Jodee who danced circles around his heart, and he wasn't interested in changing partners. Maybe he needed to find her when this was over. But now wasn't the time to think about it. It'd have to wait.

If he succeeded. Because if he failed, there'd be no point, no proof of the change in his life.

No proof he was worthy of her attention.

The bartender, Wiley, wasn't one for chatting. Or thinking if Blue gauged right.

He'd given up trying to engage the man in conversation, weary of the man's grunted out single syllable answers. If Wiley had been female—he shuddered at the image—, Blue might've had better luck, despite what he'd told Matthews earlier.

He picked up the bottle of Lone Star and raised it to his lips again as he turned his back to the bartender, pretending to take another drink as he scanned the room. Faking a drink wasn't all that hard. The hard part was letting the taste hit your tongue and refusing to let it go any further.

The hardest part was knowing this was about the twentieth one he'd bought, and he hadn't enjoyed a single sip. Another life.

Money down the drain if he didn't find something useful soon.

The temptation to take the drink was stronger tonight. Why did he have to run into her now?

He'd convinced himself he'd let her go years ago, but tonight was bitter proof that Jodee Trevaine was not a woman he could let go of. He may have pushed her from his head by filling his brain with other things, but she'd never left his heart.

His jaw clenched. He could think of her some other time, but not tonight. The window was closing on his mission.

Some mission. All he was doing was snooping, and he was failing at that.

The absence of the usual tough guy employed as a bouncer interested him. In the two weeks Blue'd been coming in, he could be certain Rusty would be hovering somewhere close by.

"You runnin' the show all by yourself tonight?" he addressed Wiley.

The man grunted, continuing to wipe the counter with the dingy rag.

"How about Nolan? He around? He owes me a game of pool."

Wiley gave a single shake of his head.

Blue swiveled back around on the barstool to study the rest of the crowd and planted his feet. A few regulars were seated farther down the bar, but most were out-of-towners.

The jukebox was thumping out a pseudo-country line dance tune when Rusty Boggs, the absent bouncer, appeared in his peripheral vision, followed by Nolan DeGroot.

His radar pinged on Rusty's sour expression. Nolan walked with his head down as though hoping to go unnoticed. Blue's radar went from pinging to whirring with curiosity.

Wiley stole a glance at the pair, then cut his eyes to Blue.

Blue opened his mouth to speak to Nolan as he walked past, but one look at the man's troubled appearance silenced him. Nolan was twitching like a fly caught in a spider web as he followed behind Rusty.

Blue feigned disinterest in everything but the bottle in his hand.

Rusty strode behind the bar, poured two fingers of Jack Daniels in a shot glass, then shoved it at Nolan.

Matthews had informed Blue that twenty-three-year-old Nolan DeGroot was the drug addicted son of the county judge, Harrison DeGroot. He'd popped in and out of rehab numerous times, but from what Matthews said, he'd stayed clean since coming out this last time. Offering him alcohol wasn't a good idea. Blue knew what it took to turn a life around.

The urge to stand up and knock the glass out of Rusty's beefy hands steeled over him. But he wasn't here to rescue Nolan.

Not yet anyway.

The young man hesitated a moment as though wrestling with his demon, then knocked the drink back in a single swallow. The empty glass thudded against the bar top.

"I don't like it. That wasn't supposed to—"

"Shut up!" Rusty's voice was low but filled with threat. Blue had been chased by pit bulls with a friendlier growl.

Nolan sank onto a stool several seats down without acknowledging Blue.

Something was up.

He made a show of spinning the bottle as though he was too lost in his own sorrows to pay attention to anything else going on, though anticipation zinged through him.

Rusty spoke into his phone, his back to Blue. The man's shoulders inched toward his ears as he hunched his body in a posture that implied submission. He hung up and glared at Nolan. Then he nodded toward the door to the storeroom.

Blue waited until they were gone, then moved to the jukebox. He dropped a quarter in the slot and hit B9. The smooth voice of George Strait belted a sad refrain about a man with a fool-hearted memory. He tipped his longneck toward the record machine in a show of camaraderie, then strolled to an empty table on the opposite side of the room and seated himself with a view of the door Rusty and Nolan had passed through.

If Wiley hadn't been sticking to the same spot behind the bar like a cocklebur, he might have faked being drunk enough to follow them. No chance he could pull it off with the dead-eyed little man standing there now, though.

Ten minutes later, the front door opened again. He checked his surprise as Judge Harrison DeGroot walked in. The perpetual scowl the man wore on his doughy face was no different tonight, except maybe darker. Wiley nodded in the direction of the storeroom, a movement so subtle anyone else would have missed it.

DeGroot headed around the crowded dance floor, stopping to shake a few hands and tipping his hat to a few of the females.

No one in this town—or what was left of it—remembered anyone ever owning this bar before the DeGroots. From what little he'd learned from his grandmother, Blue knew the original building had been meant as the county courthouse until a fire destroyed most of it in the late 1800s. By the time it was rebuilt, the county seat had moved to New Plenty, and the structure ended up being used as a jail of sorts. The *of sorts* part was one of the reasons people around here still tended to be skittish. No one really understood who had jurisdiction over the jail. Or who made the rules that got folks locked up inside.

In more recent times, the small brick house outside had been used for sobering up young men so full of themselves they didn't have sense enough to avoid trouble. That part Blue knew from personal experience. A shiver raced down his arms at the memory.

He knew too well that even though the building might have stopped being a jail, the bar remained a prison for a lot of people.

Wiley's back faced Blue as he inventoried the contents of the shelves. The mirror on the wall behind the rows of liquor gave Wiley full view of the bar and dance floor behind him, but Blue doubted the man could see him in the dim lighting.

Blue pulled out his phone and clicked on the camera, switching to portrait view as though he planned to take a selfie. He grumbled at the thought, but it offered a discreet way to observe DeGroot. The image of the man walking down the hall behind him appeared on the screen. DeGroot stopped beside a door at the far end, glanced back toward the dance floor, then unlocked the door and disappeared.

His intuition hummed like an angry hornet's nest. He itched to see what was on the other side of that door. With beer bottle in hand, he headed toward the men's room down the same hall, staggering just a bit on purpose.

Once inside, he splashed some of the beer on his clothing and mussed his hair. He stared at the liquid soap dispenser. Regretting his decision even before he finished it, he rubbed a tiny bit of soap into his eyes, then bit his tongue to keep from swearing. Eyes squeezed shut, he gripped the edge of the sink until the fire in his eyes subsided. One look in the mirror confirmed the red eyes that followed a few drinks too many. He hoped it was worth it as he slipped back into the hallway, trying not to draw attention.

"Blue Sunday!" A coy female voice sang down the hallway.

His fists balled in frustration. He shook them out and turned to see which past mistake caused him present day trouble.

An old girlfriend, though her name eluded him, swayed up to him as though her legs connected to her waist by well-oiled ball bearings. If the low cut, fitted top, tight fringed skirt, and high-heeled boots only hinted at what she was after, the swing of her hips and lick of her lips made it clear. She wanted his full attention.

He'd been afraid this might happen. The trail he'd left was just too long.

"Hey, darlin'," he slurred his words.

She didn't stop until she was as close as she could get without climbing into his clothes. His arm slid around her waist while he regained his balance.

Her arms twined around his neck as though seeking a kiss. Instead, he turned his head and coughed. Her hold loosened.

"Hey, cowboy. It's been a long time since I've seen your sexy-as-ever self around here." Her eyes flashed with meaning he wished he didn't understand.

Actions had consequences. Repenting of the actions didn't take away the consequences. If there was one thing Matthews had drilled into his head, it was that. And the proof of just how accurate his statement was clung to him like static electricity. One wrong move and he'd get a painful shock.

"You here for the rodeo?" She ran her hands down his chest, hooking her fingers in his belt loops with a tug. "You need your good luck charm? Maybe a nice rub down when it's over?"

Say something. He'd never been at a loss for words before, but his tongue glued itself to the roof of his mouth.

A nefarious idea poked its way through his consternation. A bad idea, but . . .

Lord, forgive me for what I'm about to do.

"Looks like my luck's improvin' already." He disentangled her arms and grinned, avoiding her eyes.

He wasn't proud of it, but he'd figure out how to make it right later. He pulled her toward the door the judge had gone through. With no idea what was on the other side, a drunk seeking some privacy offered the best cover he had.

Finding the door unlocked sent mild surprise rippling through him. The stairway on the opposite side brought a new challenge.

The woman with him—Niki?—pressed against him in all the right *wrong* places. A quick glance confirmed Wiley's back was still to them. He wound his arm around her waist, shifting her to a safer zone by his side as he scooted her through the door. Inside the stairway was dark, the only light a soft glow emanating from somewhere at the top. Silence met his ears.

"Shhh," he whispered, as his hands held her waist, guarding the space between them.

"I'm sure happy to see you. I'm needing all the good luck I can get." He reached up and swiped his sleeve beneath his nose as he sniffed. "Darn cold's got me feeling a little off. Pretty sure it's not the . . . ya know. I think I was exposed a few days back. That wasn't much fun the first time I had it." He gave her a charming smile as he leaned in as though he were about to kiss her. "You got the cure for that, too?"

"What is wrong with you? You're trying to kill me!" She planted her hands on his chest and pushed, leaning as far from him as she could. He might as well have confessed to having the bubonic plague.

As expected, his comment killed the mood. Now he needed to keep her quiet.

He sank down on the stairs and put his head in his hands. "I'm sorry. Guess I've had a little too much to drink already. That and seeing you looking so . . ." He gave his head a shake and blew out his breath. "Made me forget about being sick."

He reached for her hand, but she jerked away, fanning the air in front of her as if to wave away the contagion. "You can't tell anyone. I gotta ride. I need the money bad. They'll kick me out if they find out I'm sick." He gave her his most pleading look. "Promise me. I'll make it up to you as soon as I'm all better."

She bit her lip but stopped short of pouting. If he recalled right, she'd had it bad for him before, but no more than she had for the rest of the saddle bronc riders on the circuit.

"I'll call you," he said.

"Don't bother," she said as she left. His hand shot out to grab the door she meant to slam, and he eased it closed instead.

There'd be some serious repenting for him soon, but right now — well, desperate times called for desperate measures, right?

He glanced up the staircase.

Actions have consequences. He prayed this one wouldn't come back to haunt him.

CHAPTER 7

Surely man was not created to be an idle fellow; he was not set in this universal orchard to stand still as a tree. ~Thomas Dekker

*J*odee shivered as a cold rain beat against her face. She blinked at the dingy walls—no, not walls—trailers. She was on the ground surrounded by semi-trucks. Why? Had she passed out?

We're not finished yet. The words hissed through her memory. Someone wanted to hurt her. Where were they now?

She rolled to her side, wincing as a stabbing pain knifed through her. A fear she didn't understand molded itself around her.

Biting her lip, she pushed to her feet, body tensed for whatever came next. But there was no one else around.

Unsteady, she braced a palm against the trailer for support, then inched her way down its side. Pain shadowed her every movement.

Where had she parked? Her thoughts were jumbled, like the pieces of a dozen different puzzles trying to form a coherent picture.

There was something she needed to do, something to find. Something taken must be rescued.

Her body quivered with a desperate sense of urgency. Why couldn't she remember?

Rain-soaked hair plastered to her face as her wet clothes clung to her.

The tree. She could start over once she found her way back to the tree. Maybe then she'd understand what had happened to her—and how to find and recover whatever it was that had been taken.

A breath of relief burst from her lungs when she spotted her truck. She fumbled the keys from her pocket with anxious hands that shook as though they were someone else's. Once inside, she locked the doors and stared through the rain at the parking lot around her. Then she looked at the building.

Tendrils of dread wrapped around her. This place wasn't safe, and neither was she as long as she stayed here.

It didn't matter that she didn't know why. The certainty of the sensation convinced her it was true.

An itchy apprehension electrified her nerves like lightning that struck too close. She had to move.

Wind whipped against her truck as she pulled onto the access road. The fluttering in her heart raged with a new ferocity. She blinked hard and leaned forward, squinting through the wall of rain until she found the road that would take her back to the tree.

Rain fell in blinding sheets as the road wound up the plateau.

At the bottom of the S curve called Jacob's Ladder, a thin thread of relief unspooled inside of her. Almost there.

With a fierce grip on the steering wheel, she headed into the last bend as headlights from an oncoming vehicle swept around the turn. The other car slid on the wet pavement, swerving into Jodee's lane. With nowhere else to go, she shifted the wheel, hoping to create enough room for the vehicles to meet without touching. Instead, she found herself skidding toward a guard rail she hoped would hold her. Metal screeched as the rail tore into the side of the still moving truck.

A gust of wind broadsided the truck, tilting it onto its side until gravity sucked it over the short rail. The truck scudded down the steep embankment. A stand of shrubby junipers snagged it, jarring the vehicle to a stop. It took a moment for her to realize she hung upside down.

Held in place by the seatbelt, Jodee gulped in shallow breaths and tried to loosen her fingers from the steering wheel. Tree branches pressed against the windshield so that even without the rain or the dark, she wouldn't have been able to see. There was no way to grasp the reality of her position.

Releasing her hold on the wheel, she eased one hand to the ignition and killed the engine. With smooth, steady movements, she worked to undo her seat belt, but it wouldn't budge.

A flicker of orange soon turned into a fiery glow as flames darted from beneath the hood.

With a new urgency, she reached for the knife she wore. The seat belt dug into her hips, pinning her knife sheath beneath it. Dizziness started to creep over her as the blood made its way to her head.

The flames grew hungrier. She thrust an arm through the steering wheel and flexed, relieving the full weight of her body from pressing against the seat belt and creating enough room to free her knife.

Rain sizzled against the hood of the truck as the fire heated the metal. With a few quick cuts, she sliced the seatbelt and dropped free.

Snapping the blade closed, she struck the windshield, shattering it until she had an opening she could crawl through.

The heavy rain saturated the inside of the cab, making every thing slick. Her foot slipped. She tried again, and once more her boot careened into the air, banging her shin against the steering wheel as heat from the aggressive flames warmed her.

A gloved hand appeared from the darkness. A man reached for her. She seized his hand and found herself pulled free. Then the world shifted into slow motion as the sensation of flying took her away from the wreckage.

The shriek of metal ripping exploded behind her. She turned to see the truck engulfed in flames as it slipped over the edge into the ravine.

In the distance, a siren wailed.

Where was the man who'd rescued her?

She was alone.

CHAPTER 8

*First I shake the whole Apple tree, that the ripest might fall. Then I climb
the tree and shake each limb, and then each branch and then each twig,
and then I look under each leaf. ~Martin Luther*

Blue's pulse thrummed as he climbed the stairs. No place
to hide and no plausible reason to be here—and a confident feeling his presence wouldn't be welcome. His one excuse—
flimsy as it was—disappeared with Niki when she'd huffed out,
colorfully declaring him the worst sort of a scoundrel. Not her exact
words, but he'd tidied them up a bit.

He blew out another breath.

Best just to avoid getting caught.

Worn carpet covered the hallway at the top of the stairs—the
kind that wouldn't muffle a mouse's steps much less the steps of a
grown man. The thump of the bass carried up from the jukebox
below, vibrating through the soles of his boots. He flexed his hands
open, stretching his fingers wide before shaking them out. He
wasn't jumpy or anything. Must be the music buzzing through him
that had him ready to jitterbug a hole in the floor.

He'd been in more precarious predicaments. But those times had always dissolved into a good, old-fashioned brawl and the occasional night in a drunk tank. This was different. This time he cared about something other than himself.

A wedge of light slipped from a door at the far corner of the hall. It drew him like a fly to a fresh pile of manure. He gritted his teeth as his every step seemed to echo down the dark hallway. Museum-like relics and stuffed animals lined the walls like morbid soldiers in a hellish army.

He reached the door and pressed his back to the paneled wall, straining to block out the steady hum of the music while listening to sounds coming from the other side of the door. A grunt, followed by something heavy sliding over carpet. A metallic click. His fingers curled into tight fists as the urge to look battled with his need for caution. Patience had never been one of his virtues.

A creak on the stairs behind him announced he was about to have company. Time to move—and fast. A mounted grizzly bear at the far end of the hall offered the best chance of concealment. The massive paws, forever frozen with its three-inch claws spread wide, along with a massive display of incisors gave the bear a ferociousness even in death.

"Nice bear," he whispered as he slipped behind the animal. He rubbed his hand over the coarse fur, disturbing a layer of dust particles.

Wiley stepped into the hall carrying a crystal decanter on the silver tray. He headed to the open door.

Blue pinched his nose, holding off a sneeze.

The bartender returned to the hallway minus the tray. He stopped, his gaze sliding along the passage as though he sensed Blue's presence. Then he headed down the stairs. Blue waited, then followed to be sure Wiley was gone. The sharp click of the lock below inched the peril up a notch. Matthews' warning about breaking and entering echoed in his head.

No one had said anything about breaking and exiting. He hoped that gray area worked in his favor tonight.

He returned to his place by the office door. The silence encouraged him to brave a peek inside. Empty.

Halfway through the open door, he halted, arrested by the idea there might be security cameras. For show he staggered, then leaned against the wall as he scanned the office interior. If there were cameras, they were well hidden.

An oak desk surrounded by bookshelves and a couple of file cabinets. A high-end leather sofa and two wingback chairs circled a cowhide rug. Western artwork and trophy head mounts lined the walls. In the corner, a wooden hat rack displayed a couple of worn felt hats—the kind worn decades ago—, an old lariat, and a hand-carved wooden cane.

Other than the metal file cabinets and a few more modern titles on the bookshelf, Blue might have believed he'd traveled a hundred years back in time.

The large desk presided over the room.

No papers. Only a leather ink blotter and a computer monitor, along with the untouched drink tray left by Wiley. Undeterred by the desk's locked drawers, he turned his attention to the secret passageway begging for his attention.

He grinned, but the humor faded as he recalled Matthews' words. This wasn't a game they were playing.

Decades worth of mysterious disappearances, unsolved—sometimes uninvestigated—murders, and shifts of power that always flowed in the direction of the DeGroot family. People here lived with a vague sense that something wasn't right, as though a generational curse had sunk its roots deep into the West Texas soil of El Hueso, twisting the lives of those who lived there into a misshapen world. The sense of a fracture deep beneath the surface of their understanding had become such a part of their DNA they no longer questioned its presence. Like confused tenants in an uncertain world, their peace was never more than a fragile hope.

Blue rubbed his jaw, then shook his head at his analysis. Deep thinking for a cowboy, but four years in the Army had given him a fresh vision when he returned.

He stared at the open door into the secret passageway. If he wasn't allowed to let himself in through locked doors, he'd better take advantage of them when they were *unlocked*.

But if he messed up tonight and tipped the judge off to the fact people were asking questions, he'd have wasted his time and let his friend down. And if what Matthews said was true, the entire state might soon suffer for it.

He hesitated. Whatever resided at the bottom of these stairs required a hidden entry for a reason. He put his hands on his hips and stared into the opening that would take him deeper in more ways than one.

As if he weren't in deep enough already.

He might not have another chance to see what secrets lie buried at the other end of the passageway.

With shoulders squared, he headed through the opening like a reluctant paratrooper on his first jump over shark infested waters.

Stone walls lined the narrow passage. His shoulders brushed against the sides. A secret passage built for function and not fashion. The question of what that function might be whispered in his ear, but didn't talk him out of continuing.

Yellow light filtered from below, casting sinister shadows along the walls. A spider web appended itself to his forehead. He batted it away, spewing out insults concerning the judge's short stature having failed to clear the webs away when he passed through, leaving Blue to catch a face full. He brushed his short sleeves and ran a hand through his hair. Blue wasn't scared of much, but he'd just as soon not fraternize with spiders.

The light grew brighter as he neared the bottom.

On the last step he rounded a corner and drew back, his body tensing as he found himself face-to-face with a life-sized cutout of John Wayne. The legendary cowboy stared as though sizing him up. A relieved sigh whooshed from his adrenaline-charged lungs.

With his breathing righted once again, he gave a nod of respect to the Duke. After all, they were on the same team, right? The ones wearing the white hats.

He scanned the room and found himself standing in the middle of a small, domed chamber, eight feet across and twelve feet tall.

Four doors lined the circular enclosure. But other than the cardboard cowboy, there was nothing else in the space.

DeGroot's voice echoed from the direction of the only open door. The abrasive tone of his words indicated this wasn't a fun conversation. He recognized Rusty's voice as well, but the words were too muffled for Blue to make out.

The door that opened to where the voices originated led to a tunnel. How close did he dare to get?

He looked again at John Wayne. "You got my back, right?" Blue asked, hoping his humor—even if he was only amusing himself—tempered the misgivings he had about what he was about to do.

"Get back to the house and don't leave until I tell you to. And don't talk to *anyone*. Do I make myself clear?" Judge DeGroot spoke.

A long silence followed. Blue itched to know what it meant.

"You said no one would get hurt. And no one would call the law —" Nolan's voice cracked as his words sent a new unease through Blue.

"And if you keep your mouth shut, no one will," DeGroot said.

"What about the woman?"

"Are you arguing with me, boy?" The sneer in DeGroot's voice stole over Blue. "You know what happens to people who can't follow orders, don't you?"

"Yes, sir," Nolan answered, his words weighed with equal measure of fear and loathing.

The scrape of shuffling steps across the cement floor that followed sent Blue scurrying for a place to hide. Not enough time for the stairs, he ducked behind the Duke, thankful the man was larger than life in both flesh and cardboard.

Nolan opened the door on the opposite side of the tunnel he'd exited. This must be the way to enter from the storeroom where he'd seen the two men disappear earlier.

Blue waited for the others to appear, but when they didn't, he once again crept closer.

"I want the video from the store. We need to find out who she is and ensure she doesn't talk," DeGroot said.

"Want me to get rid of her?"

"Not yet. I don't want to draw any extra attention if we can help it. And I need you to keep an eye on the other two. I also don't need any more *complications.*"

The faint squeak of a metal hinge pinged down the tunnel made of stone.

"Want me to lock up the safe?" Rusty asked.

"Leave it open. I may need you to grab something in a hurry," DeGroot said. "If so, be sure you get the Makarov. It's untraceable."

"Yes, Boss."

"And see to it Nolan won't be a problem. Supply him with some drugs if need be. Only not from our inventory." Keys rattled as the men walked toward the tunnel. "He inherited his mother's disposition. All nerves and moral confusion. It's not complicated, is it Rusty? Survival of the fittest. Sometimes I wonder if that boy's really mine. The DeGroots did not get to be where they are by being weak."

Blue retreated behind the Duke again, full of conviction that he was on the right path. And that Matthews was correct in his suspicions. This man needed to be stopped.

But was what he'd heard enough to convince anyone else?

No. It'd be his word against theirs. And even on a good day, his credibility didn't carry much weight thanks to his past and his last name.

DeGroot took the stairs back to his office, while Rusty followed Nolan. The door at the top of the stairs thumped shut. No doubt the bookshelf would be back into place covering the secret door.

He checked the time. Until the bar closed, he was stuck. After that he'd still be stuck, but without an audience for his great escape. Maybe he'd have a plan by then.

He closed his eyes and rubbed his forehead. His ability to anticipate consequences still needed more work.

In the meantime, he could do some exploring and see what turned up.

He clicked the flashlight icon on his phone and headed down the passage where the meeting had taken place. Something DeGroot had said would get Matthews' attention.

The Makarov.

Blue wasn't an expert with handguns, but the name of the Soviet made firearm was one he'd heard recently. Sheriff Matthews had referred to it when he told Blue about the Witt County Sheriff's Deputy murdered in cold blood in 1976. The only thing law enforcement had to go on at the time was that a round extracted from the wall in the deputy's living room was from a Russian Makarov—the kind of handgun a lot of young men brought home as souvenirs when they returned from Vietnam. Back before it became illegal to do so.

Harrison DeGroot hadn't served in the Vietnam War, but the man's father had.

Blue shone the light from his phone on each of the pistols in the open safe, studying their make, careful not to touch.

"Bingo." He stared at the Makarov. The gun DeGroot had told Rusty to bring him *if he had to handle something in a hurry*. But was it the one used to kill the deputy?

A cold sweat dampened his forehead.

Only a ballistics test would tell them, but Blue couldn't just carry it into the Sheriff's office to demand they test it.

He took his time searching everything he could find that wasn't locked—which wasn't much.

He checked the time again. The bar would be closed now. Time to get out of this place and the sinister feeling that hovered inside it.

In a show of hope, he tested the door to DeGroots' office to be sure, then returned to the domed basement room after finding it locked as anticipated. "So, Duke, you got any suggestions?" The cowboy stared back at him. He pressed his fist into his palm and threw his head back.

The vague outline of an opening caught his eye. He inspected it with the light from his phone, then did a mental calculation.

He grinned. The jail cell he'd spent his cold night of sobering up courtesy of Oliver Matthews was right above him. He remembered the round opening and how much he wished he could escape through it as he lie shivering, but it had been sealed shut then.

Even if it wasn't now sealed shut, he didn't know how he'd be able to reach it.

The low battery light on his phone blinked at him. No time to waste debating his options. He hit the emergency number Matthews had given him.

"Yeah, I'm sorry to bother you, but I've got a little situation here." He rubbed the back of his neck.

An hour later, the grate in the floor above him lifted off, a blinding beam of light cutting through the darkness. A rope ladder unfurled before him.

"You gonna camp out down there or get to climbin'?"

"Hawk? Man, am I glad to—"

"Quit your yammering and let's get out of here. I ain't got all day."

Blue didn't bother to point out it was the middle of the night.

He'd taken pictures of the Makarov, along with several of the curious metal boxes stacked on shelves. Something about the padlocked boxes labeled with a combination of numbers and letters unsettled him.

The old man rolled up the ladder, then studied the night outside. "Let's go."

Blue held up his phone. "Wait. You gotta see this."

Hawk studied the screen as Blue scrolled through the photos.

"And?" the man asked, nonplussed.

"What do you reckon's in the boxes?"

The look Hawk gave him both baffled and chilled him. What had he gotten into?

"Ain't enough. Ain't going to do it." The old man turned and walked away.

Hawk might be right.

Cold steps of trepidation marched through Blue's soul, leaving him with the vague sensation it wasn't a matter of what he'd gotten into, but what had gotten into him.

Like a messenger of an imperiled fate, Jodee's name whispered through his mind.

CHAPTER 9

Texas 1858

Even if I knew that tomorrow the world would go to pieces, I would still plant my apple tree. ~Martin Luther

*W*ill squinted at the doe as she grazed in the tall grass seventy-five yards away.

"You got eyes like a hawk but take your time. Make it a clean shot so she doesn't suffer," Abel Charidy whispered from behind.

He inhaled the peace of the crisp, clear autumn day, the kind of clear where a person feels like he can see clean into tomorrow. But he'd seen enough in his short nine years of life to keep him from wanting to see tomorrow. His todays had always had enough trouble of their own.

If he were the smiling kind, Mr. Charidy's praise might have earned one. The man's patience had allowed Will to stalk the deer for the better part of the morning. So far, half a day was the only thing he'd killed on this hunt.

Instead of a smile, he frowned. The second half of the man's statement dragged up an image Will had spent the last three years trying to unsee. *Make sure it's a clean shot so she doesn't suffer.*

His nostrils flared as though he might draw in enough air to snuff out the emotion swelling inside him. He blinked at the burning in his eyes that threatened to blur his vision. *Think about the deer.*

Winter would be here soon. They needed the meat. With six mouths to feed—though he wasn't sure little Rose with her birdlike appetite counted for much—hunting was a part of the circle of life. Still, Will was grateful Mr. Charidy had let him follow the doe long enough to be sure she didn't have a fawn trailing after her. It wasn't right to take a momma away from young'uns who needed her—no matter what species.

The smooth wooden gunstock pressed against Will's bony shoulder. He'd fattened up a bit since the Charidys took him in, but he was still small for his age. Knowing that fed his determination to either grow or be the best at whatever he did. A good shot despite his size, he struggled to hold the heavy gun steady for long. He raised the rifle, then let his left eye close. Adjusting his head so he stared straight down the smooth metal, he covered the doe with the barrel.

A breeze rustled through the meadow, hiding the doe in the swaying grass. The air stilled and she reappeared.

Will's heart kicked against his chest like it always did right before he took a shot. He wasn't scared. According to Mr. Charidy, he was as good a shot as any man. But a person ought to respect the power they held over another life.

As soon as he squeezed the trigger, the air would crack open. Just like it had the day his momma died with a red patch of hatefulness spreading on the front of her dress. Her pain-filled cry—more guttural and wild than human—as she watched his sister die had almost knocked Will from his hiding place in the hayloft. But he'd done what she said. He'd stayed put no matter what.

For him, the atmosphere truly had cracked open that day, splitting his life in two as he watched his mother die. The memory of her gurgling breaths still came to him at night, awakening him in a cold sweat that made him shiver.

Momma had never wanted to leave her home back East for the *uncivilized frontier,* as she always called it. Pa argued that a man had a responsibility to provide for his family the best he could. That's the way of the world, he'd say. One man takes and another man gives. Ain't nothing ever stayed the same since the beginning of time, and he reckoned it never would. Then he'd ask if she'd rather they'd stayed back where she could have watched her children starve to death.

And that would be the end of the conversation. Will had heard a preacher say one time that a woman was supposed to respect and obey her husband. Even though he sometimes wondered how moving one's family to the very edge of civilization helped a man provide for them, he knew Momma trusted in the words of the Bible, so her argument had never moved beyond a soft-spoken observation, and it never ever moved beyond Pa's reply. Maybe it should have.

Head down, the deer twitched her tail as she grazed, a sign she felt safe. Perhaps that's why his heart always thumped harder in the moment before the shot.

The target never knew what was coming.

Will loosened his thin arms growing tired under the weight of the Kentucky long rifle, so they would absorb the recoil. He settled his finger over the trigger, feeling its resistance as he squeezed.

The shot shattered the air as the deer dropped. And just like that, there wasn't another tomorrow to see no matter how clear today was.

So big it would take three grown men to wrap their arms around it, the old oak was the biggest tree Will had ever climbed. The place where the branches met formed a bowl spacious enough for four or five kids to sit in at once. Not that he planned for that to happen.

53

For one thing, he didn't know four or five other kids his size. And for another, he had no intention of sharing his hiding place.

He set aside the McGuffey Reader he'd been studying his letters in, stretched out, folded his arms behind his head, and examined the canopy of dark green above him. Unlike other species of oaks, live oaks didn't shed their leaves all at once during winter so he would have this place to himself for as long as he wanted. The cradle of the trunk sank just deep enough to hide his small body.

Maybe the tree would continue to grow along with him, and he could go on hiding in the safety of its embrace for the rest of his life. Of course, he wasn't hiding. He was more or less just being. The tree offered a world unto itself, and it had welcomed him into its silent bosom, cradling him like a mother would hold a child. Lying on his back looking up, he saw nothing but limbs and leaves. A mother hen sheltering her chicks beneath her wings.

He stifled a laugh. He'd tried to snatch some chicks away from their mother hen once. The flogging he'd received had broken him of the desire to ever try that again. But the idea of the tree—his tree —chasing after someone, branches flapping as it pecked at the person like an angry hen, painted a humorous image in his head. It probably wasn't right to say so, but if that ever happened, he hoped it'd be Luther DeGroot receiving the flogging.

He pinched an ant crawling up his arm and flicked it away.

The tree was also the reason Mr. Charidy had chosen to settle here. Standing on top of a rocky plateau, it towered over the other trees. Mr. Charidy said for a tree to grow that big, it must have found a source of water, something absent on top of the ridge. A few hundred yards from where the Charidys had built the single room house and barn, Will could look down over the edge and see the river bottom and the green ribbon of trees that lined the river. But that water was over a mile away, down and back up the hill—a trip they'd been forced to make at least once a week with the wagon to fill up the wooden barrels with the water they needed.

The lack of water was one of the reasons no one else had wanted this piece of property. From appearances, there was little that could be done with it. Whoever thought that didn't know Mr. and Mrs. Charidy's determination and capacity for making things happen.

Will lifted himself up enough to see the other boys, Luther and Cub, using the iron bar to pry rocks from the soil that would become Mrs. Charidy's garden next spring. Luther looked his way, and he ducked. It seemed impossible Luther could know he was there, but the bigger boy still intimidated him with his cruel smile and dark eyes. Eyes behind which he always sensed the calculation of something mean.

The Charidys had taken in the brothers when they passed through the German settlements on their way west. Orphans, same as Will. But not the same.

Luther bullied everyone smaller than him. When the adults weren't watching, his abusive spirit came out as he unleashed it on both Will and his own brother, Cub.

He rubbed his shoulder where a dull ache reminded him of his last encounter with the older boy. He settled back into the oak and willed his little body to grow.

One day he'd get even.

The place around the massive tree had also been an old Indian camp. Comanches, Mr. Charidy reckoned. They found broken arrowheads, grinding stones, and beads. That was the other clue Mr. Charidy needed to convince him there was a source of water closer than the river.

It took some time, but he'd located a small cave, barely big enough for a man to fit into. Inside the cave, water seeped from the rock to form a pool. Mr. Charidy had sealed the entrance of the cave and dug down from the top until he had a nice cistern of cool, clear water for them.

Soon the pounding of the sledgehammer breaking the unearthed rocks filtered through the leaves into Will's sanctuary. Luther was busting the rocks so Will and Cub could carry them where Mr. Charidy would use them to line the inside walls of the cistern.

The steady crack, crack, crack lulled Will to sleep.

Sometime later, he awoke to another sound. The noise of

busting rocks had ceased. Instead, voices trailed up to him, rousing him from his nap.

He swatted at a fly that buzzed too close to his ear, then wiped the sweat that trickled from his hairline.

"Have you told him yet?" Mrs. Charidy asked.

Will started to make his presence known. It wasn't right to listen in on a conversation when no one knew you were there.

"Will Charidy has a nice ring to it, doesn't it?" He froze.

"He'll be a right fine son, especially since I'll never be able to—" Her voice tightened with emotion, and she sniffed. "Well, I'd love nothing more than for him to think of us as his family."

He pinched himself to confirm he was awake and not still dreaming.

"He's a good boy. Gonna grow up to be a fine man. But the decision will be his. He's old enough to have a say in whether he is adopted or not," Mr. Charidy said, his voice lilting in the teasing tone he often used with Mrs. Charidy.

Adopted. The word hit him with more force than Luther smashing rocks. His head spun a little, but before he could figure out how he might feel about that, a wave of guilt swallowed him. He wasn't meant to hear this conversation. Shame nailed him in place.

"If we're in agreement about the money, I thought I'd take him with me to Weatherford next week. We'd be gone a couple of days, but it would give us time to discuss it *man to man.*"

"Abel, he's barely nine years old." Mrs. Charidy scolded him in the playful manner she often used with the Rose and Will.

"Well, he shoots like a man. I don't think I could've brought that deer down yesterday," Mr. Charidy's voice grew soft. "Besides, he's seen things in those nine years a lot of grown men couldn't have handled."

"That's exactly why he needs to be a boy now. His childhood was taken from him, but that doesn't mean we can't give a bit of it back to him."

Mr. Charidy sighed. "Darling, you have the biggest heart for true motherhood of any woman I have ever known. And my own momma was a good woman."

The rustling that followed made Will imagine Mr. Charidy pulling Mrs. Charidy into his arms.

After a moment, the man continued, "But dear, once a boy becomes a man, he can't go back to being a boy. It doesn't work that way. Though I do believe you'd take in every stray you could find and smother them all in love."

"Oh, I don't know about that," her voice pinched with worry. "I wouldn't mind being rid of those other two . . .or at least the oldest one. Something doesn't seem the same with them as it does with Will. How do you think they'll take the news when they learn you want to adopt Will as your own?"

"I've thought about it, but I've kinda got the impression they wouldn't be keen on being adopted themselves. I reckon they'll handle it like young men. Luther is fifteen, after all."

"Another thing I'm not so sure about."

"All we can do is take his word on it. Some boys are big for their age. Now, back to the question of your inheritance money. I think it will be safest to deposit it in a bank in Weatherford now that we're settled. I'm not convinced any of the smaller banks around here could keep it safe."

"I agree. I'm thankful you found a good hiding place away from the house, but I'll rest even better when it's safe in the bank."

Will had overheard the conversations about Indian raids coming from the Brazos Reservation several miles to the north. He'd also heard the whispered speculations that some of those raids were just white men dressed up as Comanches to get folks riled up enough to force the government to do away with the reservation. Or to cover for their own misdeeds.

While the idea of Indians swooping in to kill them kept Will awake some nights, there was also a niggling sense of empathy. A whole people with no control over their lives, forced from what had been their home by a people bigger and stronger, and made to live on the charitable nature of others. Something about that felt too familiar.

The Charidys were quiet for a few minutes, but Will could tell they hadn't left. Probably kissing, which he thought they did too much of. His parents had never been ones to show much affection to each other. He'd been fine with that since his mother chose to pour her affection out on him and his little sister.

"Essie, don't you think we ought to give this grand ol' tree a name?"

"You want to name a tree?"

"It feels like it's meant to be part of the family. Look how much time we spend here in its shade. Don't tell me you aren't drawn to it too."

"It is a lovely *tree.*"

"How about Moses? That's a good strong name."

"For a *man*, not a *tree.*" Will could tell Mrs. Charidy had her hand in front of her mouth, trying not to laugh like she always did. "Abel Charidy, I do believe the heat is getting to you."

"Are you happy here, Essie?" A note of worry tinted his words.

"I will always love any place where I'm with you. This place is lovely, but lovely in a way that tells me we'll have to work and face hard days. I worry if it'll still look as beautiful to us five years from now after we've truly tasted its harshness instead of only the happiness we have now."

"It's a good place to raise our family, but I won't stay here if you're not happy."

"Well then, I guess you better finish unpacking your bags so you can stay awhile because I *am* happily in love with the best and most godly man I know."

"If I'm the best you know, I'd say you need to meet more people. But the truth is, I don't want to share. I'll be completely happy for you to continue in your misguided overestimation of my worth." He clapped his hands together once and rubbed calloused palms together, a sound that had become comfortingly familiar to Will. "Now back to the tree, can you just imagine if it could talk? What things it must have seen. What new secrets will it keep two hundred years from now?"

"If it were talking to me right now, it would be telling me I need to get back to the kitchen and get the bread rising for supper. Rose will be up soon. And I still have more of the meat from the deer y'all brought home to get tended."

"I'll walk with you. We need to make plans for me to be gone for a few days."

Will listened as their voices trailed off, waiting until he could no longer hear them before sitting up. He moved to slide from his hiding spot but stilled when something rubbed against the bark of the tree beneath him. He peered over the edge and found Luther staring up at him through squinty, hate-filled eyes. The older boy winked and walked away.

Will's heart thumped against his chest. Had Luther heard everything Will had?

The possibility made prickles of unease march up the back of his neck.

But just as quick the word adopted sprang back to mind. The Charidys wanted him to be their son. He wasn't sure how he was supposed to feel about that.

He had watched his mother die the day those men came to rob them. She'd put up a fight. Whether they had meant to kill her or not, he wasn't sure. But it didn't make her any less dead.

His father was a different story. He'd just disappeared. Folks speculated he'd fallen into the flooded river and been swept away. His body had never been found.

Out of respect for Will's mother, they'd waited a while before declaring him dead. But Will hadn't let go of his hope that easily.

How would his father ever find him if he let someone change his name?

CHAPTER 10

Every tree is valuable to the community and worth keeping around for as long as possible. And that is why even sick individuals are supported and nourished until they recover. ~Peter Wohlleben

Something was wrong. Something Jodee didn't want to know about. If she left now, she'd never have to hear them say it.

She found her green Forest Service uniform pants and hiking boots, bagged and tucked beneath the hospital bed. The shirt was a total loss, so the gown would have to do. She knotted the tie of the over-sized cotton garment tight around her waist. Every movement sent a throb of pain through a part of her body. But it was the ache in her middle that seized her heart, stirring an even greater anguish.

Thinking hurt. Her thoughts remained fuzzy and confused as they tumbled around in a brain that felt as though it were caught in a woodchipper.

She dug the polished white stone from her pants' pocket and rubbed her fingers over the smooth surface. What was it supposed to mean? Paul had promised to tell her when he came home.

But he hadn't come home. He'd left her fatherless in a world that was cold and cruel to daughters without fathers.

All she had to show for his presence in her life was a stupid rock. And yet it was a rock she couldn't let go of. It whispered to her of a secret truth, and if she held it long enough, it would one day tell her.

Trees whispered things to her, too.

Trees never disappeared. Trees stayed. They helped her make sense of the world—or at least, believe she might one day.

The front door of the New Plenty Regional Hospital clanged shut behind her, and she drew in a deep breath of rain-damped air. The storms had moved through, leaving the world around her washed with new life. Instead of bringing comfort, the impression intensified the sense of grief weighing her down. Her fingers squeezed the stone, pressing it into her palm until her hand ached.

Life was too much about loss.

Puddles of water dotted the evenly mown grass and the uneven sidewalk that bordered it, reflecting the glow of the streetlamps. Her steps sloshed as she headed to a red oak in the hospital yard. She placed her hand on the rough, wet bark, seeking comfort in the touch, but the tree had no way to console her in this moment.

Trees had often sheltered her, welcomed her, whispered things into her soul. But in this moment, the tree had no comfort to offer. It remained a cold, impersonal creature, unable to recognize the pain growing inside her.

She walked across the street to a bench positioned under the overhang of the Barely Awake Coffee Shop and sat. With her elbows on her knees, she hung her head as regret gripped her. Leaving the hospital was wrong.

She was like a wild animal—always running until cornered and forced to fight.

Only hours ago, she'd wrestled with a possibility. A possibility that offered choices that terrified her not matter which path she might take.

But something felt different now, as though the thing she feared had been uprooted and snatched from her. Instead of relief, her heart thrashed with agony while anger simmered in her veins. But who was she angry with?

Her knuckles went white in her fisted hands. She needed to know who to blame. Something was wrong with her memory. A giant hole existed. A hole that made her pulse race and her muscles quiver as though her body knew things her brain had forgotten to save.

She'd never experienced memory loss before, at least not one that wasn't alcohol induced during a low point in her life. This was different. This memory loss came with an urgency to remember.

Tires hissed over the wet street, drawing her attention. A black truck drove by, the only other thing that moved beneath the glow of the streetlights.

Her heart raced like a steeplechase, making random hops and lurches in between dizzying sprints. She should go back inside the hospital.

She closed her eyes. Her heart wasn't what concerned her. If she went back, the doctor would talk to her about the *other*.

And she wasn't ready to hear it.

"There you are." The nurse who'd been attending her since she arrived, Grace, crossed the street. When Jodee didn't speak, the woman sat beside her without another word. The silence she let linger became fertile soil for companionship to take root.

After a few minutes, Grace asked if she were waiting on someone to come for her?

Jodee shook her head.

"Are you sure about that?" Grace stared at her as though the woman could read her heart, understanding things even Jodee hadn't yet realized.

Because yes. She'd spent every day since her stepfather left—maybe even her entire life—waiting on someone to come for her.

"You have somewhere to go?" Grace asked.

"Sure." It wasn't a lie. Technically, she had places she *could* go if she chose. Which she wouldn't.

"May I speak bluntly?"

BENEATH THE BROKEN OAK

"Why not?" She surrendered to the fact this woman probably lacked the ability to *not speak* bluntly.

"You need to come back inside and face whatever needs facing."

She stared at the distorted light reflected in a nearby puddle.

"Do that, and when Dr. Hyson releases you, you can come stay at my house for a few days." Grace stared at her with a mix of compassion and concern and a dare for her to try to do otherwise. "Or as long as you like. My home is open to you, and it's a B&B, so the accommodations aren't so bad. I'm told the food is decent. Might be a good place to rest and recover while you get your thoughts together."

She looked at the hospital. Inside it awaited a truth that might not kill her physically but could be the fatal blow to a soul already fractured.

"Flowery wallpaper?" she asked.

Grace rocked back on the bench and laughed. "Not at all. Textured and painted in earth tones. I prefer the rustic look. Truth be told, I think it helps me pretend the world is still moving at a slower pace in a simpler time."

Jodee didn't need a slower pace. She needed a total rewind. The word yes came out before she could stop it. "Let's get this over with then."

"That's the spirit," Grace teased as she placed an arm around Jodee's shoulders and walked beside her.

Dr. Hyson greeted her when she stepped through the door.

"Ah, the prodigal returns." He winked, as though people disappearing AMA then popping back in happened all the time.

He waved her into the room she'd just left. "How're you feeling right now?"

"Like I've been sideswiped by a freight train." She pressed her hand against her stomach without mentioning her racing heart.

"I see." He pulled out a penlight and shone it in her eyes. Then he seated himself on the edge of the bed. He flipped through the papers on his clipboard.

She'd only been here for a little while. How could there be that many pages? Was he trying to kill an entire forest on her behalf?

"Do you remember what happened to you before your accident tonight?"

She'd already told him everything she could about the accident. Once again, she recounted stopping at Tooley's. Omitting the part about seeing Blue, she relayed everything until she lost sight of the cowboy who'd warned her about the coming storms. The next thing she remembered, her truck was skidding out of control as she swerved to avoid an oncoming vehicle on the road to El Hueso.

"Anything else?"

She shook her head. "Why don't I remember?"

"You took a significant blow to your head. Now I think you're experiencing what is known as transient global amnesia."

"You can you fix it, right?" The need to remember overwhelmed her.

She looked away, hoping he wouldn't see her fear—a level beyond what she could explain.

"Young lady, you're not a car to be fixed. The human body is far more complex and mysterious than that." Dr. Hyson smiled. "I can do everything in my ability to make the conditions right for your memory to return. Whether it does belongs to a higher power. I have every reason to be optimistic though."

His soft-spoken words were meant to comfort, but they were like flannel worn too thin. How could he comfort her when he couldn't know the thoughts she'd entertained?

"Let's talk about something else for a minute," he continued.

No. Let's don't. The words rested bitter on her tongue, but she didn't speak them. She steeled herself for what he would say.

"How long have you been having heart trouble?"

She rocked forward on the table. This wasn't the question she'd expected.

He looked at her as though she hadn't heard the question—or didn't understand it—then repeated it.

All my life, she wanted to say, but that wasn't the kind of heart condition he referred to. "I haven't... I mean I don't... didn't." Her hands sought for the reassurance of the rock, but she'd already tucked it back in her pocket.

"You've never noticed any symptoms like an irregular heartbeat or a fluttering sensation in your chest?"

"Just today. I'm probably just tired, or maybe I had too much caffeine. Nothing to worry about, right?" She wrung her fingers as though they were a wet rag.

"I'm afraid it might not be quite that simple. Have you ever been told you have Wolf Parkinson's White disorder?"

Her fidgeting stopped. "A few years ago. But since I've never had any symptoms, I figured it was a mistake."

"I see," Dr. Adams said. "We found it on the ECG we performed when you came in tonight. Any family members with it? WPW is often hereditary and if it is, everyone in the family will have it."

She shook her head, not that she would really know. His scrutiny now made her squirm as though she had given the wrong answer.

"Is it serious?"

"It can kill you." A uniformed officer stood in the doorway, his flint-like words tumbling to the floor like marbles.

Dr. Hyson shot him an irritated look before answering Jodee. "Yes, it can be fatal, but all of living is."

CHAPTER 11

The woods are lovely, dark and deep, But I have promises to keep, And miles to go before I sleep . . . ~Robert Frost

*L*ogan braced himself. Dr. Hyson wouldn't be happy he'd bulldozed himself into the middle of the doctor's consultation with his patient.

Hyson turned to Logan, a frown burrowing into his face. "Good morning, Sheriff Adams. I wasn't aware you'd joined my private conversation with my patient."

"My apologies. The nurse's station was empty, so I let myself back." He fingered the brim of the hat he held in his hands.

The doctor's scowl deepened as though Logan's reply sparked the fire of a different displeasure. "Perhaps you'd like to close the door and wait in the hall until I'm finished."

"Actually, if she's able, I'd like to ask Miss Trevaine some questions now. I wouldn't interrupt if I didn't think it was urgent." He'd spent the last couple of hours in the rain asking people who never saw anything to tell him everything they saw. His patience had dried up, leaving behind a brittle irritability. He was no closer to knowing the true whereabouts of the boy than when he'd started.

Dr. Hyson looked at Jodee.

"I didn't get a good look at the other vehicle. I think it was a pickup, but I couldn't really see anything," she said.

"I'm not here about the accident."

She shook her head, confusion playing over her face.

"I'm here to ask you about what happened at Tooley's," he prodded.

"And that I for sure can't tell you. I don't remember."

They never do. Logan's fingers stilled their thrumming of his hat.

"She's right. There's nothing she can tell you about what happened right now. In fact, it might be a couple of days before she's ready." Dr. Hyson dipped his chin, looking up at him over the top of his glasses.

"Doc, can I speak to you privately for a minute?" Logan nodded his head toward the hall.

"If it's about me, I'd rather you just get it over with right here." She stared at him. The lift of her chin revealed a pridefulness that said she'd be a challenge to interview if he gave her a reason.

Okay, if that's the way she wanted it. He faced the doctor. "All right, how do you know she can't remember?" He shifted his gaze to Jodee. "Or if she doesn't want to remember?"

"Are you questioning my diagnosis?" Dr. Hyson arched an eyebrow.

"No sir. Just questioning if there might be a reason Miss Trevaine would prefer not to remember."

"I'm sure if someone assaulted you in such a manner, you might prefer not to remember some of the details."

And you'd be assuming wrong. Logan kept the thought to himself. He glanced at the clock on the wall. Two AM. The boy had been unaccounted for now for over four hours. His deputies had scoured the area around Tooley's and along the roads and Interstate, but the heavy rain and the mother's insistence all was well had made it a waste of time. Still, he wasn't ready to let it rest, especially not with an unknown wild card in Jodee Trevaine. Victim or criminal? He ground his teeth. He didn't even know for sure if a crime had been committed. Or at least he hadn't until he saw her.

Exhaustion and a rain induced chill had him running on empty when it came to leniency right now. He needed a cheeseburger and a very large, very hot, very, very strong coffee.

And he needed to shift his approach. The possibility he was letting his emotions interfere with his judgement jabbed at him like a dirty needle. He softened his tone. "I had to ask."

"Just doing your job," Jodee offered, though clearly still irritated by his insinuation.

"Do you remember what you were doing at the truck stop?"

"What do people usually do at a truck stop?"

He folded his arms over his chest and scowled.

She sighed. "I stopped to use the restroom and get a snack."

"What brought you here? And don't tell me your truck," he countered before she could give him another smart aleck answer. Her uniform and the reports from the crash confirmed she was with the Forest Service, but he wanted to hear how she explained her presence in the area.

"I went to El Hueso today to inspect a tree—a potential Heritage Oak, to be exact."

A few of his muscles relaxed. His Aunt Grace had been the one who contacted the Forest Service about the tree. She'd been gathering research for the project for months now.

"Do you remember seeing anyone when you stopped?"

"Just a few people inside. A little boy." Her eyebrows drew together, her features tightening. After a second, she looked at him again with a shake of her head.

"Can you describe the boy?" he asked.

Jodee gave him the description, including the toy cars. But her inability to produce details about anyone else that she'd seen frustrated her.

"Who put their hands around your neck and tried to choke you?" Logan pressed.

She frowned. "No one."

"The bruises on your throat say they did, whether you remember it or not."

Her hands went to her neck, a new look of concern darkening her features. "I thought it was just the smoke from the wreck making it hurt. I should remember something like that, shouldn't I?"

"It's to be expected that your throat will feel sore for a few days, both inside and out," Dr. Hyson explained. "And along with the WPW symptoms, you had your brain rattled this evening. But rest at ease. I suspect the memory loss won't last. Transient global amnesia—TGA for short—usually clears up within forty-eight hours or so."

"Anything we can do to speed that up?" Logan asked.

"The best thing you can do is not interfere. Let nature take its course to do the healing." Once again, he looked over the rim of his glasses at Logan. "The human body has a miraculous ability to heal itself in times like this—*if we let it.*" His words carried a not-so-subtle warning. "Now, I'm keeping you a little longer for observation. And I won't be happy to hear of any more disappearing acts. Understood?"

But something else troubled him. He looked at Jodee. "Mind if I ask a couple more questions?"

Again, she only nodded, as though unable to speak.

"Wolf Parkinsons White . . . how common is it, Doc?" Logan chided himself for asking the question he already knew the answer to, but he wanted to see her reaction.

"It's not unheard of. Maybe one to three in every one thousand people."

"And what causes it?"

Hyson arched his eyebrow, giving him a meaningful and pointed look. "I believe you're familiar with its origin, but to confirm, it's a hereditary condition, meaning at least one parent carries the trait in their genes."

Hyson turned to Jodee. "Most cases of Wolf Parkinsons White respond well to treatment. Until we get your symptoms under control, I'll have to put a restriction on your activity. You'll need to follow up with a cardiologist. I'll make the referral unless you have another primary care doctor you'd like to speak to first."

"There's no one."

"All right, then let's keep watching this head injury." Dr. Hyson glanced at Logan with an unspoken warning. "I'm writing you a prescription for propranolol until you can see a cardiologist. Any questions?"

The question wasn't directed at Logan, though he still had plenty of his own. Asking them now wouldn't accomplish much more.

Was her job the only reason she had for being in El Hueso tonight and for stopping at Tooley's Truck Stop? The concern on her face as they discussed her diagnosis seemed genuine.

But he'd learned the hard way to never trust coincidence.

"Yeah, Sheriff, thanks for calling me back. I didn't mean to wake you. Figured you'd get the message in the morning." Logan stepped away from the hospital door and moved to a place in the yard that gave him a clear view of the surroundings and enough distance he wouldn't be overheard. "I hate to bother you with what may be nothing, but I got a hunch that won't go away. You're always telling me to go with my gut."

"Ain't been sleeping much lately, so spill it." Matthews hadn't lost his fondness for getting straight to business.

"I don't know if anything happened at all. It just doesn't sit quite right. Grace got a call earlier tonight from a hysterical mother, said her six-year-old son went missing from Tooley's. But when I got out to the truck stop where she works as a cashier, she changed her story. Said it was all a mistake. She and the father aren't together and her story is that his dad picked him up for a visit. She insisted everything was fine now, but I don't like it. She acted pretty nervous."

"How so?"

"All the usual signs of deceit. Fidgeting, no eye contact, counted the ones in the cash register five times, and I bet she still couldn't tell me there were twenty-three one-dollar bills in the drawer." He exhaled. Was he reading too much into this? Or reading the wrong message into her reaction to him? "Of course, someone did put it into her head CPS might take the boy away."

"And where's the boy now?"

"Now she's saying he's gone to stay with his dad for a few days. The problem is the dad's number isn't in service, but the mom swears everything's fine. We checked around the truck stop and at their house. No signs of the boy or of any foul play."

"Any history?"

"None that would warrant concern he was in danger."

"You know the law. Ain't nothing more you can do about it yet."

"Yeah, I know. I just don't have to like it. That's why I called you." Logan turned in a slow circle while he talked, scanning for anyone who might be within ear shot. "Something else happened at Tooley's tonight. I want to request the video from their surveillance cameras. I believe a woman was assaulted, but she doesn't remember anything."

"If I had a nickel for every woman who said she was assaulted at the truck stop then said she couldn't remember because she didn't want to get the guy in trouble, I'd retire a rich man. Frustrated, but rich. Even though the majority of them are legitimate complaints, it's a slippery slope to go down when they're scared in both directions. If she's telling you she doesn't remember, what makes you think she was assaulted?"

"I'll send you some pictures as soon as we hang up." At least she'd cooperated by letting him take pictures of the bruises on her neck.

"You check for drug use?"

"Doc ran all the tests and says she's clean. But she did take a pretty good blow to the head. He says she's got something called transient global amnesia. Said her memory should return in about forty-eight hours."

"So, you think maybe she saw something, or she's somehow involved with the kid's possible disappearance?"

"I'm not sure what to think other than it's suspicious she was around at the same time but can't remember anything. Kind of a stretch to believe two things happened at about the same time and place but aren't connected somehow."

"Stranger things have happened. If you really believe there's something to be concerned about with the boy, do you think you can keep her close by, not let her leave town until her memory returns?"

"I can try. She's at the hospital now. She wrecked her truck up on Jacob's Ladder. Her phone was destroyed in the attack and hospital staff says she hasn't made any phone calls. The emergency contact number in the DMV goes to a guy who died eight years ago." Another thing that nipped at Logan's doubts.

"Keep an eye on her and get ahold of any video footage from the cameras at the truck stop—if any of them were actually working."

"Yeah, that's another problem."

"You got anything that isn't a problem?"

He ignored the sarcasm—Matthews second language. "The manager isn't willing to cooperate without a warrant. "

"Probably afraid we'll get a look at the drug dealing he does out the back door." Neither of them said what both were thinking—their shared suspicion the judge they'd need to sign a warrant was benefitting from the back door business at Tooley's.

"You said it, sir," Logan answered.

"May need to talk her into pressing charges and see what happens. It'll make it harder for him to squirm out of it if she does."

"That's my thought, too. I will sir."

A female voice interrupted Matthews on the other end of the call. Several seconds ticked by before he returned. "Keep me posted. I gotta go let 'em jab another hole in me now. But Logan, we need to talk about something else soon."

"There's one other thing, sir. She has WPW."

Matthews inhaled, the sound raspy and faint. Several breaths filled the space between them before the old man responded. "Well, that sure thickens the stew, don't it?"

CHAPTER 12

As the twig is bent the tree inclines. ~Virgil

𝓗e tapped the tip of his middle finger against the solid oak desktop, his attention riveted to the computer screen in front of him. Could what he saw be right? She really was here.

Right in the middle of something she shouldn't have seen. Which made her a problem.

Or an opportunity? Maybe the time had come. She might be the last hope he had left.

Fate was a funny, illegitimate little thing. A throaty laugh escaped.

He always did have a fondness for the illegitimate. A rap on the door broke up his musings. "Yeah."

The burly half-wit he employed entered, his asymmetrical face in its constant frown. Rusty Boggs was stronger than an ox and had about as much sense. But he was extremely tractable. As long as he let the man have a little rein to release his passions on occasion.

Except for what he'd just seen.

What he'd seen sparked an anger best not fed. Not yet, anyway.

He steepled his hands, tapping his fingers against his pursed lips as he stared at the man. He needed him to finish his current *project*. Once it was over, well, that would be a different matter. "Anything new?"

"The woman's at the hospital still. Adams came around the truck stop asking some questions about the boy, but the mother stuck to the story that he's with his dad."

He didn't ask if Adams believed the woman. It didn't matter what the law enforcement officer believed. With nothing else amiss, there wasn't anything he could do.

"Nolan?"

"Taken care of."

"And this girl—who is she and why was she there last night?" He already knew the answer but wanted the satisfaction of hearing it confirmed.

"My friend at the hospital says her name is Jodee Trevaine. Don't know much else yet, but she was driving a Forest Service truck when she wrecked."

"Forest Service, huh?" His heart raced. It was her. The tree brought her to him. He knew it. But why?

It wasn't possible that she would know about the box, was it? "Anyone with her?"

"Alone, no one came all night. Adams went in a little while ago, but he's the only one."

He worked his jaw as though he chewed an imaginary piece of gristle. He clicked on an image and angled the monitor for Rusty to see. "You see this guy there last night?"

"Don't recall seeing him there, but he was at Roots."

"What was he doing?"

"Sitting at the bar like usual. Drinking alone. Been in several times lately."

"You got a name for him?" Ah, yes. He'd seen him, too. Sitting at a table near the back, still alone.

"Blue Sunday." Sunday. He had connections here. And maybe a purpose. If he could play this right, Sunday might be the perfect scapegoat for the dilemma created by last night's fiasco. He watched the video play again, studying the interaction between Blue Sunday and Jodee. Another reason he didn't like the guy.

"What's being said about her attack?"

Rusty's mouth drew up in a crooked grin. "Ain't nothing to say. She don't remember nothin'."

He flattened his palm against the leather ink blotter. The brute had hurt her. If he'd done permanent damage, he'd see to it Rusty Boggs experienced terminal damage.

"See if Wiley can tell you anything else about Sunday. Then get back over to the hospital and keep an eye on her. But make sure no one sees you."

"You want me to take care of her?"

Silence filled the room as seconds ticked off the antique grandfather clock. "Don't touch her." The finger tapping on the desk started again. "At least not yet."

CHAPTER 13

The tree that is beside the running water is fresher and gives more fruit.
~Saint Teresa of Avila

"You ready?" Grace asked.

Jodee clicked the seatbelt in place, then adjusted the sunglasses on loan from her self-appointed new friend and caregiver. She suspected from the more-than-casual scrutiny, her words weren't what Grace needed as affirmation. She mustered a smile. "Let's do this."

It had required a great deal of persuasion—and an even greater amount of flat-out begging, which she hated—, but she'd finagled her way out of the hospital by promising to remain in Grace's keen-eyed custody. No driving, no technology, no loud noises.

"Good! Let's get you to the house so you can get a hot shower, a decent meal, and more rest."

Jodee pulled in a deep breath. "I—"

"Don't say it. This is not an act of charity." Grace flicked her hand in the air as though waving away a gnat. "If I were in your shoes, I'd want someone to do the same for me. We just keep rescuing each other. It's the way the world should work, though it doesn't happen as often as it should. One day you'll have the chance to do the same for someone else."

Jodee wasn't sure about that. So far, she'd had more success with ruining lives than rescuing them. More disconcerting was the way Grace seemed to always read her mind.

"Besides, I'm responsible for your presence at the truck stop last night. If I hadn't been worried about the tree, you wouldn't have come here." Grace gave her head a quick shake. "I feel like a sentimental old fool. Trying to save a tree and nearly getting someone killed in the process."

"Not your fault. I love what I do. Trees are my life." The word stalled on her tongue. She didn't miss the odd look Grace gave her.

"Well, I really do feel bad this has happened to you because of a dying tree." Grace glanced at her. "It is dying, isn't it?"

"I'm not sure." The samples she'd collected had been lost in the wreck. "Something is keeping it from thriving, but I can't really tell what's going on beneath the bark until I see the results of the tests. Which I'll have to start over with. I apologize for the delay."

"Now it's my turn to say *not your fault*. Let's get you healed before we worry anymore about the tree."

Jodee turned to look out the window. She'd rather worry about the tree.

"I'd love for you to stay as long as you like. I can't wait for you to see the house. I was always drawn to the old Charidy House." She laughed. "Call me crazy, but it seemed like it had a secret it wanted to share. My husband bought it for me, one last gift before he passed away. But it's a lot of house for one little old woman, so I turned it into a bed-and-breakfast."

"Seems like a lot of work, in addition to the time you spend working at the hospital."

"El Hueso isn't exactly a tourist destination. I get a few thrill seekers who've heard the town is cursed. They come looking for a ghost and secretly hoping they don't see one," Grace laughed again. "I've even been advised to advertise that I have a ghost to attract more customers."

"The whole town is cursed, huh?" Jodee had grown up forty miles away in the small town of Murchison. There had always been an intense rivalry between the two towns and a sort of unspoken admonishment that people needed to steer clear of El Hueso. One her mother had been almost fanatical about enforcing.

"No more or less than any other place. Not since what happened in the Garden of Eden."

Jodee knew the gist of the story, but she wasn't interested in a Sunday School lesson right now. "Why don't you advertise having a ghost?"

"There's only one ghost in my life and he doesn't allow room for any others." Grace turned to her with a smile. "And it's not about the money. I've lived in El Hueso for so long I don't want people coming here seeking a thrill and missing the best part. I want people to appreciate the beauty. The sunsets are gorgeous. The peace, the view from the top of the hill at the edge of town, the determined old-timers that keep hanging on even though there's not much left to hang on to. There's so much good here, but we have to look for it." Grace stared at the road. The wistful expression on her face stirred an unfamiliar envy in Jodee. "El Hueso is a place where people can slow down and remember their roots. Maybe that's what I want to say. Maybe that's what I'm trying to hold on to myself."

"Sounds . . ." Normally fine with the silence, Jodee shifted in the seat as she dug the white stone from her pocket. The familiar touch soothed her.

"Crazy? I know. Hanging onto something whose time has passed. I just can't shake the impression that El Hueso isn't finished yet. It's like a place waiting on *something*." Grace slowed the vehicle to weave between a series of potholes. "I hope this bouncing around isn't causing you too much pain."

Jodee ran a dry lip between her teeth. Grace could be speaking of the bumps in the road or of the unsettled sensation left by her speech.

They crossed the river, then a second bridge carried them over the interstate separating the two towns.

The land flourished in the fertile river bottom soil where New Plenty resided. But the fertility passed away as they wound up the side of the hill on the road to El Hueso as though the terrain had been wrung out from the top, squeezing the rich, life-sustaining soil and nutrients into the river bottom below. The massive oaks and pecans gave way to scrubby cedars and limestone rocks where prickly pear cactus and beargrass thrived.

"So, you like El Hueso. That's why you want the oak registered as a Heritage Tree—a way to preserve the town's history?"

"I believe remembering our history is important. You know, so hopefully, we don't make the same mistakes twice. Although, in the case of El Hueso, it's not a very pretty history. I think I like what El Hueso could be, but . . ." Grace frowned. "There's something rooted in here that holds it back."

They wound past a few old houses and abandoned mobile homes. At least they appeared to be abandoned. Grace had said there wasn't much industry. Jodee guessed she had deliberately not counted the meth labs in her report.

While New Plenty learned to adapt through the lifeline of weekend tourism—small shops with repurposed antiques and eclectic handmade items, historic homes turned into quaint bed and breakfasts, and a bar-be-que joint that had been featured on Texas Country Reporter—El Hueso was a dying town situated on top of a hardscrabble pile of rock. Vacant buildings constructed decades earlier lined the Main Street. A few bore evidence of an attempt at repurposing, but most were shuttered. The town's precarious position made it an unlikely place for visitors who weren't already on a mission.

"Oh dear."

Jodee followed Grace's gaze to see an elderly woman wobbling down the street, a small box tucked under her arm.

"It's Tillie Calderon."

Dressed in a Navajo print western shirt several sizes too large, a pair of faded denim skinny jeans, and fuzzy topped UGGs, the woman tottered along in the middle of the street as though no one else was expected to use it. Her long gray braid swayed side to side in rhythm with her rocking gait. No bigger around than a toothpick, she looked like she might blow away in the next big gust of air. Blow away, but not break. She also looked as wiry as a cedar switch.

"Poor Tillie," Grace said, slowing her SUV. "Her husband passed away last week."

"Is she . . ." Jodee didn't want to say sane . . . "all right?"

"I suppose that depends on your definition of all right." Grace gave her a knowing look. "Tillie and her husband Ship own the antiques store, although I'm not sure *store* is the correct word. It's rarely open, and I've never heard of them selling a single thing from their collection. It's more like a storage place for the discarded remnants of El Hueso, maintained by the keepers of the town secrets. I guess eccentric hoarders might be the best description. But with hearts of pure gold. I'm going to miss Ship."

"Does she have family here?"

"Their daughter lives in Lubbock. Ship had been experiencing the onset of dementia. He had hip surgery a few weeks ago and was confined to a nursing home in New Plenty for the past few weeks. They said he passed in his sleep."

Isn't that what they always say? But something about the way Grace said it captured Jodee's attention. She turned to Grace, who sighed.

"That's not what Tillie believes."

Grace lowered the window as the car pulled alongside the woman. "Where are you headed, Tillie?"

"Been to see Ship. Headed home." The woman kept walking.

Jodee had noticed the cemetery at the edge of town. A fresh grave covered in wilting flowers must have been Ship's resting place.

"Hop in and we'll give you a ride." Grace stopped the car.

Tillie leaned down as though suspicious of who made up the second part of *we*. A look of surprise flashed over her face. She opened her mouth only to snap it shut, her eyes darting around as though she expected to find someone watching.

"This is my friend Jodee Trevaine. She's visiting me for a few days," Grace said.

Tillie climbed in, clutching the little box like a child with a new toy. As soon as Grace had the car in motion, the old woman leaned forward, her mouth inches from Jodee's ear. "They kilt my Ship. Murdered him in his sleep 'cause they wuz scart of him."

"Tillie, you remember what Dr. Hyson said? Ship passed in his sleep," Grace spoke with a matter-of-fact calmness as she tried to redirect Tillie's thoughts.

"I remember. But I ain't believing it. They's scart and they kilt him."

"Who was scared of him, Tillie?" Grace asked, glancing into the rearview mirror.

"The King, the Big Man, the Potentate."

Grace shook her head and offered Jodee a look of apology.

Intrigue captured Jodee's attention. "Who's the king, Tillie?"

"Oh, you'll know him when you meet him. Everybody knows him. Ship told me he'd be back to get him. He was right." Tillie slumped against the seat and turned to face out the window. "Shh. We can't talk, or we'll be next."

Ship had dementia, so who knew what he'd told his wife. Whatever it was, Tillie believed him. Maybe she was experiencing the onset of dementia herself.

Inside, the car grew quiet, and no one seemed eager to destroy the hushed atmosphere that filled the space.

They rounded the corner and Grace tapped her brakes. Jodee recognized the tree she'd inspected yesterday now split in two. Half of its limbs sprawled across the road.

"Guess both of us have been wasting our time. Looks like lightning struck the tree last night." Grace maneuvered her car around the scattered limbs. "I'll need to get someone over to get this cleared up before dark."

A screech from the backseat made them both jump. "It's here. It's here. I knew it. The reckoning is upon us."

Tillie bounced up and down in the backseat. "Mark my words, the past has come home. The roots will reveal the truth."

The frown on Grace's face deepened at Tillie's cryptic words, but whatever she was thinking, she kept to herself.

As the old woman settled back into her silence, Jodee stared at the building down the street. She'd been so focused on the tree she hadn't noticed it before.

The sign hanging from a rusty metal pole drew an unexpected shudder. One word—Roots—hovered just above a picture of tree roots digging deep in the ground like a hand made of bones. The chipped, peeling paint deepened the weathered sign's ominous appearance.

Her elbows pressed against her sides, her fingers curling around the stone in her hand.

The sensation of an unseen force reaching inside, as though the image of the roots grabbed for her heart, paralyzed her.

"You okay?" Grace asked.

She exhaled the breath she didn't know she'd held and nodded.

"What is that place?"

"A mini Sodom and Gomorrah—our local watering hole." Grace turned the car down a side street where few houses stood. "Originally, El Hueso was the county seat. A courthouse had been built there until it burned down in the late 1800s. So sad to think about all the important records and documents that were lost in that fire. Anyway, the citizens voted to move the county seat and courthouse to New Plenty before they could finish rebuilding it here, so they ended up using it as a jailhouse, instead. There's a rather unpleasant story about a body being found in the old cistern being part of the reason people opted for New Plenty over El Hueso. If it's true, I can't really blame them. Anyway, now the building is a bar."

"Kind of big for a jailhouse or a dive bar."

"There's a lot of speculation about its original purpose, and who exactly was in charge of the jail. There are some not so nice stories that go with it, I'm afraid." Grace pointed to the small square rock building standing near the bigger one. "Until recently, they still used that building as a sort of drunk tank alongside the bar. It's built over the old town cistern, though I believe that was filled in decades ago."

Jodee pulled her attention from the sign to look at the building Grace indicated, but the gnarled shapes on the sign still reached for her.

She shuddered. Or were they already rooted inside?

CHAPTER 14

Texas 1858

It is in the roots, not the branches, that a tree's greatest strength lies.
~Matshona Dhliwayo

The first thing the Charidys built when they settled on this hill was the barn. It came even before the house. It was important to take care of the things that took care of you, Mr. Charidy said.

So, of them all, Daisy the milk cow became the first to sleep under a roof once they arrived in Texas.

Will hadn't minded. Even now with the house finished, he still slept best in the crook of the giant tree or here in the barn.

He nestled in the straw a few feet from the Jersey cow. Mr. Charidy said she would calve tonight. Will wanted to be there to see, so he'd snuck out of the house. The Charidys didn't like for anyone to go outside after dark. There was still the threat of Comanches, though Mr. Charidy said rogue bands of white men stirring up trouble and blaming it on the Indians were a more likely threat.

Guilt pinched his stomach. What if they discovered he'd slipped out and decided they didn't want to adopt him after all?

He still hadn't decided how he felt about it, but that didn't mean he wanted the possibility taken away from him.

Daisy stood, restlessly tramping in the stall. Her tail hung at an odd angle, part of nature's plan for the calf's arrival, and she twitched it.

"Easy girl. It'll be over soon, and you'll have a new baby. I bet it'll be a boy," he said, though he knew a heifer would be better.

The cow paid him no mind but settled back down on the bed of straw.

Spent from a day of hauling busted rocks to make a garden fence, Will leaned against the wooden slats behind him and closed heavy eyelids.

The conversation he'd overheard beneath the oak never ventured far from his thoughts. He turned it over and over again in his mind, like finding a fossil and trying to imagine what the creature that made it must have looked like.

Did he want Mr. Charidy to be his father?

Did he even *need* a father? He was getting by pretty good right now without one. Another round of guilt pinched even harder in his middle. He had a father.

He didn't mind Mrs. Charidy's mothering ways. She reminded him a lot of his own mother. He'd even grown familiar with her touch, though it differed from his real mother's. He felt the love in both.

And Rose would be his little sister. He'd nicknamed her Little Bud because she was hardly big enough to be a rose—and because even though she was only four, she hated the nickname. His own sister's name had been Louise, and one thing he knew for sure. He did not want another little sister. Though if he were honest, he'd admit he missed her like the dickens.

How would it feel to be called Will Charidy?

Would it be as if Will Sunday never existed? Maybe then everyone would forget about Will, the orphan. The one whose daddy disappeared without a word. The one sent to live in the orphanage because no one wanted him after his mother and Louise were killed while he watched from the hayloft and did nothing to protect them. Yes, his mother had ordered him to hide there. But that didn't change the fact he'd hidden like a coward when he was supposed to be the man of the family. At least that's what everyone told him after his daddy left.

No wonder he'd been sent to the orphanage. Who wanted a coward for a son?

Maybe making Will Sunday vanish wouldn't be a bad thing.

He frowned as Luther's face punched into his thoughts. Somehow, the older boy knew too much about Will's past. He wouldn't be one to let it go. He must have overheard a conversation between the Charidys, because Will didn't believe for a second Mrs. Charidy would've told the bully. He was pretty sure she didn't like Luther, either.

It didn't matter *how* he knew, though. The problem was *that* he knew. He knew about Will being blamed for starting the fire at the orphanage.

His face grew warm.

And worse, Luther knew Mr. Charidy had rescued Will from the auction block after he'd been accused of setting the fire. Sometimes when no one was around to hear, Luther taunted Will by rattling on in the singsong voice of an auctioneer.

Daisy stood again. Her head bobbed as she pulled against the rope tying her to the stall. She sidestepped, wide-eyed and nervous.

Smoke—not the normal scent of the fireplace where Mrs. Charidy cooked their meals—assaulted his nose.

He rubbed his face. His mind was playing tricks on him. He'd just been thinking of the fire at the orphanage, after all.

But the smell persisted. Soon after came the click and snap of burning wood. The noise shook him from his sleepy stupor and sent him scurrying to the barn door. The sight that met him burned away the last of the grogginess and sent him into a wide-eyed moment of panic.

Tongues of fire snaked out from beneath the roof line and lapped at the sides of the wooden structure. The fierce orange glow made menacing shadows dance across the hard packed ground between the house and the barn.

Frantic, he searched the area for the Charidys, along with Luther and Cub. They weren't there. The realization knocked him from the momentary state of shock. He grabbed a shovel, though he reckoned it would do little good against the flames already reaching into the night sky.

Whatever happened, he didn't plan to watch while people he loved perished this time.

He skidded to a stop when the heat met him like an angry fist, pushing him away.

With his shirt pulled over his nose, he forced himself closer, shovel lifted high above his head as though he might intimidate the inferno into submission.

Smoke clouded the heavens above him, blocking the light of the full moon and casting a hazy gray over his surroundings. Except for the house where the flames still leapt in mockery at his powerlessness against them.

He raced to the corner of the home where the Charidys slept.

The flames hadn't found their way there yet. Why weren't Mr. and Mrs. Charidy trying to escape?

He yelled, swinging the shovel against the wooden wall of the house. He continued calling until the smoke and the heat parched his throat. They had to wake up.

The fire was growing too big. Soon the whole house would be engulfed. The heat blistered his skin as he swung the shovel again and again.

A movement to his right caught his eye. The wooden shutter banged open, and a small form emerged from the opening. Rose. Her muslin nightgown gave off an eerie glow in the fire's hateful light as someone dangled her from the opening.

He tossed the shovel aside and sprinted to her, catching her in his arms just as the flames nipped at the sleeve of her gown, setting it on fire.

She didn't cry when Will dropped her to the ground, smothering the flames consuming the arm of her gown with dirt. The girl's eyes were wide, the white rimming them like the first snow of winter.

He turned, expecting to see Mr. and Mrs. Charidy hurrying to them. But there were only flames.

"Mr. Charidy!" Will yelled above the fire's roar, but fear squeezed his parched throat so that what came out was a croaking noise even he didn't recognize.

Maybe they couldn't find the window because of the smoke. He called out until the smoke stole the last of his voice.

Rose whimpered, and he looked down at her. He followed the direction of her gaze. Luther DeGroot.

The glow of the flames gave him an even more menacing look.

"Luther," Will cried out. "Mr. and Mrs. Charidy—we have to get them out."

"They ain't comin' out. They're dead. I killed them just like I'm about to kill you." Luther lurched toward them. Will grabbed the shovel he'd dropped and swung, striking the bigger boy on the shin. Luther seized the injured leg, staggering. Will drew the shovel back again, bringing it down on top of Luther.

The boy fell to the ground, his arms flying up to cover his head. As his words registered in Will's head, a white-hot rage burned through him. He took another swing, catching Luther in the face. Blood spewed from the boy's nose. The guttural cry that followed snatched Will from his fury.

A yell from the corner of the house rose over the roar of the fire. "Luther!" Cub shouted.

Will prepared to swing again if Cub came near them. Instead, the other boy went to his brother. Even in the smoky haze, Cub looked pale.

Luther spit out words Will couldn't understand, but their meaning was clear. He dropped the shovel and scooped Rose into his arms. Only four years old, but a lot for Will's undersized nine-year-old frame to carry.

Still, he had to get her away from the fire and from the DeGroots.

"That's right. You'd better run 'cause when I catch you, I'm gonna kill you and that little runt, too." Luther remained on the ground, struggling to his knees while blood poured from his nose, staining his shirt. Cub stood frozen in place beside him.

With Rose in his arms, Will backed away as the roof of the cabin collapsed, bringing down part of the walls with it. If the Charidys were still inside, they were dead now.

Luther found his feet. He took a lurching step toward them, almost falling when he put weight on his injured leg. He cursed.

Will moved away until the darkness hid them.

Luther's words reached through the curtain of black. "If you tell anyone what happened, I'll say it was you done it. Just like what you did at the orphanage. Now you done gone and done it again. That's what everyone will believe."

Will swallowed the acid burning up his throat. Maybe people would believe he'd done this.

Rose was too little to tell anyone otherwise.

He looked down at the little girl he held in his own childlike arms. Her wide eyes blinked now and then. He couldn't leave her with the DeGroots. He was the one to save her.

Mr. Charidy's words came back to him. *He'll be a right fine son.*

Sorrow squeezed his heart. First his father, then his mother, and now the Charidys.

Will Sunday was no one's son.

And from this moment forward, that would never change.

CHAPTER 15

But when the sun was up they were scorched, and because they had no root
they withered away.
~Matthew 13:6

Jodee stared into the steamy mirror as she ran the towel over her hair once more. The hot shower made her feel human again. It had also offered her the reprieve of some time to herself in the privacy of Grace's guest bathroom. She'd been in no hurry to get it over with.

The meaty aroma of a simmering pot roast skimmed beneath the door. Her stomach growled.

She picked up the white stone. Another measure of tension slipped away as her fingers slid over the cool, smooth surface. The last thing the man she'd known as a father had given her. Three days later he was gone.

But unlike her fiancé, Chris, who'd died in an accident that haunted her still, Paul had simply vanished.

Not being her biological father hadn't stopped Paul from being the best thing that ever happened to her. And when he disappeared days before her twelfth birthday, he became the worst. She'd never believed he'd just up and left. She resented how her mother accepted it without question.

Her mother.

She should call her mother. If anyone had tried the emergency contact last night, they had met with failure. The emergency contact number listed with the DMV went to Chris's number, or what had been his before he died. A childish act of rebellion taken during days of numbing grief and self-destructive anger. Another thing in the long list of endeavors she regretted. No one ever imagined actually needing the emergency contact when they filled out the paperwork. Mad at the world and filled with self-loathing, she hadn't wanted anyone to rescue her. Whether to punish them or her, she couldn't say. By the time she'd come to her senses a few months later, she'd forgotten about it.

She hung the wet towel on the rack and looked again at the purple splotches circling her neck.

If her mother didn't know, there was no reason to involve her now. Her mother kept secrets from her, not the least of which was the identity of Jodee's biological father.

Now it was Jodee's turn to have a secret.

Something had fractured when Paul left, splitting her life into a before and an after. She'd never been able to stitch the two sides back together. She didn't like the person she'd become, but there was no way back to who she'd been. Not after what happened to Chris.

She tucked the rock into her pocket and headed down the stairs. The stair runner, a beige carpet covered in the brands of famous Texas ranches, cushioned her steps. But it didn't hide the hushed voices below.

"Please tell me you have good news," Grace said. "Waiting on the other will waste precious time."

"You know I can't discuss an ongoing investigation with you," Logan's voice was low. "And we don't know if she even saw anything."

A twinge of guilt made her hesitate. Were they discussing her?

She pressed her hand against her stomach. This town had stolen more than a few hours of her life, and she wanted to know what it had done with the time besides leaving her beaten, bruised, and broken. She stayed put and listened.

"When has that ever stopped you, and does this mean you're actually investigating?"

Logan exhaled, a sound more weary than frustrated. "No. There's no open or official investigation yet."

"Nothing? Something happened to that boy. I know it."

"I'm not saying you're wrong. I'm just saying that by the law, I don't have a case to investigate yet."

"What about the school? Did you check there?"

"He wasn't at school today, but he hasn't had enough absences to warrant a truancy visit. The counselor said if he's not back by Monday, then the truancy officer will pay them a visit."

"That's too long."

"You know I trust your instincts, but there's a way to go about things," another long exhale, "and a way my hands are tied. I have another idea, but so far, it's not coming to fruition without a fight. Just be patient."

"I don't know if I can."

"Understandable." The creak of leather reminded her Logan was probably in uniform, service weapon at his side. Was he here on law enforcement business or just visiting his aunt?

The quiet that followed left Jodee stuck on the stairs. Now wasn't the time to make her appearance in the kitchen.

"Now, do you think it's a good idea to take this woman in?" he asked.

And there was her answer. Official business. He didn't trust her.

"I wouldn't have asked her if I didn't."

"What are you up to?"

"She doesn't have anywhere else to go. And it's my fault she was in the wrong place at the wrong time. If I hadn't been concerned about that old tree, she wouldn't have been anywhere near El Hueso or Tooley's Truck Stop."

"I think it's more likely she doesn't have any place else she *chooses* to go." His judgment rubbed over Jodee like sandpaper. The fact they were talking about her behind her back poured salt into the wound of betrayal she kept raw by her own judgments. "She has a job—a government job—, so I really doubt she's homeless."

"Dr. Hyson doesn't want her driving and she shouldn't be staying alone after having a head injury."

"What makes you think she'd be alone? It seems a little too convenient if you ask me."

"Are you saying you think she might be involved in something criminal?" The metallic creak of the oven door snapping shut punctuated Grace's words. "That's a pretty big supposition in light of everything else that happened last night. Highly circumstantial evidence and implausible, don't you think?"

"What if someone is after her? She could be bringing trouble with her."

"But you've already done a check and haven't found anything, or you would've told me so."

"You know I can't discuss it with you."

"You don't have to. I know you well enough."

"I'm just not sure this is a good idea."

"There's a little boy out there somewhere who needs our help. I'm sure of it. And I'm not so certain there isn't a young lady upstairs who isn't in need of help too. We don't have time to wait around for good ideas. We have to take action now." Water splashed into a sink as though a pot had been dumped in. "Stir the gravy while I get these potatoes mashed before the rolls come out of the oven."

"You know I'm on duty, right?"

"You're always on duty, so, Mr. Public Servant, serve a tax paying member of your public by keeping the lumps out of my gravy." Grace's words swished a note of teasing over the troubling conversation. A spoon scraped against metal. "She might know something. When her memory returns, she might remember an important detail."

Jodee covered her mouth with her hand and sank back against the wall. Did Grace mean to say she might be involved somehow with a child in trouble? Whatever the woman was saying, they were keeping information from her.

She just wanted the truth. For once in her life, she wanted someone to treat her like she could handle the truth.

A knock at the door interrupted her. From her place on the stairs, she caught a glimpse of the visitor through the sidelights. All it took was a shoulder and a few curls of sandy blond hair.

Why was Blue Sunday knocking on Grace's front door?

If she answered the door, they'd discover she'd been eavesdropping on their conversation. Her back straightened. Well, she had no regrets since what she'd heard was information someone should have shared with her too.

"I've got it," she said, taking the final stairs in a staccato of steps.

She opened the door enough to slip through, then closed it behind her.

"What're you doing here?" She spit the words out as though having to ask filled her mouth with something sour. It wasn't just Blue's presence. It was everything that had happened—even the parts she didn't remember—barreling over her all at once, triggering a fight response.

The past, the present, and the future twisting around a black hole in the center of her memory. A black hole that had swallowed up something she didn't want to think about but couldn't bear not remembering. Still, it was there, fear fermenting just beneath the surface of her consciousness.

"Easy there!" Blue placed his hands on her tense shoulders as though she were a frightened colt he aimed to calm. But the expression on his face mirrored the swirling emotions inside her. "What the heck happened to you?"

The snarl of emotions drained as swiftly as they'd come, leaving Jodee hollow in their absence. But this was Blue. The one person she trusted with everything but her heart.

When she was a little girl, she'd thought of Blue as a big brother.

That had changed when she stopped being a little girl. But there comes a time when reality has its way, and girlish dreams awaken to the heart-rending truth. Some paths were destined to never cross because if they did, it would be a perilous road hurtling toward a destructive cliff.

"You told me to make new friends. Apparently, it didn't work out," she said. The truth hit her. She remembered that much. The memories of last night were there. She just needed to reconnect the pieces. First, she had to find them all, but she would. Eventually.

For now, her thoughts still tangled up in the news she might have seen something connected to a child in trouble.

She sat on the swing at the far end of the porch.

"I'd say it didn't." Blue followed her, his usual loose-jointed gait a bit less loose-jointed than usual. Did this upset him?

He studied her, then seated himself beside her with a deep sigh. "Guess you'll have to stick with me after all."

"I'm recovering from a head injury. You're not supposed to upset me. And how'd you know I was here, anyway? The hospital wouldn't have told you—pretty sure HIPAA laws apply even here in the country." And what could have made him look for her in the first place?

"Never underestimate a Memaw with a scanner."

Blue's grandmother, Dovey Sunday. Now there was a fiery, strong-willed woman.

Great. The whole county knew. Probably they knew more about what happened than she did.

"You want to tell me what happened?" he asked.

"If I could, I would. But I don't even know." Afraid to witness the pity she feared seeing in Blue's eyes, she stared straight ahead. She hated the vulnerability that settled over her like a soul-sucking mantle. But what if he knew something? If a boy was in danger, then this went beyond just knowing who had hurt her. "I remember talking to you." She shook her head. "Everything after that is just broken pieces that don't make sense." She inhaled, her hand brushing against her neck, before she tugged at the collar of the borrowed shirt she wore. "Did you see anyone following me? Or maybe someone suspicious looking last night?"

"If I'd seen anyone following you, I'd have warned him he was biting off more than he could chew." He gave her thigh a soft tap with the side of his fist. "But no, I didn't notice anyone but you." His voice pinched a little over the last of his words, as though maybe he'd said something he hadn't meant to. "I may not be the sharpest pencil in the forest, but I can take a hint. I finished filling up and left."

The normal honeyed smoothness of his speech was missing. In its place was a grit she didn't expect or understand. He stared at her neck. The concern in his eyes uprooted her like a tender flower, plucked from the earth. She thirsted for the water she would die without. She imagined how it would feel to rest her head on his shoulder. The thought scared her for reasons she didn't quite understand.

"I'm wishing right now I wasn't quite so good at taking a hint." He lifted his arm and draped it over her shoulders.

Jodee swallowed. The very thing she craved was right there, the sip of life that would ease her parched soul, but she refused to drink it in. She just sat there with her heart aching to be comforted, but unable to escape the stiff, impenetrable shell she'd created for it. The pain she'd risk was too great.

"You can't help that you've had lots of practice taking hints." She tried to laugh, then winced, her hand going to her bruised neck. She refused to have an emotional conversation with Blue. Her feelings hovered too close to the surface right now. She nudged him with her elbow as she steered the conversation away from the rawness. "Maybe I should have taken you up on your offer."

"What offer? All I said was hey." He leaned away until her eyes met his. The connection sparked by his gaze stole her power to look away. Something volatile simmered in his eyes, something that both drew her in and made her want to run away.

"Yeah, like I said, with you hey is never all that's being said." Even she could hear that her voice held less defiance and more confusion.

He smiled. But his look held something other than flirtation. A wistful sort of melancholy. He pulled her against him, and she let him, though she fought the urge to melt into him.

"So, I'm an open book and you're a locked box," he said.

"Well, currently the box is empty. I don't remember what happened to me." Did he know about the boy?

"I heard." His fingers tugged a few strands of her hair, the touch tender as he repeated the motion.

The faint scent of baking bread wafted over her. Grace's yeast rolls. But . . .

She bolted upright. That smell. The sensation of being unable to breathe gripped her again, pulling at other memories. She remembered the cruel touch of malicious hands around her neck, squeezing.

A tear slipped from her eye as the fear of that moment rekindled, her pulse racing even though the danger had passed.

Then she'd seen the man standing in the shadows and the pain had stopped.

A sense of peace she couldn't explain had wrapped around her, warm and soft, and safe. She'd both wanted to go to him and been too awestruck to move.

She gripped Blue's forearm. "A man in a brown leather duster. Did you see him at the truck stop?"

The muscles in Blue's arm tensed beneath her fingers. "No. Is he the one who did this to you?"

"I think he rescued me."

"If leaving you lying unconscious in a dark truck stop parking lot constitutes rescuing you, we need to talk."

A black four-door Chevy truck drove by.

Blue's gaze tracked it until it reached the end of the street. "When is Helen coming to get you?"

"I haven't told her. No need to worry her when I'm fine." Jodee ran her tongue over dry lips, as though wiping away her uncertainty.

"Look, I don't know what happened between you two after —"

"Don't go there. Not right now."

"Fine, but you need to go home." The seriousness in his voice was out of character.

How could she tell him that she didn't know where home was right now? And it wasn't the loss of memory, it was something much deeper pulling at her from within. The image of the root-bearing-sign flickered through her. She shuddered. "I can't. And even if I could, I don't want to. No good would come of it."

"No good will come of you staying here. Go home, Jodee."

She stared at Blue. In all the years she'd known him, he'd never cared what anyone did as long as it didn't interfere with his plans. What difference could her staying with Grace possibly make?

"Please, I'm asking as your friend." His glance followed the truck again.

It pulled into the parking lot of Roots and a lithe young woman with jet black hair bounced out. She turned her head toward Grace's, but the distance was too far for Jodee to guess what she might be looking for. Or who she might be looking at.

"You didn't ask. You told," Jodee said with considerably less warmth.

"It's always got to be an argument with you, doesn't it?"

Jodee smirked. "If I say no, then I'll be right, but it'll look like I'm proving your point."

"You are the single most frustrating woman I have ever known. Why do you have to be so . . ." He shook his head, his words trailing off.

She took his hand and smiled. "I learned from the best."

"Oh no. I'm not taking the blame for your mule headedness." He sighed and tugged another strand of her hair, with more firmness than before. He held on until he'd finished his statement. "I can't explain why yet, but do it for me. Please go home."

"It's not that easy." What if there was a boy who needed her help? He needed her to remember and to be here when she did.

"Then stay with me. You don't even know these people." His gaze drifted to the window behind her, then he leaned close but raised his voice. "Ya know, I've got a double bed in my camper. It'd be real cozy."

The abrupt change in his demeanor splashed against her like ice water.

"No thanks. I imagine that bed is a little worn out for my tastes." Saying the words hurt more than she expected. She'd always loved Blue. She just loved him too much to be one more in his long line of conquests. Tears welled in her eyes.

He hadn't changed a bit.

"Jodee." Her name slipped from his lips in a husky whisper. "I—" His phone chirped. "I need to talk to you, but I can't now. Please, just trust me and go home."

She couldn't imagine what Blue had gotten himself into. "I can take care of myself." She sat up, her spine straightening. From the corner of her eye, a subtle shifting of the curtain suggested they weren't alone.

"Yeah, you've always made sure that part was clear. I'm just wondering how far you have to go to convince yourself." Blue stood. "Please Jodee, just go home."

She frowned at the hardness in his tone.

The door opened before she could respond. Grace stepped onto the porch. "I was wondering who'd knocked on the door. Why, you're Dovey Sunday's grandson, aren't you?" Grace's hospitality rang through as though random people showed up on her porch all the time. On second thought, from what she'd seen of Grace so far, they probably did.

"Yes, ma'am."

Logan leaned against the doorjamb behind his aunt.

"I was just coming to tell Jodee supper is on the table. Why don't you join us? We have plenty," Grace said.

Logan's eyes narrowed as he rubbed his chin.

She could sense the gears turning behind his scrutinizing regard.

"I didn't realize you two knew each other," he said, pushing off the doorjamb.

Blue looked at her. It was just a look, but she felt it in her bones.

"Old childhood friends. I heard what happened last night. Just wanted to check on her." He lifted his cap and nodded to Grace. "Thank you for the offer, ma'am, but I best be going." He turned back to Jodee. "Please."

It was all he said. She could fill in the gaps.

And she already knew her answer was no.

CHAPTER 16

If you would know strength and patience, welcome the company of trees.
~Hal Borland

For the first time since agreeing to do this, Blue had regrets, fueled in no small measure by the bruises on Jodee's neck and the fear he saw in her eyes. Fear wasn't something she showed.

But the hardest part was playing the role of his former self in front of her when he wanted her to see he wasn't that guy anymore. There was more to him now.

When she asked if he'd seen anyone following her, he glimpsed a vulnerability that could drive him to distraction. But he also recognized a glimmer of her search for a hero in him. While he wanted to tell her he'd die fighting with the last ounce of life for a chance to show her how much he loved her, he couldn't. Not yet anyway. There was too much at stake.

What he'd seen last night left him *het up* as his Memaw used to say, or a more accurate word was spooked. He'd been in some creepy places, but the secret space beneath that bar took the cake, not to mention the punch and cookies—and most of the rest of his appetite.

He didn't believe in ghosts, but that didn't mean he didn't recognize the presence of evil when he met it. Something haunted him about the place beneath Roots.

He raked a hand through his hair. He'd always seen Jodee's stubborn streak as cute, a sort of game to play, a wall to wear down, a victory to win. But right now, it wasn't so cute. Darn it all, she could have been killed last night.

The reality of how much that possibility wrecked him kept him frozen beneath the Texas sun, one hand on his truck and one splayed across the top of his head.

The notion to march back across Grace's porch and tell her how he felt wreaked further havoc on his decision-making. He jerked the truck door open, not chancing a look back for fear seeing her would turn him into a blithering idiot. He had somewhere he needed to be, and it wasn't a meeting he'd relish the consequences of missing.

He'd agreed to this task to repay an old friend. It was a debt he could never come close to repaying, but doing this was the best he could offer. The guilt of not finishing what he'd promised would devour him if he didn't see it through.

Matthews had approached him because Blue was familiar with the area thanks to his grandparents having lived there. That made him local enough to be included, but not local enough to be entrusted. The locals remembered him as a cowboy with a good heart—at least he hoped they did—and a wild hair—that part they definitely remembered.

He'd changed, which was part of the reason he felt indebted, but he could still slip right back into the Blue of old.

The El Hueso Old Settler's Reunion this weekend offered the perfect reason to be back in town. Of course, to make it look real, he'd entered the rodeo. His saddle bronc riding days were over, and he wasn't looking forward to the beating he was about to take on the back of fifteen hundred pounds of bone jarring horseflesh.

He'd need to bribe someone to plow the arena deep before his ride.

But he couldn't get Jodee out of his head. Was she still in danger? He'd hauled his camper trailer onto the back of his grandparents' place for the weekend. If she'd just trust him and stay with him.

He scoffed. *Whose fault was it that she didn't trust him?*

Besides, could having her close jeopardize his work or put her in danger?

He gunned the engine and headed to the interstate. He needed to think this through.

But until then, he had a meeting he wasn't looking forward to.

A half hour later, he sat at a diner table across from a man in a starched faded denim shirt. But the casual dress didn't hide his identity. He might not have dressed in the traditional white shirt with the shiny five-pointed star pinned to his chest, but everything about him said law enforcement. Texas Ranger, to be exact.

Dead flies dotted the windowsill, the tiny legs jutting upward. And the glass on the front door looked like it hadn't been cleaned since the Carter administration. The smell of manure wafted into the diner every time the door opened to allow in more flies that would eventually join the ranks of their comrades on the windowsill graveyard.

Sale day wasn't until tomorrow, but already pens were filling up. The noise of cattle being unloaded and driven to their pens—truck engines humming, metal gates clanging, cowboys hollering in the vernacular that only cows understood—drowned out most of the conversations around him.

It was a good place for a meeting that required secrecy and the cover of being something other than what it was really about.

They waited until the waitress took their orders and departed for the kitchen.

Blue fanned a fly away and took a sip of the sweet iced tea from the chipped red plastic glass in front of him.

"Matthews explained who I am and why we're here, I assume?"

The man across from him sipped his own tea. Even the flies seemed to know better than to mess with him.

Not only had Matthews told him the Ranger's name was Tom Fowler, but he'd been quick to point out that the man sitting across from him was named after a World War II hero and Congressional Medal of Honor winner. Curious, Blue had looked up the name. If this man lived up to his namesake, he'd be the kind who would charge the gates of hell with a water gun. "Yes, sir."

"Call me Tom." He reached across the table and shook Blue's hand. "We're here to talk about you hauling some cattle for me. You got a trailer?"

"I can get one."

"Great." Tom's smile quirked. He cast a casual glance around at the smattering of other customers. They were seated in the corner booth in the almost empty diner. "Now how about you tell me what you saw last night, and how you came to see it."

Blue leaned back in the booth. He'd told some lies in his life, some downright big ones. But this wasn't one of those. It was a truth so outrageous he couldn't imagine saying it. "I think it was . . ." he paused, cinching up his courage to say the rest, "some sort of secret meeting."

"What makes you think that?" Tom didn't bat an eye, as though he heard bizarre stuff like this on a daily basis.

"Took place in a hidden cellar or basement."

"Beneath this bar called Roots?"

"Yeah. But they used a secret passageway." Blue cut his eyes up to Tom. Did he believe him? His story sounded ridiculous even to him.

This time Tom quirked an eyebrow, questioning Blue before the words had left his mouth. "How'd *you* find it?"

"I followed DeGroot to his office upstairs. There's a bookcase on rollers used to hide the door, but it was out of place last night. I just kept going until I ended up down in this cavern thing."

"You didn't break any laws to get in, did you?"

"No."

Tom's eyes narrowed. "Go on."

"I could hear them talking, but I couldn't get close enough to see them. I recognized DeGroot's voice. The others with him were Rusty Boggs and Nolan DeGroot."

"They see or hear you?"

Blue shook his head. "I don't think we'd be having this conversation if they had."

"How'd you get out?"

"Don't ask questions you don't want an answer to."

Tom chewed on that for a minute. "Matthews says I can trust you, picked you for this assignment himself. Don't screw this up." He gave Blue a pointed look. "And don't get yourself locked up for breaking the law."

"Last thing I want."

A couple of old cowboys sat down in the booth behind them. They let the conversation wander through other subjects like the price of feed, cattle exports, and the weather prediction for the rest of the growing season and into the coming winter. When the waitress deposited two plates of chicken fried steak smothered in cream gravy alongside french-fries, green beans, and a thick slice of Texas toast, they dug in.

Finally, Tom swiped the last of his toast through the remaining gravy on his plate and circled back to the reason they were there. He lowered his voice. "Doesn't seem like much to go on. I mean, a secret meeting is suspicious, but they could've been planning a surprise birthday party for all we know. How about the pictures you took?" He popped the toast in his mouth.

Blue handed him his phone, then sipped his tea while Tom scrolled through the photos.

"All this is interesting, but nothing we can act on."

Blue folded his arms on the table and leaned in. "It just feels so suspicious. If we could see in those boxes, I bet we'd find something there. Or maybe get that gun and see if it matches the one used to kill the deputy."

"Doesn't matter. I can't get a warrant to go in based on the fact something *feels suspicious*." Tom stood, pulled some bills out of his wallet, and set them on the table. "You find someone who can tell you something that we can corroborate, then we're in business."

Blue exhaled. He itched to know what was inside those boxes with the weird coding, but both Matthews and now Fowler had made it clear he had to stay inside the law. Opening locked doors without a key somehow fell into the category. Frustration that he couldn't make that happen chafed like starched underwear. He stifled a grin and shook his head. Well, he always did love a good challenge. "So, you got any suggestions on what I should do next?"

"Keep watching and listening. Hang around the bar—but don't do anything stupid. Sooner or later, you'll find someone who'll talk."

Blue nodded, but inside he cringed at the idea of spending more time at Roots.

"You hear about the woman assaulted at the truck stop?" Tom asked.

He debated telling him just how well acquainted he was with that news, but Tom continued before he could answer.

"People think these small towns are problem free, but they're wrong. We want to take this guy down, Blue. But I don't want to lose you to do it. If the rumors are true, he plays for keeps."

As Fowler walked away, Blue was certain of two things. He had no idea what he was doing, and he had to get Jodee out of the way.

And that meant out of this town.

CHAPTER 17

Texas 1858

When my heart is overwhelmed, lead me to the rock that is higher than I.
~Psalm 61:2

 louds rolled in to block the moon. Will sniffed the air for rain, but the acrid scent of smoke saturated their clothes until it was all he could smell.

Painful cramps drew the muscles in his arms into hard knots he feared might keep him from ever getting them straight again. He'd carried Rose for what seemed like hours.

The little girl held tight to him, her arms around his neck, her face pressed against his bony chest. Now and then she whimpered when a branch touched the burn on her arm, or when he stumbled and almost dropped her. It would help them both if she would walk, but every time he set her down, she shook and clung to him even harder.

He didn't blame her. Losing your parents set your world off kilter, making you hang on to anything you could.

A loose rock rolled beneath his foot. Will stumbled again.

Without the moonlight, the rocky, uneven terrain added another danger to their desperate trek.

He knelt, untangling Rose's arms from around his neck. She quivered. The dark didn't hide the fear in her wide eyes or lesson his understanding of the shock that glazed them.

"Shh." He patted her head. "I just need to rest for a bit so I can reason what to do next."

He was the man in charge now. The responsibility of protecting Rose rested on his shoulders. But he wasn't a man. He was a boy.

Once a boy becomes a man, he can't go back to being a boy. Mr. Charidy's words rattled through his head. Anger stung his eyes. He squeezed them shut, gritting his teeth in determination.

His heart pounded, blood thumping against his eardrums like an Indian war dance. He inhaled deep and steady until the noise subsided. Then he listened.

Had he broken Luther's leg when he'd hit him with the shovel? The possibility pleased him, though it seemed unlikely. Somewhere in the dark, Luther and Cub were looking for them. If they found them . . . Will picked up a rock and held it in a fierce grip. The knowledge he'd taken down Luther with a shovel earlier emboldened him. His chest puffed.

He strained to listen through the night sounds but gave up. Every sound seemed to be a furious, cruel Luther DeGroot crashing through the brush as he rushed to kill them.

He let the stone drop. He couldn't carry Rose and a rock. They had to keep moving.

How long had they been walking? He didn't know. But he did know he needed to get Rose far away from the DeGroots. And from her murdered parents burning inside what had been their home.

Acid scorched his throat, and he swallowed down the urge to vomit.

Just think about Rose.

Rose needed someone to tend her injured arm.

Where could he take her? The Charidys had been so busy with their own work, building a barn and a house and preparing for the winter, they'd not yet interacted much with what few neighbors they had. To the north was Graham, but they'd have to pass through the Brazos Indian Reservation to get there. He heard of a place called Collins Post somewhere east along the river. But nothing he knew of the place was very nice. Instinct told him not to take her there.

Will looked at Rose, knowing her arm must hurt, though she hadn't cried. He'd heard of people being burned so badly the nerves were seared over and they didn't recognize the pain. During his stay at the orphanage, he'd seen a boy with a burned foot. The infection came fast until the doctor sawed off the boy's foot. "I won't let that happen to you, Little Bud." He whispered the words as though making the promise to himself even more than to Rose.

Maybe she hadn't been burned so bad, but he wouldn't know for sure until daylight when he could get a solid look at it.

A trail of lightning cut across the western sky. He needed to find shelter for the night. Someplace Luther couldn't find them.

Rose wrapped her arms around his leg, once again sticking like a wad of cedar sap to his britches.

To his right a rock clattered, dislodged by something . . . or someone. He reached for Rose, catching her attention so she could see the finger he pressed against his lips, hoping she understood.

Another sound, like the whisper of a cedar branch brushing against a passing object. The sound closer.

Lightning flashed, this time to the south. He prayed the storm would miss them. But in the burst of light, he gained his bearings. A few more yards and he would find the deer trail that led to the seasonal creek. And at the bottom of the trail was a boulder. The creek was low right now, though rain upstream could send a flood raging down the narrow channel. But the boulder was large and secure. And the tree limbs that hung over it from the bank draped it in the best hiding place he could think of.

Will spent hours sitting on top of that rock, watching, listening, pretending. *Wool gathering*, Mrs. Charidy would have said. But she always winked when she did, making him think she was fond of wool gathering herself.

A raw ache pierced his heart, followed by the pinch of understanding that his chance to be adopted, to have a new family and a new name, had been turned to ash by the meanness of the DeGroots.

He let several minutes of silence pass before picking Rose up, inching his way toward the trail.

If they could get to the rock, they'd be safe—or as safe as he could make them. Hope vibrated through his small body.

On the rock, nothing could touch them.

CHAPTER 18

So, let's get back to why the roots are the most important part of a tree. Conceivably, this is where the tree equivalent of a brain is located. ~Peter Wohlleben

odee followed Grace up the steps to the run-down rent house. A rusty bicycle lay on its side near the sidewalk. The paint on the siding and the grass in the yard seemed to suffer from the same sort of contagion, making both of their coverings sparse and splotchy. Someone tried to keep the home tidy, but previous years of neglect had left little to work with.

After a tense meal where Grace tried too hard to put her at ease and Logan didn't try hard enough, Jodee hungered for time alone. But the suspicious way Logan watched her at dinner left her wary of another question-and-answer session. Instinct convinced her that as long as she stayed close to Grace, he'd give her some space.

After she'd done the painful job of letting her employer know about the accidental destruction of government property, where she had to admit she had operated the vehicle in a semi-impaired state because of the blow to her head, she'd let Grace talk her into this outing.

Anything to take her mind off her future.

Now she stood in front of the dilapidated little house with the smell of fresh-from-the-oven chocolate chip cookies swirling around her. While Jodee fidgeted, snugging the aluminum foil tighter around the edges of the plate she held, Grace acted like this was the most natural thing in the world—having dragged a person with amnesia, loaded down with a platter of cookies, to visit a stranger.

Nothing like walking across town—brief though the trek had been—carrying an armload of food to a stranger's house to provide proof she was out of her element in the company of a woman like Grace.

Jodee shifted her feet and scanned the surroundings for an escape route. A sagging chain link fence extended from the corners of the house, and the sidewalk in both directions bore evidence of roots dislocating the once level slabs of concrete into a fragmented fall hazard.

Grace glanced at her watch. "Kimberly works two jobs so she might not be home, but her son, Aidan, should be here. He isn't supposed to answer the door for strangers, but he knows me."

A fretful, hesitating note tightened Grace's words. Her shoulders pulled tight in a way that indicated a tension Jodee didn't understand.

The woman knocked and they waited. She knocked again. On the third try, the door cracked open a half a face wide. A pale, haggard looking face. A single narrowed eye, shadowed by the dark circle beneath it, stared out, darting between Grace and Jodee. A hint of shock flickered over the visible portion of the woman's face, replaced by an even greater wariness. The look sent another round of unease up Jodee's spine.

Then recognition came to her. This was the same Kimberly she'd seen working as the cashier at the truck stop, the one she'd given money to the night before. She ran through their interaction, struggling to recall anything that might cause the woman to be so guarded now. Unease prickled along her arms. She'd been in her Forest Service uniform last night. As often as she was mistaken for law enforcement when wearing it, who knew what might be upsetting the woman now.

But along with the remembrance came another emotion—a cold, swelling sensation of panic. She squeezed the plate in her hand to stifle the tremor that vibrated along her limbs.

"Good evening, Kimberly." Grace held up the basket of food. "I brought you some leftover roast. It's more than we can eat, and I don't want it to go to waste."

The door opened just wide enough to frame Kimberly's thin body, not wide enough to give the impression they were invited in. She didn't reach for the basket. If anything, she hugged skinny arms around her middle tighter.

"This is my friend Jodee. She's visiting for a few days."

Kimberly nodded without looking at her, even though Jodee felt certain she recognized her.

A look of concern deepened the lines on Grace's face. "Is everything okay?"

"Yeah." The woman's stare bobbed up to Grace's face before dropping back to the basket.

"I brought a surprise for Aidan, too. I thought you both might need a little treat after last night." Grace craned to peer over Kimberly's shoulder into the house. "Is he home?"

"He's still with his dad." Kimberly didn't make eye contact.

Grace tilted her head. "In the middle of the school week? Are you sure that's a good idea? You did tell me he's having trouble settling in."

The girl stiffened, her shoulders inching up in a body that appeared to be just as tight as Jodee felt. Why did the name Aidan set alarm zinging along her limbs? She stared at the doorframe above Kimberly's head, combing through everything she remembered. She walked through the details with a fresh scrutiny.

"I'm sorry. Here I am sticking my nose in someone else's business. I just want you to know I'm here to help however you need."

Grace's voice softened, returning to the same calming tones that had lured Jodee back into the hospital.

Grace shifted the basket of food to her free hand, then patted the disheveled looking woman's shoulder, ending the touch with a gentle rub. "I know this must be very hard on you both. It's like uprooting both the past and the future all at once. Maybe it'll do him some good to spend time with his father. It'll give you some time for a little rest. And I can help him catch up on schoolwork when he gets back, if you'd like."

Jodee's gaze swung to Grace at the odd way she pronounced *when,* as though the word held an unspoken question.

The young mother didn't respond, and Grace continued. "I guess you get all the cookies for yourself this time. Oh, to have a youthful metabolism again. Do you know when Aidan will be back? I'll bake him some more."

"We may be moving."

"Moving?" Grace's eyes narrowed. "Are you sure you're alright? Are you in some sort of danger?"

"We're fine. I'm just … I need to get some sleep now. My asthma's been pretty bad working at the truck stop."

The woman fiddled with something in her hand.

Jodee stared. A red toy car.

A weight settled on her chest as an image took shape. A boy on a floor with a red toy car.

Her heart stutter-stepped. She needed to move—move or explode. Thrusting the plate of cookies on top of the basket Grace held, she excused herself and hurried down the sidewalk with long strides, arms wrapped around her middle as though cinching herself together.

A boy playing with a toy was not a troubling memory. Why then was her body responding as though she should be afraid—as though a fight-or-flight response had been triggered?

The simple toy was the key turning in a rusty lock. Whatever she would find on the other side, it wouldn't be good.

Around the corner, a short stone wall bordering the yard of an abandoned house offered her a place to sit. She doubled over, her hands tangled in her hair, eyes closed. Something happened. Something that scared her.

Breathe and think. And remember. Please remember.

Pressure built around her. The memories came like a wave far out in the ocean, bearing down on her, lapping at her memory, swelling to a savage height. It was coming, and all she could do was brace for impact.

The waves of recall sucked her under like a riptide. She couldn't breathe, couldn't orient herself as she spun in their clutches. Broken bits and pieces, scattered images, and rage sliced through her like splintered glass.

"Jodee, sweetheart, breathe." Grace materialized at her side. Her hand moved in calming circles on her upper back, her voice soothing, a life preserver in the midst of her drowning. "Are you okay? You're as white as new cotton."

The crushing waves ebbed away, and her breath returned to her burning lungs. She sat upright, staring but seeing what wasn't there. Her hand went to her throat. Fearing a danger that had already passed was illogical. She was safe. But the fear didn't leave.

"The toy car—the red one she was holding. I saw her when I stopped last night and there was a boy playing with a red toy car. His name is Aidan. I saw his name on his backpack." Jodee shivered.

The fear hadn't left because it wasn't a fear for herself. She pictured the boy, his wide, dark eyes and freckled face. Her heart skittered in her chest.

Another memory, a much more recent one, exploded in her head. Grace and Logan had been discussing a missing boy and the chance that Jodee might have seen something.

She wanted to keep doubting that to be true, but she couldn't. She didn't yet fully remember what she'd seen, but she knew she'd seen something terrible.

Grace watched her with eyes radiating the warmth of true concern and friendship. "Yes, it's Aidan. Do you remember anything else?"

"Nothing that makes sense, but the rest will come, right?" Because knowing only in part seemed even more terrifying than not knowing at all.

Grace rubbed her arm with a motherly touch. "I think so. But we should probably get you some rest."

Jodee stared at her. "I heard you and Sheriff Adams talking about me. It's true, then, that I might have seen something related to a child abduction? It's Aidan, isn't it? Kimberly's son."

Grace sighed and stared across the street. "Oh."

"I need to know what's going on. You didn't ask me to stay with you out of sympathy. You're hoping I'll remember something that helps them find Aidan," Jodee stated the truth without emotion. It wasn't the idea they were using her that stung. She'd do the same given the opportunity.

But the fact they didn't think her worthy of knowing the truth ripped open old wounds. "If there's a child missing and I might be able to help find him, then I need to know what's going on. Nothing else matters."

"I'm sorry you had to hear it like that. It must have seemed a rude thing to do to a guest, but the less you hear from others, the more your memory will be free to remember things as they happened. I don't want your memories to return tainted by my assumptions, if that makes sense."

Jodee inhaled and closed her eyes as she released a long, slow breath. It did make sense. Why did she always assume the worst?

Not assigning motives to the actions of others was a skill she needed to improve upon.

"I remember the boy, and I know something scared me. I can't shake this sense of fear, but I still don't remember what I saw. Nothing other than an old cowboy waring a gray hat and a duster who I have the impression somehow saved me." She frowned, her eyebrows drawing together. "But maybe he was one of them."

She rubbed her forehead, smoothing the worried knots that only added to her growing headache.

"I'm afraid I may have let you overdo it today. Let's head back.

I'll let Logan know, and maybe he can stop by in the morning to visit. Maybe someone else noticed the man."

They headed in the direction of Grace's house, their steps unhurried, the woman's voice soft. "Kimberly and Aidan haven't lived here very long. She's working two jobs to make ends meet. It's not the best for Aidan. He has a habit of wandering off. Searching for treasure to help his mom, he says." Grace laughed, but it held more sadness than humor.

She continued, "He's a bright kid though, smart for his age. Just a bit of a mischief maker with his disappearing acts. Yesterday morning I caught him playing by the culvert at the far edify the road, hiding his latest find, I suppose. I had to shoo him on before he missed the bus."

The sun sank low against the horizon, tugging a blanket of shadows over the decaying community as the day slipped away. Jodee wasn't ready for the day to end—not until she had answers. But exhaustion pulled at her just as determinedly as the sun pulled at the darkness.

A black pickup drove by. The same truck that had driven by the house earlier today claiming Blue's rapt attention. Just as before, it turned into the gravel parking lot of Roots.

Before she could stop herself, she scanned the lot for Blue's truck.

The relief of not seeing it was small and short lived. Blue was like a shiny piece of hematite. Pretty to look at, but just when you thought it was yours to hold onto, it was pulled away by the magnetic allure of trouble.

CHAPTER 19

Emancipation from the bondage of the soil is no freedom for the tree.
~Rabindranath Tagore

The sidewalk brought them to the splintered oak.

Grace walked over to the tree and shook her head, a gesture filled with more sadness than Jodee normally witnessed in others on behalf of a tree.

She cleared her throat, hoping to rid the emotion that knotted up within it. "Watch your step. There's a hole over there. I stepped in it yesterday."

Grace gave the tree a pat. "This ol' fellow has seen a lot happen on this rocky hill. The state historical society estimated his age at around four hundred years. Though they can't really tell on a Live Oak unless they cut it down. He's still a baby by some standards. But so, I don't know . . . necessary."

Grace gave Jodee a sheepish smile. "Of course, you already know that. I'm being sentimental, aren't I?"

"I understand what you mean," Jodee said.

The sound of an approaching vehicle interrupted the conversation as Logan's patrol unit pulled to a stop beside them.

He lowered the SUV's window. "Evening ladies."

"Are you heading out again so soon? You've hardly had a moment's rest in the past twenty-four hours," Grace said. "How are you holding up?"

"I'm fine. Just a part of the job. Your dinner recharged me." He winked at his aunt. "And I may have caught a little catnap after y'all left. Of course, I'd be doing better if I had some of those chocolate chip cookies I smelled." He patted the doorframe where he rested his forearm. "Where did they disappear to, anyway?"

"I shared them with a friend. Nothing cheers folks up like fresh baked cookies."

"This friend have a name?" He raised a dubious eyebrow.

"Of course." Grace pressed her lips together and arched her eyebrow to mirror his. Where his had been a question mark, hers was a period.

Logan sighed and shook his head. "You remember what I said?"

Grace patted his arm. "I do. And just so you know, I'll need to bake another batch. That's if they don't move."

His eyes narrowed. "Move?"

"She mentioned the possibility. What happens if she leaves town?"

He rubbed his hands over his eyes and stared at something in front of him. "Nothing good."

"Has anyone mentioned seeing a man in a brown leather duster at the truck stop last night?" Grace asked.

"No, why?" Logan's gaze bounced between the two women.

"I think a man wearing a duster and a cowboy hat stopped my attack." Jodee tensed, anticipating more of his skepticism. "So, he might have seen the abduction, too. But he definitely saw whoever attacked me."

"Alleged abduction." He stared at her for a long moment. The dim evening light shadowed the features of his face, but it was still a mask of scrutiny. "Can you describe him other than by his clothes?"

She frowned. The open lots around the tree gave her a clear view of Roots as Blue's truck pulled into the parking lot. Like hematite to a magnet. How naive could she be?

Turning to Logan, she shook her head.

He stared, silent for a moment. "I'll check into it. Anything else?"

She refrained from voicing the words rolling through her head. *Yeah, stop treating me like a suspect if you want my help.* "Maybe Kimberly saw him."

A white super duty Ford truck—King Ranch edition—pulled to a stop beside Logan. The driver lowered his window. "Evening Grace, Logan." His gaze went to Jodee. "Ma'am."

"Harrison, this is Jodee." Grace made the introduction. "She's staying with me for a few days."

Her hand pressed against her chest as her heart started its frustrating flutter again. She needed to fill the prescription Dr. Hyson had given her.

His stare narrowed. "Now, why does that name sound familiar?"

"She's the woman who was attacked at Tooley's last night," Grace said.

"Is that right? I am truly sorry for that, ma'am." He removed his hat and pressed it against his chest. An expression of commiseration that seemed a little too forced, as though the timing of his speech and his actions didn't quite fit together. "You doing all right now? Grace will take care of you better than anybody else could. El Hueso always takes care of its own, including it's guests."

Jodee offered a weak smile, ready for the conversation to end. The entire conversation gave her the sensation of being pandered to. Was he worried about her somehow suing the town or tarnishing its reputation? She commended herself on not laughing at the idea.

Her emotions for the last twenty-four hours had battered her into a state of numbness that made it impossible to understand the strange reaction slinking through her limbs. The sight of Blue ducking into Roots added an ache she couldn't bear much longer.

"I'm sure sorry to see your old tree go down like this, especially after the amount of work you've done on its history. Guess you'll be looking for another project to tackle now, since the storm put an end to this one," he said.

"I hate to see the tree go, but the history of El Hueso hasn't fallen along with the tree. It's still worth documenting. I'll probably keep digging around with it some. Someday somebody might care to know." Grace stared at the tree stretched out like a fallen soldier.

"I'll have some of my boys come over and clean it up for you." Harrison tapped his middle finger against the truck door.

"That's not necessary. I'm sure you have plenty to do with the Old Settler's Reunion coming up."

"Nonsense. It'll be an act of community service to clean it up before the reunion kicks off."

"Thanks, but we got it." Logan had been quiet, but now that he spoke, his words carried a sharp quality that no one else appeared to notice.

Harrison didn't look happy yo be turned down. He looked at Logan as though weighing out whether to push the issue. "Well, I'll leave you to it then. You folks have a good evening." He smiled at Jodee. "Sorry about your misfortune, but glad to have you around for our big reunion this weekend. You will be staying for that, won't you?"

Jodee shrugged.

"I'd sure appreciate it if you would. Let me know if there's something we can do to make up for what happened."

Silence lingered between the three of them as he drove away.

The pressure in Jodie's chest eased, and she inhaled.

"I need to get going," Logan said. "We had an anonymous call to do a welfare check on Tillie. I told 'em I was in the neighborhood, so I'd look into it."

"We saw her earlier today. A welfare check is a good idea," Grace said.

Jodee wanted to ask why someone would make such a call anonymously, but given the often-delicate nature of the cooperation needed for living in a small town, she let it go.

"I'll ride over with you. It might be good if I sat with her a while just to make sure she gets to bed all right." Grace turned to Jodee. "Why don't you head back to the house and get some rest? Your room's ready and those dark circles under your eyes are telling me your body is too. I'll stay with Tillie for a little while, then head home."

"So, I'm being promoted from kitchen help to Uber driver?" Logan smirked.

"Don't be silly, dear. People pay Uber drivers." Grace headed around to the passenger side of the Witt County Sheriff's unit.

She paused to look at the tree. "I hate to lose this old tree," she said. "I guess I'll need to call someone to come saw it up. Might make good firewood we can give away."

"I can't get to it until after the Old Settler's Reunion this week-end." Logan's eyes cut to Jodee. "And even that depends."

Her defensive nature charged her tired body with a fresh, but feeble energy. He didn't say on *what* it depended, but his meaning was clear. Her memory, Aidan, and whatever sinister plot he imagined tied the two together.

Contrition gnawed at her. She'd assigned motives to actions—or in this case words—again. Being suspicious is part of his job description, right? It's nothing personal.

But it was.

"Bill Miller will probably do it for you if you split it with him," Logan said.

"He left yesterday to visit his daughter in Galveston. They have a new grandbaby."

Jodee detected a wishful note in Grace's words.

If Logan did, he chose to ignore it. "There's an old guy staying out at the Travis place. He passes through now and then. Goes by the name Hawk. He's been picking up a few odd jobs around. I'll see if I can find him tomorrow. I've visited him a few times, and I trust him. But that doesn't mean to let your guard down for this, either." He looked at Jodee again, his warning clear.

Grace opened the passenger side door of Logan's patrol SUV and climbed in.

He took another look at the tree before putting the vehicle in gear. "Can't say I'm going to miss that old tree, though. Something about it always gave me the creeps."

CHAPTER 20

For a tree to become tall it must grow tough roots among the rocks.
~Friedrich Nietzsche

Jodee let herself in through Grace's back door. A door Grace shared was never locked. How many people knew about that?

Her hand lingered on the doorknob, considering the stark contrast between Grace's open and welcoming home and the shuttered house she'd lived in with her mother. She'd grown up in the world of locked doors and closed blinds. Her mother had always seen a monster in every shadow. A trait that worsened after Jodee's stepfather disappeared.

She released the doorknob and headed up the stairs.

In the bathroom, she studied the bruises on her neck in the mirror. What happened last night? Had she seen something she shouldn't have? Is that why someone had done this to her? Would they have killed her if he—whoever he was—hadn't shown up?

He might have been one of them, but that conclusion didn't sit right. It contradicted the peace he'd elicited. A peace unlike anything she'd ever experienced.

She gave her head a quick shake to clear the thoughts away. She wasn't making any sense.

In her room, she stretched out on the bed, staring at the ceiling as unanswered questions wrestled around in her mind.

She didn't like the niggling fear that kept her from relaxing. When she closed her eyes, the sensation of the rough, suffocating hands tightened on her neck again. Though exhaustion pulled at her, she didn't want to sleep. Her memory of Aidan's upturned freckled face clung to her.

The aroma of baking bread filled the room. The inexplicable smell wafted up from her memories, blanketing her in the longed-for peace she didn't understand. It fostered the fanciful notion that someone was watching over her. Relaxing, she let the feeling wrap around her exhausted body, finally drifting to sleep.

She startled. The disorientation she experienced in the abrupt awakening evaporated as her subconscious registered alarmed.

She held her breath, listening. Movement downstairs indicated she wasn't alone. She exhaled. Grace had promised to let her know when she returned home.

The seconds ticked away, but the woman never came.

Shivers raced up Jodee's arms with the premonition that someone other than Grace was making the noise. The rustling noise was too restless, too urgent to be Grace.

Logan?

Her frayed nerves triggered a foreboding, but she couldn't sit here on the bed waiting for the next bad thing to happen.

She eased herself up, wincing at the squeak of the old bed frame, then slipped from her room and down the stairs. A thin slice of light came from beneath the door to Grace's office.

She opened her mouth to call Grace's name, but a hand clamped over her face before she could.

"You're going to learn to stop showing up in places where you ain't wanted," a voice growled against her ear, wet and angry.

The words *This ain't the end* screamed to life inside her. With it came a wave of memories that twisted in a cyclone she couldn't sort through now. She remembered enough to recognize the grave danger she was in.

She kicked back, connecting with her attacker's knee. He rocked forward in pain, and she planted the foot, swinging her elbow up before driving it into his ribs. His thick arms came around her, clamping hers to her sides. Off balance, they staggered until he found his footing. He reared back in an attempt to lift her off her feet.

For once, Jodee was thankful for her long legs and above average height. Almost equal in height, he couldn't lift her as far as he might have if she were shorter. Her long legs swung and kicked, striking him in the shin, though she would have preferred a target a little higher. The contact sent pain shooting up her leg, but she didn't stop.

He gave her a violent shake. The room spun for a moment as flashes of light blinded her. Then anger snapped her from the addled haze.

She tilted her head forward, then slammed it back against his face.

Pain shot through her skull, dancing on a fresh starburst of lights as the cracking of a bone told her she found her mark.

A string of curse words sliced the air as he threw her against a chair.

The impact sucked the air from her lungs as she slid to the floor. She kicked as he reached for her, but she wasn't fast enough.

He seized her ankle and jerked her toward him. Blood dripped down his face as he heaved a booted foot into her already bruised side. Whether it was pain or fear that choked her, she couldn't scream. She could only pray, *please don't let this happen.* Crouching beside her, he drew his fist back, preparing to strike her. She twisted and his fist struck the floor instead. More cursing vibrated from the walls.

Cradling his now injured hand, he rose. Jodee spun to wrap her arms around his ankle, letting her weight drag as he lifted his foot to stomp her. He toppled backwards, crashing into the wall.

"Jodee!" Grace's voice carried in from the back door.

The man swore as he staggered up. "I'll get you for this." He lurched out the front door as the back door slammed behind Grace.

Dizziness swept over Jodee as she struggled to her feet, staggering after him. She couldn't catch him, but she wanted a look at the scumbag who kept attacking her.

With no streetlights in El Hueso, he disappeared into the darkness before she had a chance. The urge to follow him darted through her, but the anticipation she might vomit at any second kept her from it. She leaned against the doorframe, letting her breath settle back in her chest.

The living room lights came on.

"Dear heavens! What happened? Are you okay?" Grace hurried to her in nurse mode, her eyes scouring Jodee in search of injuries.

"I'm fine. But you better call your nephew."

"First, you're going to have a seat so I can get a good look at you. Did he hit you?"

"His nose hit the back of my head."

Grace's eyes narrowed, then an understanding smile took hold. "Your poor head. Let me get you an ice pack, then I'll call Logan. Then I'll get the first aid kit. Though I think we'd better plan a trip to the hospital, too."

Ten minutes later, Logan stormed into the living room where Jodee rested on the couch, an ice pack pressed against the back of her head. The nausea had subsided, and her heart must be too exhausted to engage in its favorite galloping gait. She'd chalked the temporary feeling up to being overly tired and overly excited—with a bit of terrified thrown in.

"What happened?" The formidable scowl on his face wasn't encouraging.

She recounted the same story she'd told Grace, including the frustrating truth that she'd only seen his silhouette in the dark room. And the conviction this was the same man who'd attacked her the night before. "He's about my height, with a beard and a busted nose."

Was that a glimmer of admiration in Logan's eyes when she mentioned the busted nose?

"Anything else?" he asked.

"I got you a blood sample. Can't you figure it out from that?" Her head hurt. She'd taken the beating. Couldn't he take it from here?

"Yes, but that takes time." Logan stared at the drying drops of red on the hardwood floor, then he radioed dispatch to send CSI.

"We'll need to swab your scalp as well, so don't wash." He turned to Grace, worry sharpening the angles of his face. "You'd better check around. See if anything is missing or looks wrong, but don't touch anything."

Then he turned to Jodee, stance wide, hand resting on his holstered gun while his fingers tapped an unknown rhythm against the polished leather. "Okay. I want to know what's going on. Who are you, why are you here, and who is after you?"

Jodee bristled. While a part of her might concede his suspicions were reasonable, the fact that she was on the receiving end of multiple attacks in less than twenty-four hours ignited her indignation.

"*You* have my ID. *You* are the one who wants me to stay close so you can keep an eye on me. And this is *your* county. Now you tell me who's after me and we'll both know."

"Don't get smart with me. You put someone I love in danger tonight. I'll find a reason to lock you up if that's what it takes."

"Might not be a bad idea since you can't seem to protect me any other way." Jodee had bounced through so many emotions in the past twenty-four hours she had nothing left to offer but a bad mood. And a deep regret that she'd ever stopped at Tooley's Truck Stop. But if she hadn't been there, what might happen to Aidan?

"Logan, I think they were after something other than Jodee." Grace looked between the two.

Jodee wasn't yet ready to regret what she'd just said to Logan, but she wished Grace hadn't heard it.

"Come with me."

Logan followed his aunt down the hall with Jodee close behind. In the room she used for an office, desk drawers hung open, their ruffled contents spilling out. Cabinet doors stood ajar, and the contents of an emptied box scattered across the floor.

"I can't imagine what they were looking for in here. There's nothing but my research on El Hueso." Grace shook her head.

Logan exhaled. "I know you were trying to finish something my mother started years ago and never got to finish, but at least now you can quit worrying about doing this. The tree's gone, and not too many folks care to remember El Hueso's past."

Jodee supposed he was trying to comfort his aunt with his remarks, but if that was his goal, he stunk at it.

"Hmmm." Grace wasn't listening to him. "But if they were after Jodee, why do all this?"

Logan stared at the mess. Then he looked at Jodee. "She believes this was the same person who attacked her last night. Maybe they decided to rob the place when they came here after her. Or maybe it's just to cover up their real motive."

His pointed look held an edge of animosity, but she didn't blame him. Grace could have been hurt tonight instead of her.

"And if they were here after me, it must be because I did see something that would identify the people who took Aidan." Jodee sank into the desk chair. "I remember hearing the man talking to Aidan about a red car. I heard a truck pull up and stop, and then I heard the man apologizing to the boy. At least it sounded apologetic. I couldn't see them from where I was, so I ran toward them." She swallowed, her eyes meetings Logan's. "And that's when he attacked me."

Jodee turned to Grace. "I need to use your phone."

She wasn't excited about it, but there was a double bed in a camper where she knew she'd be welcome.

Not that she planned to share the bed, but she'd deal with that later.

At least there she wouldn't be the one bringing trouble.

Trouble had a way of gravitating to Blue Sunday.

Or like her grandfather used to say, he had a way of always extending it an invitation.

A shiver buzzed through her. He'd invited *her*.

Trouble.

CHAPTER 21

The greatness of man is great in that he knows himself to be wretched. A
tree does not know itself to be wretched. ~Blaise Pascal

The cold touch of the amber-colored bottle welcomed
Blue's fingers like a long-lost friend. The kind of friend
that would stab him in the back and take his milk money. He swallowed the longing that danced over his tongue, pulling up old
memories of times when alcohol seemed to ease the pain.

The smells, the sounds, dim lighting, country songs about lost
loves, coarse laughter, and coy smiles. The distinctive pop of a metal
lid lifting from a long neck bottle, the clunk of a mug hitting the bar
top. The cloying scent of heavy-handed colognes and perfumes
intermixing with the musky smell of the beer as the liquid courage
drew couples to the dance floor.

Funny how he could remember the things he did—all the tiny
details he didn't know he'd noticed—when all he'd done was set out
to forget.

So, which was it tonight? Remember or forget? Remember why
he was here and what he promised to do? Or forget that Jodee

Trevaine had kicked open the door he thought he'd nailed shut, waltzing back into his heart to hogtie him in the same old knots.

One required him to stay sober and alert. The other required a state of alcohol induced oblivion. A sarcastic half smile moved over his mouth. Even the strongest of whiskey had never washed Jodee from his mind.

He faked a drink from the long neck, frowning as he set the bottle down. Tonight was for his friend, Oliver Matthews. But he couldn't reach the end of this endeavor fast enough. If he never set foot in another bar or faked another drink, he'd be just fine.

Syrah had flounced in about half an hour ago, seating herself on the barstool next to him. But so far, she'd paid more attention to the guy on the other side of her. Occasionally, she looked around as though searching for someone. Once or twice, she'd cast a glance at Blue over her bare tattooed shoulder. The dark ink stood out against her pale skin, making it easy to discern that the floral design intermixed with the phases of the moon.

Did it have meaning, or was it just a clever design? That was the problem with tattoos. He never knew if they were meant to make a spiritual, mental, or fashion statement.

He stared at the bottle in front of him. Charming a girl—attached or not—had never been a problem for him. Of course, he'd never had to do it sober before either. He had to figure out how to make something happen without getting himself tangled in a knot he couldn't get out of.

Running into Jodee hadn't helped. If anything, it made it exponentially harder to go on playing this role. Seeing her made him eager for her to see the changed man he'd become.

A feminine hand touched his thigh, and he jumped. He worked to hide his surprise when he found Syrah staring at him, a vampish look of amusement on her face.

"Something wrong? You look like the devil done stood you up."

This was the part he hated. He wasn't going out of his way to lead her on, but neither had he discouraged her. "I've been stood up by worse." He winked. "All better now."

Syrah was an attractive woman, but Blue had to wonder just how old she was. Younger than him, he'd guess. But her eyes held a hardness and knowledge she attempted to hide with dark makeup.

Whereas Jodee was a no nonsense, headstrong, determined-to-be-independent fireball that often scared the daylights out of any man who dared approach her, Syrah had a seductive quality that invited men to come closer. It was like comparing a cactus to a leather jacket.

The leather jacket might be easier to get into, but it was still a hollow shell that could slip away as fast as it came.

The cactus, on the other hand, took great care, patience, and the willingness to risk being hurt, and once the thorns got in you, you couldn't shake them loose. Blue smiled. Who knew he was a cactus man?

Syrah must have interpreted his smile as an invitation. She swiveled her stool to face him, and he mirrored her movement, noticing for the first time that Nolan hovered a few feet behind her. The man pretended to be interested in anything but Syrah, which made it obvious she was the only thing he was interested in. How long had he been standing there?

He'd picked up on the man's infatuation with Syrah. Blue sorta felt sorry for the lovesick fool. A likeable enough fellow, Nolan probably had a good heart somewhere in there.

The younger man shifted, ran his fingers around the inside of his t-shirt collar, then rubbed the back of his neck while chewing on his bottom lip.

Blue gritted his teeth. The guy was tweaking like he had his finger in an electrical outlet. He remembered what he'd heard last night. Blue's own father had been a no-good scoundrel but would still have been a better man than to have someone provide drugs to his addicted son. Maybe later, he'd find a way to help this guy.

The bartender set a glass of red wine in front of Syrah.

"A wine drinker, huh?" He'd have taken her for a whiskey girl.

"Not just wine. Syrah."

"Like your name?"

"Exactly."

The bartender let his gaze linger on Blue for a little too long. Blue picked up the bottle in front of him and lifted it to his mouth.

Syrah sipped her wine, licked her lips, then set the glass on the bar, spinning the glass stem between fingertips covered in nails painted with dark glittery polish.

"And what exactly is a Syrah?" Blue stared at her, keenly aware of Nolan's presence a few feet away.

She leaned close, the tight-fitting tank she wore offering him more than he wanted to see.

He concentrated on faking another sip from his beer.

"It means I'm good to have around when you want to relax and have a good time."

Blue nearly choked on the pretend drink of beer he'd taken.

She laughed and sipped her wine. "So, tell me, you've been hanging around for a few days. You're practically a local now. What're you doing tonight?"

Getting in over my head was the first response that came to mind.

The jukebox picked that moment to twang out Johnny Lee's song about lookin' for love in all the wrong places.

That about summed it up. He shook his head at the irony.

"Same ol' same ol' I reckon." He looked around the inside of the bar, spotting an empty table near the corner. "How about we take this conversation to that empty table over there?"

He swiveled and found Nolan still standing there.

Nolan looked at Syrah as though she were the moon, and he could only orbit at her command.

"Why don't you head upstairs and rest a minute? I'll come up and check on you soon." A note of annoyance edged her words as she addressed Nolan.

Nolan's eyes moved back and forth along the bar, bouncing to the doorway and back to the bar. "Where's Rusty?"

"Taking care of some business," Wiley answered, causing Blue to wonder if the man listened to everything they said.

Nolan shifted glazed eyes between Blue and Syrah, then, like a well-trained puppy, turned and headed to the hallway on the opposite side of the dance floor. No doubt about it, the boy was high.

Blue itched to get back into DeGroots' office. His mind spun with ideas on how to make that happen. Upstairs with Nolan seemed like the best option he had going.

Before he could act, Syrah leaned closer. "Nolan isn't feeling well tonight. He has this chemical imbalance, makes him moody and confused sometimes."

She was right about that. Nolan had a chemical imbalance. One his own father had brought on.

Blue had known Syrah for all of four days, and every time he'd seen her had been here at Roots. She came and went with a familiarity that said she was more than the customer of the month. "So, you're his sister, his nurse ? His girlfriend? Maybe we should go with him."

"You mean maybe we should go somewhere else, too?" Her eyes darted to something behind Blue, darkening.

He sensed the bartender's presence.

She took another slow sip of wine, staring at Blue over the rim of her glass. "I'm not supposed to stay long tonight." She lifted her chin, a spark of defiance flashing in her eyes. "But I *am* feeling kinda restless. I could probably be persuaded if someone took the notion." Her eyes flickered to a spot behind him once again before settling back on Blue.

He had no trouble reading the look she gave him, so the fact that she rested her hand on his knee was unnecessary. A fiery shiver of warning raced down his limbs. He twisted on his stool. The adjustment wasn't big, just enough to unsettle her hand and make it awkward for her to return it to a place not appreciated.

"I think he likes you." Blue faked another sip of beer. Instead of returning it to the bar, he let his hand drop to his side, away from the bartender's watchful eyes. With his left hand, he picked up Syrah's glass of wine and made a show of examining it, hoping it drew enough attention that no one noticed him lifting his jeans high enough to allow him to pour half his beer into his boot. It wasn't his first choice but spilling it on the floor would draw unwanted attention. Wiley's frequent antagonistic glances made him wary. "I never did see why folks liked to drink wine. I never liked the taste of it myself."

"You've just never experienced the right one." She tucked a strand of hair behind her ear with a manicured finger in a move that was anything but accidental. "I bet you'd change your mind if you did."

That she said experienced instead of tasted suggested it wasn't wine she was talking about.

She slid from her stool. Resting her elbows on the bar behind her, she faced Blue, sending his discomfort level into the red.

It took everything in him to hold her gaze and think about Jodee at the same time. He needed a cactus right about now. *Lord, help me do what is right. Keep my thoughts pure.*

It wasn't the first time he'd prayed such a prayer, but the need for it had lessened the more he listened to Matthews and followed Christ.

"Well then, tell me something. What's a fine wine like yourself doing in a dive bar in this sorry little town?"

"I have my reasons." She rolled her bottom lip through her teeth. "What's a fine-looking cowboy like yourself doing alone *in a dive bar in this sorry little town?*"

He saluted her with the long neck. "I have my reasons."

She arched her eyebrow and stared, telling him she could get away with a non-answer, but he couldn't.

He lowered his voice. "I'm needing to stay off the radar for a bit, if you know what I mean. You wouldn't happen to know where I could find a little work around here, would you?"

"I might." She shoved off the bar, grabbed his hand and started tugging him in the direction Nolan had gone. "How 'bout we finish conversatin' upstairs?"

Her smile held the promise of a long and busy night. For a man other than Blue Sunday. Not since he'd discovered the truth—the only thing that made life make sense of the mess he'd made. Still, he felt a thin layer of sweat making his shirt stick to his body. He needed to get out of this before it went any further, but he needed to do it in a way that wouldn't keep her from talking to him later. *Lord, I need a rescue—pronto.*

The phone behind the bar rang. Wiley answered, then turned to glare at Blue for a second before extending it in his direction. "Blue Sunday?"

He swallowed and nodded.

His *thank you Lord* was short-lived as Jodee laid out her request to stay at his place.

Out of the frying pan and into the fire.

CHAPTER 22

Notice that the stiffest tree is most easily cracked, while the bamboo or willow survives by bending with the wind. ~Bruce Lee

Inside Grace's house, the CSI team swabbed blood stains and dusted for fingerprints. They'd taken Jodee's already. She waited on the front porch steps for Blue to arrive. She closed her eyes. The cool night air brushed against her. In the distance, a barn owl called, and beyond that, coyotes yowled their lonesome songs. If she could block out the hustle going on inside the house, she could almost imagine herself in a different reality, as though something inside her knew she had been created for something more. The thought was deliciously hopeful and upsettingly vague. What more could there be? How could her heart long for something she'd never known and couldn't imagine existing?

Convincing Grace she didn't need to go to the hospital had taken effort undergirded by her stubborn refusal. Neither had the woman been keen on Jodee's decision to stay with Blue. Still, she'd packed Jodee an overnight bag with a change of borrowed clothes and a toothbrush. The duffle bag sat at Jodee's feet.

If she could stuff all her problems, her doubts, her longings for what would never be into that bag, maybe then she could hold on to this interlude. Because already she sensed it was nothing more than a broken piece of time, a shard disconnected from the reality of her life. The peace she sought always seemed to float just out of reach, drifting further away the harder she strained to take hold.

The hissing and screeching of cats tangled up in a fight a few streets away seemed to prove her point.

"You recognize this?" Logan stepped on the porch behind her, and she turned to see a ball cap in his gloved hand.

"It's a ball cap with a Hooey logo just like half the county wears." Just like the one Blue had been wearing earlier today. She faced back into the night and tried to appear nonplussed. "Pretty common around here."

"Seen one recently?" If the scowl he wore indicated anything, it was that she'd worn his patience thin.

She shouldn't blame him for his reaction. His aunt could have been hurt tonight. She didn't want that any more than he did. She ran her tongue over her swollen lip. "Blue was wearing one earlier today."

"Good answer."

Jodee squinted at him, wondering how that was a good answer.

"Found it on the floor in Grace's office." He pulled a piece of paper from inside the flap. "A gas receipt from Tooley's for the same night you were attacked. Wanna guess whose name is on it?"

"You don't really think Blue did this to me?"

"Who knows," Logan shrugged. "Maybe you did it to yourself to cover for him."

"I guess that makes me quite the brute then." She laughed. "But Blue has an alibi for tonight. He's at Roots." She nodded her head toward the building in the distance.

"Not his best option, but you can be sure I'll check that out."

"Never doubted that you would. Blue wouldn't do this. Not to Grace and not to me."

"Logan!" Grace stepped from the house. "You're out of line. I won't have you treating Jodee like a criminal in my house."

"Aunt Grace—"

"No. Not another word." Grace stood in the doorway, arms folded over her chest.

"It's all right *Acting* Sheriff Adams. I'm not staying." Jodee turned to face Grace. "I appreciate your hospitality, but we don't know who did this or why they were here. Logan's right. I don't want to put you in any danger."

"I'm not afraid. I've survived in this county for too long to let something like this scare me. But what does frighten me is the idea of . . . well, we don't know what's going on or who's behind this."

"I'll be fine," Jodee said. "Blue's been my friend for a long time. I trust him." Did she or was he just safe in that he was familiar? They weren't a couple of teenagers with no responsibilities, with heads full of dreams and a world full of opportunity before them anymore.

As if on cue, the headlights from Blue's truck cut a swath across the yard.

"My knight in shining armor has arrived." Jodee rose, hoping she could reach Blue before Logan did. If he at least had a warning about what was coming his way, maybe this wouldn't end up with them both sleeping at the county jail tonight.

"Don't be too sure about that." Logan's voice was low and full of insinuation. "Keep your seat."

"What's that supposed to mean?" She knew, but she didn't like where this was headed.

A mix of things Jodee couldn't pick apart clouded Blue's expression as he stopped several feet from the porch.

"Sheriff Adams." His gaze flickering from Jodee for a second to acknowledge Logan. "You okay, Jodee?"

"I'm fine, just—"

"Miss Trevaine is fine," Logan cut her off. He held Blue's cap up in the light. "But did you lose something?"

"My respect for your sheriffing if you took that cap out of my truck." Blue rubbed his jaw. To his credit, he held Logan's stare. To his detriment, he did so with a challenge sparking in his dark eyes.

Jodee cringed. She'd already used up Logan's patience for smart aleck answers. Blue better tread easy.

"When was the last time you saw *it in your truck?*" Logan's skepticism stamped itself into his last words. Challenge accepted.

"I left it on the seat right before I went into Roots. Swapped it out for this here hat." He reached up to tip the brim of the straw hat he wore.

"Anyone else have access to your truck?"

"I reckon everyone who can figure out I keep the spare key under the right rear fender well. You're probably familiar with the places folks might hide their spares, aren't ya Sheriff?"

Logan didn't respond. Seconds marched by like the footfall of giants.

"You want to tell me what makes you sure that's my cap and how you came to have it?" The accusation in Blue's tone didn't bode well for a pleasant conclusion to the evening.

"It has a gas receipt with your name on it from last night. They found it in Grace's office," Jodee blurted out.

Logan stared at her. He hesitated, then shook his head.

"Also in my truck when I last saw it." Blue planted has hands on his hips, elbows wide. "Now, can I have my cap back?"

"This sure is a nice Hooey cap. You know what a hooey is, don't you, Blue?" Logan made a show of examining the cap's logo.

"Yes sir, I believe I do." Blue's posture bristled along with his words.

So did Jodee. You don't grow up around rodeos and ranch hands and not know. But she'd said enough already.

"A hooey is that final tie a cowboy makes when he ropes and hogties a calf. The final tie that just," he paused, "holds it all together." The smugness in Logan's voice raked across her.

She closed her eyes. *Please, don't let him get to Blue.*

"What are you getting at?" Blue asked, his lazy smile returning.

A fresh apprehension gripped Jodee at the unexpected shift in his demeanor. The barely contained anger morphed into the devil-may-care swagger Blue was most known for.

"Nothing. Just thinking it was interesting." Logan held the cap up, moving it around as though examining it. "I think I'm going to hang on to this a little while longer. You two can go now. Just don't go far."

Jodee expected either a lecture or flirting—Blue's native tongue. Instead, the brooding silence made her uneasy. Blue couldn't be angry with *her*, could he? This wasn't her fault.

She sniffed. "You smell like a brewery. You shouldn't be driving."

He tensed like a rope with the slack yanked out of it. "Thanks for noticing. I'm fine."

"You don't smell fine."

"It's not what you think. I'm fine." The curves of his face flattened, the tightening lines evidence of his frustration.

"I think you smell like you took a bath in Coors Light."

"Told you it wasn't what you think. It's Lone Star."

"I'm not going to ride with someone who's been drinking. Pull over and let me drive or let me out."

"I haven't been drinking. Just trust me, would you?"

"Let me out."

"Not happening, so how about you just sit quietly and try real hard not to insult me anymore tonight? As I recall, you called me for help, not the other way around." He cut her off, the sharp edge in his words biting into her heart.

She glanced at the speedometer. His speed was normal, his driving was steady, and his words weren't slurred.

But tonight opened the door into a night long ago, a nightmare they both lived to forget. "Blue—"

"Don't go there." His tone silenced her as much as his words, leaving her to fight through the memories alone.

In a flash, she was back at that night when the last thread holding her life together had died in her arms. And all the while, Blue stayed passed out in the truck.

Grief could be a bridge or a wall. In the case of her and Blue, it had become a wall.

A taciturn half hour later, he parked beside a camper at the end of an overgrown pasture road. A few trees and a weathered old barn with a collapsing corral were the only other things in sight.

"Wait here." He reached into the pocket of the driver's side door and retrieved a Glock. "I'll turn the lights on. Can't have you stepping on a rattlesnake in the dark."

She nodded, in no hurry to expose her foot to the bite of a venomous viper, or her heart to more of Blue than it could stand. He'd always been a pretty easy book to read, but she began to wonder if the cover no longer matched the contents. Maybe he wasn't such an easy read after all.

His choice of location for his camper perplexed her. This was the kind of spot where someone who wanted to hide out would be, just one step away from going completely off-grid.

He disappeared inside and an exterior light came on.

Was coming here a mistake? Just how many mistakes could a person jam into less than thirty-six hours? She was on the fast track to find out.

She closed her eyes and pressed her hand against her stomach. So many life-changing mistakes. Tears stung her eyes, and she hurried to wipe them away before he returned. *Jodee Trevaine didn't cry, especially over a man.*

A sudden longing for Grace's presence consumed her. Grace with her reassuring words, her warmth, her what? Her faith? She hadn't mentioned it to Jodee, but the peace she exuded was something different, contagious.

The truck door opened. Blue offered her his hand as she climbed out. His brown eyes were clearer than she would have expected from someone who smelled as much like beer as he did. Nothing he had done hinted at him being under the influence of anything but a sour mood.

She followed him toward the camper. The question pestering her for most of the drive grew more persistent with every step. She trusted Blue. It didn't matter if he acted differently tonight. He was still Blue, and she was still Jodee.

And they were still never meant to be.

"Why was your cap at Grace's house?" She didn't mean to sound distrustful, but the squaring of his shoulders told her she missed the mark.

He grabbed the door latch without using the steps and glared at her. The look was cold, but she didn't miss the hurt hovering in the depths of his gaze.

She opened her mouth to respond, but he cut her off.

"Save it." The little camper shook as he stomped up the steps and through the open door, returning seconds later with a pillow and a blanket. "I'll sleep in the truck."

Not to be outdone, Jodee pounded up the steps and slammed the door behind her. She paced the length of the small space a couple of times. How could he make her so angry and so sad at the same time?

Sight of a Bible on the nightstand snagged her attention as she sank onto the bed.

She put her head in her hands. There were glimpses of the person Blue used to be, but intuition kept telling her Blue wasn't the same person as before. She might not know what had changed—how he'd changed—but she knew he'd never hurt her. Not physically and not intentionally. He wouldn't hurt anyone outside of getting into a barroom brawl.

In a moment of painful honesty, she faced the truth. She'd made a life out of hurting Blue and everyone else who loved her by withholding her trust from them. But it had also been the only way she knew how to protect her heart.

Now she was punishing him for her weakness. It wasn't his fault her heart wanted what it couldn't have.

Returning to the door, she inhaled, then opened it and leaned out. The light from behind her spilled onto the cab of his truck. The windows were rolled down but no Blue. "Blue?"

"What?" His gruff response came from inside the truck where he had reclined the seat.

"I don't want you to sleep out there." She cleared her throat. "I'd feel better if you were closer. I'll take the couch, and you can sleep in your bed."

He released a frustrated sigh as he stirred from where he reclined. She waited while he climbed from the truck and walked past her without glancing her way.

"I'll take the couch. You sleep in the bed. And close the door. You're letting mosquitoes in."

She closed the camper door and locked it, once again wondering if this was a mistake.

As he settled onto the couch, Jodee worked to pull the curtained divider that separated the two rooms closed. It wouldn't budge.

"It's broken." Blue clicked off the light from the living room. "But don't worry. I'm not looking. Your virtue is safe with me."

She slipped off her jeans in the dark, then slid beneath the quilt and stared at the ceiling. How had everything gotten so complicated? Her mind trailed over the events of the evening, certain of one thing, but baffled by the why of it. "You're being framed."

"I know. Good night, Jodee." His words closed the door on further conversation as though her concerns were nothing more than pesky mosquitoes of a different kind. The springs under the sofa squeaked as he adjusted himself.

She continued to stare into the darkness.

No, it wasn't a *good* night. The person she most wanted to trust was keeping something from her.

The smell of beer-soaked leather was too much. Blue sat up, tugged off his boots, then pealed the wet sock from his foot. He went to the door and tossed both outside, then settled back on the torture rack of a sofa for a sleepless night.

Uncertainty nibbled at him. Who would set him up and why? Maybe the answer to that one was obvious. But how did they know?

And more concerning, what if they succeeded?

He didn't want to drag Jodee into this anymore than she already was.

The fact that the only woman he'd ever loved slept a few feet away, a front row seat for watching the trajectory of his probable failure, added shame to the toxic emotional concoction brewing within him. Since all of this had been for a single purpose—to prove he wasn't the same ol' good-for-nothing he had been—anger at himself came close to overtaking his anger at whoever was doing this.

He couldn't stop the memory of that night years ago, not that most of what he knew came from his memory. He only knew what they told him, but it was enough. The old familiar guilt washed over him. His jealousy had gotten his best friend killed. And it had stolen something from Jodee he could never repay. He didn't deserve to be free of that debt.

And yet he was. According to the mercy he'd been granted, he was a free man.

Free to love Jodee. And he did. He always had.

He just didn't plan to ever let her know. Because in doing so, he'd have to be honest with her about what happened that night. And once that happened, she'd be lost to him forever.

Like the searing touch of a hot coal to tender flesh, love for her burned his heart with a longing that would leave him forever scarred.

He'd tried to get her to go home. He'd told himself it was because he didn't want the distraction of her presence. But the truth was that he didn't want her to see him fail. No matter how much confidence Matthews and now Fowler put in him, he couldn't forget who he used to be. There was more possibility of failure than success with this. And now, there could be the possibility of arrest if whoever tried to set him up was determined enough to keep trying.

Someone wanted to hurt her. He didn't know if it was connected to what he was doing. Until he knew she was safe, he wouldn't let her go.

And once she was safe, he wouldn't be able to hold her.

CHAPTER 23

Texas 1858

It is like a mustard seed which, when it is sown on the ground, is smaller than all the seeds on earth; but when it is sown, it grows up and becomes greater than all herbs, and shoots out large branches, so that the birds of the air may nest under its shade. ~Mark 4:31-32

Will woke before sun up, thankful the rain clouds passed to the south. Once in the night, he'd smelled the moisture, but no rain had fallen where they were.

Rose snuggled into him, whimpering in her sleep.

He'd tried to stay awake, but exhaustion had overtaken him. With Rose's warm body resting beside him he'd drifted into sleep and dreams of family: his Ma, Mr. & Mrs. Charidy, even Will's Pa was there, which when he thought about it, roused a strange emotion. Was he happy his Ma and Pa were together some place, or sad that his Pa must really be gone? Even though he didn't understand the purpose of the dream, he knew that's what it must mean.

He wanted to go to them now, but they seemed to be shooing

him on. They were waiting on him in an unhurried, timeless way at a family gathering he couldn't yet join.

A hot, wet tear slid from the corner of his eye into his hair. He jerked upright and rubbed the offending tear away. Real men didn't cry, and that was what he was now. He had Rose to take care of.

"Will," Rose's tiny, sleep clogged voice murmured. She sniffled. "I wanna go home."

"There isn't any more home to go back to," Will said. Saying the words made everything real. The stinging in his eyes intensified. Maybe he shouldn't have said that, but it was the truth.

He shrugged Rose off and sat. He had man-sized decisions to make. His stomach growled. Rose must be thirsty and hungry, too. He'd learned to ignore the feeling while living on the streets. But Rose had never known real hunger. He looked at her small face. They were just the same now. Orphans without a family or a home. Fingers of worry wove through him, knowing what life as an orphan would be like. He couldn't let that happen to her.

He looked at Rose's arm, seeing the extent of her burn for the first time. The ragged, blackened remnant of her sleeve clung to the patch of red marring her forearm. Already blisters oozed over her skin.

Today. He'd do whatever it took to get Rose some place safe today.

They would follow the creek bed. Whatever neighbors there were would probably be settled somewhere near water. Unless they were like Mr. Charidy.

He looked at the creek and watched the sun lifting itself like a flower unfurling over a new day.

Were the DeGroots still searching for them? And if so, where? He grit his teeth and put it out of his mind. Dwelling on it would only keep him frozen in fear.

They'd go south.

He reached over and tugged at a strand of her hair. "Okay Little Bud, we're going to find us some food today, but we better get going."

She'd have to do some of the walking on her own if they were going to reach another house before dark.

He wondered where the DeGroot brothers were and remembered poor Daisy. Tied up in the stall as she gave birth. Alarm triggered in him that the barn might have caught fire and burned down too. Even if it hadn't, would Luther and Cub have checked on her and the calf? Had they bothered to water her? He turned his back to Rose to hide the tears he couldn't stop.

He hadn't yet shed a tear for the Charidys. Now the grief for them and the angst for Daisy mixed and ran together. But it was the guilt of not yet knowing what a man was supposed to be and do to protect his family that ravaged his young soul.

He swiped his sleeve across his runny nose, dried his face, and turned to see Rose staring not at him but at the hideous burn on her arm.

He shouldn't have let her see. He'd only been thinking about himself, but he couldn't do that. Not until he got Rose to safety. She must be terrified.

"I'm hungry," she said in the thick clunky words of a child her age.

Will sighed and patted her head. "Me too Little Bud."

He crawled to the edge of the rock. It was higher in the daylight. Pushing Rose up had been easier than lowering her down would be. He shimmied down, staggering as he dropped the last foot. Then he piled more rocks against the bigger one until it was tall enough for him to stand on and coax Rose to the edge.

"Guess we might better get going so we can find us some breakfast, Bud."

She scooted to the edge and reached for him. Will inhaled. He wouldn't drop her. He wouldn't.

When her feet were firmly on the ground, he exhaled. Rose wobbled and banged her injured arm on the rock.

Tears filled her eyes, but her lips set in a firm line. She didn't cry. She just looked at Will with more trust in her eyes than he had ever seen.

Though he didn't share the same confidence, he loved her for it.

CHAPTER 24

Such partners are often so tightly connected at the roots that sometimes they even die together. ~Peter Wohlleben

Jodee snuggled into the pillow wrapped in her arms, pulling it close and inhaling. The first good sleep she'd had in what seemed like a week. She didn't want to let go of the dream that enveloped her in the soothing scent of Blue.

Reality popped the dream bubble she floated in, and she bolted upright. She was in Blue's bed. She was—her head spun to the noise beside her.

Half-dressed, Blue stood with his shirtless back to her.

"What are you doing?" She tugged the quilt higher. Blue in a dream was one thing. Blue in the oh-so-real-looking flesh was another.

"Getting clean clothes. Didn't mean to wake you." He rifled through a drawer.

The cold indifference in his words stung. "Blue, about last night—"

"Nothing more to say."

"Yes, there is. Stop being mule headed and admit asking how

your cap made it to Grace's house without you is a reasonable question."

"It's reasonable." He tugged a gray T-shirt over his head, then rotated to face her, arms crossed over his chest. "Just not coming from you."

"You think I'm accusing you of putting it there?"

"Actions speak louder than words." The smirk contradicted the hurt in his eyes.

"You don't even know what you're mad about, do you? It was my *words* that offended you. There were no *actions*." She dipped the last word in sarcasm before hanging it out to dry in the heated air between them.

"I know actions when I see them." He mimicked her use of the word. "You think I can't read you like a book?"

"And yet here I am, alone with you and sleeping in your bed—the ultimate expression of trust with you." An exasperated exhale blew away the tension. "Sheesh, Blue, you don't even read books."

"Maybe not, but I guess I read you well enough." He braced his hands on the mattress and leaned close. The smoldering look in his eyes sparked a flame that scorched her cheeks. "I mean, I did always say I'd get you in my bed one day."

"In your dreams." Or maybe those were her dreams. She swung the pillow and hit him. "Stop trying to avoid the issue. I'm being serious. Someone was in Grace's house last night. They attacked me and left your cap there to set you up. I have a right to know what's going on."

Blue sighed and ran his fingers through his hair, leaving it sticking out in damp, spikey angles, then sat next to her. "I left the cap in the truck before I went into Roots. I didn't even notice it was missing."

"So, anyone could have taken it and left it where it would be found at Grace's. But why?"

He looked away, but not fast enough to hide the troubled look that darkened his eyes.

"You're being framed. Why? What aren't you telling me?" Because without a doubt, Blue Sunday had a secret.

The silence stretched as though he were debating with himself. "Go home, Jodee. Please."

"I can't. There's a reason why I'm here." The idea skipped through her mind on wobbly, uncertain legs. What reason could there be? She could walk away right now, couldn't she?

She couldn't. A missing child might be in danger, and somehow, she fathomed he needed her. And maybe Blue needed her, too. "Why'd you smell like beer last night when you hadn't been drinking?"

"You just can't let yourself trust me, can you?" He stood, then leaned over to kiss her on the top of her head. "I have to leave for a little while. I hung a clean towel in the shower. Why don't you rest up and when I get back, I'll take you into New Plenty for lunch and whatever other girly stuff you need?"

Though innocent enough, his kiss left her too captured by an impossible dream to speak. She stared after him as he walked out the door into the early morning darkness.

Where could he be going at this time of day?

A new understanding gripped her like the first icy wind of winter, making her muscles tense as she braced against the cold.

Blue was shutting her out, refusing to let her into his secrets.

Just like she'd been doing for years. Just like she was still doing.

A thump jostled Jodee from sleep. She smiled as the beckoning aroma of baking bread awakened her senses.

A growling, hissing noise snatched her from the surreal moment.

She rubbed her eyes to clear them, then swept her damp, tangled hair from her face, expecting to see Blue. Instead, she found a wall of orange flames dancing along the walls between her and the living area.

Scorching heat fanned over her as the flames swept closer.

Get out! Her own voice screamed inside her head. She couldn't die here. Not now.

Smoke stung her eyes. She tugged her shirt over her mouth as she searched for the emergency escape.

Her fingers groped until she found the red release latch, but the window didn't budge. She slammed her shoulder into it but still nothing. Coughing, she spun to kick at the window. The safety glass didn't give. Heat consumed her as the fire raged closer.

Don't look!

She ran her fingers around the windowsill again. Already the aluminum frame of the camper grew hot to the touch. There had to be a way out. Her fingertips raked across a soft plastic. The wedges used to secure the window for transport were still lodged in place.

A spark landed on the bed, bursting into an angry flame. She kicked the comforter away, then clawed at the objects that kept the window from opening, flinging them away.

She kicked the window wide with her bare feet, then flipped to her stomach, preparing to slide out feet first. Blue's Bible lay on the bed where she'd been reading when she fell asleep, her white stone on top of it next to the dog tags she'd found inside it. She snatched all three, clutching them to her chest as she swung her legs through the open window.

Movement caught her eye, and she glanced at the raging fire. A man in a duster stood between her and the flames racing from the living area of the camper. He didn't move.

Intense heat parched the scream building in her throat. The sound came out a wild mix of shock and fear. Who was he and how had he gotten into the trailer?

If he came to kill her, he wouldn't have stood between her and the flames like he was somehow holding them back to buy her time.

Her hold gave way. She landed hard, her legs buckling. Rolling to her hands and knees, she scrambled away from the burning camper before looking back. But he wasn't there.

Had he made it out when she wasn't looking? She searched through the smoke filled dark, but just like before—she was alone.

She dropped to her knees. She was hallucinating, right? But three times now? What was happening to her?

Headlights spread across the scene. A pickup slid to a stop, the dust it churned mixing with the smoke already thick in the air. An old cowboy leapt out. Jodee stepped into the glow of the fire and he turned to her.

"Blue with you?"

"He's not here, but I think there's a man inside." She squeezed her eyes closed, hoping to squelch the image from her mind.

"You *think*?" The man looked at the camper now engulfed in flames, then back at her.

She shifted, tugging at her shirt before crossing her arms over her chest, painfully aware of being underdressed. "Yes, I saw him right before I jumped out."

"Who is it?" he asked, striding back to his truck.

"I don't know. I've never seen him before." Only that wasn't true, was it? She had seen him. The duster, the way his face was never quite visible. At the truck stop the night of her attack. Then again at the wreck. Was she losing her mind? Had the blow to her head made her crazy?

He returned with a tattered Mexican blanket covered in dog and horsehair and a pair of rubber boots. Handing them to her, he asked, "And you are?"

"A friend of Blue's. Jodee Trevaine." She slipped her feet into boots several sizes too big, then wrapped the blanket around her, suddenly conscious of the chill soaking into her now that she was away from the fire's heat.

Then she stared at the camper. The intensity with which the flames billowed over the camper's ravaged body made it too late for anyone still inside. A shudder rattled down her limbs and didn't stop.

She pulled the blanket tight against her, but the shivering persisted.

He walked to his truck once again, this time returning with a thermos of hot coffee and a command. "Folks call me Hawk. Drink this."

The coffee was strong but smooth. Perhaps the best she'd ever tasted. But then a near death experience probably made everything that came afterwards *the best ever*.

His was a face lined with the stories of a full life. A lean face with a gray mustache and closely cropped beard and with eyes that said they'd seen the worst of humanity and still found a reason to keep living. His presence eased away the terrified emotions boiling inside her. An odd sense of familiarity settled over her.

The aroma of baking bread rose through the acrid stench of smoke.

"You hurt?"

"No." Jodee coughed.

"You sure?"

"I'm fine . . . at least until Blue finds out."

"This your fault somehow?"

Was it? First Grace's and now this. Was she bringing trouble with her wherever she went? Was she the reason bad things kept happening, bringing trouble and suffering to those around her? But why?

Her mumbled *maybe* intensified his scrutiny, but he didn't say anything.

With no way to put the fire out, they could only let it run its course until there was nothing else to consume.

Where had Blue gone when he left? The prospect of telling him he was homeless daunted her. Whatever else he had going on seemed to trouble him enough.

Sirens howled in the distance. "Looks like company's coming."

A half hour later, Jodee sat beneath the awning of the old barn, watching as Blue and men from the volunteer fire department doused the camper's charred remains in water. The hot metal hissed and popped, sending plumes of steam snaking upward in the pale light of dawn. They hadn't found a body—or what might have remained—inside the blackened debris.

She shivered at the recognition of how close she'd come to being a part of the ashes now swirling on the breath of morning.

Had the blow to her head addled her so much she was seeing things . . .people . . . a man . . . when no one was there?

Blue'd arrived moments after the fire department. The relief in his eyes when he found her sent a warmth through her the even the raging fire couldn't have stirred. But realizing the extent of his loss must have unleashed other emotions—emotions that seemed to propel him away from her instead of closer.

Shutting her out even more when what she wanted most was to . . . what? Tell him she loved him? A confession like that would be the final nail in the coffin of their friendship. No matter how different things had been these past few days, Blue Sunday wasn't the kind to form lasting attachments. He'd never been bashful in making that known. How could she think any of that would have changed?

The fact he seemed to be ignoring her now spoke volumes.

She flicked at a wad of ash that had landed on the blanket covering her lap.

Blue gripped the side of the pickup bed, then shoved away to walk in a circle. He stopped, throwing his head back as if searching for answers in the midmorning sky.

A memory floated up. Their last conversation before they'd gone separate ways, the pain of Chris's death still bleeding out between them. She remembered the horizon first.

The late day sunset had brushed across the vista in shades of pale pinks and oranges as though anticipating the coming goodbye and wanting to soften it. Side by side, they'd leaned on the corral fence as though mesmerized by the display of changing colors in the sun's swift descent.

Looking back, she wondered if maybe he'd been the one to see it best, even though he was looking at it through the tinted brown glass of the beer bottle he sipped from.

They'd lingered in silence as though letting the last of their friendship drain into the red dirt beneath their boots. It was like the moment when the movie was over, but you remain seated as the credits scroll, hoping somehow you can hold on to the magic of the happily-ever-after ending a little bit longer.

She'd been the one to break the silence.

"Don't wait too long, Blue."

"Too long for what?" He stared over the open pastureland that stretched between them and the backdrop of the setting sun.

"To find your way home."

Her words were a joke, though she wouldn't have admitted it at the time—how wrong they had been. She hadn't seen then just how lost she'd been. Even with a plan in hand.

When your roots are shallow, no ground will hold you.

"So, this is what you want? To leave the ranch, your family?" Blue's eyes had locked with hers. "You're sure that's what you want . . . just walking away?"

"Yes."

What she had wanted was to run far enough the pain and the guilt couldn't find her, but she couldn't tell him that.

The image of him as he turned back to staring into the distance, taking a slow drink before his final words seared her. "Well, then . . . you're a thousand miles ahead of me."

He'd said the words as though running from life's pain was the goal. But she hadn't been *ahead* of him, had she? She'd only been better at lying to herself, whereas Blue was honest with everyone, including himself.

Now Blue's voice carried to her over the noise from the scene of his camper's destruction.

She couldn't do this. Blue Sunday remained a mystery she'd never unravel. A dream she'd never hold on to.

He'd let her walk away before. He'd do it again.

She looked away when he turned and marched in her direction. Gone was the look of relief that warmed her earlier.

"Why didn't you just go home like I asked you to?" He stopped a few feet away, hands on his hips, elbows out, and glared.

"How would that have kept your camper from burning down?" Like a cornered and wounded animal, her defenses rose. His hostility perplexed her when what she'd seen in his eyes when he first arrived was anything but anger.

"It's not about the camper, Jodee." Frustration strained his words.

"Then what, Blue?" She bolted to her feet, mirroring his stance as she faced him.

The emotion in his eyes stole her breath just as he'd stolen her heart long ago. He'd taken it, held it in his greedy hands, preventing her from giving it to anyone else. Because it wasn't her heart he wanted. Hadn't that been life's lesson all along?

"You shouldn't be here," he said. "That's all I can say."

"Then say what you really mean. I shouldn't be here . . .or you *don't want* me here? There's a big difference." Challenge dripped from her words.

"Could you stop making everything so difficult?"

Memories of her stepfather leaving raced through her. She'd asked him to give her his name—to adopt her—, and then he disappeared. At least Blue was honest about his feelings when he said he didn't want her here.

With more force than necessary, she slammed the Bible she'd rescued against his chest with a satisfying whump. The dog tags slipped from her hand to land in the dirt.

He stooped to pick them up without saying a word.

"A Bible? The Army? Now running around like you have some big secret you can't tell me? I don't even know who you are now."

"And whose fault is that? You're the one who left after—"

"Stop! Everything between us always comes back to him, doesn't it? He's like this giant wall we run and hide behind every time our emotions get to be too much. Well, you know what? That's never going to change. Chris isn't coming back."

She pressed her lips tight, clamping her next thought inside. *And you'll never stay.*

Brushing past him, she headed toward the firemen busy reloading their equipment. She waved her arm to get their attention before they could drive away.

"What're you doing, Jodee?" Blue grabbed her wrist and spun her back to face him.

"I'm leaving. Giving you what you want, right?" Her words were cold and flat, sounding as though they originated from a hollow place deep within her.

His grip on her arm loosened, but he didn't let go.

"No. That's not what you're doing." He released her, his hands falling to his sides, drooping under a weight she didn't understand.

He scrubbed his palm over his face, as though attempting to wipe away the emotions stirring chaos in his eyes. "When are you going to stop living like you're broken, and that it somehow makes you less?"

Jodee preferred the chaos over the sorrow that met her when he looked up.

"We're all broken. We're dumped into this world in the care of people who were dumped into the same jacked up mess. We're raised by people just as screwed up as we think we are." He sighed. "How long until you let yourself heal, Jodee?"

Trees don't heal, they seal. The oft repeated line of arboreal wisdom echoed in her head. The truth that the wounds they experienced accumulated until they weakened the tree beyond repair soon followed. Had she gone so far she was beyond repair now, too?

He stepped close, lifting her chin with a tender touch until her eyes met his. "Every now and then we get a glimpse of something truly good. Don't let anger or fear or whatever this is make you miss it."

Taking her hand, he placed the Bible in it.

Jodee choked on a sob as he walked to his truck. He didn't understand. She wasn't the one missing it. She was the one watching it walk away.

CHAPTER 25

A fool sees not the same tree that a wise man sees. ~William Blake

Logan stared at the cap on his desk. No doubt evidence. But evidence of what?

Had Blue been the one to leave it there? The bartender had suggested that Blue had disappeared for a period last night, though he said they'd been too busy to say for sure how long.

If Blue was the one to leave it there, what was he looking for in Grace's office? The majority of what she kept in her office pertained to her historical research for El Hueso, a project she pursued in her effort to have the oak registered as a Texas Heritage Oak.

The part that left him most skeptical that it was Blue who had left it there was the attack on Jodee. For one thing, she would have been more apt to recognize him, even in the dark.

Unless she was just a really good liar.

Even more convincing was the way Blue looked at her. It wasn't the look of a man who had harm in mind.

Or she was a part of this and the repeated physical attacks were just their cover.

Still, why?

Aidan's disappearance, the break in at Grace's. Jodee and Blue had been connected to both. And Logan made it a rule to never trust a coincidence.

A call came through on his radio. There was a camper on fire. A camper belonging to Blue Sunday.

He lifted his hat from the rack by the door and slammed in onto his head with more force than he intended.

Never trust a coincidence.

Blue pulled into the parking lot at the New Plenty Dollar General. The tension between him and Jodee filled the cab like a swarm of angry bees, and he definitely didn't want to get stung. He'd hurt her. It hadn't been his intention, but maybe there really was too much history, too much pain, too much fear between them. Maybe this was all they could ever be.

"You haven't asked about the dog tags?" He tried one more time to bridge this new divide between them.

She folded her arms over her chest and stared out the window without responding.

"Well, since you insist. Four years in Uncle Sam's Army." He placed a hand against his chest in mock humility, his voice now animated. "Some of the best and worst time of my life. But it was, in fact, exactly what I needed."

That wasn't an understatement. After his *come-to-Jesus* meeting orchestrated by his Memaw and Oliver Matthews—a long, cold, wet night in a dark jail cell—he'd seen the light and decided to change his ways. Truth be told, they'd frozen and starved the pride right out of him and left him with nothing to do but face the truth. He knew he wasn't being the man he was capable of being, and he'd had to admit the way he was living was nothing but an attempt at never failing.

The Army had been the best place to solidify his new awareness that he was created to be something more than a rebel rousing drunk. It had taught him structure and self-discipline. He thirsted for her to know that about him.

Memaw had a saying she was fond of using. *Steaming mad.*

Jodee was definitely steaming right now and obviously nonplussed by his admission. Maybe when she was less steamy, she'd recognize the thirst in her heart. Her fingers had spent the better part of the drive in trailing along the gold embossed lettering on the front of the Bible he'd placed in her hands, occasionally thumbing at the gilded edges of its pages, but never opening it.

In her other hand, she held a white stone.

"Hungry?" he asked. Perhaps the hunger in her stomach would be an easier approach.

Her stomach rumbled in reply, but he wasn't sure she heard anything he'd said.

"Are they sure there wasn't a body in the camper?" She stared out the window, but whatever she saw existed in the private confines of her thoughts. "It was him again. I saw him."

"Him again?"

"The man at the truck stop. The one who stopped the attack." She hadn't made eye contact with him since the episode after the fire. "And then again at the wreck."

"There wasn't anyone else in there, Jodee." His words were tired. He didn't want to cause any more damage to whatever this was between them. But still, he needed to be honest. "You think you might have just imagined it? Some sort of hallucination or something due to the blow to your head?"

"No."

"Come on Jodee. Think about it. You needed a rescuer, so your recently addled brain saw one."

She stared at the Bible in her lap. Blue had no idea what kind of storm brewed behind her dark eyes. Without warning, she opened the truck door and climbed out.

He did the same, hurrying around the truck to intercept her. He was in way over his head when it came to the complex issue of wanting to make things right between them and keeping her out of harm's way at the same time.

She stopped on the sidewalk and cinched the blanket she'd been clinging to around her waist.

He wanted to tell her how adorable she looked with her mussed hair, wearing an old Mexican blanket for a skirt and finishing off the look with rubber boots that made her look like she had clown feet. He grinned and looked away, hoping she didn't notice his ill-timed amusement.

"Is there an ATM around here?" she asked.

"Not likely. I got it, though." He held the glass door open for her.

"I don't want—"

"I said I had it." He placed a hand on her back and ushered her inside. She didn't shrug the touch away. A good sign, right? "You can pay me back later if it makes you feel better."

"It won't." She stalked toward a rack of discounted t-shirts as though completely unaware of her unusual get-up.

He exhaled and left her to round up her purchases alone while he grabbed a couple of bottled waters, a protein bar, and two packages of peanut butter crackers. Then he waited at the checkout stand.

"Why, Blue Sunday," Syrah's voice snaked down his spine as though he were a mouse about to be devoured.

His lips pressed together. *Not now.*

Inhaling, he turned to Syrah wearing a lopsided grin. "Why not?"

There was no way this was going to help the situation with Jodee. But he had to play through using the hand he'd been dealt— which was, first and foremost, the task Matthews had given him.

The young woman looked up at him with hungry eyes. Dressed in cutoff denim shorts and a tank top that revealed the elaborate tattoo on her shoulder—along with a few other places of interest— she had danger stamped across her like the hazardous chemical warning on a tanker truck.

She reached over to tug at the front of his shirt. "You took off so fast last night, we didn't get to finish—" her eyes flickered to something behind him, "Conversatin'. We ought to see about finishing our talk later. I will see you at Roots tonight, won't I?"

He dipped his head, looking up at her like a shy schoolboy and gave a single shoulder shrug.

The heat of Jodee's ire behind him seared his back like a blowtorch.

He didn't need to see her to have confirmation of her presence. She dropped her items on the counter with a thud and cleared her throat.

A challenge glistened in Syrah's dark eyes. He risked a glance at Jodee and winced. An ice cube would've looked warmer.

The *he's-all-yours* look that soon followed didn't surprise him. Neither was he surprised when Jodee held Syrah's stare without blinking.

He shifted in an attempt to block their view of each other.

Syrah leaned to see around him. She ran her gaze over Jodee, then turned cat-like eyes to Blue. She patted his chest with a seductive wink. "I'll see you tonight." She walked away, pausing with a single glance back, as though to confirm he was still watching.

He was, but only because he wasn't ready to face what stood behind him.

Rubbing the back of his neck, he opted to face the cashier instead. The woman's expression told him he wouldn't be getting any discounts today as he handed her his credit card. She could charge him a thousand dollars right now and he wouldn't notice. He had only one thought in his head. Jodee.

Syrah's timing added fuel to the inferno already turning their fragile relationship to ashes.

He hurried to catch up with Jodee as she strode out the door. He opened the truck door for her as she climbed in, then handed her the bags with her purchases.

"That Care Bear T-shirt is going to look great on you. But are you sure there wasn't a Hello Kitty or something with a mutant turtle on it? You never quite struck me as the Care Bear type." His attempt at levity fell flat, but if he were honest, it wasn't completely a joke, though Hello Kitty wasn't her style either.

"It was all they had. Besides, looks like you already have Hello Kitty covered with your new friend there."

"It's not what you think." His answer came in a quiet, measured tone he hoped hid his annoyance.

"I'm told that happens quite a lot." The piercing stare she leveled at him hit him like ice water. "But I'm more inclined to believe it happens not at all."

CHAPTER 26

As a terebinth tree or as an oak, Whose stump remains when it is cut down.
So the holy seed shall be its stump. ~Isaiah 6:13

*A*fter the unpleasant encounter at the Dollar General, Jodee had insisted Blue take her to Grace's. With no one at home, he'd dutifully checked inside before leaving her, something he seemed reluctant to do.

Yet he did it anyway.

Now Jodee sat on the ground beside the broken tree. Trees don't heal, they seal, carrying their wounds with them for the rest of their lives. Often with no outward sign they're dying inside until it's too late.

The damaged part of this tree could be removed, and the tree might linger for a few more years like a battle-scarred old soldier. But it would never again thrive.

Trees don't heal, they seal.

The bark—a rough exterior—hid the inner hurts and wounds that would never mend. Death could come in a thousand little ways often overlooked by those focused too narrowly on a single source of affliction.

People were like that, weren't they? Rough exteriors hiding a multitude of hurts that were slowly eating them alive.

A single tear traced a lonesome path down her cheek.

Did the tree know it needed to heal? Did it believe it could? Did it understand what had happened and what would come?

She sighed. The outcast acorn that grew into this oak hadn't chosen this place for its home. Whether a storm carried it here or a bird dropped it, it had been forced to face the world in this solitary state. When trees stuck together, they helped each other in times of need, sending nourishment through their root systems to help their neighbors survive. There should be trees doing that for this one now.

It stood alone. Now it would have to face death in that same state of loneliness.

Daily dying on the inside while others passed by without noticing.

Blue had noticed.

An aching despair stole through her, stirring a new hunger. She needed roots, and she needed to let them connect with others.

A sea of regrets crashed over her. Like the night she'd spent with a firefighter named Caleb six weeks ago. She'd expected it to fill the hole in her heart and drive away the pain, at least for a little while. She'd thought wrong.

With her eyes closed, she pressed her hand against her stomach. At least trees didn't inflict their own wounds.

Always paying the price but never satisfying the longing? The conversation started in her head but moved to her heart.

What is it that you really want?

I want my life back.

You never lost it. You just surrendered it to the wrong things. It's time to accept the gift, Jodee.

She exhaled. It's hard to accept it when you don't know what it is.

"There you are." Grace's voice broke through the whirlwind inside her.

She carried a glass of iced tea in her hand. "Thought you might like some iced tea." She reached into the pocket of the scrubs she wore and pulled out an apple. "And something nutritious to eat." She seated herself on the ground beside Jodee. "You know, they say an apple a day keeps the doctor away—if you throw it hard enough."

A grin quirked at the corners of Jodee's mouth, but the quiet *thank you* resonated up from her broken, humbled spirit.

"I called Logan and told him you wanted to talk. He's headed over now."

She nodded, rotating the apple in her palm, noting the smooth, firm feel.

"You doing okay?" Grace asked.

"That must be the million-dollar question, judging by how many times I've heard it in the past few days." She bit into the apple and the tangy sweetness raced over her taste buds, bringing a new delight. She held the bite she'd taken on her tongue to savor it.

"Well, I've got some news for you. You asked me to check the results of the lab work done when they first brought you in." Grace sighed and let her hand rest on Jodee's shoulder. "Your pregnancy test was negative. I'm sorry no one thought to tell you."

"So, I wasn't . . ."

"No. You didn't lose a baby, because there wasn't one." Grace reached for her hand and squeezed.

She should be relieved, right? So why did this feel like another blow to her battered heart? Unexpected grief threatened to drown her. She rocked back and forth, arms wrapped around her middle. Why did she feel this pain when what she should be feeling was relief? Tears formed. She blinked, trying to hold them back. In the moment, she recognized that the seed of a hope for something more, a life that mattered, had germinated within her when she thought she might become a mother.

Why did she always give her heart to things that didn't last or weren't real to start with? Surrendering her heart to the wrong things— childish longings and impossible dreams? *What is the right thing? Tell me and I'll do it? I can't live like this anymore.*

A breeze stirred through the leaves of the oak and brushed against her face, the aroma of baking bread caressing her senses.

Accept the gift.

The salty taste of tears she didn't know were falling surprised her.

"It's all right. Cry all you want." Grace held her, patting and rocking and humming a quiet song. Jodee recognized the hymn, though she couldn't recall the name.

The grief receded, leaving her hollow inside. She straightened, wiping her face with the hem of her new shirt. This time the hollowness didn't frighten her but instead invited something new to fill it. "What is that song?"

"An old, old, hymn called I Heard the Voice of Jesus Say." Grace cleared her throat and softly sang the words "I heard the voice of Jesus say, Behold I freely give the living water, thirsty one; stoop down and drink and live." She ran her hand over Jodee's hair, then nudged her with her shoulder. "You can stay here with me as long as you like. I hope you know that."

"But what about—"

"No. Not another word." The older woman stood.

Jodee rose but didn't move, as though the tree somehow held onto her.

"You know trees, they don't get to move when the going gets tough," Grace said as though reading her thoughts. "All they can do is bend in the wind and let the environment shape them as it will— for better or worse. Not so with people. We get a choice as to what kind of soil we sink our roots into and how we let the world shape us. Yet so many people just stay rooted in the wrong place as though they haven't been given the freedom to change." She slipped an arm around Jodee's waist, and they started to the house.

"If you don't like where you are move. You're not a tree." Jodee recited the familiar quote though she couldn't remember who said it.

"Exactly" Grace gave her a gentle squeeze. "We have been given a gift. All we have to do is accept it."

Jodee inhaled the words now being repeated as though they were a healing balm.

Out of habit, she reached into the pocket of the new pants she wore for the white stone, clutching it in fingers hungry for something she couldn't define.

Was that the gift? The ability to change? What would it cost her to accept the gift?

Jodee ran her palms over her jeans. She patted her thighs, then stood to pace the length of the porch for the dozenth time. The Care Bear shirt didn't instill the perception of her being a credible witness.

She'd spent the past thirty minutes sharing everything she could remember of that night at the truck stop. A few of the details remained elusive, but the most important part seemed clear enough.

Yet Logan just sat there, scribbling on his notepad without speaking. Well, it might have been a verbal silence, but his body language and scowling face spoke volumes. Wasn't he supposed to be asking questions?

Across the road, Hawk had arrived to clean up the broken tree. The same man that had shown up after the fire this morning. He'd been on his way to Grace's when he'd seen the smoke. In a way, the damaged tree might have saved her life if she hadn't already escaped the fire. The interconnectedness of life struck her with its perfect mirroring of the interconnectedness of tree roots.

The chainsaw roared to life, and she flinched.

She turned back to Logan, frowning to find him still writing.

Grace gave her a don't-worry-this-is-just-the-way-things-work look and patted her shoulder.

It wasn't the way things worked for Jodee, at least it wasn't the way she expected them to work. Jodee Trevaine against the world. The cold shiver of abandonment rippled over her. But something was changing. She looked at the haunting sign down the road. *Roots.*

Maybe like a tree in its proper ecosystem, she wasn't completely without a support system. And maybe she was stronger because of it.

Logan set his notepad aside and picked up a folder he'd brought with him. He flipped it open and handed Jodee a picture of Aidan. "Is this the boy you think you saw being abducted?"

"Yes. It's the same boy I saw playing at the back of the store."

Logan retrieved the picture and returned it to the folder. "You're sure you saw this boy being put into a truck?"

She started to nod but paused. She hadn't actually seen his face at that moment. Blue jeans and Nike tennis shoes were all she'd really seen. If she was imagining the man in the duster, did she dare trust any of her memories?

Still, she knew it was him. The red car proved it, right? "I didn't see his face when they put him into the truck, but that's the boy I saw playing with a red toy car. I heard the man talking to him about a red car. It's him."

Logan stared at her, the muscle in his jaw twitching.

"What aren't you telling me? I know what I saw. If the boy is safe with his dad like his mother claims, why won't you just say so?"

"Because we don't know where he is."

"Have you found his dad and confirmed the story?"

"I skipped that day of training at the academy." The sarcasm in his voice set Jodee back.

"I'm sorry. I'm just—" What was she *just*? Was she mad, or was it her wounded pride that simmered just below the surface? But this wasn't about her. It was about Aidan. She needed them to believe her. He needed them to believe her.

"We haven't been able to get ahold of the dad, but according to the mother, he might not have good cell phone service."

"And you believe that? You're not even looking?"

"I didn't say that, but sometimes police work isn't all black and white, cut and dried like everyone thinks."

"So, you're busy being concerned about who attacked me, even though I'm fine. But forget about a missing child who's probably in danger?" The image of his frightened face intruded, piercing her heart. The prospect he could be hurt opened the raw aching wound that never seemed to heal. She wrapped her arms around her middle. Memories raked over her. Alone. Weak. Too unworthy to be wanted. To unwanted to be rescued. The crushing shame though she didn't know what she'd done wrong.

"*Are* you fine?" His pointed question stung. His stare cut at her like a draw knife stripping the bark off a tree. "You've been assaulted twice and barely escaped a fire. You do realize that's not normal?"

Aware of the self-soothing motion of rocking herself, she halted, responding with a forced laugh. "You don't know me. How do you know it's not normal?" She pressed her lips together, on the verge of either crying or laughing hysterically. Neither would do her any good or help the boy. "I'm sorry. I just know Aidan was abducted. What if he's—" The words choked in her throat.

"I know the what ifs, but we have to make sure we do everything by the book in case there is criminal activity."

"Criminal activity? Of course, there's criminal activity!"

Logan gathered his notes into the folder he carried. "We can sit here conversing and speculating all day, but I think we'd both rather I got back to work."

"Wait! *Conversatin'.* The woman who helped take Aidan used that word." The memories rattled and spun like rocks in a tumbler.

"It's a pretty common word," Logan said.

"Not the way she said it. I recognized her voice. I heard her say it again today when she was talking to Blue at the store." Jodee described the woman, annoyed that her attention to detail had been spurred by jealousy.

"I know who you're talking about. I'll have a talk with her. But as of right now, we have no report of an abducted child other than by you." He glanced at his aunt before looking back at Jodee. The look in his eyes revealed his assessment of her credibility. *You . . . the one who was physically attacked for an unknown reason by an unknown assailant. The one who keeps imagining she sees a man who no one else ever seems to see.*

"You don't believe me," she said.

"Let's just say you've had a lot going on in the past forty-eight hours."

"What about video cameras? Can't you look at the security camera footage from Tooley's?"

"Another day at the academy I guess I shouldn't have skipped." He shook his head. "But since you brought it up, I could use your help with that. I need you to agree to press charges on the assault so I can get a warrant for the security video." His words softened as he attempted to solicit her help. "The owner isn't willing to provide it without a warrant, and I can't get a warrant without a reason. Since the child isn't officially missing—"

"How can you just sit here and go about everything so calmly?" Jodee said, interrupting him.

"Part of my job description says I'm not allowed to lose my cool in a crisis."

She looked up to find him teasing her.

Grace reached over, putting an arm around Jodee's shoulders. "It's okay dear. You have a lot of emotions rolling around inside. And rightfully so," Grace said, comforting her.

"As of right now, you're the only one claiming anyone's been abducted. Could have been the boy's father picking him up just like his mother claims, for all we know. The only possible crime we have is the attack on you." He sighed. "And the owner of the truck stop isn't being cooperative in releasing the surveillance videos. Not that I think they'll be of good enough quality to help much, but it's the only next step I have. And I need a warrant to make it happen."

She pulled a knee up to her chest, a barrier to the world as she retreated into the teenage girl whose father had disappeared. Or so she'd believed until yesterday. The abandonment she'd experienced had left her feeling things she never wanted to acknowledge. Did Aidan feel any of those things now?

"Okay, tell me what to do," she said.

"Come with me to the station and we can get the paperwork started."

"What about the blood sample from Grace's floor?"

"We're a small department. It takes time to send our evidence off and get the results back." He leaned forward, resting his elbows on his knees, and stared at her. "Getting the video might help us move faster."

She nodded, not trusting her voice around the growing lump in her throat.

The only one to claim he's been abducted. She couldn't let Aidan down.

She would make sure he was found if she had to do it herself.

"Jodee?"

She realized Logan had asked her another question.

"What about the fire this morning?" he repeated.

"I just woke up and the camper was on fire."

"You were there by yourself?"

In the distance Hawk continued stacking lengths of wood he'd cut to fit in winter fireplaces. He looked up as if he felt her eyes on him. He was far enough away he couldn't hear them, still the timing of his look unsettled Jodee even more than her silent debate on how to answer.

Had she seen someone? If so, how had he gotten out unseen—or alive?

Condensation ran down the sides of the glass of iced tea, moistening her palms as she picked it up. "I was alone."

"Where was Blue?"

"He didn't say."

"Had y'all had a fight?"

Her head snapped around, her gaze boring into him. "Blue did not do this."

Though what business he had at that time of day provoked a long string of questions she didn't want answers to.

"You don't find it a little curious, him being in the proximity every time something happens to you?"

"No." Her answer came fast, maybe too fast. Did she find it curious? Her gaze drifted across the opening toward the disturbing sign. The word Roots made her shiver again. "Roots."

"What?"

She sat up, the glass slipping from her hand to shatter at her feet. "Roots. The man who attacked me had a shirt on with some sort of tree and roots. Like the sign." Her stare met Logan's.

He sighed. "They sell T-shirts and sweatshirts with their logo. A lot of folks around here have one."

Along with that memory came another, that of his hot breath against her cheek as he whispered, *I'm not through with you yet.*

She should have seen him, should know his face. But she hadn't been looking at his face, had she?

She stared down the street at the weathered sign in the distance, her gaze fixated on the image of roots reaching into the ground like decaying hands seeking to pull the dead from their graves.

CHAPTER 27

Learn character from trees, values from roots, and change from leaves.
~Tasneem Hameed

Jodee stared at the shattered glass, then rose to pick up the pieces.

Grace placed a gentle hand on her shoulder and urged her back onto the swing.

Grace had moved into nurse mode, a thinly veiled look of concern on her face as the woman stared at her and not the mess at her feet. When she headed inside for the broom and dustpan to sweep up the shards, Jodee found herself alone with Logan, who didn't have to slip into LEO mode. He lived there.

The disposition of his face confirmed he, too, regarded the broken glass as something more than a clumsy fumble. He listened as she did her best to explain her reaction, his expression unreadable. He tapped his pen on his notepad, no longer busily taking notes. The sound added to the jumpiness already coiling around her like a giant spring.

His eyes narrowed as something behind her caught his attention.

"Excuse me for a minute," he said as he rose to step off the porch.

"Take as long as you want," Jodee mumbled the words under her breath. She caught the quick grin that flashed over his face, so maybe it hadn't been as under her breath as she intended.

He headed toward where Hawk stood beneath the tree.

She pulled the familiar white stone from her pocket. Its smooth, cool touch settled her nerves back in line.

She needed to talk to Blue. The problem was, she didn't *want* to talk to him. They'd played this game of cat and mouse—that's how she'd come to think of it—for so long she didn't know how to stop.

But this wasn't about her. And as much as he hurt her, she really had no one else to turn to.

Grace returned, a fresh glass of tea in one hand and her phone in the other. "It's for you." Jodee didn't miss the look of apprehension on her face as she handed her the phone.

Logan was the only one who might have a reason to call her on Grace's phone, but he was still within shouting distance. Why call when yelling would do just fine?

She took the phone, holding it to her ear with the same eagerness of pressing a hot coal to her cheek. "Hello."

"Jodee Rose Trevaine!" The outrage in her mother's voice scalded her ear. "Why haven't you called me?"

Grace may not have understood the words, but the tone was loud and clear enough to carry. She signaled to Jodee that she'd be in the house.

"I lost my phone." Jodee inhaled, holding her breath in preparation for what would follow. Saying it was lost sounded much better than admitting it had been demolished by the dirtbag who attacked her.

"What a shame no one had one you could borrow." As always, her mother moved seamlessly from the accusation of crime to the trial where she then presided as prosecution, judge, and jury.

Jodee ignored the barb, a skill she'd perfected as a teenager. It was no credit to her that she often brought this side of her mother out on purpose. Ever since Paul disappeared. "How'd you find me here?" The question was more rhetorical than necessary. She was pretty sure she knew.

"Is that your biggest concern? Someone tried to kill you."

"We don't know that. If they'd wanted to kill me, they could have." Jodee sat up straight, her feet planted firmly on the porch, stilling the movement of the swing. "I was just in the wrong place at the wrong time."

"I couldn't agree with you more. You are most certainly in the wrong place, and I can't for the life of me understand why you went there. You know the things people say about that place. Do you think they make up those stories for no reason?" A sharp inhale carried over the airwaves. "You're coming home."

"My job brought me here. As a government employee, I don't really get to pick and choose which people I serve. But I'm fine. You don't have to worry. Grace is taking good care of me." What her mom said about El Hueso held a measure if truth. She'd felt unsettled ever since she got here. Maybe that was why she didn't want to leave.

"How well do you even know this woman?"

Her stomach tightened as heat surged through her. Maybe it was her protectiveness of Grace or her own defensiveness. Everything about her mother provoked her to be disagreeable. "We met at the hospital. I didn't bother running a background check, but she seems nice enough, and she's a really good cook."

"Why are you doing this? Why do you always push me away?"

She stared at the boards beneath her feet. She'd fought this battle for so long it no longer made her eyes burn. But the door had been opened, and she was forced to acknowledge she'd honed shutting people out to an art, never thinking about the damage it might be doing. Not until she'd experienced the same from Blue. Her intentions were to help him, but his lack of honesty with her meant— what? That he didn't trust her?

We're all broken, Jodee. His words came back. Was her mother broken, too? Had she been missing the bigger picture all along? She sank back onto the swing.

"Are you still there?" her mother asked, interrupting her moment of epiphany.

Did she trust her mother? Did she really need to know every secret her mother kept? Was she being selfish to demand something her mother wasn't willing to give? That wasn't trust, was it? Her anger bled away in the discovery of her hypocrisy. "I'm here."

"I'm in Houston on business, but I'm trying to find a flight to Abilene. Unfortunately, the weather down here has most of the charter planes grounded. I can call someone to get you and bring you home. Then I'll be there as soon as I can."

"You're overreacting a tad, Mom. I promise, I'm fine," she said.

"You have amnesia from being beaten. A head injury, Jodee."

Meaning my opinion is not to be trusted. "I've recovered from the amnesia. My memory is fine."

"So does this mean you know who did this to you?" The faint quiver of fear she detected in her mother's voice differed from the note of relief she had expected.

"No. That's still a mystery."

"Then it's not safe for you to stay there. You're coming home."

Jodee wanted to say she was twenty-eight years old and past the point of letting her mother run her life, but she didn't. "If someone really is after me," which she couldn't quite make herself believe, "then I'll be in danger no matter where I am."

"Jodee . . ."

She sighed. "I'm fine. But I'm not coming home right now."

"You shouldn't be there. Come home away from that place." A sniffle whispered through the phone, so faint she wasn't sure she'd heard it.

A new idea rushed over her. The years of lies, so many lies. What if the truth could be found here in this place? Why did she detect fear in her mother's words as she begged Jodee to leave? Would she beg her to leave if it was some place other than El Hueso?

"Why shouldn't I be here? Why shouldn't I stay in El Hueso? Maybe I'll be as much at home here as I ever am anywhere else."

"You do not belong there, and I won't listen to you say that again." Her mother's voice was tight as though straining against something she didn't want to say.

"What does this place have to do with anything?" Why wouldn't her mother tell her the truth?

Silence stretched between them, until she finally said, "You aren't going to find him."

"Who?" Jodee asked.

"That's why you're there, isn't it? You think you'll find him." Her mother's voice cracked. "You don't want to find him, Jodee. Please just come home."

"Who are you talking about? Paul? Why on earth would you think I might find him in El Hueso?" Tension radiated up her neck as the muscles in her shoulders tightened. Cold chilled her like a hoar frost clinging to her skin. Her heart skittered into its hastened beat, reminding her she needed to fill her prescription soon.

Her mother swallowed as the seconds ticked by. "Please come home."

"How do you know I won't find him here?" Jodee's words were tentative, treading carefully, trying not to push her mother away when she seemed so close to the edge of the truth. Though she would never believe the man she called her father would just vanish without a goodbye, the notion she might find him here had never crossed her mind.

But was uncovering the truth worth putting her mother through this obvious pain? Shame twisted through her, and she crumpled like a wrung-out rag.

Her fingers flexed around the white stone, squeezing. "Why won't I find him here, Mom?"

"Because he's dead." Hollow, defeated words from a woman exhausted by the secrets she'd been keeping.

"What are you talking about? He was never found."

"There was proof. I lied."

"Why would you do that?" The earth seemed to tilt. The rock slipped from Jodee's fingers as she grabbed the side of the swing to brace herself.

"I didn't want to hurt you."

"Letting me believe the man who raised me had abandoned us wasn't supposed to be painful?"

"I knew it hurt you, but it was for the best."

"How was it for the best? I loved him."

"And he loved you. He would have agreed with what I did. I had to keep you safe. Now, not another word. I need you to come home immediately. You can't stay there."

"Shouldn't," Jodee whispered. Until her mother told her the whole truth, they'd never be healed. What did El Hueso have to do with Paul? And was Paul the one her mother had meant when she said she wouldn't find *him?*

"What was that?"

"*Shouldn't.* You want me to believe I *shouldn't* stay here."

"What are you trying to prove? That you can be the most stubborn daughter in the world? That it doesn't matter who you hurt as long as no one tells you what to do?"

If there had been tears left to cry, she might have let herself. "I love you, Mom. But I'm not leaving yet."

She disconnected the call and placed the phone down on the swing beside her.

The bright colors of the spring day around her faded to sepia. She shivered.

Grace stooped to retrieve the stone that had fallen from her fingers. "A white stone. It must be special." She handed it back as she seated herself beside Jodee.

"It was a gift from my stepfather. The last thing he gave me before he disappeared." She wasn't ready to accept he was dead.

"I see," Grace said. "That is an interesting gift. Did he tell you if it had a special meaning?"

She shook her head, memories like rain clouds rolling through her. "He said he had something to do and when he returned, he'd tell me what was special about the stone."

"Mmm," Grace smiled.

"It was my fault he left."

"Why would you think that?" Compassion filled Grace's words.

"I had asked—more like begged—him to adopt me so I could have his last name."

"He didn't want to?"

"No. I believe he did, but it just seemed like it was taking so long, and I had a deadline?"

Grace looked at her, full of curiosity.

"The Father Daughter Dance. You have to be twelve to go, and my twelfth birthday was coming up just days before the dance that year."

Grace inhaled and ticked up a bit straighter. "I think I may know the meaning of your special gift, then. Would you like me to share?"

She hesitated. *Did she want to know?* She rubbed the white stone, then nodded.

"And I will give him a white stone, and on the stone a new name written which no one knows except him who receives it." Grace smiled. "It's from the Bible. The Book of Revelation."

A single tear trailed from the corner of Jodee's eye as she stared at the stone in her palm. *A new name.* Was it possible Paul hadn't left to avoid giving her his name? That he really had died before he could adopt her?

"I don't know what your relationship with God is like, but I do know He wants to have one with you. You're His daughter."

"I don't know. After Paul left, God kind of disappeared with him."

"We can shut Him out if we choose, but God doesn't disappear. Even in the worst and most painful parts of our life, He's still there."

And remember, behind every patch of bad weather, the sun's still there.

What if she had seen Him? The image of the man in the duster— the one no one else seems to have noticed—the one who neither escaped the fire nor died in it.

But what she'd seen wasn't the same as what Grace spoke of. Jodee had seen what wasn't there. A hallucination conjured up by a frightened mind. Besides, God couldn't be a weathered old cowboy in a duster now, could He?

"God often uses others who he places in our lives to be His hands and feet. Maybe Paul was such a person for you. The verse about the new name on the white stone, it starts by saying it is for him who overcomes." She reached to brush Jodee's hair over her shoulder, her touch tender with love. "Sweetheart, we can't overcome by running from what hurts us. We overcome by letting Him into our wounded places and believing the truth. Talk to Him."

Jodee rubbed her fingers over the stone. A new name. Paul's gift to her had been a new name, but he'd died before giving it to her.

Accept the gift.

Something bothered her about his death, but she couldn't identify what.

She looked toward the tree where the two men stood side by side like chiseled statues staring at something on the ground. Logan glanced their way, then scratched his chin. A few minutes later, he rejoined them on the porch. Grace exchanged a questioning look with her when he shuffled his feet instead of speaking.

"What is it?" Grace asked.

"We have a problem with your tree." He removed his hat, giving Jodee the impression of a deliverer of bad news. "I'm going to need to notify the Texas Historical Commission, and well, I don't know who else just yet."

Grace tilted her head to the side. Her confusion matched Jodee's.

"Did you know there are four graves beneath the tree? The headstones look like they've been covered for some time, but the date on each is 1858."

Grace frowned. "I had no idea. Are there names on the markers?"

"Yes. Three members of the Charidy family—Abel, Essie, and Rose—and one Cub DeGroot."

Grace's hand went to her chest. "That would have been enough to establish this as a Heritage Oak. How sad that it's too late now."

Logan settled his hat back on his head. "I told you that tree always gave me the creeps."

The cold shiver Jodee experienced minutes before morphed into something far more foreboding. When it came to trees, you could trust there was always a lot more going on in the root system than was visible above ground. Seems it worked that way for people too.

Rose Charidy Trevaine. Her great-great-great grandmother's name.

But this wasn't where her great grandmother was buried.

"Is the name Charidy very common?" she asked.

"Not around here, especially not with that spelling. In fact, as far as I've discovered, there was only one other Charidy. A man by the name of Will Charidy who built this house."

Driven by the rapid cadence, her heart rushed blood through her veins until the sound filled her ears like a tree full of locusts on a hot July afternoon.

Had there been more than one Rose Charidy?

Or did this have something to do with the reason her mother didn't want her here? What about Paul's disappearance? There was something in El Hueso that Jodee needed to know.

The sign for Roots caught her eye again. The sinister sensation of fibrous roots twining through her tightened her chest. For the first time in her life, she couldn't run from what scared her.

Whatever held her in El Hueso wouldn't let her go until she faced the truth.

But first she had to find it.

CHAPTER 28

Texas 1858

They have in me struck down but the trunk of the tree; the roots are many and deep - they will shoot up again! ~Toussaint Louverture

Though the sun shone bright and strong against the blue sky, the dips and shadows still held the cool air of fall. Will led Rose along a deer trail through the tangle of briars and brush along the creek bed until they reached the top of the bank. Warm sunshine greeted them like a hug.

He scanned the horizon looking for smoke. Nothing but a clear, brilliant span of blue sky.

Rose sat in the dirt. Her hair was ratted and mussed, and there were smudges of ash streaking a face that grew paler by the minute. He sat beside her, twisting a stem of dried bluegrass in his hands. He didn't like the blank look that had crept into her eyes. She didn't seem to notice him until he tickled her nose with the grass.

It was a brief sound, but the giggle that erupted somehow comforted him and made him stronger. He knew how to make Rose laugh.

"Come on. We better keep going until we find someone to take care of your arm."

She looked at her arm as though the knowledge something was wrong was new to her. He helped her to her feet.

"You sure are a brave girl, Bud. You just gotta be strong for a little while longer. We'll find someone soon." He could find someone faster if he didn't have to go at her pace. But leaving her so he could go in search wasn't something he could do. She was all he had left in the world.

They walked on. Sometimes he carried her. Sometimes he left her sitting while he ran up a rise to look around. Always he listened. The sun passed midday and worry that they might have to spend another night in the cold crept over him. He'd been relieved when he'd found what might be a wagon trail. If it was, it hadn't been used in a while, but it was still the best chance they had.

He stilled as the breeze carried a sound to him. Not a bird, he decided. The noise was out of place in nature. He hurried to where Rose dozed in the tall grass. "Bud, wake up."

She opened her sleepy eyes and blinked, then started to close them again.

"Rose, I think someone's coming, but we need to hide until we can tell if . . ." His words trailed off. She'd just had her first lesson in the existence of bad people in the world. He didn't want to add to it. "If they might help us."

He pulled her up and swore she was getting heavier, which seemed impossible since they hadn't eaten in nearly a day. Together, they climbed over the creek bank. He motioned for her to lie down, and she dropped to her back. Will rolled to his stomach and inched up just far enough to watch the road. The sound came from the west, growing closer. He hoped that was a good sign. Maybe homesteaders heading east for supplies.

Or maybe a band of outlaws who wouldn't mind making a few dollars by selling a couple of orphans. He swallowed the lump in his throat and licked dry lips. Then he bit down hard on his bottom lip because he wasn't going to cry. He wouldn't. He was going to take care of Rose, and he couldn't do that by bawling like a newborn calf looking for his momma.

A wagon crept into view, but still he waited. Having a wagon sure didn't make you a good person. Lot of people had wagons. As it drew closer, he made out the milk cow tied behind. The wagon jostled over a bump, and he heard the agitated clucking of chickens. A woman in a bonnet sat on the buckboard.

Hope bubbled up inside him, swelling like Mrs. Charidy's yeast dough sitting in the sunshine.

"Bud, I'm going to walk over there by the road and check things out. You gotta stay down until I come for you, understand?"

Her eyes widened. "Don't leave me, Will. I love you."

Fright made her little girl voice quiver as her words tied his heart to hers with an invisible thread. *I love you*. Her words made his eyes burn.

He patted her head. "I won't leave ya." The look in her eyes pulled him into his own memories of being abandoned. "I won't ever leave you, Little Bud. I promise."

His promise didn't erase the doubt in her eyes. But her world had just been tumped over like a bucket of fresh milk on dry ground. Her home and family evaporated into brown earth and soon there'd be no record of them left at all. That's what happens when one becomes an orphan.

He gave her another pat, then scrambled over the top of the bank and made his way to the road. In the shadow of an oak tree, he waited for the wagon to get close. Mrs. Charidy had instilled in him the beginnings of a prayer life. He reckoned now was as good a time as any to practice on his own.

As the wagon approached, he ambled from his hiding place.

The man leading the team of oxen pulled them to a stop.

Ten minutes later, the woman, Mrs. Muellar, had Rose seated in the back of the wagon while she cleaned the burn.

"I covered the burn with some egg white, but she needs more than I can do, Johnny." The worried lines of her face made Will nervous. "She's running a fever already."

Mr. Muellar scratched his head, then looked at Will. "What happened to your folks, son?"

"Indians." Will hated himself for the lie that rolled off his tongue like a glass marble, especially since his lie made someone else look bad. But while the Muellars had been fussing over Rose, he'd thought this through. If he told them the truth about their names, they'd figure out what happened to the Charidys. He had no doubt Luther would make good on his threat to blame it on him. Telling the truth wouldn't bring Rose's parents back. It wouldn't do them any good at all.

Cold chills trickled over his body. Luther had meant for Rose to die in the fire. He'd left her inside after he'd killed Mr. and Mrs. Charidy.

A new question jolted him. Something he'd been too frightened and exhausted to think about until now. *Who helped Rose out the window?* It had been a man, but his hands were not Mr. Charidy's hands.

At the word Indians, Mr. Muellar took a keener interest in the surrounding landscape. He turned to his wife. "We best keep movin'. Got a ways to go before we reach Murchison."

Mrs. Mueller must not have heard him as she disappeared inside the wagon to return with dried peaches and crackers. She waved Will over to sit in the shade and handed him some of both. "Johnny, fetch some drinking water. These two look plumb starved. Let me get some vittles in them and then we can go on. Sure wish I could build a fire and cook a proper meal, but Mr. Muellar's right. We best not tarry too long. We can have us a nice dinner when we stop tonight."

The Charidys had passed through Murchison on their way to their homestead months ago. Would someone there recognize him?

Maybe they'd arrest him and send him to prison. Surely they wouldn't hang a boy his age. Although they might send him back to an orphanage. But who would take him after he'd been accused of setting the last one on fire? And if Luther told everyone it was Will's fault the Charidys were dead, he'd be in deeper hot water than he'd ever been in.

He didn't know what might happen to him. But he did know Rose was safer if no one knew her name.

He also knew he wouldn't be keeping the promise he'd made. He couldn't if he wanted to keep her safe.

Before the moon had lifted itself a quarter way up in the sky that night, Will placed a feathery kiss on Rose's head, then he gave her hair a gentle tug. "Take care and grow up real strong and pretty, Little Bud. It's better this way."

As silently as a wild cat, he slipped away while the Muellars and Rose slept.

He wished he hadn't shot that deer.

CHAPTER 29

Only the love that flows from the heart of Christ can heal. Only He in whom that love flows, even as the sap in the tree or the blood in the body, can restore the wounded soul. ~Ellen G. White

𝒰prooted.

Like being jerked from the barren soil she'd planted herself in and tossed on the ground to wither and perish if she didn't find answers soon.

Barren soil did not produce life, yet that's where she'd rooted herself while wallowing in lies and self pity.

A chill soaked into her bones. The white stone lie beside her. A blessing or a curse? Or perhaps a tangled mix of both?

She picked it up. The same cool, smooth surface she remembered still existed. Same size and weight. Yet somehow changed. She squeezed the stone in her palm until it bruised her hand, letting the pain refocus her.

From her perch on Grace's front porch steps, her gaze wandered back and forth between the tree with its hidden graves and the sign for Roots standing in the distance. Why did it feel like the answers she needed hung somewhere in between?

Stop acting as though your brokenness makes you less. Blue's words played on a repeating loop in her head. He'd made his brokenness a weapon of self-destruction. But something had changed. He'd changed.

His observation of her brokenness stung. He'd hit too close to the truth. A truth she hadn't realized until she saw it reflected to her in his eyes.

Her stare landed on the tree. Broken, but she would still try to save it, wouldn't she? Was she any less than a tree? Was she more?

Just ask Him, Grace had said. Easier said than done.

Accept the gift.

She stared at the stone. What was *the gift?* Surely it must be something more than a rock.

A new name which no one knows except him who receives it.

How could a new name possibly change anything? There had been a day when she had believed it would.

Rust bled through the white of the painted tree with its roots extending downward like a fiendish hand. Maybe the sign had looked less wicked when it was freshly painted, but now the tree took on a sinister appearance against the backdrop of the faded and peeling black paint.

Her gaze shifted to the real tree, now roped off with yellow crime scene tape, even though Logan assured the nervous gawkers who turned out to investigate that this wasn't a crime scene. The rust red in the veins of its leaves—venal necrosis, a sign of the unhealed wounds slowly killing it—mirrored the rust on the painted sign. She shuddered at the impression the graves below somehow connected to the bone-like roots on the sign.

Was the sign omniscient?

Knowing one of the markers bore a name identical to her great-great-great grandmother unnerved her. What if it wasn't an accident? What if her mother was right and she really shouldn't be here? She chewed at the corner of her mouth. Was she in danger, or was Blue the target?

Her leg bounced.

Maybe she couldn't know the answer to that question, but she did know Aidan was in danger.

She pressed the white stone into her palm, then relaxed her fingers to stroke its polished surface before repeating the process. Her leg continued its frantic up and down motion.

The late afternoon sun tipped the day toward dusk. The dark ink of night soon would soon spill out.

Grace was at work again after another nurse called in sick. Apparently, the coworker had made a habit of it these past few weeks. Melody the Malingerer, Grace had called her.

After asking Jodee no less than a dozen times if she would be all right by herself, she'd left early to check on Tillie before heading to the hospital.

"The reckoning is upon us." Tillie's strange words rang inside her head.

Like a giant jigsaw puzzle, the pieces of the past few days lie scattered at Jodee's feet. She had the feeling there were pieces to more than one puzzle in the heap.

Start with the corner pieces, her grandmother had always said. Right now, the only corner piece she trusted was that she'd been attacked at the truck stop when she tried to stop a boy from being abducted. Correction . . . *allegedly abducted,* according to Logan and pretty much everyone else.

Like the electricity of a lightning strike, the emotions of her day sent an energy through her limbs that couldn't be fidgeted away. She had to move.

As painful as the meeting might be, she needed to find Blue. She could swallow the pride that hung in her throat like the pad of a prickly pear, making her chest ache. She had to if she wanted help in finding the boy.

And right now, finding Aidan was the only thing she would allow herself to think about. The only thing that mattered. The rest was too much.

Blue would do it for the boy, if not for her. Locating him would be the challenge. After all, he didn't have a camper to go home to anymore. Syrah's face sashayed through her head with a smugness that fueled Jodee's dislike of the woman.

An older model Ford Bronco parked on the far side of Grace's driveway drew her attention. She had an idea where to start looking. Having a vehicle would certainly help.

The idea swarmed around her like a gnat.

Inside the kitchen, she searched for key hooks and dug through drawers until she found a set of keys. Hope ballooned at the sight of the Ford logo.

Please let this one be the one. She drew in a deep breath and closed her eyes as guilt spidered up her back.

The idea of going to prison for grand theft auto didn't appeal to her. And she felt sure Logan was just looking for a reason to get her away from his aunt by locking her up.

Grace understood about the missing boy, though. She would understand why Jodee took the vehicle. Even if she didn't, there was a child in danger—and a very confused woman who had nothing else to lose and maybe everything to gain in searching for him.

The premonition she was embarking on something important in ways she didn't understand hummed through her. But it didn't matter. She wanted—needed—to find Aidan. After all, who she was didn't matter near as much as what she did.

She scribbled a note to Grace, then paused. Was she ready to face being arrested for the unauthorized borrowing of Grace's vehicle?

Well, if she felt confused about her identity, letting the state of Texas assign her one in the form of an inmate number was better than nothing, right?

Whatever penalty she might face, it would be more bearable than trying to live with herself after doing nothing.

Outside, the truck's door creaked from lack of oil and use when she pried it open. She flinched, certain the entire town heard the noise. Sliding into the driver's seat, she closed her eyes. If she needed to start talking to God, maybe now was as good a time as any. She said a quick prayer the old Bronco would start while wondering if prayers for help in committing crimes were automatically denied.

The engine coughed to life like an old smoker climbing out of bed in the morning.

She couldn't restore Blue's house, force her mother to tell the truth—a truth which now seemed to stalk her like a zombie fresh from its grave, or make anyone believe she'd witnessed an abduction. But she could find the boy. Syrah held the key.

Find Blue and find the woman. Deep inside, she hoped not too close together.

Because guarding her broken heart was a goal she wasn't sure she desired anymore.

She put the Bronco in reverse, then glanced in the rearview mirror to find her path blocked.

Blue's truck lurched to a stop behind her and he pounced out. The anger in his steps was nothing compared to the wrath in his eyes.

He jerked her truck door open. "Out."

CHAPTER 30

Life without love is like a tree without leaves. ~Himanshu Acharya

Trepidation pawed at Blue as Jodee complied without an argument. Like a rodeo clown who just opened the chute gate to a raging bull, Blue stood in dumbstruck paralysis as she climbed from the truck to face him. The confusion of knowing whether he was the clown or bull kicked at his confidence.

An enraged bull, seething at her inability to let *him* love *her*. Or a clown for loving a woman who would never love him back.

The thunderstruck expression clouding her face seemed to render her speechless, though his momentary advantage wouldn't last long. Jodee was all fight or flight, with no middle ground. And she was feistier than a feral cat when it came to landing on her feet.

With a firm grip, he held the Bronco's door open and widened his stance, blocking her escape. He hadn't forgotten her ability to go from zero to squared up and primed to fight. It was the ability that had gotten her removed from the varsity softball team her senior year.

"Helen called," he said, displeasure dangling from his words.

"You had no right to call her." She planted her feet and squared her shoulders, painting her reply in an equal measure of displeasure. "I'm an adult, not some runaway teenager."

His jaws clenched, muscles taut as he fought the urge to throw her over his shoulder and physically haul her away from here.

"Interesting choice of comparison." He moved closer, standing tall, shifting into a posture intended to intimidate a guy looking to fight, painfully aware that the person in front of him was for dead certain not a guy.

She lifted her chin and stared him in the eye, her expression morphing into a familiar stubbornness. No doubt still angry from the shopping fiasco earlier. And possibly something he'd said.

"And I didn't know I needed a *right,* since I had a pretty darn good *reason.* Someone tried to kill you—multiple times. What if something happens? She's your family. For Pete's sake, Jodee, let someone love you."

"It was my call to make, not yours." She leaned toward him, their faces only inches apart.

The impulse to kiss her stampeded over him, dragging his gaze to her lips. The effort it required to tug his attention back to her eyes and focus on the purpose at hand drained a measure of his anger away. Love ignited some fires and extinguished others. Her hostility told him more than he wanted to know. The fire in her eyes wasn't a friendly kind of fire.

Do not think about kissing her. He needed to break eye contact, to look away from the hopeless abyss he was sliding into. But if he had, he would have missed the storm of emotion softening her features.

"What if it's you they're trying to kill?" Pain rippled over her face. The change in her demeanor sent him sailing through the air like a cowboy who just experienced an unplanned dismount from an unhappy bronc. He braced for a hard landing as he concentrated on one thing. *Don't stay down long enough to get stomped.*

The light in her eyes dimmed as though a gust of wind had snuffed out the fire in her eyes and replaced it with a smoldering coal of fear. She stared at his collar, giving him the impression she'd let him see more than she meant to.

Okay, he wasn't an expert in fires. Was the concern scrawled across her face a sign she had feelings for him? The good kind of feelings?

"I think your head injury is impairing your judgment," he said, unsure if he meant her statement or his interpretation of her reaction. He cleared his throat, purging the uncertain quality of his words.

"I'm fine."

The hollow sound of her voice kicked him in the gut. The urge to hold her burned along his arms and made his fingers tingle. Not good. For her safety and his, he needed her away from here, even if it meant destroying what was left of them. With a forced curtness, he continued to push her. "Then why are you still here?"

"Grace said I could stay," she said, defiance once again palpable in her words as her chin lifted. Feral cat landing on her angry little feet once again.

"And Grace—the *nurse*—said you could drive her truck? This ain't my first rodeo with head injuries, and I'd bet money the doctor told you not to drive until he releases you." Not that he ever followed the doctor's orders for care of a concussion to the letter. But this wasn't him they were talking about.

"The doctor's orders say I'm *not allowed* to. That's not the same as *can't* as in *lacking the ability to.*"

"Spare me the grammar lesson." Of course, she'd avoided the question concerning Grace's permission to use the truck. Thoughts of physically hauling her away loped through his head again. "Where were you planning to go?"

"I'm going to find your girlfriend." The challenge in her eyes might have been cute if he weren't so confounded about how to get her to leave.

"My *what?*" His eyes narrowed.

"The dark-haired little hottie with the tank top and shoulder tattoo. Don't pretend you don't know who I'm talking about." The stubborn set of her jaw matched the wrath in her eyes. "Syrah. Named for a wine. How clever." She rolled her eyes. "Is it her bold,

198

full-bodied self with just the right touch of pepper that has you hooked?"

He ducked his head, rubbing his chin to hide the grin he couldn't stop. *Jodee Trevaine, jealous?* Maybe her having feelings for him wasn't such a far-fetched proposition after all. But her statement riled him. "She's not my girlfriend. Trust me, you don't understand what's going on here."

"Oh please, I know exactly what's going on here. Same ol' Blue up to his same ol' ways. I guess it's true that leopards can't change their spots?" She folded her arms over her middle and cocked her head at a smug angle. "Although I always saw you as more of a whiskey girl kind of man. I guess tastes can change though, huh?" She leaned forward, the heat of her accusation warming him for reasons he knew she didn't intend. "But by all means, go ahead and lie to me about this and everything else. Everyone else has for almost my entire life."

"Stop feeling sorry for yourself, Jodee. It doesn't suit you." He resisted the impulse to reach out and tug a soft strand of her wayward hair. Heck, he was resisting the impulse to curl his fingers through the whole mass of it as he held on for dear life. "And for the record, you really *don't* know what's going on here."

He drew in a long breath, then continued. "You're right, though. A person's tastes can change." He smiled. "And yet you're also dead wrong. With the right perspective, people *can* change. I'm not the same guy I used to be, though you're free to believe whatever you want about that. What you aren't free to *doubt* is that when I asked you to go home, it was for your own good. El Hueso isn't a place anyone visits for a happy-go-lucky vacation. This town is full of secrets and few of them are good."

Something in his tone must have hit the mark.

She leaned back against the truck seat, her thoughts veiled.

His arms twitched, the urge to hold her now shooting fire down his arms. But he knew better. She needed a moment to process something she'd heard. He could only hope and pray she reached the conclusion that he loved her and was trying to protect her.

"So, what is this magical perspective that allows people to change?" she asked.

"You really want to know?"

"I asked, didn't I?"

He checked his inclination to roll his eyes in exasperation. He was being given a moment, a single moment that would impact every moment of the rest of her life.

"It's coming to understand the truth about who you really are and accepting it."

She shook her head in doubt.

"Who are you, Jodee?" he prodded.

"You know who I am."

"Yes, but I don't think you do?"

She laughed. "We both know I don't. I'm the girl without a father, remember? Even my stepfather left me." Her words sobered. "And when God took Chris away . . .that's when I knew."

"Knew what?"

The look in her eyes dared him to deny her words. "That God made me unlovable." Her eyes misted.

The longing to tell her how wrong she was filled him, but this wasn't the time for that. She was on the edge of understanding something more important. He couldn't let his selfish desires keep her from it. "You've let that become your identity, but it's not the truth. You're not fatherless. You never have been."

"How about we change the subject and stop talking in riddles?" She stared at him as though he'd turned purple. Her arms cinched tighter around her waist. "You're not making any sense. Sheesh, I'm the one with the head injury."

"How about we—" A burst of wind swept by, tossing leaves and dirt into the air, blinding him as he shielded his eyes.

"How about we find Syrah?" she said.

"Why are you so determined to find her?"

"There's a missing boy, and I don't want him growing up thinking he was unlovable because no one came for him. And I sure don't want him dead. I won't leave until he's found." Determination etched into her features. "Syrah knows something. I heard her voice coming from the truck that night. I'm sure of it."

Blue drew in a breath, then let it escape in a long exhale. Her words sank into him like hot coals, fanning the flames of the fire he found himself stuck within. He should have suspected there might be a connection between the boy's mysterious disappearance and the reason he was here. Syrah might be even more treacherous than he'd guessed. "Stay out of it, Jodee. Let Logan do his job. Just stay out of it."

"Hold on a minute, cowboy. Don't think you get to suddenly waltz into my life and start giving orders when we haven't even spoken in—how long has it been?"

He leaned down to face her, his own emotions now snarled into an aggravating knot. A vein twitched above his collar. How far could he push her without pushing her away forever?

"Technically, it was you who waltzed back into my life." Like a runaway train, he wanted to add. "And whose fault is it that we haven't spoken in years?"

"Cut it out, Blue. I don't understand why you're suddenly here trying to play the hero, spewing out heroism and church platitudes when we both know that's never been your M.O."

The muscle in his jaw twitched. He didn't want to scare her off, but he also didn't want to lose the chance to help her start healing. *Desperate times call for desperate measures,* his Memaw always said. "You really don't get it, do you?"

She froze beneath his touch as his hands slipped up her arms to pull her to her feet. He cradled her face in his hands. His thumbs caressed her cheeks. He took his time, savoring the moment of her stunned silence. When he kissed her, it was tender, less than he longed for, but far more than he ever believed possible. The heartaches and hurts of the broken world around them faded away until it was only him and her. The sweetness of her kiss when she responded was almost his undoing.

He leaned back, ending the kiss long before he wanted to.

"I guess I don't." Confusion edged her whispered words.

"I love you, Jodee Trevaine. I always have. And right now, I have the only chance I may ever get to make up for what I've done to you in the past." He searched her face, hungering for something he wasn't sure she could give and fearing she wouldn't even try.

Her eyes glistened, but she didn't look away. His breath caught at the fragile hope he saw in them.

"I don't want to fight anymore. Not with you. But I don't understand what you're saying. I'm not even sure I know who you are anymore," she said. She backed against the truck bed and sank to the ground.

He hesitated, knowing what he needed to do and dreading what might happen when he did.

After a few minutes of silence, he sat beside her. "The night Chris died—" His voice cracked with raw emotion.

"Don't. Please don't go there." Jodee drew her knees up, wrapping her arms around them to pull them tight against her chest. "I don't want to talk about it."

"I'm not asking you to talk. I'm asking you to listen. You said that it's always the thing between us, that we use it as a hiding place when our feelings get too honest. And you're right. This has been a long time coming, but I'm not going to keep lying to you." His eyes lingered on her face.

"The night Chris died—" He swallowed again but refused to stop now. "He was going to propose to you." His head dropped back against the metal, and he closed his eyes. Something would change between him and Jodee tonight. He just wished he knew if it would change for the better.

A soft, anguished sound followed by a sob shuddered up from deep within her. "Why are you telling me this now? It can't change anything."

The brokenness he recognized like a fresh wounding consumed him. He didn't want to hurt her. He wanted her to heal. "That's not true, Jodee. Getting the truth, no matter how ugly, out in the open changes everything when you let it." He searched the lines of her face, hungering to see her made whole again, even if it meant ripping out his own heart. "I need you to know the truth before you destroy yourself. Trust me. I know first-hand what that looks like."

He swallowed the emotions building in his throat, then thumbed at a piece of dirt clinging to his jeans, only to find his fingers curled in a fist. Better a fist than to reach for her. His wouldn't be the comfort she wanted after she heard what he had to say. "Want to know why I got drunk that night?"

She buried her head in her hands as though already fearing what he would say.

"I didn't want to be sober when he asked you to marry him. And then I thought if I could get myself good and drunk, Chris would be too busy taking care of me, and maybe it wouldn't happen."

The tears she shed seemed wretched up from a place deep within, but he had to keep going.

"It should've been me. I should've been the one driving that night. I should've been the one to get out and help at that accident. Y'all shouldn't even have been there." The emotions he'd swallowed twisted in his stomach, his throat tightening as though it longed to seal his words inside. "I should've been the one the car hit. I should've been the one to die that night."

Sobs shook her and he took a chance, wrapping his arms around her and holding her close. The tear-stained eyes that finally sought his face brought a fresh ache to his chest. Not the anger or hatred he expected—deserved—filled them, but a guilt-ridden pain that matched his own.

She placed her hand against his cheek. "Not you. Never you. It wasn't your fault. It was me. I made him take me to the rodeo that night. If I hadn't insisted, we would never have been on that road."

He took her hand, rubbing his thumb across her knuckles. "That doesn't make what happened your fault."

"You don't understand. I wanted to be there because of *you*." Tears streamed down her face in trails that ended in dark splotches on her shirt. "I . . .didn't know he planned to propose. But I knew that night it was you I loved. I knew I should break up with him, but

I was afraid to let go. Afraid I'd be all alone again. Chris was the first steady person in my life to love me after Paul left."

Her words melted through him, molding him into the man he wanted her to see, the man he wanted to be. But remorse still held him in its grasp. Sometimes being able to forgive even yourself was a process of repeated choice.

"Chris was a good man—a better man than me. He loved you. He was the one you needed, not me." His words were soft, spun up in a melancholy that even he recognized.

She settled against his shoulder with a hiccup. "Why are you telling me this now?"

"My mom loved my dad and ended up married to a man who destroyed her. Back then, all I knew was that I couldn't be the reason that would happen to you. I wouldn't be the one to destroy you, and I would have." He shifted to pull her closer. "But I couldn't tell you about Chris. I couldn't stand what you'd think of me once you knew what I'd done. I couldn't stand having you know my selfishness was the cause of your pain." He inhaled. "I'm not that man anymore."

He caressed her cheek with his free hand, compelling her to look at him as he spoke. "And I think you need to know he loved you. A good man loved you, Jodee Trevaine. If you'd stop running long enough to see how very loved you are, it would change everything."

"But did *you*, Blue? Did you love me too?"

He swallowed the emotions continuing to build in his chest and stared at the horizon. Was now the time? Could he tell her the truth without risking losing her?

"No. Not *did* as in the past tense. No matter what happens between us, it will never be a love in the past tense." He kissed her again with a slow and gentle touch. "I found forgiveness, Jodee."

She pulled away, reaching into her pocket to pull out the white stone. Questions filled her eyes.

"You can be too." He tugged a strand of her hair. "I want that for you. More than anything, I want it for you. But there's something else." He covered her hand with his, stilling her fingers, then he rotated her palm up until the white stone was visible. "I want you to know who you are." He ran a finger over the stone, then pressed her fingers closed around it, giving her fist a squeeze.

"And if you're not going to leave, then I need you to know you may see some things or hear some things about me that aren't true. I can't explain yet, but soon." If the fire now burning inside him could warm her to the idea, he'd gladly combust. "Please trust me. This town is a flesh of distrust clinging to the skeletal bones of evil."

She nodded, then licked her lips. "I trust you. But I can't leave. There's a boy who's missing. I'm afraid he's in danger."

Blue sighed. He was asking her to trust him, now he needed to trust her as well. If she believed she'd witnessed the boy's abduction, then he needed to stand by her. Even if doing so might be the primer strike that blew everything he was working for to bits.

"I think I know how to find him," she said.

He frowned. He trusted her, but he didn't have to like the consequences. "How?"

"Syrah," she said. "The one who's *not your girlfriend.*"

Blue opened his mouth to respond but caught the trace of a teasing gleam in her eye. The arrival of a Sheriff's Department SUV, followed close behind by a second one driven by Logan, silenced them both.

"Rolling up two deep. This can't be good." Blue stood, pulling Jodee up beside him. He tugged his phone from his back pocket and slipped it into hers. Leaning close, he whispered, "Keep this safe. Don't let anyone get to it or see what's on it. And Jodee, please just trust me."

Logan stepped out of the SUV and settled his hat on his head. "Blue Sunday. You're under arrest."

CHAPTER 31

Love is flower like; Friendship is like a sheltering tree. ~Samuel Taylor Coleridge

"Under arrest? For what?" Blue's shoulders rolled back, arms wide.

Logan rested one hand on his hip, the other on his holster, his fingers drumming against the leather in a way that prickled Jodee's unease.

"Arson and attempted homicide," Logan said. He stared at Blue as though analyzing the details of his response.

"What are you talking about?" Jodee's voice pinched. "You can't be serious!"

"I'm afraid I am." His stare remained fixed on Blue.

Blue raked his hands through his hair and sighed. "What arson, and who am I being accused of trying to kill?"

Logan glanced at Jodee. "I warned you every time you were threatened or hurt, he was there."

"Is this about his camper? Blue did not burn his own camper down, and he did not try to kill me! He wouldn't."

"The truth will come out. It always does," Logan nodded toward

Blue. "Now, up against the car so I can do a pat down before we take a ride. I believe you're familiar with the drill."

The expression on Blue's face was an unreadable mask as he followed Logan's orders. Then he looked at her. "Stay away from the wine until I get back." The pointed look he gave her let her know he wasn't speaking of actual wine.

Logan escorted Blue around his SUV as the other deputy opened the rear passenger door to allow the prisoner into the backseat.

"And get some rest." Blue winked at her. "Don't reckon I'll be gone too long once these yahoo Barney Fife's realize they got the wrong guy."

"What is this about? Why are you arresting him?" Jodee couldn't let it go as easily as Blue seemed to.

With Blue seated in the vehicle, Logan faced her, stance wide, arms crossed. "You should know. You're the one pressing charges."

The look in his eyes troubled her. It didn't match the confident authority of his actions. A question lingered there. She was certain of it.

"Yes, so you could get the video from the truck stop to help find the boy, not to get Blue arrested. He hasn't done anything."

"The video tells a different story." He cocked his head to the side. "And I'm left wondering what your role in all this really is." He pulled the keyring from his pocket and twirled it around his finger a few times before snatching in mid swing as though to punctuate his comment. "I reckon we'll find out soon enough."

He reached to close the door, but before he did, Blue inserted one final comment. "Be careful, Jodee. You don't know who you can trust around here. Isn't that right, Sheriff Adams?"

Jodee paced across Grace's driveway. She pressed her fingers to her temples. How long had she been at this when she should have been taking action?

Blue liked to have a good time, and sometimes that had made

him color outside the lines. But that was different from the kind of trouble Logan suggested now.

He'd implied Blue's arrest had to do with something on the video.

The memory of his arms around her just minutes ago slowed her steps. She'd felt secure, accepted—genuinely loved. But it was his tender gaze that reached into her soul, touching her in a way his hands never could.

She folded her arms over her middle, shrinking in on herself. What showed up that video? What had Blue gotten himself into?

Whatever they thought, they were wrong. But what could she do that wouldn't make matters worse?

She could find Aidan.

But where to look? Blue had told her in his encrypted way to steer clear of Syrah until he got back. He'd asked her to trust him, so okay, maybe she'd give that a try.

But if she wasn't looking for Syrah, then who or what?

Everything started at Tooley's Truck Stop, and if the video from the truck stop led to Blue's arrest, then it seemed like as good a place to start as any.

She eyed Blue's truck still parked behind the Bronco. A warning skittered through her when her hand touched the door. If someone was after Blue, would she be putting herself in danger by driving his truck? She decided in favor of the Bronco.

Twenty minutes later, she circled through the parking lot in the *borrowed* vehicle. She'd made two passes already. If she made another, she'd be the one acting suspicious on the surveillance video. She parked where she could see inside the building. A larger crowd than before milled around inside.

A thin teenager with stringy blonde hair worked the register this evening. Jodee wandered around the inside. The restrooms were empty. After several minutes with no sign of Kimberly or anyone else she remembered, she grabbed a bottle of water and headed to the register.

The young man looked at her T-shirt and snickered.

"You have a problem with Care Bears?" she asked.

"Pretty lame, especially on someone…"

"Someone, what?" Jodee gave him a teasing smile. "Someone my age?"

"Hey, you said it, not me."

"Yeah, well, I actually agree with you, but it was a gift." Technically, not a lie since Blue paid for it. She handed him her money. "Kimberly around tonight?"

"Nope. And if she pulls another sickie, I'm out."

"She's a working mother with a young boy to take care of. You might show a little compassion."

"Her choice, not mine. I had to cancel my date tonight."

If he'd really found someone willing to go out with him with this disposition, then maybe he should've quit. There couldn't be too many women out there looking for such a rotten attitude backed by so little ambition.

"And for the record, I can take my Care Bear shirt off. That Tommy and Chuckie tattoo is something you're stuck with for the rest of your sad little life."

She saluted him with the bottle of water and left.

No weathered cowboy in a duster held the door for her tonight.

This was a waste of time.

That Kimberly had called in sick for a few days stirred her curiosity. Was she really sick or was there, as her intuition suggested, something else keeping her from work? If Aidan was with his dad, why didn't she come to work? From what Grace said, she didn't have the money for the luxury of days off.

Maybe the next thing to do would be to drop by Kimberly's. Enough sunlight remained in the day that Jodee felt safe. Still, she made frequent scans of her surroundings as she drove up the hill to El Hueso.

She parked in front of the house she'd visited with Grace. Kimberly's car still sat parked in the same place as before. The living room light was on, but the curtains were drawn, and shades closed.

She knocked. No television or radio noise carried from inside.

She knocked again. What if she was sick or hurt? What if she's hurt herself? Acid burned Jodee's mouth at the idea that she might have even hurt her own son. But she had seen him being abducted. A wicked truth scorched through her. Some parents sold their children.

She silenced the macabre thoughts whispering in her ears. Aidan was alive and she would find him. She had to believe it.

The woman was home. Her intuition made her certain of it. But short of busting the door down, there was nothing she could do if Kimberly refused to open. She smacked the door harder. "Kimberly, I know you're in there. Open up or I'm calling the cops for a welfare check!"

After letting a minute or more tick by, she turned to leave.

A burst of a raspy, wheezy cough rattled from inside the house. The click of the door unlocking followed. Kimberly stared at her through puffy eyes in the narrow slice of opening.

The woman didn't say anything. Dark circles deepened the shadows beneath her eyes. If it was possible for her to look any paler, she did.

"Kimberly?"

She didn't respond.

"I saw you that night. I saw you and I saw Aidan." Jodee shifted herself so she'd be ready to stop the door from closing if needed. "Please, talk to me."

"There's nothing to say." Kimberly's gaze flickered up and down the street. "Everything's fine."

"But you haven't been at work? Are you sick?"

"It's my asthma. I'm used to it."

Jodee tried not to scowl. The girl looked like death warmed over, as her grandmother used to say.

"Look, it took me a little while to remember, but no one's going to believe me unless you tell the truth."

"There's nothing to tell. I can't."

"Can't or won't?"

"You don't know everything there is to know. Please stay out of my business and leave me alone."

"Is someone threatening you? I want to help you get your son back." Jodee looked away, then looked back. "That's a lie. I wouldn't be doing any of this for you. But Aidan, your son, he's alone out there somewhere. He needs to know someone is coming for him not hiding out in their house."

The flash of pain that swept over Kimberly's face left an ashen trail of grief in its wake. "I said I don't need your help. Everything is fine. Please, just go away." She closed the door. The clank of the dead-bolt sliding into place confirmed the visit had reached its conclusion.

Nothing had been gained from the conversation, but the trace smell of cigarette smoke that wafted out around Kimberly created new questions. She'd told Jodee it triggered her asthma that night at the truck stop.

Was Kimberly alone in the house? Or did she have a visitor she didn't want anyone to know about?

She drove around the corner and parked, positioning the Bronco where it wouldn't be seen but still allowed her a view of the drive-way. Kimberly wasn't alone, but was she in danger?

Waiting for nightfall would require another half hour of patience. Her leg jiggled, and she patted her thighs. She wouldn't last for thirty minutes. A scan of the few houses around led her to believe that most were vacant or occupied by people who wouldn't feel compelled to call the cops at the sight of someone lurking about. Of course, that also meant they might be ones most inclined to take matters into their own hands. The memory of having a shotgun aimed at her sent ripples of unease over her and prompted her heart to skip into its rapid, unsteady rhythm.

Closing her eyes, she breathed in a calming breath. With it came the memory of the conversation she'd had with Blue. If she'd been foolish enough to follow her heart to Blue back then, they'd only have inflicted more damage on each other than what they started with. Chris was a good man, but would he have stayed a good man if he'd married her? If she'd brought all her baggage—the unspoken and unhealed wounds and the lies she believed about herself and everyone else—into a marriage? She had needed him to fill a hole in her heart he wasn't meant to fill.

That didn't mean Chris deserved to die.

She pushed back in the seat, overcome by the truth that she never looked for healing for her wounds. She ran from them. It was a bitter irony that even though she ran from them, she carried them with her. Time had not erased them, only buried them. Like the oak tree who'd spent its life sealing over its wounds instead of healing, the accumulation of life stressors made her vulnerable. And like the storm-torn tree, it made her easy prey for the root rotting fungus that wanted to destroy her.

Did she want to know the truth, or was she afraid of what she might find?

She was tired of running. She was tired of being afraid.

Pocketing the keys, she took a long sip of water, then stared down the street in both directions. Nothing moved. In the distance, the sound of the national anthem blared from the speakers high on their poles at the rodeo arena. It was a fair guess that most of the town would be packed into the bleachers tonight.

She wished she were one of them. Instead, she crept through the shadows, analyzing fences and trees, moving between them until she could approach Kimberly's house unseen.

Her heart thrummed in her ears, threatening to drown out every other sound. With cautious steps, she moved along the side of the house. She only needed a small peek inside to confirm the presence of someone else. Then she'd—what? Call Logan?

The last time she'd trusted him, he'd arrested Blue and blamed it on her. If she told him what she'd done now, he'd probably lock her up as a stalker.

The shades were lowered, but no light slipped from the edges. One by one, she moved to each window, leaving the front porch and living room for last, even though that was where she would most likely to find what she was looking for. She considered her present maneuvers like a courage-building exercise, strengthening her nerves before she attempted the place with the greatest risk of discovery.

She ran sweaty palms down her jeans.

Behind the house, a small square slab of concrete served as a porch. The back yard sloped so that a couple of cement steps were needed.

But the curtain over the back porch window was an ill fit, leaving an inch wide gap for the curious. Mouth drier, pulse faster, palms sweatier, she froze. Her erratic heartbeat added a trace of dizziness.

A rundown chain-link fence surrounded the yard but lacked the ability to restrain much with the gate hanging by one hinge. It wouldn't take a lot to hop over it if needed and given enough head start. And if they didn't just shoot her instead.

She pulled in a long, deep breath, then exhaled.

With an escape route firmly in mind, she stepped onto the porch to position herself for a closer look. She planted her feet, pressing her back against the house where she was out of sight, and stalled.

In the past forty-eight hours, someone had threatened to kill her at least twice. Maybe three times if the fire at Blue's camper had been aimed at her and not him.

She inhaled again, filling her lungs in an effort to settle her pulse. Her hand went to her stomach, and she froze. The involuntary touch triggered her determination to save someone else's child.

She slid along the outer wall until she could see inside. Nothing but a view of the kitchen counters and sink. Crouching beneath the window, she shifted to the other side of the door, hoping to get a better look.

A chair scraped against the floor, and she ducked.

A male spoke, and though she couldn't make out the words, the terse tone spoke volumes. Footsteps thumped in the direction of the door.

She leapt from the porch, darting around the side of the house to dive between a couple of overgrown chokeberry bushes.

The door slapped shut. The gritty scuff of lazy steps crossed the cement porch before stopping at the edge. A faint clicking sound, followed soon after by the smell of cigarette smoke.

She squatted, pressed against the house with her knees tucked tight against her chest. In a panic, she'd bailed off the porch on the wrong side—the side without a gate.

A demonic laugh convulsed in the darkening night.

CHAPTER 32

Unless a tree has borne blossoms in spring, you will vainly look for fruit on it in autumn. ~Walter Scott

Three rings before answering. Completely unacceptable. His mouth set in a grim line. He didn't have long to make this call. He'd finished his official duty of riding in the Grand Entry, but his guests would expect him in his box seat soon.

"Yeah, Boss," came through the line.

"Yeah, Boss? That's what you say after taking your time to answer the call?" He fisted his hand, squeezed, then released as though letting go of the anger. He had enough of a mess on his hands at this moment. When it was over, changes would be made.

"Sorry, Boss." The man's expressionless voice didn't reveal whether he was sorry or not.

"Any news?"

"Nothing new from the boy. He's sticking to his story."

His jaw clenched. The boy told the truth. He didn't believe for a second a child his age could stick to a lie like this when they'd made it clear what was at stake if he didn't tell the truth.

"His mother had a visitor, though."

"A visitor?" Making him dig for answers was not going to end well for the man on the other end of the line. The tension crept from his clenched jaw to travel down his neck into his shoulders like a noxious vine.

"Trevaine. The woman from Tooley's."

"I know who she is. What did she want?" The creeping vine of tension clenched him even tighter. He rolled his shoulders, trying to release the stiff muscles.

He was still in control. He'd just have to adapt his approach.

"Wanted the boy's mother to go to the police."

"And?" This was a problem. She'd already inserted herself into what happened at the truck stop, but that she was pursuing the matter created another knot in his plans.

"And she got the door closed in her face." The man chuckled. "The mother must be enjoying my company."

His hand fisted again, wrapping itself around the bone deep desire to break his hired man's neck. He didn't ask Rusty if she'd bought it. He knew better. Jodee was too smart to fall for that, even if she needed to think on it for a bit. Cleverness and intelligence were in her DNA.

"You want me to take care of her?" Rusty continued when he didn't respond right away.

"Lay a hand on her and you're the one who'll find out what it's like to be *taken care of.*" Permanently, he wanted to add. But not yet. Not until he had everything that was his. "We stick to the plan. Are Nolan and Syrah where they're supposed to be?"

"Yep, at the farm keeping an eye on the boy."

"You make sure they don't hurt him but keep him out of sight." He tapped his middle finger on the desk. "And don't let anyone see you, either. You look like you've been kicked in the face by a mule."

The sound of Rusty swallowing thumped from the phone. He pursed his lips at the idea Rusty might be holding something back. "You have something else you ought to tell me?"

"No, sir. Just wondering how long you think until Sunday is out again?"

He'd planned to have Sunday behind bars and out of the way for a few days. But if he were forced to put his backup plan in motion, he'd need to have the man released. He'd see to it that his bail was set low. Then he'd follow Sunday to whoever he was working for. The man was up to something. He could feel it in his gut. Maybe setting him up for whatever was about to happen with the boy and his mother would eliminate two problems at once.

Plus, it was only a matter of time before they showed the video to someone who might figure out it had been doctored. Time was not on his side in this.

His jaw clenched again. And he wanted Blue Sunday away from Jodee.

He didn't know how to make that happen, but he'd think of something. His ancestors always had. For generations, they'd been solving their own problems. Protecting what was theirs. "You let me worry about him. You take the mother and head to the farm. Maybe she can get the boy to give us the answer we need. I want this resolved before sunup tomorrow."

There had already been too many missteps. Using the distraction of the Old Settler's Reunion as a cover wouldn't work if this went on much longer.

"When do you want me to head out with her?"

"Do it now while everybody's at the rodeo. Less chance you'll be seen." He wanted to pummel the man himself for letting her bust his nose. He'd had to keep Rusty out of sight ever since. "Maybe you can keep this woman from getting the best of you this time."

He hung up, a smile emerging in place of his usual frown. She was a fighter.

He liked that about her. She'd soon know just how very much he liked that.

CHAPTER 33

For a good tree does not bear bad fruit, nor does a bad tree bear good fruit.
~Luke 6:43

"Yeah, you might want to think twice about making fun of Rusty Boggs, *Boss.*" Gone was the respectful deference to whoever "Boss" was. He dipped the word in sarcasm as thick as tar so that it hung in the air with a tangible menace.

Jodee assumed that meant he was no longer actually speaking to the *boss*.

"Don't care what you say, me and her are going to have ourselves another meeting real soon and she'll understand who she messed with." He spit. "Ain't no female getting the best of Rusty Boggs. She's gonna find out the third times a charm and when done she'll be the one looking like she got kicked by a mule or worse." His malicious laughter scuttled over her like fire ants.

He was talking about her. Sweat beaded on her forehead with the understanding. Her breath froze in her chest.

Movement on the other side of the fence caught her attention. A chihuahua materialized from a pet door in the neighboring house.

Three pounds of dog wrapped around a ton of attitude. The scrawny little dog stared from its place across the fence, clearly not expecting or pleased to see a human staring back. Even from the distance, she could see the hair lifting on its neck, its tiny lips curled back as a low growl crawled from its throat. She gave her head a slight shake. *Please don't.*

Cheering erupted from the rodeo grounds. She flinched. The little dog launched himself from his place on the porch next door and raced across the yard to the fence between them, yapping with such ferociousness his paws lost touch with the ground.

"Shut up, you—" The man rounded off his command with a string of curse words.

The mutt took up a position opposite from where she hid, continuing its yipping with no regard to the command to shut up.

If he came to investigate what had the dog riled up, he'd find her.

She tensed, biting down on her lower lip until the pain blocked out the escalating fear edging her toward panic.

Heavy steps stomped her way. She held her breath and tried not to shiver. Through the dense leaves, she could make out the leather work boots he wore. She braced herself, muscles coiling in preparation for the fight she would give if discovered.

A second later, a sharp crack exploded from the other side of the house. The dog yelped and retreated to the safety of his own porch.

Did he actually shoot the dog? She recoiled, biting her lip until it drew blood.

Another curse word rattled in the air.

The roaring in her ears made hearing a challenge as he ground the unburned stub of his cigarette into the dirt in front of her. Then he turned back to the porch. The click of his lighter told her he planned to enjoy another smoke.

But she didn't plan to stick around and enjoy another near miss.

A scan of the yard fence confirmed there was no gate on this side. No gate, but a gnarled section of fence offered her an escape route. The work of a previous canine resident expressing his refusal to be held in by digging a hole beneath the fence to her right. Along with the packed dirt, the dog had managed to bend and twist the wire until there was just enough space for a midsized dog to slip out.

Jodee estimated she would fit, but she wasn't sure she could do it without making any noise.

She crawled to the scratched-out opening. On her back, she wiggled under, wincing as a jagged piece of wire raked across her, sending a burning streak of pain down her arm. Another wire snagged at her t-shirt. She cringed at the ripping sound that followed.

Courage restored, the yapping dog returned to his station at the fence, sounding his alarm at full throttle—definitely not shot. If anyone looked out a window, they might see her.

She shimmied the rest of the way through the opening and rolled to her feet.

"Shut up you stupid mutt!" The man shouted again. The screen door at the back of the house slammed closed.

An old Ford pickup drove by. She jerked back as another gunshot burst from the street. But it wasn't a gunshot. And neither was the sound she'd heard earlier. Not a gun. A back-firing clunker.

She recognized the truck as it rounded the corner at the end of the street. Hawk.

A feeling of having been protected overcame her. The sense she wasn't alone gave her a new belief that she was doing the right thing.

The faint smell of cigarette smoke closed in on her. A twig behind her cracked.

She bolted from the yard, racing down the middle of the empty street as footsteps pounded behind her.

An alley opened up and she took it, hoping to lose her pursuer in the shadows. The steps began to sound farther away as she outdistanced him, but she didn't waste a second to look back. She rounded another corner and slipped into an unfenced yard to hide behind a shed.

His heavy breathing gave him away before she saw him. He

paused, his chest heaving, and scanned first the alley and then the yard where she hid. With no exterior or security lighting, he wouldn't see her unless he walked over.

She snuck to the other side of the rundown shed, only to find her way blocked by a mound of aluminum beer cans piled higher than the top of her head.

Her scalped tingled. Trapped. She leaned just far enough around so that she could watch him, her vision tunneling until he was all she saw.

He removed something from his pocket. She flinched as the light glinted off the blade of a knife. When he moved in her direction, she made a panicked search of the area around her for anything she could use as a weapon. Whatever she might find would do little good against a knife in the hands of someone intent on harming her. But she would go down swinging. The only things close by were an old hubcap and some plastic toys, none of which would help.

The aroma of baking bread wafted in the air. The deep breath she held siphoned out in a steadying stream. She looked for the source of the smell and found a walnut tree nearby. The results of its self-pruning scattered at its feet. She moused her way beneath its crown, searching for a limb big enough to prevent her from becoming a carving dummy for the lunatic after her.

Armed with a thick branch, she maneuvered to the darkest shadow and pressed her back against the side of the shed. The tree bark dug into her palms as she clutched the makeshift weapon. She'd only get one chance at surprise and only one swing. The rest depended on her ability to dodge his knife and run.

The steps shuffled closer. He was moving along the side of the building. Only a matter of seconds until they'd be face to face. There'd be no chance at surprise. He knew she was here.

Instinctively, she dropped into a crouch. He wouldn't be looking for her down low. He'd be expecting her to be standing.

His steps halted just around the corner. She could hear his breath and held her own.

"Come on out now. It's time for us to have a little fun," he teased, his words slithering over her.

She raised the stick she held and tapped it lightly against the building in the spot where her shoulders should have been.

He lunged around the corner, slashing the air with his knife.

With a fury charged strength, she swung the branch, connecting with his knees.

He crashed against the building, blistering the air as he voiced his rage. She jumped to the side as he staggered forward, still slashing with his knife.

She ran, not stopping or looking back until she reached the Bronco.

Out of breath, she leaned back against the side of the vehicle, pressing her hand over the stitch in her side. She slammed her fist against the metal, sending pain shooting up her arm. Instant remorse gnawed at her. A broken hand would not prove useful.

She clambered into the vehicle and drove to the most inconspicuous spot she could think of—the parking lot at Roots.

He couldn't know what she was driving, but would he be looking for her? On his phone call, he'd said something about *heading out with her*. That had to mean Kimberly. What were the odds he'd take her to where Aidan was?

If Aidan still was. The suggestion squeezed her throat. She forced the thought away as the boy's precious face materialized in her mind. No. She refused to even consider that possibility, going all in on the odds being in her favor.

She frowned. Was Kimberly a part of this? Instead of being a victim, was she as guilty as the rest of them?

The chance wrenched her heart open all the more for Aidan— the little boy looking for a treasure so his mother wouldn't have to work so much. Her determination to find him solidified.

If the man who'd identified himself as Rusty Boggs was headed out with Kimberly, she needed to follow them. She left Roots and drove back to the place down the street where she could watch Kimberly's house.

All she could do now was wait. And pray, she supposed. If she knew how . . .

Lord, not for me. I don't deserve it. My mess is because of choices I made. Not Aidan, though. He doesn't deserve any of this. Please Lord, help me find him. And until I do, let him know he's not alone.

Warmth like a cup of Mexican Hot Chocolate poured through her. Not sweet, but strong. *Not alone.*

Hawk. The man at Tooley's, the fire, the backfiring truck today. Who was he? And how did he always appear when she needed him most?

The door to Kimberly's house opened, and they stepped out. The man following her hobbled as though he were in pain.

Jodee looked at the man who *wasn't done with her yet.*

The smile morphed into an expression of solemn determination. She wasn't done with him yet either.

CHAPTER 34

All that is gold does not glitter, not all those who wander are lost; the old
that is strong does not wither, deep roots are not reached by the frost.
~J. R. R. Tolkien

The black Nissan turned on a dirt road, accelerating so that it stirred a rolling cloud of dust in its wake. Despite the heavy rain a few days ago, the caliche roads were dry enough to create a plume of dust that hovered in the twilight.

Pulling to the side of the narrow country road, she put the Bronco in park. The powdery white cloud stirred by the Nissan would be easy enough to follow, but she didn't want to create one of her own.

When the dust had cleared to a thin veil, she resumed driving. The A/C in the Bronco didn't work. With the windows rolled down, the chalky grit whipped in to cling to her face and hair, intensifying the parched sensation claiming her throat.

Several miles slipped by before the dust cloud ceased to move. The notion that they might have hit pavement again roused a new angst. She increased her speed, decelerating as she rounded a corner near where the dust cloud stopped. The Bronco' was too old to have automatic headlights. She flicked them on now in case someone looked out and saw her drive by. No lights would make her look suspicious.

Mountain junipers lined the sides of the road in a bushy wall of green. The trees hid all but the roof of the old farmhouse ahead until she was nearly in front of it. The Nissan sat in the driveway along with two other vehicles, one of which was the familiar black truck.

No movement caught her eye, raising hope they were already inside.

She drove another two miles before coming to a second road that cut to the right. A check in her rearview mirror assured her she wasn't being followed. She shook out each hand one at a time to rid herself of the tension squeezing her muscles. She was a forester, not search and rescue personnel.

A dip in the road took her over a wash where rushing rainwater would cut across during a heavy downpour. The recent rains had gouged large ruts that jostled and bounced her, kindling fresh pain in the aches and bruises she'd acquired during her recent attacks.

A hundred yards beyond, she found a rusted gate into an overgrown pasture. Briars grew thick along the fence. It would have to do as a hiding place for the Bronco. She backed it into as much concealment as she could find without obstructing potential escape routes in case she needed to leave in a hurry.

Standing beside the vehicle, she tilted her head back to examine the growing number of stars populating the darkening sky. She rubbed her arms in the cool evening air. A perfect night for sitting in the bleachers watching a rodeo. She shivered, recalling another night at a rodeo.

The things Blue told her—was that just today?—had catapulted her heart into a sea of emotions. But given everything that had happened since, she'd been forced to leave it bobbing in the turbulent waves, fighting to stay afloat.

The desire to explore what it all meant tugged at her heart, but right now, she could only focus on one thing. Aidan.

She could follow the road back to the house, or she could cut across the pasture in front of her. She'd hazard stepping on a rattlesnake if she cut through the pasture in the dark. But she'd hazard being caught by a different kind of snake that scared her more if she didn't. Rusty Boggs was in that house.

A half hour later, she'd had one close call with a prickly pear, one moment of shared surprise with a jackrabbit, a stinging slap from a mesquite tree, and more tangles with the prickly scrub brush covering the hill than she could count. But the light from the rundown old farmhouse met her as she stepped through the thick line of trees lining one last briar covered fence.

From here, the silhouette of a barn loomed fifty yards behind the house. An empty chicken coop rotted itself into disrepair to the east of the house. Several pieces of old equipment rusted away in grass no taller than carpet, the result of over grazing and poor land management.

The assessment nicked her ire. People who had no respect for the land weren't to be trusted.

Darkness would be her friend—and her enemy.

She stilled, thinking. She hadn't seen a dog, or any sign that one lived here when she drove by.

Her hand pressed to her chest. *Not now.*

The aggravating tremors—tremors now named Wolfe-Parkinson-White Syndrome—bumped to life in her heart. A few steadying breaths didn't make them go away, but it helped her forget about the WPW and stay focused on finding Aidan.

Swinging wide around the back, she used the barn as concealment.

A security light pole blanketed the area between the house and the barn in an artificial glow that reached neither the house nor the barn.

The barn faced the house, its door hanging like a loose tooth, thrown wide and half off its hinges. Inside, the shadows wrapped around her, allowing her to breathe easily for a moment. She waited for an inspired idea to guide her next steps, but all she heard was a cynical voice with the words, *who do you think you are?*

Who did she think she was? She was starting to understand that better, but right now the question was what she was capable of?

An odd sense of relief and comfort drenched her. The erratic beating of her heart ceased.

She was about to find out just what she was capable of, and in doing so, she might start to believe something new about herself.

A shuffling behind her triggered a fresh fear. She tensed, wondering if she'd really heard anything.

Then it came again. It sounded like . . .sniffling?

With stealth, she moved into the obsidian darkness in the depths of the barn.

Another faint scratching stilled her. Something moved in front of her. An open stall door in the far corner of the barn drew her to it.

She eased away from the wall and peered into the stall, inhaling sharply as the form of a small child took shape. Forgetting caution, she flew through the opening and knelt beside him.

"Aidan?" She placed a hand on his forehead. It seemed warmer than it should have been. "Aidan, can you hear me?"

Confusion clouded his wide eyes.

"It's okay. I'm here to help you. Do you remember me? From the store. You were playing with your toy cars, and I told you I liked the red one."

He blinked, a glimmer of recognition in his eyes.

"I'm going to get you home now, okay?"

Had she just promised more than she could deliver? Her jaw set. No, she hadn't.

The ratty blanket covering him left his bare feet exposed, drawing her attention. A closer look revealed a mass of black and blue toes crusted in dried blood. She swallowed. Now was not the time.

A moaning from near the far wall startled her.

She jerked around to find Kimberly bound and propped up in the corner.

Going to her, she gripped the girl's shoulder. "Kimberly?"

The girl wheezed in air as though breathing through a cracked straw. "You have to get Aidan out of here. He needs a doctor."

"Sounds like he's not the only one." Jodee reached to untie the rope that bound her wrists.

Kimberly shook her head. "You don't have time. You have to go."

"I'm not leaving you." Jodee took in the bruising on her cheek and the busted lip. Kimberly had fought back.

"You have to. Asthma attack," she gasped. "I won't make it far without my inhaler. But Aidan . . ." Tears glistened in her eyes. "I was only trying to protect him, to do what was best for him." The tears broke free and ran down the girl's cheeks. "I failed."

"We can tally up our mistakes and failures over a big steak dinner after we get out of here. But for now, we need to move."

"Please go. You won't make it with me." The rattling sound coming from Kimberly's chest made her wonder if any of them would make it. But Jodee had made a promise. She wouldn't give the possibility of failure a foothold.

Aidan's little body twitched, his head spinning to the doorway. Footsteps.

"Syrah's coming!" Kimberly's eyes widened in fear.

With nowhere else to go, Jodee shifted into the darkest corner at the front wall of the stall. At least she'd see Syrah before Syrah saw her. Her toe stubbed against something solid. She reached down to find a hammer. Gripping it with both hands, she flattened against the wall and waited.

"You better not have wet your pants again. I can't stand the smell," Syrah said before she entered the stall.

The rage churning inside of her at the sight of Aidan boiled over as Jodee positioned herself to take action.

Syrah entered the stall, a wad of silver tinfoil in one hand and a lantern in the other. A bottle of water was tucked beneath her arm. "I got you something to eat. You better not waste it this time." She waved the foil-wrapped package in front of him. "If you'd just tell him the truth, Boss'd let you and your mommy go home. You don't want something bad to—"

Gripping the cold steel of the hammer head in her hand, Jodee drew back. She wanted to hurt Syrah, but she didn't want to kill her. Then she brought the wooden handle of the hammer down on the woman's head.

Syrah swayed and Jodee swung again. The woman crumpled to the ground.

A check of the unconscious woman's pockets failed to produce a phone or anything helpful—like an asthma inhaler.

"Hey Syrah, hurry up. I gotta go," a man called.

Okay, then go. The words screamed through Jodee's head as her eyes locked with Kimberly's. "How many are in there?"

"Just Syrah, Rusty, and Nolan."

The man kept up his dialogue even though he'd received no response. "You might as well give up. He isn't going to change his story." The voice hadn't moved. "Fine. Suit yourself. Stay mad at me, but you're not going to change my mind. You shouldn't have done that to the boy. I'm going to town to get some medical supplies and bandages. Just don't do anything else until I get back."

Jodee exhaled a shaky breath. The voice wasn't Rusty's, so this must be Nolan.

At the sound of the door slamming, she hurried from the stall. Whoever it was had gone back inside. But knowing there were at least two people in the house meant going out the front would be risky.

Too risky while carrying the boy.

She'd have to go with Plan B, which was hard to do since she didn't even have a Plan A.

Blue's phone.

She jerked it out and clicked on the screen. No signal. But was there something on here that might help since he'd insisted to hold on to it? The bright bubble of hope burst as she stared at a request for his password. She tried a few obvious possibilities, but nothing worked. A fine time for Blue to be clever.

"Kimberly." She knelt beside the girl, not liking the way her breathing came in raspy bursts. The girl sounded as though she really wouldn't make it far in distance or time. But could she just leave her?

"You can't fight all of them. You have to save Aidan." Kimberly's pleading voice sliced through her heart.

But the girl was right. Odds of getting all three of them to some place safe without detection were slim. If she could get Aidan to the Bronco, she could get to town and send help. "I don't like the idea of leaving you. What will they do to you?"

"I'll pretend I was passed out and didn't see a thing. I fainted once already, so they'll believe me."

"What do they want with you and Aidan?" Jodie asked.

"I don't know. They keep asking about a box, but I don't know anything about it." The string of words left the girl winded. "Now, please go. Aidan needs medical attention."

Jodee retrieved the bottle of water Syrah had brought. Had they drugged it? The possibility made her uncertain.

When she offered, Kimberly shook her head. "Aidan needs it more."

She scooped up the foil wrapped food that slipped from Syrah's hand and shoved it in her pocket.

Her fingers raked through her hair, holding it away from her face while she looked for another way out of the barn. There had to be a way. There was something different about the back wall. Going to it, she found a shorter wall with an opening for feeding animals running along the bottom. The top of this interior wall didn't reach to the roof. A wooden trough ran along the bottom, allowing feed to be poured in on this side while the animals ate on the other, just like the one in her grandfather's old barn. Aidan might fit through the feed slot, but she couldn't. She'd have to go over the top.

"Aidan, you be brave. No matter what happens. You're a fighter,"

Kimberly's words were urgent. "I'll be with you soon. I promise. I won't leave you" "

The anguish in the mother's voice ripped at Jodee's heart.

Aidan's voice cracked. "I don't want to leave you."

"You have to. Go with Jodee. She's going to take care of you. You be strong like you always have. Now please, just go before they come back."

The boy looked up at Jodee as though seeking proof that he could trust her. She nodded but doubts still filled her. *Can I do this?*

She knelt beside him, averting her eyes to hide the hot tears pooling in her eyes. "I'm going to get you out of here, but it might take a little bit of work. Have you ever heard someone say *it's about to get Western?*"

He shook his head.

"Well, it means things are about to get rough, and we're going to have to be strong and brave."

"That's not what it means," Aidan said.

"You said you didn't know," Jodee replied.

"I forgot, but now I remember. It means there's going to be a gun fight."

About the same level of difficulty as what we're about to do. "A gun fight, huh? Did you bring your six shooters?"

He shook his head.

"Me either, so I reckon we best just get out of Dodge." She looked at Kimberly, who nodded. She didn't need light to see that the woman was crying silent tears. "We'll send the whole posse back for your mom."

Her hand cupped his cheek. "Ready?"

He looked at Kimberly and received her reassuring smile.

Was she doing the right thing leaving her here? It didn't feel like it.

"Okay, buddy. Let's be brave and tough and strong and . . ."

"All the superhero things." He finished for her when her throat squeezed too tight to get the words out.

She scooped him up, but instead of heading to the door, she moved to kneel beside Kimberly. He wrapped his arms around her neck, and Kimberly kissed his forehead. "Remember, be strong. I will come for you."

Moving Aidan as gently as she could, Jodee placed him in the feed trough and helped him wiggle through the opening.

She looked back at the lantern lying next to Syrah's unconscious body. It would be a huge help in seeing their way. But it would also be a beacon to their pursuers. And sooner or later, they would be pursued. She righted it on the ground. At least, she could give Kimberly the comfort of being out of the dark.

When she stepped on the trough and reached for the upper edge of the wall, she found it just beyond her grasp. She backed up and took a running jump, her fingers hooking over the top as her bruised body slammed into the solid wall of boards. She dangled for a minute, catching her breath, before leveraging herself over the top, only gasping once as the boards dug into her tender ribs. Lowering herself feet first, she landed on the ground with a thud.

Aidan sat up, watching her.

"Do your feet hurt really bad?"

"Real cowboys don't feel pain," he answered.

"I think they do. That's what makes them real. They just keep going in spite of the pain." She wanted to ask if he was hurt anywhere else, but fear made the words stick in her throat. Instead, she motioned him onto her back.

"What about Kimber?" His fragile voice trembled.

"We're going to get help for your mom." She turned her back to him and knelt, waiting for the feel of his thin arms around her neck.

As she hoisted him onto her back, his words whispered in her ear.

"My sister."

CHAPTER 35

Texas 1874

I said to the almond tree, 'Friend, speak to me of God,' and the almond tree blossomed. ~Nikos Kazantzakis

*W*ill handed the leads to the boy who met him at the corral gate. His backside was ready to part company with his saddle. And his stomach was ready to enjoy the company of a hot meal.

And he wouldn't mind a hot bath and a shave. But all that would have to wait until he'd finished with his business.

He swung out of the saddle and flipped his reins over the rail as the stable owner walked over.

"You weren't lying. Some pumpkins these here horses are." He shook hands with Will, then walked over to inspect the horses up close.

"I ain't ever hornswoggled anyone. Least not when it comes to horses," Will said. He loosened the cinch strap on his saddle, then dug a sugar lump from his pocket and held it out for his mount to take.

"Town sure has changed," he said. Murchison wasn't a place he'd ever planned to visit, but the deal he'd been offered for the four horses he'd brought with him had been too good. It was more than the money, though. Something else had compelled him to return. Curiosity, perhaps.

The buyer lifted one of the horse's heads, pulling back the muzzle to examine the teeth. He ran his hands along the horse's flanks and patted the animal's rump. After he'd repeated this with each of the four horses, he turned his attention back to Will. "Right fine animals you got here." He reached in his coat pocket, then handed Will a bag of coins. "Pleasure doin' business with you."

"And with you. Wouldn't mind if you'd spread the word." He'd found his passion when he'd started working with horses. After just a few years, he'd established his reputation for quality horseflesh and fair dealings. He considered himself a blessed man with a good wife and a healthy strapping son, along with a house and enough land to raise his horses. But of all the good things that had come his way, his reputation was the thing he was most grateful to have. It hadn't always been that way.

His throat tightened. He meant to give his son what he never had. A secure home, loving family, and the favor of having a father other folks respected.

Pretty much all an orphan boy could dream of. Even if Will always felt as though a part of his heart was missing. He loved his wife, Amanda. He'd never betray her. But he couldn't deny that there was a part of him that he held back, as though it were reserved for another. Sometimes he thought of Rose and wondered what had become of her. Was she happy? Did she remember him?

But those memories always led back to the destructive tangle of guilt and shame. He'd long ago discovered the irony that his fear of being blamed for something he didn't do had made him do something that left him in a state of self-condemnation and dishonor. The burden he never shared remained a heavy yoke, a torment that never left.

"Where's a good place to grab a hot meal around here?"

"There's a nice widow lady—heck of a cook—runs a fine café down across from the hotel. I like to send her business every time I can. Ain't been easy for her since her husband got killed eight months ago."

"Thanks. I'll give it a try."

"I'll have the boy brush down your horse and get him fed. How long you stayin'?"

"I'll be heading back in the morning. You got room for a man to bunk down in the barn?"

"Help yourself."

Will thanked him again for the business, hoisted his saddle bags over his shoulder, and headed in search of his dinner.

The town had grown up since he'd last seen it. Of course, he'd been just a boy then. There were lots he didn't remember. There were also lots he tried to forget.

Guilt niggled under his skin. Had he truly earned the right to a good reputation?

As always, he came back to the same answer he told himself. He'd had no choice. He'd only been a boy, barely nine years old. What could he have done differently?

The pleasure of the sale he'd just made dissipated into the dirt at his feet. He'd left her. At the time when she'd needed someone familiar the most, he'd broken his promise and run away like a coward. Even more convicting was the truth he'd let the DeGroots take what should have been hers. They'd murdered her parents and stolen her inheritance, and he'd done nothing to stop them other than to get in a couple of shovel swings.

His appetite left him. If his son ever learned the truth of who his father was, he'd know he was a fraud.

A fraud with no way to change the past and no chance to change the future.

Only a handful of diners occupied the café when he arrived. It was not yet time for dinner, but he wanted to start out before daybreak for the two days ride back home. Turning in early for the night held a certain appeal.

A woman carried plates of food to a table of men on the opposite side. A couple of elderly ladies sat at a table near him eating pie and sipping coffee. He rolled his shoulders and tried to shake off the melancholy mood that had crept over him.

Another woman in a calico apron appeared in front of him with a pot of coffee and a china cup in her hands. "Coffee?"

She filled the cup she set in front of him and left. If the food lived up to the aroma filling the dining area, he had no doubt he'd enjoy this meal. His stomach growled, his appetite returning.

The woman who'd served the men their food now moved to the table where the women sat. She chatted with them for a moment, then reached to remove their empty plates.

Will couldn't keep himself from sneaking glances at her while he sipped his coffee. Something about the way she moved, like a prairie flower in the evening breeze, captured his attention. Not her carriage, but the delicate lines and angles of her face felt familiar.

He wasn't a man with a wandering eye. When he'd taken his wedding vows, he'd meant them and that was never going to change. It irritated him now to find his gaze drawn to her.

She reached for the empty plates in front of the women, causing her sleeve to move up her arm revealing a nasty scar.

"Bud." The murmured name slipped out before he could stop it, as though his heart recognized her before his brain accepted the truth. He rose in haste, bumping the table, causing the dishes to rattle. Like a man who'd just been kicked in the head, he lunged from the cafe in a daze.

Bracing a hand against a porch post, he worked to settle the emotions scrambling themselves in his head.

"What did you say?" The feminine voice behind him broke through his fluster with the quiet strength of butterfly wings.

He inhaled, wanting both to find what he expected when he turned around and to be mistaken at the same time. His movements faltered as he turned to find her holding the hat he'd left in his hurry to get away.

She held it out. "You forgot this." Her guarded expression held a thousand questions he didn't want to hear and couldn't bear to answer.

Her sleeve slipped up from her wrist again as he reached for the hat. Once again, his gaze fixated on the scar.

"You said Bud." She released her hold on his hat and tugged her sleeve back in place, tears glistening in her eyes.

His tongue became too thick for speech. He could only stare at the woman before him, suddenly feeling like a nine-year-old boy with the weight of the world resting on his shoulders.

"Will?"

He closed his eyes and lowered his head for a moment before attempting to look at her. "It's you, isn't it? Rose Charidy."

She turned her face away from him as though his words unsettled her. "Charidy. I haven't heard that name in so long I'd forgotten it. I've been Rose Muellar and then Rose Wilkins for as long as I can remember."

Her gaze fixed on him, accompanied by a broken laugh that spilled out of emotional turmoil, as though she didn't know whether to be happy, afraid, or just plain sad.

He broke free of the feelings that held his tongue captive and smiled. "It is a good name. An honorable name."

She offered a thin smile, reaching behind her to untie the apron strings as she swept back inside. "Wait here."

Will stepped from the porch of the café. Gripping the hitching rail with both hands, he ducked his head. *Why was his heart racing like a herd of wild horses?*

Twenty years of guilt and shame fermenting inside of him simmered on the verge of boiling over. But there was something more. Something like the dovetailing of planks fitting perfectly together as they had been designed to do.

A fresh source of remorse stampeded through him. The wrenching pain of a heart ripping in two staggered him.

He should walk away. He could be gone before she returned. Just saddle up and head back home. But wasn't the fact he had abandoned her once before the source of his torment?

"Will?" Her presence behind him warmed him like an August Texas breeze. A wind that left a man spent if he tarried in its presence too long.

Turning to face her, the air slipped from his lungs. His Little Bud had blossomed into a Rose. A face lovely by any man's standards, but it was the grace and tenderness he saw that swept over him.

Not a praying man, Will still asked God to help him see clearly, and to think with faithfulness and honor. The smiling faces of both his wife and son rose before him. The angst inside him faded, and he smiled. "Rose. I can't believe it's you."

No longer a boy, but a grown man with a family, still he ducked his head as though shy in her presence.

"Would you walk with me, Will?"

The soft invitation from the girl who had almost been his sister opened the door to a place he'd denied for too long. He offered her his arm. "Always for you, Little Bud."

She looped her hand on his arm, chuckling. "No one ever called me that but you."

They walked in silence for a few minutes, neither seeming to know what should be said though they each had much they wanted to share.

Will cleared his throat. "I'm sorry to hear about your husband. I'm sure the past eight months haven't been easy for you."

He flinched inside. *Had he just sent the wrong message?* A pang of sorrow gripped his heart. First her parents and then her husband. How much loss could one woman endure? Especially a woman as tender and sweet as Rose.

"Eight months?" Her brow wrinkled as though confused. "I think you're referring to Edna, the owner. I work for her."

A subtle tenseness crept into her touch. "But yes. I lost my husband as well. Two years ago. Both he and our baby died of the grippe." She drew in a long breath that quivered with emotion.

"Then my condolence is doubled." The emotion in his own voice was part filled with an ache of sorrow for Rose and part for the agony of imagining how it would feel to lose his own wife and son.

"Thank you." She glanced up at him. "How about you? You have a loving family and a happy home now, I hope."

He smiled. "I do. My wife Amanda is a better woman than I deserve, and our son Jacob—" His throat tightened, squeezing the words until they couldn't come out. He allowed a few moments to pass before trusting his voice to continue. "I never even dreamed of being a father when your parents first took me in, but God has blessed me beyond what I deserve."

Her fingers clasped his arm a little tighter, enfolding him in the comfort she offered. "I'm happy for you, Will."

Silence settled over them as they continued down the sidewalk. The sun slid toward the horizon. People still bustled about the businesses lining the street. Will knew he should return her to the café before dark. It wouldn't be proper, and he wouldn't bring shame to her reputation.

"I was too little to remember much about those days. In fact, it wasn't until I became a mother that the memories started surfacing again," Rose said. She stopped and turned to face him. "Tell me about them. I want to know who my parents were, who I was supposed to be." She swallowed again. "And I want to know why you left me."

CHAPTER 36

By the fruits which it bears is the tree known.
~Jan Hus

ogan read the arrest warrant again. The words never changed. But the rightness of them dimmed every time he read it.

He picked up the Styrofoam cup half full of cold coffee, swirled the dark liquid around, then set the cup back on his desk without drinking.

The decision of guilty or innocent fell outside his responsibility. His job was the objective upholding of the law. It'd be the task of a jury to pass judgment.

Still, something wasn't right. The evidence against Blue was circumstantial at best. Logan made it his habit to study human behavior and had developed a decent ability to read people. Blue might not be the model of good citizenship, but the charges against him didn't quite fit. The itchy feeling there was something he was missing persisted.

He leaned back and stared at the picture hanging in the hall outside his office.

And then there was the other. The lie that had infected his childhood and festered still. If not for Grace, he'd be no better off than Blue.

A day was coming, and he hoped soon, when he would find the balm of justice might heal the wound, even if the scar remained.

But for now, if someone targeted Blue, the jail cell might be for his own good.

The situation with Kimberly and Aidan peppered his thoughts. Something wasn't right there, either. He scowled.

Blue, Aidan, Kimberly, and Jodee. Who needed his help most?

It didn't matter who he wanted to help the most. The oath he'd taken didn't allow his personal feelings to make his choices.

"On my honor, I will never betray my badge, my integrity, my character, or the public trust."

He meant it then, and he meant it now. Even if his doubts multiplied, his job was to uphold the law, not interpret it or put himself in the place of judgment. He picked his cell phone up to call Oliver Matthews, but it rang before he could make the call.

Aunt Grace.

"What's up?"

"Hal Collins called. He was on his way home from the rodeo and when he drove by my house, he noticed the Bronco was gone. It's not worth much, and I'm not really worried about it being stolen. It's just with Jodee and everything." She sighed. "I think someone should check on her."

He knew his aunt well enough to recognize the unspoken worry that travelled through the phone. He didn't blame her.

Since the moment he'd met Jodee, trouble seemed to hunt her down. How long before it went in for the kill?

And who else might be there when it did?

Covered in thorny shrub and riddled with loose rocks and hidden holes, the uneven terrain prevented a quick dash to safety.

With Aidan clinging to her back, Jodee lacked her usual sure footedness. Her ears sought to catch evidence of pursuit or the equally unwelcome buzz of a rattlesnake.

Don't think too much, just move. Failure is not an option.

She stumbled over an exposed root.

"Do you know where you're going?" Adian asked.

"Of course." *Though I'd have parked closer if I'd known I'd be packing out fifty pounds of frightened boy too injured to walk and too sick to wait.*

She also had not one life, but two to think of. Three if she counted her own. How long could Kimberly hang on?

Her heart kicked off its erratic cadence once again. Lowering Aidan to the ground, she dropped to her knees beside him as the list of things that could go wrong continued to grow. Did the kidnappers have night vision goggles? A tracking dog? Reinforcements to call in on ATVs that would make short work of overtaking them?

What if her own heart made her fail? She closed her eyes and reined in her fears.

Focus on what you know for certain. Don't overthink, just move.

The child weighed next to nothing, but already her legs burned from the exertion.

"You thirsty?" She looked at Aidan, his gaze riveted on the path they'd just taken. Even in the dark, she could see the worry etched into his pale face. She placed the water bottle in his hand. "We'll get her help. We will. Your . . .?"

"Sister."

"Right. Your sister. She's going to be okay." She looked away and swallowed, wondering why lying to him seemed the right thing to do when she had no reason to believe they'd make it in time. Not at the rate they were going.

Hope. The undeniable impulse wasn't an urge to lie. It was a need to fuel his determination to keep going. She plucked a piece of straw from his hair and thought of her own mother. "She loves you a lot."

The words resonated from a place inside her that had spent sixteen years longing for the same thing.

"Drink," she said, satisfied when he obeyed. She studied the wall of darkness surrounding them, listening.

"No matter how bad the weather gets, the sun's still shinin' on the other side." The old man's words spun a web around everything else in her head.

Well, Lord. I'd sure like to get to the side where the sun is shining. But I think I'm going to need a bigger umbrella for the storm I'm in right now. She bit her lip. Did that count as a prayer? Did she want it to?

She pulled the stone from her pocket, not certain that she'd witness the sun rise on another day, much less the mystical sunshine promised by his words. A new name. And more than that a belonging. Or what should have been the offer to belong.

She tucked it back in her pocket. Focus on her next step, not the mysterious meaning of a rock. Time was a commodity she couldn't waste.

With Aidan secured on her back, she continued.

Prayers sprang up from a place deep inside her she'd lost touch with long ago.

Simple words for Aidan and Kimberly repeated with each step. *Lord help them.*

She paused to get her bearings. *And if you can use me to do it, then so be it. I surrender. With all my heart, I surrender. Just don't let them die because of me.*

Not a rock, but a thought caused her to falter. How long had it been since she'd loved anyone with all of her heart? Or had she ever?

There'd always been a piece she held back, the piece that said without a father she didn't truly know who she was.

Because what if one day she knew, and it was something too ugly to bear?

A startled jackrabbit lunged from a clump of prickly pear and raced away.

We're all broken, Jodee. Stop acting as though you're the only one. Blue's words ricocheted through her.

Distracted, she didn't see the loose rock. It moved beneath her foot, twisting her ankle. She staggered, wobbling to maintain her balance. Her knees hit the ground, landing hard on a shrubby mesquite. A thorn sank deep into her knee.

"I thought *that* was about to get western," Aidan said, sarcasm clearly a skill he'd acquired at an early age.

His impish comment freed her from her brooding thoughts and drew a laugh.

"Next time you can carry me, then." She struggled to her feet once more and resumed walking until they neared the hidden Bronco, the damaged condition of his feet tugging at her heart.

No light broke through the darkness around them. Though it would have helped to see where she was going, she took that as a good sign.

Someone had to be looking for them by now. Sweat trailed along her scalp and made her long hair cling to her neck. Where were Rusty and Syrah?

When they were close to the Bronco, she tucked Aidan into a stand of tall grass and crept closer. Satisfied it hadn't been discovered, she retrieved Aidan and seated him in the passenger seat.

Without a doubt, Aidan's cowboy status was established by the way he pretended not to hurt as she buckled him in. She cranked the engine, then grit her teeth. There was no other way to get safely away without using the headlights. Tension roped through her as the beams split the night open, dividing it into the safety of the seen and the unknown danger of the dark.

She pulled onto the gravel road and gunned the engine in the opposite direction from where she'd come. Where it would take them, she didn't know, but it had to be better than where they'd been.

Aidan sat like a statue strapped to the seat, his eyes straight ahead. She needed to keep him from going into shock, but her own mind spun with too many questions.

"First one to spot a light gets an ice cream cone," she said. "Or a highway. A highway would be good too."

"Why would I want a highway?" he asked. "I'll take the ice cream. One scoop or two?"

She grinned. "Definitely two." Maybe he wasn't as near to going into shock as she feared.

Ten minutes later, they still hadn't seen another house or encountered a road sign to direct their path. If she ever wanted to go off the grid, now she knew where to go.

She checked the rearview mirror. The night closed behind them like a black curtain.

Alone again. The words whispered in her ears. But she wasn't alone. She had Aidan.

But you'll always be abandoned.

Not this time. Someone would come for them. Blue—

Blue was in jail, powerless to help them. But would he if he had the chance? Could she trust him? It was one thing to say he loved her, but a very different thing to really love her. To risk one's heart on love was not the same as risking one's life, was it? Twice before she'd heard the words and twice she'd been abandoned.

The engine coughed, then gasped its way to a stop as she maneuvered to the side of the road. The gas gauge read a quarter of a tank. She smacked the dashboard with her fist. The orange needle shivered, then came to a rest on the E.

Out of gas.

The feeling of betrayal jabbed her, and she struck the dashboard in anger.

Why God? Why? She slugged the dash again. From the corner of her eye, she caught Aidan watching her. Definitely *not superhero* behavior.

"Why don't you just call someone to help you?"

Why indeed? She refrained from telling him there wasn't any signal. Somehow it seemed like too much of an extinguisher of hope for him to have that information.

"I don't have my phone." Still she pulled out Blue's phone and stared at the screen. Was there something on there she needed to know? Something that might help her make sense of their situation?

"Yes you do."

"Okay, technically, that's true, but since I don't know the password, I might as well not have a phone."

"That's dumb. How do you not know your own password? Like it's supposed to be something you remember, like your birthday or the name of your second-grade teacher. Which is also dumb because some of us haven't had a second-grade teacher yet."

She couldn't argue with his assessment. Pride had made her stupid—or at least irresponsible.

After all, Jodee Trevaine didn't need anyone. She could take care of herself, right?

She looked in the rearview mirror with just enough light to see her face. *How's that working out for you?*

Pulling out Blue's phone, she stared at the screen, then at Aidan. "Since you seem to know so much about it, you don't happen to be some sort of child technology prodigy, do you?"

"What's a prodigy?"

"Someone with a gift."

"I'd like a phone for a gift."

"Not that kind of gift."

She tried Blue's birthday, the name of his first horse, the year he'd graduated from high school, and the brand of his favorite beer—though she hadn't seen one in his hand or anywhere near him since she'd run into him at the truck stop.

She even tried the date of the accident.

A warning box flashed to tell her she only had two more tries before the phone locked for good. She tucked it back in her pocket.

They couldn't sit here on the road all night. Like ducks on the pond just waiting for the hunters to arrive. But the Bronco itself would be a dead giveaway they were nearby. The only option was to not be nearby.

"Looks like we're on foot again." She stared at Aidan.

"Speak for yourself." He rolled his eyes.

She laughed. "Indeed."

"But first," she dug the foil wrapped chicken from her pocket, "you eat while I think."

She searched through the vehicle for a flashlight, first aid kit, expired granola bar, or anything that might come in useful without adding more weight to the load she already carried. When Aidan finished his snack, she helped him onto her back and began her search for a place to cross the fence. They needed to get off the road and out of sight.

They hadn't gone far when headlights swept across the pasture beside them as another vehicle rounded the corner. Jodee darted into the tall grass at the edge of the road, then stumbled down a sharp incline. Her toe caught on a vine growing over the slope, and she came down hard on her knees once again. Pain exploded up her legs, but she had to keep moving.

The barbed wire fence in front of her presented a bigger problem. She had to get them both to the other side without being seen, and she had to do it fast.

Switching Aidan to her arms, carrying him in front of her, she hunched low and kept moving. How much time did she have?

Lord, help us.

The straining muscles burned as though a blow torch set fire to her back. A game trail. The kind made by wild hogs and coyotes cut under the fence. A narrow depression in the packed soil, but enough room for them to wiggle through.

She dropped to the ground. A look of panic ghosted across his face as she sat him down and prepared to scramble under the fence. *He thinks I'm about to leave him.*

The thought pierced something deep inside her. She knew that feeling. With a tender touch, rubbed his cheek. "I'll go first, then help you through. How are your inch-worming skills?"

The fear drained from his eyes.

Rolling to her back, she worked her way beneath the sharp barbs. Once clear, she flipped to her stomach and pulled Aidan through.

The vehicle attached to the headlights that sent them running stopped. They'd found the Bronco. Soon they'd start searching along the ditch.

Aidan whimpered when she bumped his foot.

"I'm sorry, little guy, but now's when it's really about to get western. Since I forgot my phone and you said you didn't have a six shooter, we're just going to have to outsmart the bad guys. Are you ready?" She sensed more than saw his head nod. "When we get away from these guys, you can cry and scream all you want, but right now, we need to be as quiet as a mouse."

Car doors slammed, followed by Syrah's voice. "They're not here."

"Hood's still warm. They can't have gone far. After what you did to the boy, she'll have to carry him. You'll be lucky if Boss doesn't do the same to you, especially after you let him get away from you. I told Boss you couldn't handle it. Told him you were a mistake all along."

She tensed. *Rusty.*

"Shut up!" Syrah's voice hissed through the dark.

Jodee whispered close to Aidan's ear."Put your arms around my neck and hold on. We've got to keep moving." As soon as Rusty or Syrah found the game trail, they'd know where to look.

With the boy on her back, she crawled along the trail.

To her left, a beam of light cut through the night. The light swung their way. She flattened against the ground. The silhouette of an overgrown prickly pear hid them from view—this time.

"Which way do you think they went?" Syrah asked. They were moving along the road now.

"Blood Cut Creek's over here." Rusty let out a string of cuss words. "She's going to know she messed up when she messed with me."

"I'll believe it when I see it. She done bested you twice," Syrah mocked.

"Shut up, you stupid—" A slap of flesh striking flesh drowned out the rest of his speech.

Syrah's pained cry stabbed the air.

Jodee's muscles quivered. Syrah was no angel, but after what she'd done to Aidan, maybe she and the hateful brute deserved each other. But no. Somehow, she sensed that Rusty acted out of hate while Syrah acted out of a desperation to be loved and valued. Maybe she could empathize with that, though she didn't approve of the other woman's method of seeking it.

Thoughts of what Rusty would do to her if he caught them ignited her desire to keep going. Thoughts of failing to get Aidan the help he needed spurred her into action.

Think. She didn't want her next move to be her last one. She had to get Aidan to safety and find a way to send help for Kimberly.

Jodee hadn't crossed Blood Cut Creek—a name she now officially hated—before running out of gas, so it must lie ahead of them. If they were headed in that direction, she'd go in the opposite. If they were following logic, she'd do the illogical. She'd head away from both the road and the creek, pushing further into the brush. As the voice of their pursuers faded, she rose, and lifting Aidan, headed into the tenuous protection of the unknown bramble before them.

The weight of Aidan's physical body seemed trivial to the weight of responsibility she felt to protect him.

The self-sufficient life she thought she'd rooted herself in crumbled away beneath her steps. She didn't know who she would be when this was over, but she knew she could never be the same.

CHAPTER 37

In a forest of a hundred thousand trees, no two leaves are alike. And no two journeys along the same path are alike. ~Paolo Coelho

Jodee stumbled more often now, her feet growing heavier with every step. How long had they been moving up the narrow wash she'd found? She wanted to pull her boots off and sink her aching feet into one of the cool patches of silt and sand still damp from the recent rains.

Aidan's grip had loosened. With one hand, she held his thin arms in front of her while she wrapped the other behind her to support him. Every few yards, she leaned forward and swapped arms as her muscles began to cramp.

Were they far enough from the road to chance resting? Would she be able to go again if she stopped now? Superhero M.O. being what it was, better to press on.

This draw gouged out of the stony clay and cobble wasn't Blood Cut Creek, where Rusty and Syrah were looking for them. The shelter of its banks gave her a sense of safety.

The moon worked its way up now. Third quarter, so she guessed the time to be after midnight. She paused to listen for evidence of someone following.

The sound that filled her ears this time, though, alarmed her just as much.

Feral hogs. Her pulse skyrocketed. She'd heard people say wild hogs were attracted to the smell of blood, able to catch the scent from as much as five miles away. She didn't know if that was true, but now wasn't the time to research the matter further.

The need to find a safe place where the hogs couldn't get them jolted new energy into her legs.

She jogged away from the sound. Pain ran through her limbs like liquid fire, but stopping wasn't an option.

The moonlight played off the limestone as she rounded a corner, making the scene in front of her appear as though painted in sepia. Her gaze landed on a large rock in the middle of the creek bed. Deposited eons ago, the boulder stood over five feet tall. They might be safe on top of it—if she could get them there.

She lifted Aidan as high as she could. "Hold on and try to pull while I push." His toes banged against the rock, and he yelped.

Behind her, a pig squealed. Things were about to get real western for sure if they didn't hurry.

The boy clung to the rock like a stick tight while she pushed him up. Once over the edge, he used his elbows to work himself to the center.

With a running start, Jodee leapt, gritting her teeth in anticipation. With nothing to hold on to, her palms scraped across the rough surface. One moment she was sliding backward and the next she felt herself being lifted. She planted her elbows and tensed her upper body. With slow, measured effort, she worked the toe of a boot over the top.

Rolling to her back, she stared up at the stars. She lay still, breathing in the night air as the pigs began to grunt and squeal as they rooted in the creek bed below.

"Jodee?"

"Yeah?"

"You know there's no such thing as superheroes, right?"

Did she know that? Maybe not superheroes, but there must be something out there. She hadn't made it to the top of this rock on her own. Or had she once again, as Blue suggested, needed a hero, so she imagined one. She squeezed her eyes shut to stop the tears. "Well, there should be."

"Are you scared?"

"Absolutely." She wanted to lie and tell him they'd be fine, but he'd been through too much and he was too smart.

"Do you think Kimber's okay?"

She drew in a long breath, then exhaled. "I do." She couldn't explain why she believed it, but she wasn't just offering the right answer to comfort the boy. "Do you want to tell me about her?"

The softness in her voice matched the softness growing in her heart. A heart she'd kept hardened for too long. Like the delicate shoots of new growth on a forest floor, new life took root inside her. And like those tender new shoots, it was fighting its way to the light.

Jodee startled awake with a sharp inhale. The darkness on the eastern horizon faded as a new day edged closer. She hadn't meant to sleep. Her pulse jerked and sped like a frightened colt. Aidan lay curled up asleep beside her. The aroma of baking bread filled her senses. Her stomach growled. What had awoken her?

The noisy grunting of the pigs receded. They were moving away. She eased herself up on an elbow and stared at the dark. Was someone out there?

Shapes in shades of black and gray still surrounded them. Trees, like stalwart soldiers standing guard.

She turned in the direction of the pigs. Her breath caught at the silhouette of a man. The edges of the duster he wore flapped around his legs as he followed behind the pigs.

The figure paused, tipping his head down as though to look back over his shoulder. Darkness hid the features of his face, but the subtle nod seemed to offer guidance.

She blinked and he was gone. If, in fact, he'd ever really been there. Perhaps he was nothing more than the lingering effects of her recent head injury. But if the peace he left her with was the remnant of a head injury, maybe she didn't mind.

You needed a hero, so you imagined one, Blue had said.

Only this was too real. It might not make sense. And she didn't understand why, but her heart leaned into his presence—real or imagined. She wanted to believe he—whoever he was—existed.

She yawned and brushed her fingers through Aidan's hair.

He was too hot. She pressed her palm against his feverish forehead. The heat radiated up her arm.

Anger welled inside her.

Her fisted hand struck the rock beneath her, but it was the blow she felt inside that knocked the breath from her lungs. The tears rained down like a summer storm that appears without warning. The hardness inside her broke.

She didn't want to keep trying to do this on her own. She couldn't.

You were never meant to.

"Then come for me. If you love me, prove it. If you won't save me, save Aidan." Her words whispered into the air as tears continued to stream from the broken well of hurt and anger inside.

In the emptiness of her broken heart, she felt a presence. No words, nothing tangible. Only the notion that maybe she'd been running in the wrong direction for most of her life.

A tugging on her sleeve drew her from the moment. She opened her eyes to find the dry creek bed stirring back to life beneath the rays of the sun.

"Ma'am," Aidan's groggy voice sought her attention.

She sat up and wiped her eyes. "Good morning, my brave little Superhero. Did you enjoy the Superhero accommodations of the Big Rock Bed and No Breakfast?"

"Better than the last place I stayed." His attempt at a smile was only half-hearted.

"Love the positivity!" She winked. His weakened condition worried her. *Stay positive.* "But as wonderful as this place is, how about we go find us a nice hot stack of pancakes? Do you like pancakes?"

"Yep." He placed a hand over his stomach. "But I don't feel much like eating right now."

She handed him the rest of the bottled water. "We'll see what we can do about that appetite, but I need you to drink some water now."

She ached to feel the wetness in her own mouth, but Aidan needed it more.

If she made a mistake now, she could walk Aidan right back into danger. Was anyone looking for them? And by anyone she meant anyone who might rescue them? Logan or Grace? Blue?

Was he still locked up?

"Jodee." Aidan looked at her. "I wanna go home."

Beloved, come home.

"Me too, kid." In more ways than one. "So that is exactly what we are going to do."

She spoke the words with a confidence she wasn't sure she trusted as she at the freckle-faced boy beside her. But she would get this right. "I promise. We're going home."

She slid from the rock and landed with a thud in the dirt. Dusting herself off, she motioned Aidan to the edge. Redness crept up his foot, the sign of a spreading infection that sent alarm racing through her. She had no room for error, but she didn't know which way to turn for help.

Never will I leave you. Never will I forsake you.

Did she believe those words? Something inside her latched onto them. She had nothing else to lose.

Knowing who they were up against might be helpful if they were going to get out of this alive. Knowing *why* they were up against them could be essential.

"Aidan, can you tell me about who took you?" Jodee had seen Syrah and Rusty, but there was one more. Someone Kimberly had called Nolan. Maybe he was the man who'd first lured Aidan from the store. Rusty had referred to someone as Boss. That title didn't seem to fit what she'd heard about Nolan so far.

"There was a nice man. He's the one who—"

She sensed him debating something in his head. "It's okay. You're not in trouble, and maybe what you tell me will help him not be too." Though she doubted that.

"He said he had a red car, but he didn't. He lied. But he was actually pretty nice. She was nice sometimes too, when she wasn't whacked out on meth."

"Whacked out on meth?" What does a six-year-old know about being *whacked out on meth?*

"My dad had a pipe just like hers."

"She was smoking meth in front of you?" Jodee was not thinking turn-the-other-cheek kinds of thoughts now.

"No, Nolan—he was the nice one—always took me to another room. They let me stay in the house. Until I tried to run away."

Cupping his cheek, she looked him in the eyes. "You're one of the bravest people I've ever known, you know that?"

His eyes clouded, the collection of many days' worth of tears brewing in a storm of emotion threatening to break loose.

"It's okay, sweetheart. I'm going to get you home and back to your sister." She stumbled over the last word, regretting the mention since the last time she'd seen Kimberly she'd been tied up in a barn in the middle of an asthma attack. They also hadn't had a chance to discuss what he'd said last night. Was she his mother or his sister?

"That woman said she'd fix it so I couldn't ever runaway again. She said then I'd be too much trouble for anyone to love me. She laughed and said I'd be just like her." His lip quivered as he fought the urge to cry. "I don't want to be mean and ugly."

"That *woman* is mean and crazy. You don't believe a thing she said." She bobbed her head to catch his gaze, forcing him to look at her. "Promise me. Kimberly loves you, and I love you too. I'm not going to give up. I will never abandon you and neither will she. So, you promise me, or I'll throw you over my shoulder and carry you like a sack of taters the rest of the way. And that would not be good for your superhero appearance." She tickled his sides, and he rewarded her with a giggle.

"I promise."

She faced up the creek the way the man in the duster had seemed to indicate she should go.

Please Lord, let me not be wrong. I don't know who this man is I keep seeing, but I'm counting on him being one of yours.

Light glistened off something at her feet. She looked down to find Blue's phone trampled in the dirt. It must have fallen from her pocket last night. From the cracks in what remained and the pieces missing, the hogs must have given it a taste test. She didn't bother retrieving it.

With Aidan on her back, they started out again. Even though she prayed, even though she'd made a promise she was determined to keep, doubt still niggled at the edges of her mind as her steps ate away at the space between them and whatever came next.

"Do you have any idea why they took you or what they wanted?" From the looks of Kimberly's financial situation, ransom couldn't be the reason. She also didn't think the boy had been trafficked. They wouldn't have kept him in the area if that were the purpose. At least that's what she wanted to believe. Plus, Rusty had been sent to guard Kimberly. That didn't fit in with the kidnapping. Unless the ransom was being demanded from someone else. The dad, maybe?

His head shook against her back. "I thought maybe it was because of my dad, but he never came."

Exhaustion exposed itself in the wavering tone of his words. Still, she needed to know. She found a stump and lowered him to it.

"Where is your dad? Why would you think he might do this?"

Several breaths came and went before he spoke again. "I'm not supposed to talk about him."

"Why not?"

He looked away. "My dad's not a nice man. That's why Kimber took me away."

"So, if Kimberly is your sister, where's your mom?"

"Dead."

If Kimberly had run away with him, she could be arrested, leaving the possibility that Aidan would be returned to an abusive father.

Taking him to the hospital could expose all of this.

She had no other choice, though. He needed medical care. His feet were too injured for home remedies.

Her empty stomach soured at the thought of saving the boy from one danger to return him to another.

CHAPTER 38

The true meaning of life is to plant trees, under whose shade you do not expect to sit. ~Nelson Henderson

The King, the Big Man, the Potentate—the prattling words of a crazy woman rattled in Jodee's head. She'd insisted Jodee would know him when she met him. *Had she met him?*

Tillie's wild claims battled their way to the forefront of her thoughts as she wrestled with the tangled web that ensnared her.

The abduction of first Aidan and then Kimberly. The break-in at Grace's house and Blue's cap. The attempt to silence her. Blue's camper fire and arrest. She had no shortage of *whys* to consider. It was becoming clear that the key to understanding *why* might be knowing *who*. But that led her back to why again. The endless loop of questions on repeat.

They'd been following a cattle trail that cut through the brush for what seemed like hours. There was less shade on the exposed path than they'd had in the creek bed. As hot as she was, Aidan had to be miserable beneath this sun. But cow trails always led to either food or water. Surely this was the most practical route to take.

The muscles in her back balled fiery pain. Her steps plodded along at a tortoise-like pace. How long had it been since she'd eaten or had a sip of water?

When she tripped over nothing for the second time, it was time for a rest.

She deposited Aidan with as much care as possible in the sparse shade of a mesquite tree, then dropped to the ground beside him. He'd stopped talking a while back. When he'd failed to respond to her efforts at humor, she'd decided the best thing she could do was focus on finding help fast.

Maybe stopping wasn't a good idea. She wasn't sure she'd be able to lift him again when it was time to move.

Traveling without him would be faster. Aidan leaned over to lie on the ground at her side, his brow sweaty, eyes closed, his face flushed. She'd never be able to leave him, though.

No sign of life anywhere. No farmhouse, no road. Just this lone cattle trail.

She lowered her eyes from the horizon and spotted a pile of cow manure. Only a few days old, and the best thing she'd seen in days. If there were cows, then there had to be water nearby.

She touched his forehead and frowned. He was burning up.

"Hang in there, buddy." She pulled the water bottle with the last of the water from her pocket and forced him to take a sip. Unable to bear the sight of his feet, she stood. It didn't take a medical professional to see that the infection was spreading.

Shielding her eyes from the sun, Jodee scanned the surroundings. "Okay, mister. Whoever you are. I need some help here."

She made a full circle. No man in a duster waiting on the horizon. She sniffed. No baking bread. "Guess we're on our own for this one."

Never will I leave you.

Yeah, well I'm feeling pretty alone right now, Jodee answered the voice in her head as though debating an actual person and not her own insanity. Only it didn't feel like insanity. The words felt real.

A flash of light caught her eye. Gone before she could see what caused it. Had she really seen it? She chose to believe she had.

She scooped Aidan into her arms and headed in the direction where the flash had been. Fifteen minutes later, she spotted the roof of a barn. Drawing closer, she saw an old mobile home nearby. A new energy propelled her legs down the slope, still following the cattle trail.

An uneasiness wormed its way along her sweat drenched spine. She angled toward the barn, studying the house, annoyed by the check in her spirit that told her to proceed with caution. Aidan didn't have time for caution. He needed help fast.

Settling Aidan out of sight in the shadows beside the barn, she surveyed the house. Ill kept and dilapidated, but there didn't appear to be a dog waiting to attack her.

She didn't have time to stall around in hopes the premonition would go away. Sucking in a deep breath, she strode to the house and knocked on the back door.

Shuffling inside told her someone was home. It was an old man who opened the door. Dressed in faded denim overalls over a wife beater white undershirt that had stopped being white years ago, he stared at her, his bottom lip sagging open as his eyes narrowed.

The theme song to Gunsmoke blared from inside.

"I need to borrow your phone. It's an emergency," she blurted.

He scratched at his unshaven cheeks, the sound elevating her wariness.

"I ain't ever seen you before. Where you from?" The smell of snuff on his breath identified the brown stain trailing down his chin.

"My name is . . . Rose." She blinked at the sound of her middle name rolling off her tongue, unsure why she'd used it instead of her given name. "I've been hiking, and I got lost. My son's hurt and I need to get him to a doctor."

The man stared. The smell wafting from inside the house carried a sense of hopelessness, as though she'd opened a door to a time fifty years ago, releasing a slowly decaying life that'd been trapped inside the dreary house for the past five decades.

"Please, I just need to call Sheriff Adams."

The man recoiled as though she tossed a bucket of spiders in his face. His eyes watered as grief stained his features. "I don't get involved. You go on and get out of here now."

He started to close the door, but she braced it with her arm. "Please, just one call and no one has to know you're the one who let me. I promise I won't say a thing."

She didn't know how it could possibly matter, but clearly it did.

The man leaned toward her, voice lowered. "The people around here who stay alive are the ones that don't see nuthin'. You go on and get away from here."

He shoved the door closed.

She looked back at the barn. The sense of foreboding that had troubled her before she knocked on the door now pressed against her. Time drained away from her with every second she spent wondering what to do.

Hurrying to where she'd left Aidan, she picked him up and headed toward the road on the other side of the house. At least that was something.

Sight of another house across the road and about a hundred yards away triggered renewed hope.

She checked to see if they were being watched. Or worse, followed. But the house with the bitter old man remained closed, curtains drawn as though light were somehow offensive to the fermenting grief that had spilled through the open door when he'd opened it.

This town is a flesh of distrust clinging to the skeletal bones of evil. Blue's words came back to her in a harsh wave of recognition.

She stared at the house in the distance.

Lord, please let this one be friendly. Because if she couldn't find a phone, even the threat of prison wouldn't keep her from doing whatever it took to get help for Aidan.

The terrain sloped downward still, requiring less effort to get there.

Again, she approached from the backside, but this time, she kept Aidan with her. A water faucet near the back door caught her eye.

The boy shivering in her arms needed fluid. She eased him to the ground, propping him against the house, and turned on the faucet until a small stream appeared from the end of the hose. She let the water run for a few seconds, purging out the warm water that would taste like a rubber hose, before holding the cool water in front of the boy. Her own mouth longed for a drink, but Aidan first.

"Aidan, take a small sip for me."

The boy blinked, his eyes unfocused, then swayed toward the water. Water trickled down his chin and dampened his shirt. He stopped too soon. She took a quick sip while he rested. The cool, water filled her parched mouth like summer rain falling on the desert floor, restoring fresh life. Then she helped him drink again.

Footsteps from inside the house told her someone was home. They'd likely been alerted to her presence by the sound of the running water. She moved so Aidan was behind her as the door cracked open. *Please don't let them shoot first and ask questions later.*

"What are you doing in my flower bed? This ain't a public drinking fountain," an elderly woman said, her voice laden with annoyance and a touch of fear.

"My name is Rose, and I need to use your phone." The name rolled off her tongue much more easily this time. "Please. It's an emergency."

The door opened enough to give the woman a better view. Her eyes widened at the sight of Aidan's bruised and swollen feet.

"Please, he's hurt. He needs a doctor," Jodee begged. "I just want to borrow your phone."

The woman hesitated. "Wait here." She returned with a cup of water and a damp cloth for Aidan. "How'd the boy get hurt?"

"Our car broke down. He tripped and fell while we were walking." She recognized the skepticism in the woman's eyes. She could say more, maybe even tell the truth, but something held her back. Once again, a premonition wiggled over her.

"What did you say your name was?" The woman's gaze traveled over the horizon behind them, as though she expected a party of Comanche warriors to come bearing down on them.

"Rose."

"You all go on up on the back porch out of the sun. I'll make the call."

Suspicion made Jodee's fingers tingle. It radiated up her shoulders and the back of her neck. But she did as she'd been asked, carrying Aidan to a wicker swing in the shade of the porch.

Soon the door opened again, though the woman stood just inside as though intent on keeping a barrier between them.

"Someone's on the way. I'll wait up front to let them know where to find you." Her eyes darted up to Jodee, then jerked away.

Prickles of unease raced up her spine. "Who did you call? Are they sending an ambulance?"

"They'll be here soon." The woman responded without making eye contact. "Is there anything else I can get you while you wait?"

Jodee shook her head, unsettled by the woman's odd behavior.

Maybe she read too much into it. The woman could be shy or maybe she had an abusive husband she's afraid of. There were a thousand reasons why she might act the way she did that had nothing to do with Jodee and Aidan. And yet she didn't think so.

She moved to the faucet, pretending to re-dampen the cloth. From there, she crept to the corner of the house that gave her a clear view of the driveway. Maybe fifty yards long and lined with a fence covered in vines.

She returned to Aidan, tenderly wiping his hot skin with the cool cloth. She tried to count the time. How long until someone arrived? She made a pattern of returning to the faucet every few minutes to soak the cloth in cool water. The heat from his body dissipated the coolness quickly, but it also gave her a way to keep an eye out for approaching vehicles.

On her fourth trip, a black pickup turned into the driveway. She pressed a hand to the side of the house as her knees threatened to buckle. The same black pickup that was always present at the wrong time. This explained the woman's odd behavior. She hadn't called for help. She'd called in more harm.

She couldn't outrun them while carrying Aidan, but she

wouldn't just sit here and wait. Sprinting back to the porch, she scooped Aidan in her arms, motioning for him to stay quiet, though she wasn't sure much of what was happening registered.

She bolted down the steps to the corner of the house. She peeked around in time to see Rusty disappearing around the other side. Her gaze settled back on the black truck. She'd never before appreciated the sound of a running engine so much.

She half shoved, half tossed Aidan to the passenger seat as she jumped behind the wheel. Slamming the truck in reverse, she spun it around in a spray of gravel. They were barreling down the driveway before anyone realized what was happening. In the rearview mirror she watched as Rusty ran onto the driveway. Even through the dust and distance, she could feel his murderous rage.

It removed all doubt as to what would happen if he caught them.

She'd be a dead woman.

CHAPTER 39

Texas 1874

A tree is known by its fruit; a man by his deeds. A good deed is never lost; he who sows courtesy reaps friendship, and he who plants kindness gathers love. ~Saint Basil

ose's request rattled through Will like a murder of startled crows taking flight. What happened that night wasn't something he wanted to remember, though he'd never forgotten. And the truth of her parent's brutal death certainly wasn't something she'd want to hear.

He didn't want her living with the truth of the night for the rest of her life. Now the only scar it had left her with was on her arm. Once she knew the details, she'd be scarred in the deepest parts of her heart.

He also didn't want her to realize it was cowardice that made him abandon her, breaking the promise he'd made. On the day after her parent's death—her first real day as an orphan—he'd left her in the hands of strangers.

If she knew the truth, she might forgive him, but she'd never respect him. How could she? Her own father had declared Will a man, yet when she needed him most, he'd acted like a frightened little boy who made promises he wasn't man enough to keep.

As he'd grown into the man he was now, life had shown him that people let others down all the time by making promises they lacked the power to keep. But it had been the last promise he'd ever made.

Until he'd married his wife. And even now he kept his promises few.

Life was too unexpected.

"Please, Will."

"It's not an easy thing to say, much less to hear." He stared down the street, unable to look at her.

"Then come back to the café. You can tell me over a piece of pie. It'll sweeten things up." The twinkle he found in her eyes when he glanced at her now snared him, though he knew there was no pie sweet enough to make what he would say easier to swallow.

Two hours later, they sat across from each other, empty pie plates in front of them and an empty café around them as he finished telling her about Abel and Essie Charidy and the life they'd planned to build on top of the plateau. She'd finagled details from him he hadn't meant to share—like those of Luther and Cub DeGroot and how they'd left her parents to burn inside their home.

He'd hoped something might draw forth a glimmer of memory from her to satisfy the question that troubled him ever since that night.

Who had lifted Rose out of the fire through the window? Whose hands were those holding her before she dropped into his arms? The more he'd thought about it, the more convinced he was that it hadn't been Abel's hands. He knew the hands that had taught him how to shoot a gun and skin a deer.

"I want to see." Rose's words broke into his thoughts.

"See?"

"Yes. I want to go there. I want to see where my parents died. I want to see this place where they planned to make a home and a life for our family."

"It won't be the same." Will himself had never been back, though he knew a community had established itself in the area. El Hueso—The Bone—the name alone was reason enough to stay away.

"I don't care. If everything you've said is true, then to walk on the same ground they did is the last connection—the only connection—I have left with the people who gave me life."

He cleared a throat clogged with emotion. "You have me."

"True, but . . . I've felt so . . . distant and unconnected from these people who were my mother and father for so long. I mean, the Muellars were good people. They took me in and raised me as their own. I had a happy life, but there was always something missing. I need to feel their presence again." She put her hand on his sleeve. "I have to do this, Will. Please."

"You aren't going to find them there." Unexpected apprehension scraped up his back. Were the DeGroots still there? What would happen if they recognized him? Even worse, what would happen if they recognized Rose? They'd meant for her to die too that horrible night.

"If you won't take me, I'll find someone who will."

The stubborn streak that had annoyed him as a boy cropped up to nettle him again. Some things a person just didn't outgrow.

"Please, Will."

The fear she would go there with someone else—someone who wouldn't know the danger—along with the intensity in her gaze, destroyed his resolve. He sighed. "Can you go tomorrow?"

El Hueso was a day's ride away. To get there and back, with time in between for her to see whatever it was she hoped to find, would be a three-day journey. Three more days away from his family, but he owed Rose at least this much. He'd let her down as a child. How could he abandon her in this one wish now?

He'd send a telegraph to Amanda letting her know of the delay. "We'll ride to New Plenty tomorrow. You can get a hotel room there, then we can go to El Hueso the next day."

He stared at the crumbs of pie on the dirty plate in front of him, the smear of cherry juice on the white porcelain glaring back at him like a harbinger.

CHAPTER 40

Love is like a tree, it grows of its own accord, it puts down deep roots into our whole being. ~Victor Hugo

The awning covered drive of the New Plenty Emergency Room greeted Jodee like the father welcoming home his prodigal son. She ran into those arms and screeched to a black cloud of smoke producing stop. The stench of burning rubber stung her nose as she sprinted around the truck to lift Aidan's unconscious body into her arms.

"It's Aidan. Aidan Truett." Jodee yelled the information to the nurses rushing for them.

"How long has he been unconscious?"

"He passed out five minutes ago." Jodee's voice cracked. Five minutes. They'd been so close. What if it had still been too far? He couldn't die. Not now. Not after all he'd survived to get here.

The medical melee that followed had her spinning in streaks of blues and greens and pinks. Pummeled with questions intertwined with sharp commands and crisp strings of numbers that communicated in a language she didn't speak. Grace. Where was Grace?

The sterile world of white walls and shiny metal bed frames blurred around her. They were taking him away.

No. She'd given him to the doctors and nurses. He needed them, not her. So why then did the absence of him in her arms create a hollow rawness in her middle? As though she were a shell. Where once she'd held something precious, now she felt empty, as though she'd been robbed of the one thing—the one worthy thing—that gave her purpose. Her arms moved restlessly at her side as though they didn't know what to do.

A hurricane of urgency stormed around her as she stood frozen in the eye of the tempest. Her heart lurched into its erratic beating. The sensation of falling into a dark vortex crept over her, and she swayed.

"Whoa there." An arm slipped around her shoulders, saving her from a fall. "Let's get you into a room and get you checked out."

The words tore through the daze, tearing her away from reality. "No. Not me. There's no time. I need—" Her words slurred together as a stabbing pain pierced her. She clawed at the invisible knife razoring deep into her chest. Kimberly. She had to get help. "I have to talk to Sheriff Adams."

The voice attached to the arm supporting her resonated from some place far away.

"Somebody get me a gurney."

Logan swung his patrol unit around, sliding to a halt behind the black truck parked under the ER awning.

Both the driver's and passenger's doors were flung open.

Through the glass doors, the organized chaos of an ER unit in action halted him. He'd received the call as soon as the hospital realized what was happening. Thankfully, he'd been just around the corner on his way to the station.

He shoved through the door as Jodee was lifted onto a stretcher.

Her lack of cooperation had them wrestling her onto her back, and still required more than one to hold her down.

"I have to talk to the Sheriff. Somebody find Sheriff Adams." The pinched sound of her voice was thick with distress. "There's a woman in danger. Stop! I'm not going anywhere with you until I talk to him."

Logan inserted himself in the midst of the medical attendants surrounding her. People trying to do their jobs though the patient refused to cooperate. "I'm here."

She turned to him, her face pale and seized with pain. "Kimberly. You have to get Kimberly." She jerked her arm away from a nurse trying to slip a needle into her arm. "Get away from me. I have to—" Her sentence ended in an agonized cry.

Logan looked at the attendant. "What's going on?"

"She's exhibiting the signs of a heart attack. We need to get her calmed down. Are you a friend or relative?"

"I don't need to calm down. I need Sheriff Adams," she swallowed, "to listen to me."

A frowning Dr. Hyson burst into the commotion, intercepting a volley of details relating to Jodee which ended with a brief summary of her lack of cooperation.

"You're having a possible MI. A heart attack. You understand that every second you delay on getting help, you take your life in your own hands?" The censure in his voice failed to affect her attitude.

"My life has never been in my own hands, and it's not in yours either." Jodee growled the words through gritted teeth. "Now please, Logan, listen to me."

"Dr. Hyson, we're ready in the OR."

"I'm going to finish what you started in saving that boy. Don't you have the audacity to die on me before I get back." Dr. Hyson gave Logan a sharp look, then took off in the direction of the OR with a nurse beside him rattling off a list of vital signs and lab results.

"Logan, listen to me." She reached for his hand and he let her take it.

She swallowed as though her mouth was too dry.

"Kimberly. She's at the farm." Jodee's eyes squeezed closed as her fingers clamped around his. "Asthma attack . . . wouldn't come. You have to . . . find her." Tears slid from the corners of her eyes.

Her words curdled in his stomach. "Where?"

He listened as she made a piecemeal description of where she'd found Aidan. He knew the place, and he knew who lived there and who they worked for. His lips set in a grim understanding.

Logan reached for the handset radio attached to the shoulder of his uniform.

The nurse began wheeling her away.

"Wait. There's something else." She licked at her cracked lips as he hurried beside her down the hallway. "Kimberly . . . not mother. Sister. Protecting him from his father. Please." Pain distorted her features. She grimaced as they slipped the oxygen mask over her mouth.

"Times up, Sheriff." The nurse pushed him away from the gurney.

As he watched them wheel her through the doors beneath a radiology sign, he radioed dispatch, putting two units and an ambulance en route to the place she'd described. "The ambulance personnel are to stay back in the vehicle until the scene is secure. We don't know who might be there but proceed as though all parties are armed and dangerous."

All except the one fighting for her life. He prayed she won the battle. For the sake of justice.

And for the sake of his heart.

CHAPTER 41

Happiness is like a tree going into the sky; and sadness is like the roots going down into the wombs of the earth. Both are needed. ~Osho

On the far bank of the river, a stream of water so clear, so dazzling that it almost hurt to look at it. A strong and steady current filled with life. Her parched soul longed for the feel of it. An irresistible desire to drink deeply drew her closer.

A pleasant awareness she wasn't alone settled around her. He was there. Her stepfather, Paul, on the opposite side, his familiar smile warming her. Behind him stood a woman beneath a tree. Someone Jodee had never seen yet felt drawn to by an invisible bond. Both Paul and the woman looked away as though something farther up the river drew their attention. His face glowed with a new radiance, and Jodee searched to see what had caused this change.

That's when she saw Him. He walked to the edge of the flowing stream of life between them. His eyes met hers and a cascade of love swept over her.

He stepped into the water, walking toward her. In His hand He held something she couldn't see. Yielding to the fierce longing within her, she stepped into the stream, moving toward where He stood in the middle. The rush of the water felt pleasant against her legs. Her lungs seemed to inflate with air as though she'd never really breathed before.

"I've always been here, Jodee." His voice floated over her.

Her legs gave way beneath the release of the burden she'd forced herself to carry. Not alone. Not abandoned.

He caught her in the tender security of His embrace.

A breeze whispered around her, fluttering through her hair, and carrying words that only her soul could hear.

"You have never been alone, my Beloved Daughter. Trust in my love."

He turned His palm up, revealing deep scars. In His hand was a stone with a name written on it—her true name. No longer fatherless. She never had been.

A longing for the opposite shore pulled at her. But something caught at her hand, pulling her back. She wanted to shake it off, make it release her. Paul and the woman disappeared. No!

The pulling persisted and she glanced back. A string of faces—Aidan, Blue, Kimberly, her own mother, fluttered before her.

"Jodee, you're home now, but your time on that side of the river is not yet done. There is still good for you to do there."

She felt herself shaking her head, not wanting to accept the words. Not wanting to leave the peace that enveloped her in its warmth.

"You're never alone, Jodee. Don't be afraid."

"Jodee, come back to us."

Where was it? She inhaled again. She needed to smell it. The aroma of baking bread. If she smelled it, then she'd know she wasn't alone. But the only smell that greeted her was that of industrial strength disinfectant and steri-tape.

She wanted it back. The dream—it had ended too soon.

Aidan. Was he okay? A firm hand rested on her shoulder, gently pushing her back onto the bed when she tried to sit.

"Welcome back. You left us for a moment." The kind voice subtly told her she'd passed out. "It took a minute to get you back, but you've been resting and stable ever since."

Was the nurse saying she'd actually died?

"Did I—"

"Did you what?" the nurse asked.

"Never mind." Maybe she didn't want to know. What difference did it make? She was here now.

She didn't know if it was exhaustion or medication that made her eyelids heavy, but it took work to get them fully opened. She looked around the unfamiliar room. How long had she been out? She licked dry lips. "Where's Aidan? Is he okay?"

"You his parent or guardian?"

Jodee shook her head, a slow movement, as though maybe the nurse wouldn't notice the negative answer.

"Technically, HIPAA laws forbid me from giving out that information to someone without his parent's consent." She cocked her head and stepped closer. "But I can tell you that all of our patients are currently stable and resting." She aimed a look of warning at Jodee. "As should you be."

"I need to talk to Sheriff Adams," she mumbled.

The nurse patted her arm. "Again? You got a crush on the man? He is nice looking."

Jodee ignored the comments. There was only one nice looking man she was interested in. "What do you mean again?"

"He was right beside you when you—"

"Don't say it," Jodee cut her off. Hearing the words actually spoken would make it too real. "What did I tell him?"

The nurse pressed two fingers to the inside of Jodee's wrist and checked her watch with her other hand.

"Couldn't say. I was focused on other things. Like keeping you from becoming un-alived." With a sly look, her eyes cut to Jodee, then back to her watch. She frowned. "I need you to stay calm now, okay? You gave us a pretty good scare when your heart stopped. Let's don't get it worked up again just yet."

"Where's Grace?"

"Grace was in the OR with your little friend. I'm sure she'll be back around in a bit."

"Aidan. His name is Aidan." Jodee's nerves chafed at the constant placating. She needed to check on him. "I must have just had a little dizzy spell. My eating and sleeping has been a little off these past few days. I'm fine now." She tried to sit.

"Girl, you had more than a dizzy spell." The nurse nudged her back onto the pillow.

It was then she noticed her shirt had been replaced by a hospital gown. "Where are my—" She stopped herself just before saying clothes. No sense creating the worry that she might be planning to escape before they made their quota. "My belongings?"

"They're in a bag beneath the bed." The nurse paid more attention to the computer screen on the rolling cart than she did the patient in the bed.

"A panic attack. That must be what happened." She'd never had one, but if it would put everyone at ease so they'd leave her alone, she was happy with that diagnosis. "I'm fine now. Really."

"Hmmm." The nurse continued tapping on the keyboard. "We'll just let Dr. Hyson double check that self-diagnosis." She looked at Jodee and winked.

"What is this?" She motioned to the bag of fluid hanging from the tree.

"Just some saline solution to get you hydrated."

"You haven't given me any medicine though, right? I don't need any drugs."

"So, you're a doctor now?"

Jodee bit her tongue at the grating remark. "I don't *want* any drugs."

"Just a few shots of epinephrine. Now rest. I'm going to step out for a minute. You're stable now, but we'll get Dr. Hyson in here to check you out soon." The nurse kicked the door stopper free and glanced back at Jodee. "Relax and don't go givin' us another scare."

The door closed, and she slumped against the pillows, eyes closed.

The soft scrape of the door opening again interrupted her prayer. She opened her eyes hoping to see Dr. Hyson. Instead, a man dressed in everyday street clothes slipped through the door. He eased it closed behind him without looking at her.

When he did turn her way, a shiver stole over her, leaving a lingering unease. "Hello, Jodee. I'm so relieved to see you feeling better. You gave me a good scare."

She frowned until she recalled meeting him with Grace and Logan that night at the tree.

Grace's refusing to accept his offer to clean up the storm damage had perplexed her. Suspicion stuck inside her like a shard of glass.

He stepped closer and held out his hand. "Judge Harrison DeGroot. We met a few nights ago out by the broken oak."

Something sinister slithered up her arm as she shook his hand. She pulled her hand away, burying it beneath the blanket as she regretted the touch.

"I hear you're quite the hero." He grinned.

"Hardly." She stared at the man, unable to discern the reason for the discomfort she felt, the unease that constricted around her heart.

He pulled up a chair—too close—and sat.

"You need your rest, and we don't have much time, so I'll get right to the point." His lips twitched as he glanced at the door. "The boy you rescued has something of mine. It's extremely important I get it back."

She stared at the machine scratching out jagged lines while she took in his words.

Aidan had talked about finding a box that he'd then hidden. But he also said he'd told Rusty and Syrah where to find it, even though he'd planned to keep it his secret. Weren't they all in this together?

He raised his hand to stop her when she started to speak.

"I'm sure he's told you the same thing he told us. And I do believe he's telling the God's honest truth."

His reference to God piqued her resentment. She doubted very much this man knew God, much less His *honest truth.*

Until the last few days, she hadn't either.

That wasn't true anymore. The understanding gave comfort. She wasn't alone.

"It's not where he insists it should be. So, either he's confused about where he left it." His head sank to the side as though gaining a better angle from which to examine her. "Or maybe someone else has it. I thought Grace, perhaps? But my man didn't find it when he checked at her house."

She stared at him, forcing herself not to look away.

"The break-in at Grace's. He was looking for it there. I guess assaulting me was just a bonus for him," she said.

"That was unplanned and frankly, unacceptable. But also, not of the same importance as finding that box. As I'm sure you've figured out, there's nothing I won't do to get it back."

She swallowed, frustrated when he noticed the subtle sign of her fear.

He reached for the cup of water on her tray table and offered it to her. She refused to take it, and he returned it to the tray.

He leaned back in the chair and rested his hands on his thighs. "Well, that puts me in a difficult position." Intimidation dripped from his sharp stare.

This time she refused to squirm.

The lines of his face hardened, contradicting the words he spoke when he leaned forward. "I care very much about you, Jodee Rose Trevaine."

A shiver skittered down her arms at her full name on his lips. "How do you—"

"We'll have plenty of time to visit about the necessary details soon. By the way, nice touch using your middle name while trying to find help. Clever. Of course, I wouldn't expect anything less. That's why I'm certain you can help me get this box."

"I don't know what you're talking about."

"I bet if you think real hard on it, you'll figure it out. Like I said, you're a clever girl." He tapped his middle finger on the edge of the bed. "Because here's the thing. If I don't get that box, I will have to start eliminating people who might have it or know about it—just to be safe, you know. You've gone through so much to rescue that boy—and don't get me wrong, I would hate to harm him—but sometimes there are things that must be done for the greater good."

She pressed back into the pillow, her breath shallow. This wasn't a dream or a nightmare. She was fully awake and staring into the face of an evil she had never seen before. Her grandmother's words came to her. *Never have a conversation with the devil.*

As if he read her mind, he continued, "You don't have to say anything. Here's the deal. You have two hours—and I'm being very generous with the time—to bring me that box. If things start to get dicey, I might shorten the time, so don't go to Adams or Sunday or anyone else for help. If I don't have that box at the end of the two hours, I'm afraid the boy's surgery . . . well, there may be unexpected and unfortunate complications. His sister will be next. On and on it will go until it's just you, Jodee."

He rose and calmly returned the chair to the corner before facing her again. The smile on his face mocked his words and the wickedness behind them. "You can do this. I have faith in you."

He reached into his pocket and pulled out a key chain. He studied it for a moment, then placed it in her hand. "In case you doubt my sincerity, here's a little reminder. I play for keeps Jodee, and I will have what is mine. I always do."

She gaped at the key chain—a flattened .45 shell casing. She dropped it as though it burned into her flesh like metal straight from the forge. This wasn't a coincidence. It couldn't be.

"Go ahead. Read the inscription," he said.

The words etched into the brass *For My Dad.* After winning her first 4H shooting sports competition—one he'd helped her train for —she'd taken a spent casing from that day and made a keychain for Paul, the man she loved as a father. "Where'd you get this?"

"Let's just say it used to belong to someone else who wanted something that belonged to me."

With his hand on the door, he paused. "Two hours Jodee. Bring the box to Roots." His smile slithered over her flesh. "Now, don't waste time wondering about what you have in your hand. You'll understand it all soon enough."

The door swung shut behind him, leaving a void as though all the oxygen had gone out with him.

Her hands shook as she examined the keychain. The growing fear inside her told her she didn't want to understand. She wanted to run.

CHAPTER 42

Texas 1874

The creation of a thousand forests is in one acorn. ~Ralph Waldo Emerson

ill glanced at Rose. He trusted the horse she rode. He'd just sold it to the stable owner yesterday after breaking it himself. Still, the ashen color of her complexion concerned him.

He reckoned he'd look the same if he'd seen his own grave.

That there might be graves for her parents was something he'd wondered about. Would the DeGroots have buried them? Maybe some neighbors? His nine-year-old brain hadn't been concerned with anything except escape back then. Though he would have bet money against it—if he were a betting man—finding them hadn't been too shocking all the same.

But seeing a marker with Rose's name on it had made the hair on the back of his neck stand up in prickles of unease. A sinister presence hung in the air beneath the oak tree where they'd found the graves. The same oak tree where he'd overheard the Abel's planning to make him their son.

Four graves. Three for Abel, Essie, and Rose Charidy marked with the date of their death. The fourth grave was for Cub DeGroot.

Two things troubled him. One, Cub had been very much alive when Will had last seen him that night. Had Luther killed his own brother? And two, Luther didn't seem like the type to bother with digging four graves and placing neatly carved markers on them. He'd been more likely to dump all the bodies together in a very shallow grave, if he did anything at all.

Who had buried them? How had Cub died? And why was there a grave for Rose? A dark cloud drifted over the day, shrouding them in a distressed gloom they couldn't ride out from under even once they were off the plateau as they made the ride back to New Plenty.

Chance alone caused them to stumble upon the graves. They'd gone to the shade of the oak tree to escape the withering midday sun. Instead of respite, they'd found a new form of torment.

By the time they reached the hotel where Will had reserved a room for Rose, he was through with the questions and ready for answers. He'd failed Rose and her parents once before. This time he intended to find justice.

He dismounted and reached to help Rose down. "You go up to your room and rest for a bit. I've got some business to tend to. I'll come back and get you later so we can find something to eat."

"Will?" The distress in her voice stung his heart. He shouldn't have let her talk him into this. The urge to comfort her, to wrap her in his embrace, filled him, but he'd promised his embrace to another woman. He could only pray his care for her resonated in his words and in the look he gave her.

"Don't worry. We'll figure this out." He reached to tug a strand of hair. "I'm quite certain you are not buried in a grave in El Hueso. You are very much alive." Emotions he wouldn't acknowledge made his voice husky. "Now go rest. I'll be back for you as soon as I'm done."

Ten minutes later, he stood in the solicitor's office before a wide-eyed young man who appeared to be caught in the clutches of a great confusion.

"Who did you say you were again?" The young man tugged at his collar as though it were shrinking by the second.

"Will Sunday. And I'd like to speak to Mr. Barnes, please."

The young man, the secretary he decided, fumbled over some words that landed in a pile of nervous gibberish at Will's feet. Then he spun and headed down the hall, leaving Will to frown in his own growing confusion.

He sat on a wooden bench and waited. It didn't take long for the secretary to reappear. Will watched the nervous man retrieve his hat, then dart out the front door without a word or a look in Will's direction. Seconds later, a rotund man in a dark sack coat, unbuttoned over a waistcoat that stretched itself until Will feared he might be injured by a flying button, strode from the dark recesses of the hall to greet him.

"Solicitor Barnes." He extended his hand to Will. "And who did you say you were?"

"There's no *were* to it. I *am* Will Sunday." Something unpleasant niggled along his spine.

"Yes, well . . . it's nice to meet you Mr. Sunday." He motioned Will down the cheaply paneled hallway to his office and offered him a chair. "What is it that I can help you with?"

Barnes seated himself behind the large mahogany desk and folded his hands across his middle.

"I'm not sure." Now that he was here, he really wasn't sure what he planned to do or what he needed to ask. "There's a grave up in El Hueso. I assume you're familiar with the town there."

"As the only solicitor in this area, I have, in fact, done some business there." He chuckled. "But I'm a barrister, not an undertaker. There are times people may wish *me* dead, but I've never overseen a burial."

"This one would have happened nearly twenty years ago. Do you know who might have been here to do that?"

"I've only been here for going on eight years now. I'm afraid that was before my time."

His thoughts scrambled around in his head as he tried to grasp how to get the information he wanted without betraying his real purpose or putting Rose in danger. The sense that Rose might still be at risk worried him. "I'm sure in your line of work that your acquaintances in the area must be vast. I'm hoping you can think of someone I might ask about the graves we found."

Barnes pursed his lips. "And which graves is it that have you so curious, Mr. Sunday?"

"It's the Charidy family. Three graves." Will leaned forward. "I think they might be distant kin. I'd like to make sure that I found the right ones." He cleared his throat. "Ma's dying wish," he lied.

"I see. I'll tell you what. I'll ask around. I might know just the person. Let me know where you're staying, and I'll send word as soon as I speak to them."

Will hesitated. He'd booked two rooms at the hotel, one for him and one for Rose. Unease held him back from an honest answer. Maybe it was the feeling in his gut he wasn't being told the straight truth. "I'm bedding down at the stables on the far end of town."

He left the meeting with the unsettled feeling that he'd somehow just poked a hornet's nest.

Bypassing the hotel, he went straight to the stable. He'd unsaddled and brushed the horses down before turning them into the corral. Now he debated saddling them again in case they needed to leave in a hurry.

"You look like a man watching his best friend run away with his dog." The gravelly voice behind him drew a smile and a prayer of thanks at the sound of an old friend.

Though he'd ridden more miles than he could remember with the man, he'd never known his name beyond what everyone called him.

"Hawk, an angel from God just when I needed one most."

CHAPTER 43

For in the true nature of things, if we rightly consider, every green tree is far more glorious than if it were made of gold and silver. ~Martin Luther

*R*unning from her fears wasn't an option Jodee could consider. How could she, with Aidan fighting for his life somewhere in this hospital? How could she when Blue was locked up in a jail cell, wrongly accused and with no one fighting for him?

The speed at which the secondhand moved around the clock hanging on the wall sent the world spinning around her. Her fingers reached for the white stone before remembering the hospital gown she wore.

The second hand continued its furious ticking. They wouldn't let her just walk out of the hospital. There'd be questions and lecturing and possibly physical restraint if Grace found out she was trying to leave.

Grace? She was in danger too, but Jodee couldn't tell her that. She couldn't tell anyone.

The blankets tangled around her legs as she stormed from the bed. She staggered and reached for the bed rail as the door swept open again.

Blue charged through, almost colliding with her and sending her to the floor. He grabbed her shoulders, steadying her as she blinked the world back into focus. Then he pulled her into a hungry embrace. "Thank you, Lord." He repeated the expression of gratitude twice more as she reoriented herself to the fact that Blue was out of jail.

Despite DeGroot's warning, she couldn't do this without Blue. She didn't want to.

"Blue . . ." She leaned away.

"Do you know how much you scared me Jodee Rose Trevaine?" For the second time in less than five minutes, she'd heard her full name. Coming from Blue, it sounded like a sultry summer breeze over moonlit water.

But that was a feeling to explore some other time. The second hand made another swift pass around the clock. She needed his attention.

"Blue!" But unlike his, her words were sharp.

It was his turn to pull back.

"I need your shirt."

His eyes narrowed.

"There's something I have to do, and I have to get out of here to do it. I only have two hours, so please don't ask questions. If I don't get this done, Aidan could die." The face of her stepfather flashed in front of her. Tears stung her eyes. "And who knows who else he'll kill to get what he wants."

"Who?" Blue tensed, his body turning to stone beneath her touch.

Jodee licked her lips. "Judge DeGroot."

Storm clouds thundered across his face, but he didn't speak.

"Blue, did you hear me? I can't stand around doing nothing."

"Where's my phone?"

She shook her head. "The pigs ate it."

A baffled look replaced the strain tugging him into tight lines. "You can explain that one later. Tell me what's going on?"

She hesitated, but the steadfast way he held her gaze freed her from the fear.

"He told me not to tell anyone, but I need you Blue." Her fingers squeezed around his arms. She did need him, and she could trust him. The comfort of the truth flowed through her like a river of living water. "Judge DeGroot wants something he thinks Aidan has —a box of some sort. He said he'd kill for it, and I believe him."

"So do I." Blue's expression looked as stony as the chiseled face of Michaelangelo's David. He pulled her close again, brushing a kiss across her forehead. "Okay. We're in this together. Tell me everything. Does Logan know?"

"No."

Blue exhaled. "I'm pretty sure we can trust him, but he's a little slow on the uptake sometimes. And I'd like to not return to jail anytime soon."

"I need your shirt. I have to get out of here without being noticed. This gown makes me look like a patient." She held her hand out.

"Which you are." He eased her back onto the bed. "You almost died, Jodee."

She sprung back to her feet and faced him. "But I didn't. I'm not going to repay that gift by letting someone else die instead."

"I can do this. Let me handle it. Just tell me what you know, then stay put."

"I trust you, Blue, I do. But we're in this together. I can't just do nothing while Aidan is still in danger." The wariness in his regard made her wonder if she should regret telling him. "Please. We can do this together."

"What exactly do you plan to do?" he asked.

"I don't know. I just know I can't do it here. And we can't risk telling someone else. Not until I know what he wants."

"And if you don't figure it out?"

"Not an option." She held his gaze, an unwavering determination burning through her. "Help me get out and then we can go to Grace's and think. Now, give me your shirt."

"What am I supposed to do without a shirt? Don't you think I'll be a little obvious walking out without my shirt on?"

"Exactly." She motioned for him to hurry.

The slow shake of his head communicated his doubt as he undid the pearl snaps to shed the long-sleeved denim shirt he wore.

He turned his face away as she changed out of her hospital gown to slip on his shirt. She dug through the bag of her belongings sitting in the corner to retrieve her pants and shoes.

"Hand me your cap, too. It'll help me hide my hair. And your truck keys."

He handed her the cap. "No keys. We're in this together, remember? Head out through the waiting room, then meet me at my truck. I'll go out by the nurse's station." He shook his head. "You know this man is dangerous, right? He's playing for keeps. He always does."

She rolled her bottom lip between her teeth and nodded. To do more would make the terrible truth too potent. Someone she cared about could die in the next two hours.

Blue walked down the hall feeling every bit of the awkward sight he made. He reached to adjust his cap before remembering that Jodee had just commandeered it. He didn't know which made him feel more exposed, being shirtless or being hatless.

Maybe he should have stopped her. This was too dangerous. Besides, she'd nearly died, hadn't she? But how could he stop her? After what she went through to rescue Aidan, she deserved to see it through to the end.

But even if it meant the end of her?

No. He wouldn't let that be an option either.

He needed to find a phone and let Tom Fowler know what was happening. Whether the Texas Ranger or even Oliver Matthews knew he'd been arrested, he didn't know. Though he was more than happy to be out of jail, it bothered him that his bail had been set low for someone facing charges of arson and attempted murder.

Knowing who they were up against now took his concern to a new level of unease. He jabbed his fingers into his hair, raking it into uneven rows.

A young female nurse stared over the chart she held in her hand. He gave her a weak smile, smoothed his hair in place, and hurried down the hall.

Judge DeGroot had threatened Jodee. Exactly the kind of thing Blue had been tasked with uncovering. He wasn't sure how happy he was to finally have it. It came with a price—Jodee.

Even worse was that he had no way to share it with those who needed to know.

His steps thudded against the tile floor as he strode down the hall. Had it been this long when he'd come in? The longer he took to get back to her, the greater the possibility she'd take off on her own. Or worse, fall into DeGroot's ruthless hands. When this was over, he planned to never let her out of his sight again.

But first he had to get to her before DeGroot.

CHAPTER 44

Texas 1874

I took a walk in the woods and came out taller than the trees. ~Henry David Thoreau

Will had done all he could. Now it was time to wait. He sat on a wooden barrel and settled into the dusky shade, hoping Rose wouldn't get anxious and come looking for him before Hawk delivered his message.

Once the sun disappeared, he changed positions. A couple of water barrels stacked near an oak tree allowed him to see both the corrals and the barn should anyone try to creep too close without him knowing.

He didn't wait long.

The sight soured his stomach and sent a flash of white-hot rage shooting through him. Cub DeGroot—very alive and not buried in the grave bearing his name—crept along the side of the barn. Will squinted to be certain, but twenty years hadn't erased the familiar sloping shoulders and receding chin from Will's memory.

Cub didn't see him as he made his way through the dark.

Instead, he made furtive glances behind him as though he expected to be followed.

He appeared to be alone, though. *Where was Luther?*

The burst of anger that had ignited inside him moments ago reduced itself to the slow burn of hatred at the memory of Luther.

He slipped the Colt single action firearm from its holster. It wouldn't be the first time he'd had to shoot a man. But the possibility never got easier to digest. With the stealth of a panther, he slipped from his hiding place and followed Cub.

"Looking for someone?" He leveled the barrel at the center of the other man's head as Cub spun to face him. "Keep it real quiet now and slowly toss that Thumb Buster to the side." Will motioned to the Colt Single Action pistol in Cub's hand.

The man shook as he complied with the order. He held Will's stare with a wide-eyed fear.

"Will?" Cub stammered, then swallowed. "It *is* you. You wouldn't shoot an old friend, would you?"

"Nope." The sharp click of the hammer of Will's gun cocking beneath his steady touch made the man flinch. "But a man who murders innocent people isn't a friend of mine."

Cub swallowed again, and Will guessed his mouth must have gone as dry as cotton. "That wasn't me. I didn't want that to happen. I was just a kid . . . just like you back then."

"Compare yourself to me again, and I'll put a slug right between your eyes." On the outside, he was controlled and deliberate, while years of anger and self-loathing roared to life inside him devouring the contrition he might have otherwise felt at his not very Christ-like thoughts.

A wagon rolled by, metal pans clanging as the springs beneath pinched and squeaked.

Vengeance is Mine, I will repay, says the Lord.

The wrath burning in Will's veins subsided. He was here for answers to help Rose regain what should have been hers. Rose's inheritance stolen by evil men.

"Keep your mouth shut and get inside." He stepped aside for Cub to pass, his gun still aimed at the man's head. "Where's Luther?"

"I don't know. He's hard to keep track of. I haven't seen him lately."

"How'd you know I was here?" Will knew the answer already, but he wanted Cub to talk.

"I didn't."

"You make it a habit to creep around in the dark in places you have no reason to be?" He didn't wait for an answer. "Why'd Barnes tell you I was here?"

The flash of relief in Cub's eyes and the lift of his shoulders bore an unintentional warning Will didn't miss. "You should ask him."

Will shifted, backing into the shadows and angling himself for a view of both Cub and the entrance to the barn.

It didn't take long for Barnes to show himself. He approached arms wide, palms out, evidencing his empty hands as though he wanted Will to trust his sincerity.

The gesture didn't fool Will. He hadn't taken Barnes for a fighter. Only a leech who used the law to drain the life from others less knowledgeable. But he'd still bet money the man had a hidden weapon on him somewhere.

"I went to see him right after you left. As soon as you introduced yourself, I knew something was wrong." He moved closer with the slow, regulated steps of someone uncertain of how far they could go but deliberate in pushing his boundaries. "Two Will Sundays in El Hueso? Something deeper must lie beneath the surface. As a man of the law, of course my curious inclination sent me to investigate."

"Two Will Sundays?" The harsh edge in his voice masked the confusion in his thoughts, though the pieces of the puzzle were coming together. He pierced Cub with a glare. "You?"

Again, Cub swallowed.

He'd soon have a belly full of fear if he kept that up.

"I'm Will Sunday," Cub said.

The pieces of the puzzle locked into their duplicitous places. The fourth grave marker for Cub DeGroot marked an empty grave. He'd faked his death and assumed Will's identity. *But why? What reason could he have for wanting to become the orphaned kid nobody wanted?* "Why?"

"With Rose gone, well, there needed to be an heir to inherit what had belonged to the Charidys."

The adoption. Mr. Charidy had read Will the letter he'd written to file for his adoption. But he'd been killed, and the letter destroyed in the fire before they had a chance. "So, you created a fake to get what you wanted."

"No. We have the letter written by Mr. Charidy stating his desire to adopt *me.* It's all legal." His voice quivered, snagging itself on the word me. "I don't know why you're here telling everyone that you're Will Sunday. Mr. Barnes was doing his job when he came to warn us of an imposter."

Will's jaw clamped shut as he ground his teeth. Rose's stolen inheritance. His stolen name. He looked at the cowering man before him, then cut his eyes to Barnes, who seemed to be undisturbed by what he was hearing. Maybe the name Will Sunday hadn't meant much to anyone when he was a nine-year-old kid, but what had the miserable, thieving liar standing in front of him done to drag it further into disgrace?

"For as his name is, so is he."

Apprehension shuddered up his back. Instinct jerked him around. A flash of gunpowder exploded in the dark just before the bullet ripped into his right shoulder, staggering him. He dropped to his knee, looking for the shooter through the red cloud of pain marring his vision. It had to be Luther.

Three against one were not good odds.

He tried to press his injured arm against his side, bracing it to take a shot. But the shredded muscle in his shoulder left him barely able to grip his gun. He struggled to switch it to his left hand as Luther stepped into view and raised his gun a second time.

Will found the trigger and squeezed. Two explosions licked through the black, sending their bullets racing for one another. Both found flesh.

The world around Will became a silent roar as the force of the bullet toppled him backward to land in the straw.

Amanda's face, followed by that of his son Jacob's, and finally Rose's. No longer the frightened little boy who ran from evil, he felt himself floating. He was a man, a good man with a good name who'd done the best he could. He had, hadn't he?

Somebody, please tell me my best has been good enough. The urgency of his need to hear an answer rode through his body on a wave of pain that had nothing to do with his physical wounds.

"Luther. Your arm. He shot you." Cub's voice seemed to echo toward him down a long tunnel.

"We can worry about it later. Let's clear out before anyone shows up," Luther's voice growled, the anger and pain intensifying his wrath.

"But he isn't dead. You can't just leave him like that." The quavering had returned to Cub's voice.

"Gut shot. He's as good as dead," Luther said.

"But—"

"Unless you're going to pull the trigger yourself, I ain't got another shot in me. My arm is busted clean through the bone."

Will clutched his stomach, feeling the warm flow of blood, and tried to breathe as the voices whirled around him. They faded into the pain until he didn't hear them. He looked to find himself alone. He had to get out of here. The gunshots would've attracted others. If they found him still alive, he might slip up and expose Rose. He couldn't let that happen.

On legs that no longer felt like they belonged to him, he staggered to his feet. Sweat ran along his forehead and into his eyes. His whole body felt slick with perspiration.

Clutching his middle, he stumbled through the shadows. He had to find Rose before anyone else did.

The same tinker's wagon that had made so much racket going by the stables earlier waited behind the hotel. No driver in sight.

Will reached for the wooden handrail that led to the second floor. The steps might have been a mile long for all the strength he had. Determination held him together when his head swam and his knees buckled.

A firm hand caught his arm and steadied him on his feet. Will twitched, afraid the DeGroots had followed him, but there was no one there. His world blurred, distorting itself so he couldn't tell what was real anymore.

Every step upward felt like a weight being lifted from his shoulders. He continued one after another, his breath labored. At the top, he leaned against the wall, resting until he had the strength to crack the door open and peer in. A man and woman walked along the far end of the hall and entered a room.

He glanced back at the wagon. Hawk stood beside it. The old man tipped his hat in a show of respect, one man to another. Will lacked the strength to return the gesture as he stepped through the door. Though he hadn't anticipated how this had turned out, he'd had the foresight to get Rose a room close to the rear exit.

She answered his soft rap as though she'd been waiting on the other side. He lurched inside, pressing a finger to his lips to keep her quiet. It took her a moment to notice the blood seeping from the wound in his shoulder and draining from his abdomen to soak his shirt.

Her hand flew to her mouth, and she backed away, tears flooding her frightened eyes. "Will!"

"Don't speak. Just listen. There's a man out back with a wagon. He's going to get you out of here. It's not safe for you to stay."

"I can't leave you like this." She reached for him as his strength gave way and he stumbled to the bed.

"You don't have a choice." He eased himself onto the bed. "And don't worry. I won't be like this for long." He ran his dry tongue over his lips, but it didn't help.

"Don't say that. I'll get the doctor."

"No. Rose, listen to me. I know what happens when a man is gut shot." He was shocked he'd lasted long enough to make it here to tell her. "You don't know who you can trust in this town. No telling who all the DeGroots have in their pockets." He paused, gasping for enough breath to finish what he had to say. "I don't think they know you're here. You can't let them find you. And Rose, no one can ever know who you really are. A secret, Rose. Promise me you'll keep it."

She sank to the floor beside him, taking his hand in hers and holding it over her heart. "Please don't make me leave you. I can't."

Tears fell from her eyes, landing on his blood covered hand in splotches of cool. He smiled.

"Why are you smiling?" The pain in her words intermixed with her anger and lack of understanding.

"Your tears . . . No one has ever cried over me like that before." His tongue was thick and heavy. "They're the last thing I'll feel." He pulled his hand away to gently tug a strand of her hair escaping its braid. "Thank you, Little Bud."

He closed his eyes. "Will you make sure they know . . . that I love them very much, and that I tried to do the right thing?"

The world around him grew dim as his life drifted away like a leaf carried on the current of a peaceful stream.

Rose's tears ran in a warm trail of love over his hand.

He hadn't restored Rose to the inheritance that should have been hers, but he'd protected her life. Had he even come close to repaying the debt he owed to the Charidys? He wanted to think so. He wanted to believe he'd done the best he could, and that his best had been good enough.

He prayed Amanda would understand he died finally able to love her with a whole heart—a healed heart. Not the heart of a broken and fearful little boy, but with the heart of a man who knew what love meant. He hurt to know his son would grow up without a father. But one day, when Jacob had sons of his own, he prayed he would tell them how their grandfather had been a righteous man, a brave man. An honorable man with a good name.

Who did his best.

CHAPTER 45

You have to work out whether your roots have become so entwined together that it is inconceivable that you should ever part. Because this is what love is ... your roots grow towards each other underground and when all the pretty blossoms fall from your branches, you find out you are one tree, and not two. ~Louis de Bernieres

*B*lue peppered Jodee with questions as he raced up the hill to El Hueso.

She braced herself as the truck slid around another corner. "Stop asking me questions so I can think."

The top of the S curve loomed ahead, taking her back to the night of her accident, and then, one after another, images exploded in her head. The ride with Grace that first day out of the hospital, driving past the cemetery, Tillie in the middle of the road. Like an electrical jolt, the memory zinged through her. "Tillie! I know where the box is!"

Blue looked at her to elaborate, but the certainty evaporated. Could she trust her memory of seeing Tillie carrying a box beneath her arm as she walked down the road?

"I mean ... I think ... maybe."

"Look at me Jodee." His words rang in the cab with an insistence made of steel. She turned to meet his stare. "Stop doubting yourself."

She took a moment to let his words fill her with determination. "Then we need to find Tillie." She looked at his bare torso. "But first we need to get you a shirt."

"No, we need to get *you* a shirt. I have one, and while I do like the way it looks on you, I am starting to feel a bit objectified."

Five minutes later, Jodee hurried up the stairs at Grace's to replace Blue's shirt with one of her own.

In her rush, the hem snagged on the corner of the built-in book-shelf, causing her to stumble. She jerked at the garment, but the piece that had caught the shirt didn't release its hold. The narrow opening widened as the trim pulled further out of place. She reached to disentangle the garment, her fingertips brushing against a piece of paper hidden behind the shelf. She nudged it, and the edge of an envelope slipped into view.

She plucked it from its hiding place to keep it from sliding further behind the shelf. The paper was yellowed with age and covered in the flowing script of a bygone era. Grace would be thrilled with this discovery. She set it on the shelf. Whatever it held, it could wait.

She flung the shirt at Blue as she raced into the kitchen where he stood downing a bottle of water. He tossed a bottle to her.

"Tillie has it. She has to." For the first time since DeGroot had entered her room, she felt hopeful.

A concern filled breath whooshed from him as he yanked this shirt on. "You think she'll give it to you?"

"I think she will. But if not, I'm counting on you to finagle it away from her." She dug a rubber band from the junk drawer and wound it around her hair. "Now let's go."

He ran his tongue around the inside of his cheek, annoyance radiating off him as he stared at her. "When this is over, I sure hope people will stop looking at me as some sort of gigolo for hire. I'm a changed man."

"I thought it was like riding a bike. Once you figure it out, you never forget."

"It is not at all like riding a bike." He grabbed her hand and headed out the door. "For one thing, when you fall off, you don't usually skin your knees."

Three minutes later, they slid to a stop in Tillie's driveway. "You sure you don't want me to come in?"

"I think it'll be faster if you aren't there for her to ogle." Jodee dropped the white stone she'd been rubbing into her shirt pocket. "Just keep the truck running, and Blue, keep your eyes open. If anything happens to you . . ." Her words trailed off in a stream of silent emotion.

"Hey, nothing's going to happen." He reached for her hand and kissed it. "And though it's not really your style, be careful yourself."

She shifted toward the door, but he didn't release her hand. Instead, he pulled her closer. His eyes spoke a language that seduced her heart into a fit of longing.

"What I said a few minutes ago. I'm not that guy anymore. I don't chase women or sleep around. In fact, I can honestly say I've been a no-woman kind of guy for the last few years. I hope that's about to change."

"Change?"

"I want to be a one-woman kind of guy. Only not *any* woman. It's you, Jodee Rose Trevaine."

She swallowed the emotion knotting in her throat as he leaned closer, his breath warm against her skin. "I'd like that."

His kiss reached into her heart. A feathery brush of his lips on hers, a silent offer of his devotion that grew into a gentle, unconditional promise of forever.

Breathless, she leaned back to study him, praying what she saw was as real as what she felt. She placed her hand against his cheek. "And I'd definitely like more of *that.*"

She savored the taste of his kiss that lingered on her lips as she moved away. "But right now . . ."

"Don't worry. I'll be waiting right here." His words rasped as the intensity of his gaze held her captive. "William Blue Sunday will always be waiting for you, Jodee Rose Tremaine." He smiled, loosening the loop on the lasso he had tangled her in. He tugged a strand of her hair that had fallen loose.

She slid from the truck, knowing as much as she wanted to continue this conversation, she had something more urgent to do. And time was slipping away. Fighting the urge to look back, she hurried across the lawn. The front door swung open a second before she reached for it.

"You leavin' that good lookin' cowboy out there all by his lonesome?" The woman peered around Jodee and waved. "Good lookin' and quite a kisser, I'd say." The woman's laughter drew heat to Jodee's cheeks.

"Uhmm." She shifted on her feet. Even if she'd had a plan, it wouldn't have included this. Flustered almost as much by Tillie's remarks as by Blue's kiss, she grappled to find two sensible words to string together.

The elderly woman winked at her. "My Ship was quite the kisser too. Ain't nothin' to be ashamed of."

This time, her words pulled Jodee back into the reality of the moment. "Maybe we can come by for a longer visit soon, but I'm kind of in a hurry right now. And it's really important." She bit her lip, uncertain how to make her request.

"Well, come in." Tillie tottered back into the house.

Jodee shot a look at Blue, then followed her.

"I really don't have much time, so I hope you don't mind if I get right to the point. I think you have a box I need. You were carrying it the day I met you. Do you remember that day? Right after the storm when we saw lightning had struck the tree?"

"The broken oak?"

Jodee nodded. "That's right. Do you remember the box?"

"Oh, I remember. Town folk think I'm touched. They may be right. But I ain't forgetful." The woman seated herself in a worn-out recliner and picked up the pipe she'd been smoking. "What do you need it for?"

"I can't say yet. But I'll pay you for it if you want. Just name the price."

"That sounds like a right fine idea. You fetch it from beneath that sofa cushion and have a seat."

Caught off guard by the ease with which the bargain had been made, Jodee lifted the indicated cushion. She hesitated for only a second before reaching for the box she was surprised to find was actually there. "I really don't have time to sit. Just tell me how much I owe you." She resisted the urge to open it now. She didn't have any money to pay her with, but she would get it. Whatever amount she asked for.

"That's how much I ask for. That you sit."

Reluctantly, and with the flexibility of a fence post, she sat. She placed a hand on her thigh to still the bouncing, trying not to look too closely at the hands of the grandfather clock flying around its face. *How could she slow the hands on the clock while making this conversation go faster?*

"Jodee Rose Trevaine. Great granddaughter of Rose Charidy."

Her attention snapped to the woman with the pipe dangling from the corner of her mouth. "How do you—"

"Tsk tsk . . . an old woman just knows things. How isn't the question to ask." She pulled her pipe to the side. The sweet, earthy scent of tobacco floated from her lips as she leaned forward. "The question to ask is *why does she know it?*"

"I don't understand."

"My name is Tillie Calderon. My husband was Ship Calderon. And his great-great-great grandfolk were the first Calderons in El Hueso." The woman rocked back in her chair and stuck the pipe between her lips again.

"And?" A growing unease fueled Jodee's impatience.

"Charidys, Calderons, and DeGroots. First folks to settle on this ol' heap of hard-luck ground." She puffed a few times on her pipe. "But everything ain't always what it appears to be." She chuckled, though Jodee found no humor in her words.

"Please, I really do need to go. Someone's life depends on it."

"You are right about that, but you have it wrong about whose life it is. The Calderons," she continued, "they were cursed to be the keepers of a secret, a very bad secret. A secret they've kept for over a hundred years. Passing it from one generation to the next, lest the secret be forgotten and the truth be lost forever." Her words sing-songed into a mystical sort of rhythm that raised the hair on Jodee's arms.

"Why . . . what kind of secret had to be kept for that long? Why couldn't they just tell someone else?" *And how could it possibly matter now?*

Tillie's laughter rattled through the room like a bucket of marbles had been kicked over. "You tell, you die." She pierced Jodee with her stare. "They ain't near as many Calderons grow to old age as they is for other families."

A jittery energy pulsed through her.

"The Calderons, they learned to be quiet so's they could survive. Waiting, always awaitin'." The woman rocked forward, resting a bony elbow on her knee. "Until Ship. The old-timers disease made him forget to keep his mouth shut. He done said things he oughtn't, and it got him killed."

Jodee swallowed the bitter taste of fear that had settled on her tongue. "I don't understand."

"Our daughter left this town first chance she got. She ain't comin' back. She's tired of the secret. Never understood why we'd go through so much to keep a secret that weren't even ours, as though we were paying a debt we didn't owe. But the truth . . . that's the only thing that matters in this old world. The only thing that can't ever be destroyed," she chuckled. "It won't stay buried forever. There're only two families that understand the secret's power. The ones that hold on to it with their lives, and the ones seeking to destroy it."

She sat back and smiled. "Ship, he knew you were coming. When I saw that old tree all broken apart, I knowed he was right. It's time to let the secret stop being a secret."

"I can call Grace for you. Maybe it'd be a good idea for you to see your doctor." Jodee scooted to the edge of the sofa.

"Phooey. I don't need a sawbones. I ain't keepin' this blamed secret anymore. Once it's out, they won't be need of any more killin' . . .'cept maybe me." She laughed again. "I might just die in my sleep like Ship." She harumphed her disbelief.

"What secret, Tillie?" Jodee's charitableness in indulging the woman had run out. If something happened to Aidan because she'd sat here listening to the crazy talk of a lonely old woman, it would be her fault.

"It's all right there." Tillie pointed at the box. "And now it's yours, but know this. Opening it is only the beginning of the end. It ain't the end."

A tremble of premonition twitched through her fingers as she lifted the lid. Inside were an old Bible, a stack of letters, and some sort of legal document dated in the 1800s.

Why was DeGroot so interested in this that he'd kill to have it? Maybe this wasn't the box he wanted. She placed the items back in the box and closed the lid.

"I'll look at this when I get home. But thank you for trusting me to keep the secret."

Tillie's face grew serious. "Beloved, you ain't keepin' the secret. You *are* the secret."

CHAPTER 46

A people without the knowledge of their past history, origin and culture is like a tree without roots. ~Marcus Garvey

"What happened in there? You're white as a ghost and you're shaking." The concern in Blue's voice charged the air, adding to the tremors already making Jodee shake as she climbed in the truck.

"Just go," she snapped.

He backed out of the driveway. "Which way?"

"Doesn't matter. Just go." The adamant words made her voice harsh, a desperate sound he'd never heard before.

"You got the box—"

"I just need a minute. Don't say anything." She tossed him a pleading look.

She stared out the window as he drove her away from the madness. Only she couldn't shake it. Tillie's words clung to her like the web of a spider.

Like a spinning wheel left untouched, her thoughts slowed. She inhaled a lungful of sanity and blew it out through her mouth in a slow breath. The tremors stopped. "Pull over."

He parked the truck at the edge of the road, and she turned to face him, unsure where to begin.

"Just go, now stop. I'm getting a bit confused here," he said. "Is this about the box?"

"Yes . . .no . . .maybe . . ." She stared at the box she still held.

"Okay." The word stretched, reflecting his confusion. A confusion that mirrored her own, though for different reasons.

"She said there was a secret that her family has kept for a hundred years." Jodee raked her bottom lip through her teeth and looked at Blue with apprehension. "She said I was the secret."

"Well, Tillie is a bit eccentric. I don't think you should worry about anything she said." He placed his hand on her back with a tender caress. "I'm sorry she upset you."

"You're right. It was just so strange." She handed him the box. "Let's just get this over with and figure out what to do next."

He removed the contents one by one and placed them on the seat between them. "How much time do we have left?"

"Not much."

She buried her head in her hands. "Just a crazy old lady, right? We have to turn this over now. But why does he want it? Why would it be worth killing for?" Blue thumbed open the Bible and read the names. "Abel Charidy, Essie Charidy, parents of Rose Charidy."

Jodee sucked in a breath. "Rose Charidy was my great grandmother's name."

A low whistle came from Blue as he stared at the legal document tucked in the pages of the Bible.

"What is it?" Unease prickled through her.

"Looks like some sort of letter for adoption . . . for my great grandfather." Blue ran his fingers through his hair. "I don't understand. My great grandfather's name was never Charidy." Wrinkles fanned from his eyes as he narrowed them to study the paper. "But how many William Blue Sundays could there be?"

She took the paper from him and examined it, then shook her

head in disbelief. "Why are our ancenstors both named in the contents of this box?"

"Jodee, there's something I haven't told you."

Intuition made her hand itch to take hold of the door and escape. But her heart remained tethered to the man now looking at her.

"I told you I was here for a reason." He exhaled. "Judge DeGroot is that reason."

His confession seemed to make the keychain in her pocket burn like an ember against her thigh. "You're working for him?"

This time she gave in to the impulse and lunged from the truck. With her hands pressed to her mouth, she paced, thinking. Then spinning as though no direction would be the right one.

In an instant, Blue was beside her, holding her arms in his firm grip. "Listen to me. I'm not working for him. I'm working to stop him."

Her thoughts reeled as Blue explained about Matthews and the Texas Ranger and his search to uncover anything warranting an investigation that could be corroborated.

"I have to find a way to reach Tom Fowler," he said. "With what happened to you and Aidan at the hospital, there's got to be enough for them to do something."

"We don't have time!" She broke away from him. "I can't wait around for you to call in the posse and hope they get here before he hurts Aidan."

"The man's a sociopath, Jodee. He's dangerous. And something's just not right with all of this. I can't let you do this."

"Do what?"

"Deliver the box to DeGroot. Don't tell me it's not what you're planning." Blue scrubbed his face as though he could wipe away the sound of him yelling at her.

"I trusted you, Blue," she whispered. "He told me not to tell anyone, but I trusted you."

He looked away, then kicked a rock. "Get in the truck."

She didn't move.

"Jodee, it seems we were in this together long before we were born. I think the only way to finish it is to do it together. Together. Whatever happens. But we're running out of time."

⸙

"I can't let you be seen with me. It was a part of his instructions, and I don't think he intended them to be negotiable." Jodee spoke as though the matter were settled. In her mind, it was. They'd debated it for the past five minutes as he drove them to a house on the outskirts of El Hueso.

"For the love of Job, I don't care what he said. He can dance the Cotton-eyed Joe with the devil for all I care." The intensity in Blue's eyes burned into her soul. "I care about *you*."

Jodee closed her eyes and inhaled. "Then care about what I care about. I have to do this for Aidan and Kimberly. I have to save them. That's it. If I can't do that—if I'm not willing to risk my own life to save theirs—then I'm nothing more than the selfish monster he is." Her eyes met his. "I won't let him turn me into something I'm not."

He exhaled. "Let me make this phone call. Then we can discuss what happens next when I get back."

At her nod, he opened the door but hesitated. "Two minutes. That's all I'm asking."

When she didn't answer, he continued, "You'll stay here? No funny business?"

"Nothing funny about any of this, as far as I can tell."

"Agreed." He left the truck running and jogged to the front door.

She couldn't see who answered, but they let him in. He wasn't going to let her finish this the way DeGroot insisted. She ran her hands down her jeans. *Think.* She didn't want to do this alone, but did she have a choice?

She picked the box up from the seat beside her. *There's a time to think, and a time to act.*

Was that from the Bible? She didn't know, but it could be. What she did know was that this was the time to act.

She reached for the door handle, her hand freezing just inches away. She and Blue—they were in this together. Charging off like the Lone Ranger no longer felt like her only option.

"Going somewhere?" He opened his door and slid into the seat.

"Only where we go together."

He gave her a skeptical look and put the truck in gear.

"And?" she asked.

"Had to leave a message. Hopefully, he gets it pronto."

He pulled out of the driveway and drove toward Grace's house.

The house was dark. Jodee couldn't stop the worrisome thought that Grace might be in trouble now, too. Surely, she was still safe at the hospital. "So now what?"

"We wait."

She looked at the clock on the dashboard. "No. You wait. I'm going in."

He opened his mouth, but she cut him off. "I'll go in, give him the box, and be done with it."

"He doesn't work that way. He'll know you know something he doesn't want you to know. And he'll want to clean up the loose ends."

"You're carrying right?"

"Yes, I'm carrying. But I wasn't planning to play Marshall Dillon today."

"Well, I always saw you as more of a Rowdy Yates, anyway." Somehow, the senseless quibbling eased her nerves. "Once I'm in and he's distracted, you sneak in and . . ."

"And what?"

"We might have to wing it the rest of the way."

"Not a chance. I don't like you putting yourself in danger like this," Blue said.

"Here's the deal, Blue. He's going to find out we have the box, and it won't take him long to find us. He's probably spotted your truck sitting here already and deduced that we're together." She turned a grim face to him. "Face it, he's coming for us, Blue. Like you said, he doesn't want loose ends. We either wait for him to surprise us or we surprise him."

Blue didn't respond.

She looked at the dashboard clock. "Do you really believe that help is going to arrive in the next six minutes? That's all the time we have left."

He thumped the steering wheel with his fist and looked away.

"Blue, if something happens to that boy because of me, you know I'll never be able to live with it." She placed a hand on his arm. "And all that we've gained in these last few days would be for nothing. Maybe we owe it to Chris or maybe somehow, we owe it to the people mentioned on the stuff in that box or we just owe it to ourselves to be what we were meant to be."

Blue shook his head and looked away, as though seeing something far into the past. "Be the best we can be and hope our best is good enough."

"What's that?" she asked, not sure she'd heard his mumbled statement clearly.

"Nothing. Just something Grandpa Sunday always said."

"I'll go into the house and wait for you to drive off. Maybe he'll think I haven't told you." She kissed him on the cheek and climbed from the truck with the box in her hands.

"You know, in the movies, that kiss right before the climax is always a lot sexier than that," Blue called after her.

"Gigolo." She didn't look back.

"Yeah, well, the clock's running and I don't come cheap."

She circled through Grace's house, pausing to watch as Blue's taillights disappeared around the corner.

The walk to Roots seemed a mile long, though it only took her a few minutes. She made a wide berth around the disturbing sign. *Were they watching her? Did they know she'd told Blue?*

Too late to worry about that now.

She stopped at the front door, staring at the closed sign as she worked up the courage to open the solid metal door.

Turns out courage wasn't needed. The door swung open, and Jodee found herself face to face with Syrah.

And the gun she held.

CHAPTER 47

For there is hope for a tree, If it is cut down, that it will sprout again, ~Job 14:7

"Well, look who it is? I can't tell you how happy I am to see *you*." Syrah motioned Jodee inside, keeping distance between them. The click of the door closing behind her echoed through the empty bar.

Jodee's arms pressed against her sides, misgivings drawing her body into tense lines. Would Blue be able to get in unnoticed?

She scanned the room. Chairs stacked upside down on tabletops, a silent jukebox near the front wall, but otherwise empty. No DeGroot.

"You don't have a hammer with you this time, do you?" Syrah rubbed the back of her head where Jodee had hit her. She indicated for her to place the box on the bar top. Then she gestured to a chair at a nearby table. "Have a seat."

The bruise on her cheek, most likely the result of Rusty's blow, stood out against her fair complexion. Was Rusty here now, too? Apprehension slipped its cold fingers around her.

Syrah leaned against the bar, retrieving a smoldering cigarette from an ashtray. She inhaled, then exhaled a long, slow cloud of smoke that wafted up from lips the color of eggplant to curl around her pale but finely sculpted face. Hidden beneath years of anger, Jodee suspected lie a great beauty.

"Where's your boss?" Jodee asked, hoping she sounded more confident than she felt.

She took another puff on her cigarette. No answer.

"What's so valuable about this box?"

Syrah's eyes went to the box. She didn't touch it, though Jodee saw the hunger in her eyes. A fearful hunger filled with distrust and desperation. A look Jodee had once recognized in herself.

She shrugged a thin shoulder. "How should I know?"

"Surely, he told you something to get you to go through so much trouble to get it?"

"Weren't no trouble at all." Syrah smiled, but the distant, wary look in her eyes never left. She dismissed the possibility with a wave of her gun. Then she thumped ashes from the cigarette to scatter across the floor.

Jodee noted that she'd switched hands after letting her in, now holding the gun in her left while she tended her cigarette with the right.

"I just thought he would've told you why if he was going to ask you to risk going to prison for kidnapping and torturing a child. Seems the decent thing to do."

Her eyes narrowed, a brief twitch at the word decent. She flicked her cigarette again, knocking more ashes to the floor.

"The police know it was you. If you turn yourself in, they'd—"

"I didn't torture that boy. He just wouldn't stop trying to get away." Her eyes were wide, nostrils flared. She leaned forward. "And I'm not going to prison. The all-powerful Judge Harrison DeGroot'll make sure of that."

"Looks like the *all-powerful Judge Harrison DeGroot* needs to buy himself a watch. I mean, it's not like he didn't know I was coming." She tried to quell the antsy feeling that incited her to fidget.

Blue was somewhere outside. What happened if he came in too

soon? What if DeGroot had seen them together and cut the time short? Was he already making good on his promise to kill Aidan? Her ears burned with the possibility, and she bit down hard on the inside of her mouth to stem the growing fear.

"Or maybe he's just letting you take the fall for all of this. The police show up and arrest you for kidnapping and he says he's innocent. You did say he was all-powerful, right? He won't go to jail, but you will, and he'll still have that box and whatever's inside that he doesn't want you to know about," Jodee said.

Syrah puffed out more smoke as her eyes cut toward the box.

Footsteps approached from behind her, crossing the empty dance floor. Shuffling steps that lacked the authority of DeGroot and the mean arrogance of Rusty.

Jodee's heart thumped, but she couldn't turn her back on Syrah. An emotionally wounded woman could turn on a person just as quickly as a physically wounded animal might. And with deadlier consequences. A wounded animal only wanted to get away. A wounded woman wanted revenge.

"Syrah, what are you doing?" The question drug out heavy with regret.

"I'm taking care of the *problem*. You heard him. He said you and Rusty were too incompetent. But I'm going to fix it."

"I think you should put the gun down," Nolan said.

Jodee allowed herself a look. Nolan would make an unlikely ally, but now wasn't the time to be picky.

He continued to walk toward them. "Syrah, this is getting insane. He's going to get you killed. I've asked you a thousand times, please just come with me. We can leave, go somewhere else, and start over as different people."

"I don't need my big brother to rescue me."

"Yeah, you keep saying that, but he never does. When is that ever going to click with you? There's a reason he doesn't call you his daughter unless he wants something." Frustration edged his words. "Maybe you deserve a better life. Maybe we both do." His voice grew loud. "Geez Syrah, you don't think I realize he dopes me up like a circus monkey whenever it suits his needs?"

"Then why don't *you* leave?" A cold dismissal of his honest plea.

"Because you're still here," Nolan mumbled. He moved to stand between the two women. "Put the gun down."

"Stop talking in front of her." Syrah shoved him aside and re-aimed the gun at Jodee.

"Like she matters. Maybe she did us a favor. Maybe we need to just go now." Nolan's voice rose with an urgency only he seemed to feel.

"And just where do you plan to go that I won't find you?" Judge DeGroot's voice bled into the room like poison.

She looked around to find he wasn't alone. In front of him stood an ashen faced Kimberly. The girl tottered, swaying as though she'd been drugged.

He closed the door behind him and slid the deadbolt in place.

Jodee tried not to flinch at the sound. Blue wouldn't be able to get in. She was on her own again, wasn't she? And now she had Kimberly to think of.

You are never alone.

"I asked you a question."

Jodee startled. He was speaking to her now.

"You brought the box?"

"She did," Syrah said.

"When I want an answer from you, I'll ask for it."

Syrah shriveled beneath the sharpness in his words.

Jodee glimpsed in the other woman the abandoned little girl she'd once thought of herself as. The one desperate for a father's love.

"I'm in a dilemma, Jodee *Trevaine*. You've caused me so much trouble. I respect that about you, but I also kind of hate it if you know what I mean. This little matter should have ended quietly and beneficially for all. Now there's just so much damage control. So much *collateral damage,* as they say."

"How exactly would Aidan benefit from *this little matter*? Or Kimberly?"

"Money. Isn't that the root of all evil?"

"I believe the correct saying is that it is the *love* of money that is the root of all evil. Is that what this is all about? Money?" Mentally, she went through the contents of the box again. There was no money—nothing of any value—inside.

"Money, my dear, is a tool—a very useful tool. Power, security, love. Everything has a price and money pays the tab." He shoved Kimberly into an empty chair and moved behind the bar where he took his time pouring an amber liquid into two shot glasses. "For goodness' sake, Syrah, put down the gun before someone gets hurt."

He looked at Jodee. "Drink?"

Her gaze flickered over the gun Syrah had placed on the bar at the Judge's orders.

"I believe I'll pass." Her voice sounded calmer than she felt.

"I insist. I think you'll be glad you did before this is over," he said.

Jodee hesitated, repulsed by the thought of getting any closer to the man. But the gun . . . She walked over to a place within arm's length of the gun, though they might not know it. Being above average in height also came with the perk of long arms.

She stared at him, pretending to be unaware of the Glock lying just a couple of feet away. Her hand itched to feel it pressed against her palm.

"Nolan, stop pacing around like that. Act like a man for once in your life." DeGroot turned to Jodee and tapped the box. "Do you know what's in here?"

She shook her head, hoping the truth didn't show on her face.

"For as far back as our family can remember, there's been a rumor of a box filled with lies that could take away all that belongs to us. Now that I have that box, what's in it doesn't really matter. Isn't that a kicker?" He laughed.

"Why'd you kidnap Aidan to get it?"

"Who said I did?"

"Kind of obvious neither of these two are the masterminds

behind it, don't you think?" She didn't bother reminding him of their visit at the hospital. He'd never actually confessed to the abduction then, either.

"I do like you." He saluted her with the shot glass before taking a sip.

"Great. Let's do lunch sometime." Bitterness seeped into her voice.

"Oh, I think we're going to do more than lunch." He swirled the liquid in his glass, then gave her a quizzical look. "You don't know who I am, do you?"

"I guess answering that you are Judge Harrison DeGroot isn't what you're looking for."

"Smart girl. You got spit and vinegar, a backbone. Like I said, I like you."

"How'd you get Paul's keychain?" The question burned through her will until she couldn't stop herself from asking it.

He ran his tongue over his lips as though mopping up the last of the whiskey clinging to them. He stared at her, a smile growing on his face like oil sliding over ice. "I think you already know."

The world around her turned to nothingness. A terrible knowing exploded inside her and she gripped the edge of the bar to steady herself. "No."

"You really didn't know, did you? Your mother, she kept a good secret. Of course, she understood she didn't have much choice, especially not after Paul's tragic disappearance."

She leaned away from him as though distance could erase the truth.

"Oh, don't be like that. We're going to get along just fine. He just wanted something that was mine. When he wouldn't take the money . . . well, I had to make another offer he couldn't refuse. That's how life works."

"You monster! You *killed* him? Why?" She couldn't stop the outburst.

"He wanted to give you his name, but you're *my* daughter."

Jodee shook her head. "No. I don't believe you."

His laughter spluttered to a halt, his smile twisting into a grimace. He hunched forward, his hand pressed against his chest.

"Your heart!" Syrah dodged to his side, but he pushed her away.

Jodee snatched the gun from the counter and sprang back, putting as much space as possible between them. From this angle, she had all three of them in front of her. Make that four. Kimberly.

"What's wrong with your heart?" she asked.

"I think you already know that, too. Wolfe-Parkinsons-White. It's a hereditary condition." He rubbed his chest with one hand while remaining bent over. "You know what they say . . . like father like daughter." DeGroot drew himself to upright, a gun in his hands. "And it's time for your first lesson."

"I am *not* your daughter." The words raked up her throat like barbed wire. "I am nothing like you."

"Really? We have a life and death situation here and all you could think about was what happened to Paul. It's your selfish nature. It's in all of us. Nothing to be ashamed of. The ones who survive are the ones who know how to feed and protect it."

She shook her head.

"It's what you've always wanted, Jodee. Don't say it isn't true. It's what every little girl longs for, right? A father. Now you have one who loves you and can show you how to survive in this unfair world."

"You don't even know what love is."

Syrah erupted in hysterical laughter. "I've spent my whole life wanting you to call me your daughter and you never have. Now you call her daughter, and she hates you for it." She doubled over, staggering as though drunk with hysteria.

Jodee's heart hammered in her chest, but its rhythm remained steady.

Disgust radiated off him as he stared at Syrah. He turned to Jodee. "You shoot her, or I will give her the gun and she will shoot you."

"I am not a murderer." She looked from DeGroot to Syrah. The girl's eyes had gone wild with the stab of betrayal. Would Syrah shoot her if given the opportunity? Not a chance she wanted to take. Still, she held fast to her commitment. "No."

"Let me explain. Someone has to die so they can take the blame for what has gone horribly wrong here. In other words, we need a dead body who won't deny our story. It's the only way to tidy up this mess. Now, either Syrah is responsible, or you are. And here's the thing, you shoot Syrah, we get Kimberly to the hospital in time to save her. If you don't shoot Syrah, you die, but so does Kimberly."

The roar in Jodee's ears threatened to drown out everything else and set the room spinning.

My Beloved Daughter, trust.

The calmness of knowing settled over her. "I'm not a murderer."

"You're a DeGroot."

"I'm a *Charidy*." She was, wasn't she? That's why she was the secret. She'd been born with the blood of both. Good and evil each dwelled within her but now the choice was hers as to which she let win. She could choose to be a cold-blooded killer or to die.

The aroma of baking bread swept over her.

"There's a war inside of you, Jodee. There always has been. Two bloodlines fighting to control you. One is weak. You don't want to be weak. You pride yourself on your independence, on being stronger than all the others. You don't have to fight it anymore. I see who you really are. You're ready to make it end." DeGroot's words coiled around her like a serpent, as though he'd read her mind. "It can all be over. You can claim your true identity—be who you really are—right now."

"I am Jodee Rose *Charidy* Trevaine. And the war is over." She aimed the gun and prayed for steady hands. Could she do it? Could she actually pull the trigger and become exactly what he expected her to be? She lifted her finger off the trigger. *I won't let him make me something I'm not.*

"Jodee, don't shoot!" Blue yelled.

Startled by his voice, she looked at Blue, failing to see DeGroot point his gun. His shot cracked through the tense air like a tree limb breaking beneath the weight of ice.

The impact of the bullet sent a sharp pain streaking through her torso and down her arm. She staggered, but didn't fall.

Another shot exploded.

Jodee stepped back, her eyes going to the gun in her hand. But she hadn't shot DeGroot. She snapped her head up to see Nolan, gun still aimed at his father.

DeGroot hunched forward. A red blotch grew on the front of his shirt. He aimed at Nolan, falling to his knees as he fired.

She lifted her hand from her chest where the bullet has struck, but there was no blood. Instead, she felt the shattered remains of the white stone.

"Everyone, drop your weapons!"

The room swarmed with armed law enforcement personnel as Jodee let the gun slide free of her fingers.

Blue snatched her into a bone crushing embrace. "What happened? Are you okay?"

She nodded as shock made her thoughts sluggish. Nolan? Why?

Pulling away from Blue, her gaze found Syrah frozen against the bar as though she'd just landed in the middle of something she couldn't understand, her eyes glued to Nolan.

Nolan's gun—a Russian Makarov—lay at his feet. "Is he dead?" He asked. Blood seeped from his shoulder the stain his shirt, but he didn't seem to notice. Or care.

No one answered. He sighed and closed his eyes. When he opened them, he held his hands up in surrender. "For the greater good."

CHAPTER 48

In nature, nothing is perfect and everything is perfect. Trees can be contorted, bent in weird ways, and they're still beautiful. ~Alice Walker

"Yes sir. Thank you for calling." Both grateful and bewildered, Jodee ended the call. She inhaled, filling her lungs as though truly free to breathe for the first time. She returned to Grace's kitchen where the others sat around the table polishing off tanother batch of Grace's chocolate chip cookies. The only one missing was Blue, but he'd been summoned to a debriefing with Tom Fowler.

"Is everything all right?" Grace asked. The concern in her voice mirrored the worry etching lines in Helen's countenance. That Jodie's mother was here with them gave the moment a surreal quality. The woman was finally free from the darkness and burden she'd carried by herself for all these years.

Though fully healing might take time, Jodee's relationship with her mother had been reborn on the wings of new understanding. Trees don't heal, they seal.

But Jodee wasn't a tree. She was a woman with the ability to mend what had been broken and make something beautiful out of what had been destroyed.

And she had a Father who made all things possible.

"I'm great, but I think Dr. Hyson is a bit perplexed." She reseated herself next to her mother and across from Logan. "The Wolf Parkinsons White is gone. He can't find any evidence of it on the tests he ran." She maneuvered the last cookie onto her plate. "Apparently that's not supposed to happen."

Grace tipped the pitcher of iced tea over Jodee's glass, refilling it with one hand while she squeezed Jodee's shoulder with her other. "Miracles still happen. I'd say you aren't the only miracle that happened that day. Nolan is making a lot of progress. Logan says he's turned state's evidence and is fully cooperating."

"And his new girlfriend is pestering me every time I walk past her cell, wanting to know how he's doing or asking me to give him a message. If I have to utter the words 'Syrah said to tell you she loves you' one more time, I'm going to charge her with assaulting a police officer."

Grace flapped at him with the dish towel. "Pooh, you old softy. We aren't fooled by your tough guy act."

He drained the last of the tea from his glass. "I'd say the real miracle is how that bullet hit the rock in Jodee's pocket and ricocheted off." Logan shook his head as though seeing a three headed unicorn would be an easier thing to swallow.

"Not a rock, a white stone." Jodee corrected as she stared at the stone laying on the table in two pieces now.

"I'll call it whatever you want if you'll just stop doing things that create more reports for me to write up."

She smiled and took a bite of cookie. "Does this mean we're friends now?"

His phone dinged, and he looked down. Dressed in a long-sleeved button-up shirt, wrinkle free and crisp, and starched jeans, he was a step above cowboy casual. Though out of uniform, he still wasn't out of his law enforcement demeanor. "They found Rusty Boggs. He was hiding out in his parent's basement over in Snyder."

He reached to put the phone back in his pocket, but it dinged again before he could. "It's Matthews. He's home now."

A ribbon of sorrow intertwined with an awareness of the fragile state of life wound its way around the table. Oliver Matthews had been sent home on hospice.

"I know it's too soon, but any word on the ballistics test for the Makarov Nolan used to shoot his dad?" Grace asked. "It'd be nice for Oliver to have the peace of mind in knowing his friend's killer was finally being brought to justice."

"Not yet, but he's good." Logan stood. "He said he's confident we've got the murder weapon used to shoot his friend in the back in '92."

"Do you believe he's right?" Grace gathered his plate and moved it to the sink.

"I never believe anything but the evidence."

"And how about you? Do you feel you have the answers you've been looking for?"

Logan inhaled and held a breath, as though looking at a memory no one else could see. He let the breath seep out as though purging the memory as well. "I reckon it's as close as I'll ever come. Finding the truth won't bring them back."

"Your parents were good people. Your brother having WPW doesn't change that. Your mother was a good, godly woman, Logan. And your father was the kind of man that would stand by her and fight to protect her. I think that's enough to hold on to, even if we don't know for certain how they died."

He swallowed and tried to hide the emotion Jodee saw rolling over his expression. He retrieved his cowboy hat from the chair beside him and settled it on his head. "Well, I believe Matthews can at least rest knowing justice is coming. I think a whole lot of people around here are resting easier now that DeGroot is dead."

Should she feel something about her biological father's death other than sorrow for the kind of man he'd chosen to be? She didn't. In her confession, Syrah had explained why she'd broken Aidan's toes with a hammer. The most relevant part was that she was high at the time.

But the idea had stemmed from a story DeGroot had told her about his grandfather who had raised him after his parents had abandoned him. The old man had made an example of what it means to be unwanted and useless by eliminating a litter of puppies in front of him.

The thought made Jodee shudder.

"Now if y'all will excuse me, I'm going to pay him a visit on my way to the . . ." His speech trailed off as though he wished he'd stopped talking ten seconds ago.

Grace turned the faucet on and rinsed the dishes. "Tell Kimberly I said hello when you get to the hospital. And let Aidan know I'll have a big plate of chocolate chip cookies waiting for him when he gets home."

Jodee laughed. "Why, Sheriff Adams, I do believe you're blushing. Is that only allowed when you're out of uniform?"

Logan returned a scowl for her laughter. "And this is why we can't be friends." He ducked his head and gave it a shake. Then gave her a wink, hugged his aunt, and let himself out the back door.

"The miracles just never cease." Grace grinned like she'd been doused in a bucket of new joy.

Jodee sat on the ground beneath the oak tree. The damaged part had been cut away, and the decision made to leave the rest, giving it whatever time it had left.

She was grateful for that. Though lopsided and disfigured, the tree still had much to teach her.

The graves had been examined, and someone had cleaned up around them, leaving flowers on the two that actually contained the bodies of her ancestors. No one really knew what to do with the empty ones—the fake graves—but the consensus was to leave them as a reminder that just because a grave has your name on it doesn't mean you're dead.

In the distance, the sign for Roots still hung like an ominous herald. But it's secret was out. The truth really had been buried in the roots beneath the tree, guarded by the bones of Abel and Essie Charidy.

She unfolded the letter she had brought with her, the one she'd discovered wedged behind the bookshelf. Though she'd read the letter several times already, the touch of the paper still took her breath.

Dear Rose,

I hope I may call you that but ask for your forgiveness if I've taken a liberty you haven't offered. Maybe by the time you finish reading, you'll understand why a name seems to me such a sacred thing.

A sacred thing that has been taken from me, leaving me adrift in a sea of uncertainty. It is a sea I'm not sure won't drown me.

I am no longer the person I believed myself to be for these past twenty-two years of my life. Instead, I have been made to understand a darkness in my lineage that I worry I cannot shake or overcome.

Elizabeth Charidy is no more. Elizabeth DeGroot has come to take her place. And I am forced now to share their story, because their story is your story.

It is true that your parents were killed when you were a child. Did you know that? I wonder how much you may remember of those days and pray this doesn't shock you too greatly.

It was an act of cold-hearted murder fueled by a love of money. A greed that, it seems, seized upon a conversation overheard by Uncle Luther in which he learned of both your parent's desire to adopt Will and a large sum of money hidden by the Charidys. I think that perhaps it was more than a greed for money, but also a bit of a jealousy. An orphaned boy with a desire to belong. Unfortunately, he allowed that desire to twist him into something so vile.

I shudder now to know the role my father, Cub DeGroot, known to me my whole life as Will Sunday, played in this evil deed.

If I might defend him—though there is really no defense for such a cruel act—he was only a boy at the time, very much under the control of his older brother, Luther, an evil man to this day.

Their wickedness did not stop with the killing or the fire, but they crafted a plot whereby they might inherit the property that should have been yours.

Here I will add that they never knew what became of you after you were rescued by the true Will Sunday.

Because they were boys and you, the only true heir, were a girl, they seized a letter written by your father expressing his plan to adopt Will. Under the guidance of Luther, the man who was to become my father assumed the name of Will Sunday. They even went so far as to claim Cub DeGroot had perished in the fire, along with you and your parents.

These secrets my father confessed to me shortly before he passed, extracting my promise that I would find you and tell you the truth of that terrible night. Looking back, I can see now how tortured a life he lived beneath the shadow of this wicked deed.

And now I must confess I have inherited my father's faintheartedness. I cannot face you and have chosen the cowardly means of fulfilling my promise by writing this letter.

Through great efforts to maintain a strict secrecy of my mission, I engaged a man who has been in my father's employ for many years and is now in mine, Mr. Amos Calderon, to find you and deliver this missive to your hand. He can be trusted.

Buried beneath the headstone bearing your name is a box. In that box can be found the Charidy family Bible, which has brought me great comfort through the years, but which I can no longer bear to touch with such stained hands as mine appear to me now. A few other papers are there as well, including the adoption letter for Will Sunday, though I can't imagine that it would have any worth to you now, especially as it is most likely a forgery.

My father has also confessed to me the tragic but heroic manner in which Mr. Sunday died. What another terrible shock that must have given you. I can only hope and pray your life since has been richly blessed, though I can hardly imagine anything would compensate for the tragedies you've experienced.

It may take some effort to locate the graves as I have had Mr. Calderon cover over even the markers until nothing can be detected of them. I couldn't bear the sight of them. Though an irrational act, I hoped that by covering them I could silence their relentless cries that now haunt me.

The truth has tormented my father's days and terrified his nights, but he lacked the courage to stand up to his brother. Until the end, when he made this confession. Maybe I give the act of confession too much credit for being courageous, since he had so little to lose at that time. But I loved my father, and believed him to be a good man, though a weak man at times.

He begged me not to have him buried beneath the oak tree beside the graves of your parents. Beside your empty grave. I shudder now to think of such a thing—an empty tomb bearing the name of a very much alive person.

But it gives me pause to wonder if perhaps this is how most of us go through life. We live as though confined to a grave bearing our name, doubting the truth that we are fully alive. Imprisoned by our circum- stances, enslaved to the name by which the world has called us, we live in the shadow of our own death, sliding further into the tomb every day. By our failure to root ourselves in God's truth about who we are, we wither day by day beneath the weight of a lie.

Oddly, it is the very picture of my soul as I try to reconcile that I am not now and never was a Charidy. How unbearable it is to know that I am a DeGroot.

To stay here would mean to continue living in the lie. There is no Eliz- abeth Charidy—there never has been. And I refuse to bring Elizabeth DeGroot into being.

What is to become of me, I do not yet understand. I know I cannot stay here. Even if I didn't fear my Uncle Luther, the shadows would still come for me. I have become a fatherless girl with no name.

All that is left for me is to go away and hope to find a place where I can one day discover who I am meant to be.

. . .

The letter ended unsigned, giving Jodee the impression it wasn't yet finished. Why had it been hidden behind the bookshelf? Was Elizabeth the body in the cistern Grace has spoken of? Sorrow, like a silken thread, spun around her heart. In her soul, she knew it was.

She startled as Blue sat down beside her. He nudged her with his shoulder.

"You doing okay?"

"So much pain and sorrow, and it all started here beneath this tree. Do you wonder what might have happened if Luther had never overheard that conversation?"

"I reckon Will would have been adopted, making Rose his sister." He took her hand and placed a warm kiss on it. "I think I kind of like the way things turned out for us, though."

A slow smile took root in her heart to bloom upon her face. "I'm the granddaughter of Rose, and you're Will Sunday's grandson, aren't you?"

"I haven't taken a great deal of interest in my esteemed lineage—somethings are better not known. But, yeah. I talked to Dovey. I am the great-great-great-grandson of the real Will Sunday. Guess I'm going to need to rethink my esteem for my bloodline. Apparently, there was some heroism mixed in at one time."

"Do you think Will and Rose were meant to be together?" She leaned into Blue, and he wrapped an arm around her, pulling her closer.

"I reckon only God knows that. Besides, if they had been together, you and I wouldn't be here." He tugged a strand of her hair. "All I can say for certain is that Blue Sunday and Jodee Rose *Charidy* Trevaine are meant to be together. What do you say to growing old together?"

She warmed at the sound of her name. Her mother had supported her decision to have her name legally changed to add Charidy. Hearing it from Blue now settled it around her like a blanket of peace. She answered him with a kiss.

Like an acorn bursting forth with new life, acceptance came first —she knew who she was now. With acceptance came contentment, then hope. She looked at what remained of the tree—one branch still strong and tall.

A truck backfired and she jumped. Rattling down the road was Hawk in his worn out truck. He looked her way, and nodded, then turned to head down the road to Jacob's Ladder. Silhouetted by the setting sun, he soon faded into the glorious light.

"Do you smell that?" She inhaled, filling her lungs with the reassuring fragrance of baking bread, understanding that it had never actually been bread she'd smelled.

"What?" he asked.

She smiled. "Nothing."

One day her life would be like a mighty oak. Her roots had found their way into the life-giving truth of her Father's love.

ACKNOWLEDGMENTS

Many lives have touched this story and I am grateful to everyone who helped me shape it. Though I may not have always succeeded in grasping their instructions, I am blessed to know so many who are willing to give of their time and knowledge.

For knowledge concerning trees and their ailments, I am grateful to Kimberlee Peterson with The Texas A&M Forest Service. For all things of a law enforcement nature, I owe thanks to Texas Ranger B.J. Hill and Sheriff Matt Coates, as well as my usual go to sources, Austin and David. Many thanks! If I've bent the procedures or blurred the lines a bit, it was for the sake of the story and not because you failed to tell me.

For the crafting of this book, I owe a great deal of thanks to both Allen Arnold and Dani Pettrey. What a wealth of knowledge and insight. To the one I bounce my ideas off of—the one who willingly read a thousand different versions of this story—and always offered constructive feedback, thank you Donna Nabors. Thank you also to Lori DeJong and Kelly Goshorn for being an endless source of encouragement.

And finally, thank you to my family. A special thank you to Emily for fielding all my odd questions and for her ability to find the holes and offer insight on how to correct them. And a very special thank you to Joe, my unwavering encourager who gladly reads rough drafts and tells me I'm his favorite fiction author.

ABOUT THE AUTHOR

Lori Altebaumer shares the joys of living a *"boots on the ground, head in the clouds, heart in His hands"* life through her writing. An award-winning novelist and Amazon Top New Release author, she writes both inspirational fiction and nonfiction. She also cohosts the *My Mornings with Jesus and Joe* podcast with her husband.

ALSO BY LORI ALTEBAUMER

A Firm Place to Stand

A Far Way to Run

Silenced Night

Walking in the Reign